Sword of The Boar.

Book two of the Soldiers of The Boar.

Copyright@Allan Harper 2022.
Cover photo Copyright©Allan Harper 2022.
Revised paperback edition 2025.

Visit the author's website at:
www.lochardfiction.co.uk

The Roman short sword, the gladius, was a brutal weapon. It had a uniform blade two inches wide, tapering to a fine point. Its purpose, like the Greek spear of old, was to make a large hole in the body of its victim. And thereby, by loss of blood, bring death. The killing stroke could be in the torso or any wound on a limb close to the bone, or a drawing across the neck.

Hail Caesar. Hail Rome.

Principal characters.

Velio Pinneius. – centurion commander of Trimontium.

Fufius Pulcher. – commander of the Trimontium cavalry.

Tacto Oscius.– senior centurion and second in command.

Dometius Barrus. – commander of Blatobulgium.

Hanno Drusus Glaccus Ticinus. – commander of Velunia.

Pomponius. – centurion and second in command to Hanno.

Servius Albinius. – legate of the Twentieth legion, Deva Victrix.

Marius. – legate in command of the Sixth legion, Eburacum.

Appuleia. – wife of Marius.

Gnaeus Julius Verus. - governor of Britannia.

Gallus Tiomarus.– senior weapons instructor, Twentieth legion.

Eidumnos. – a headman of the Votadini tribe around Trimontium.

Bractia. – his wife.

Tianos. – his son.

Voccia. – his daughter.

Orann. – his stable boy.

Segontio. – war chief and prince of the Selgovae tribe.

Aulercas. – Veniconi war chief.

Eithne. – wife of Aulercas.

Little Aulercas. – son of Aulercas. 'Little Owl.'

Ucsella. – daughter of Aulercas.

Asuvad. – Dumnoni war chief.

Orgidor. – Brigantes war chief.

Key places.

Deva Victrix. Modern day Chester. Home of the Twentieth legion.

Eburacum. Modern York. Home of the Ninth and successively Sixth legions.

Velunia. A fort on the Antonine Wall.

Pinnata Castra. A short lived, legion sized, fort built on the upper reaches of the river Tay (Tavae.)

The Bodotria. The river and estuary of the Forth.

The Clota. The river Clyde.

Trimontium. Roman fort in east Scotland, near modern Melrose.

Blatobulgium. Roman fort on west side of Scotland. Not far from the Solway.

Trimontium fort lies sixty miles north of Hadrian's stone wall and fifty miles south of Antonine's turf and timber wall. It controls the road north-south on the east side of the country. Its sister fort Blatobulgium controls the western road.

Roman gods and goddesses favoured by the army in Britannia.

Jupiter Optimus Maximus. - "Best and Greatest."

Mars Ultor. - God of War.

Fortuna. - Goddess of Fortune and luck.

Mithras. - God of soldiers, representing light, truth, and honour.

Epona. - Celtic goddess of horses, favoured by cavalrymen.

Holy Mothers of the Parade Ground. (Campestres) - Celtic goddesses linked to parade grounds and training areas for cavalry.

Aesculapius - God of healing and truth.

Brigantia. – Native goddess of the Brigantes tribe, adopted by some Roman auxiliary cohorts.

Dis Pater. - Equivalent to Greek god of the underworld, Hades.

AD 156.

Britannia has been a province of Rome for a little over one hundred years. During that time, the southern and western tribes have either accepted Roman rule willingly or been, to all intents and purposes, subjugated. A legion has been lost during the conflict and in the north two separate walls have been built by successive emperors to deal with the implacable Caledons and their allies who continue to hold out against Rome.

Those walls work efficiently as customs and taxation frontiers but neither has wholly removed the threat of the northern-most tribes as enemies of Rome. Throughout the empire the resources of the army are being stretched. Hard decisions are required.

Part one.

Landscape.

The legate of the Sixth liked a picnic as much as the next man, or woman. He liked military ones even more. If anything, he enjoyed them too much. He hammered up the Eburacum - Deva road with the entire ala of the legion cavalry towards the moors. The whole morning was beckoning. No clerks, no pens, no ink, no politics, just good company, and his favourite horse. First, there would be a spot of lunch with some decent Falernian, then a short walk before the sacrifice; a white goat to Mars. He would speak impromptu thoughts of encouragement, and then do the courage awards. More wine, then a canter back to barracks.

The praefectus drew alongside as the pace slowed to ease the horses. The legate smiled at him.

"Splendid day, don't you agree?"

"I do sir. Though I wonder if it would not be wise to send a half turma ahead to scout for us?"

The legate raised his eyebrows, and leaned over to pat the praefectus' horse.

"Very well, if you wish my dear chap. It is always good to

show the officers that even I need to take precautions. The Brigantes and all that," he said.

He knew he patronised, but did not care.

"Very good sir."

The legate heard the order trickle down the chain of command. A minute later sixteen troopers and a decurion officer trotted to the side of him, saluting with their spears as they passed. The praefectus returned it on his behalf. They did look smart.

"They will clear any obstacles on the road and wait for us at the waterfall," the praefectus said.

He nodded back.

"Excellent. Gives them a little task. Always good to mix training with pleasure."

"Indeed sir, indeed."

Three hours later the rocky outcrop that heralded the waterfall hove into view. Out of sight from passers-by on the road, water welled up from the ground, falling in a sweet tumble in several small rocky steps to a pool, where it gathered itself to its purpose before meandering across a flat piece of tussocky, bullrushed moor. A perfect spot for troops to rest their horses, gather in and listen. He suspected it was the sort of place the natives would venerate. No doubt one of their local gods resided there. So, all must be done with respect, politeness and dignity befitting a holy place. If he could find out what the deity was, he might suggest its adoption by the cavalry wing. Why not? Prayers, offerings, and praise were seldom wasted. Who was to say this little place was not the watery hearth of a Britannic Apollo?

He pulled his mount to the side and waved his men on so that he could make a grand entrance. The praefectus led the way with the ala standards at his back and the trumpeters following. The column swung down off the metalled roadway in pairs and began disappearing behind the low hump of ground towards the pool. They would be forming up in individual troops, decurions setting distances so it was all neat and tidy. He held his horse back for a moment to give them time. His boys would not want him to be unimpressed. If they could set a perfect semicircle of spears and calm beasts, they would take as much pleasure from that perfection as he would from handing out their medals. There was something beautiful about a cavalry ala that could not be expressed by any number of honest legionaries. It was simply the inherent grace of man and animal in tandem.

There were shouts of alarm. He spurred on. Down behind the hump of ground the men had formed an outward defensive arc with their spears poised. What in the name of Dis Pater was going on? He rode through a gap. The standard bearers bore waxy grey expressions. The praefectus was off his horse, kneeling on the ground. His stomach roiled with an acidic shard of concern.

'Mithras.'

There were headless cavalrymen lying all around the edge of the pool. None of them quite in the water but all left in the rushes along its edge: placed there. Like the sacrificial offering he had intended for the goat. The horses were gone. He dismounted and strode to the kneeling praefectus cradling a sawn-off corpse; the young decurion officer.

"Brigantes bastards, Orgidor, most like," the praefectus snarled.

"Any sign of them?" he asked.

"None, sir. They left them like this."

Fifteen decurions standing and one dead, their faces mirrors of pale horror. Twenty years of command experience slipped its quietening hand onto his shoulder, quelling his rage.

"Send two turmae in all four directions. Find their trail. I want whoever did this. Alive for punishment, do you hear?"

"As you command sir."

He noted the speed his order sent them flying to get away from the gory bodies of men who had been friends this morning. Around the pool the grass was churned in blood, but he had nearly five hundred horses stamping about. The grass could tell him nothing useful.

It was an hour before the first of the four patrols returned.

"They've gone west into the high ground. Perhaps a hundred of them," a decurion reported.

"Do we pursue sir?" the praefectus asked.

He reached a swift decision.

"Get these lads secured on some horses. The savages will split up before we can get close. They have too much warning."

"I thought the Brigantes had finally decided on peace? I thought Orgidor was dead of old age by now," the praefectus said.

The legate waved a hand at his fallen men.

"We will bury these lads in Eburacum and then we will come back and deal with the Brigantes."

"And the ceremony sir?" the praefectus asked.

He shook his head.

"I do not know why Mars punishes us today," he said, "we must do something to put right whatever it is we have done wrong. The awards will have to wait a little longer."

He looked at the waterfall and the pool. The water was tumbling and falling over its little, insignificant, picnic-place steps as though nothing had happened. He fancied it was laughing. The atmosphere seemed to change. He made the stiff finger sign to ward it off. Whatever deity held this place, it was no friend, and it did not seek new followers. If he had forbade the scouts, they would still be alive. He was not so cold hearted to think he would sleep well tonight. All in all, it had rather spoiled the day.

Chapter 1.
Trimontium fort.

Velio stood watching the day's light fading through the small glass window of his office. He could feel his mood sinking with the early winter darkness. A thin grainy snow was beginning to smooth away the roads inside the fort. Not the usual big wet fluffy flakes; this was the stuff to block roads and drift over streams, bringing a beautiful white treachery to the landscape and breaking communications in every direction for days. There was an order from the governor on his desk. It took no account of snow.

"Hail and Greetings Centurion Velio Pinneius.

I hereby order and confirm you are to support the withdrawal of all our forces back from the lines of our beloved emperor Antoninus Pius. Your cohort will ensure and maintain the road leading to and from the defence lines of Hadrian at all costs – may he rest quiet and serene.

Your sister cohort in Blatobulgium is receiving identical orders to maintain the western road. Our emperor is confident of your success."

It was cryptic to the point of a death sentence. Then, below his signature, Gnaeus Julius Verus struck a longer, much more personal note in his own hand.

'Velio,

This is my first direct order to you since your appointment and your legate assures me you will succeed in every endeavour. Be assured Servius Albinius knows my mind on what I am about to convey. Seek further clarifications as you may require from him. Know this, the tribes to the south of your position continue to test my patience and further intelligence tells me the defences of Antoninus Pius cannot last much longer without my sending further troops as reinforcements. I have decided that doing so would leave the rest of the province naked. Our beloved emperor Antoninus Pius reluctantly permits withdrawal of all cohorts back to the lines of Hadrian. Save all that you can.

You act as my support to the northern lines, but I cannot give support to you. May Mars and Jupiter keep you strong. I pray Fortuna covers you and your men with her cloak. I place my faith, as I always do, in the Twentieth legion.'

So that was it. In a handful of sentences. It was to be whole scale retreat of the army from the north. He shook his head in disbelief. Make a retreat in winter with uprisings happening in both directions? If you sought a bad alignment of omens this would do it. To cap it all, his legion commander Servius Albinus had once been his tribune during the construction of Antoninus' wall. Quite what his views were about its abandonment so soon was anyone's guess. But knowing Servius he would not be thrilled at the prospect, but neither would he comment; an order was always an order.

"Be assured Servius Albinius knows my mind on what I am about to convey."

'I bet he does, governor, and I daresay you know his feelings about it as well. I bet the air was black and blue.'

The snow kept hurrying down.

"This is going to lie Marcellus," he said.

His clerk looked up from his desk wondering whether to agree or say something more optimistic. Laying down his pen, he decided to use his privileged position to offer some advice.

"You've raised every order you can sir. This will turn to rain. It always does. And that's just as bad."

"I don't think this is going to turn to rain Marcellus," he replied.

He turned.

"At least not tonight. Are the sentries set outside?"

Marcellus knew he was referring to the headquarters itself and the room of the cohort standards but played the soldier's card.

"All evening sentries will be in post sir."

"Then that will do for now. Marcellus, finish up and go and feed yourself. We'll begin again tomorrow once I've seen what this stuff turns into."

He gestured at the white enemy whispering on the window

glass. Donning his cloak, he went for his usual end of day prowl around the ramparts, checking the walls were secure, all gates bolted shut. As if they would not be? The helmet gave him away. There was not a legionary, nor a trooper caught unawares. He overheard a few voices impeaching Boreas for a bit of mercy, but the god of the north wind was not listening. Torches lent a wild atmosphere to the evening. He nodded to those involuntary clusterings at these small sources of warmth and found his corner; usually a pleasing view overlooking the curl of the river around the fort. He began ticking the list he had already formed in his head.

Six centuries of 'Boar' infantry.

Four troops of Augusta Vocontiorum, good horsemen all.

Fighting strength: six hundred men. Forty-three assorted support staff.

Horses: two hundred and seventy all counted, including mine. Two for every cavalry man plus a small reserve. Seven greys: excellent for parades and useless for scouting. The time for parades has passed, Velio.

Waggons: twenty heavy waggons with horses to pull and twice that number of carts.

Mules in plenty.

Fort defences: excellent.

Weaponry stock: excellent.

Moral: perfectly satisfactory, discipline is good.

Quantity of laid in forage for the animals: acceptable and the grass will be growing soon.

Quantity of grain in store: good.

Immediate threat from local population: non-existent.

So why?'

Marcellus would be eating by now. His sentries saluted just to keep warm as he passed headquarters towards his house.

"Call me if anything changes," he said.

"Sir," they replied.

They only relaxed when he disappeared through his own doorway.

*

He woke the next morning and listened to the fort. It was quiet. 'First bugle' had not sounded. He smiled at the satisfaction of being up ahead of his men. He dressed, eating the food Lentulus had left on the table. Cold food on a cold morning. Piping hot porridge with a dash of honey later. He picked up his cloak before venturing into the white shroud. He returned the greetings of different sentries and strode the few short steps next door to the fort's headquarters building, inhaling the zesty air, rich with the smell of fresh snow, so cold it caught his lungs. Fabulous in its purity. He loved it. But it was deep and soft enough to sink into. If it was bad here it must be worse up on the wall or even over on the signal hill.

Marcellus was already there at his desk.

"Get me every map we have of the land between here and the two walls," he said, "I want a meeting of the centurions this afternoon. We have work to do."

Chapter 2.

Velio's was not the biggest garrison the fort could accommodate. Rebuilt from the first small wood and turf affair dating from Agricola's campaigns before being enlarged in stone, it could house eight-hundred infantry and two hundred and forty cavalry. That would have been a worthwhile command. For four months he had been trying not to wonder too much about why he was here. Beyond the obvious, that he was a soldier and he had been ordered. Now, he knew why. It was not the temporary *'get some experience of commanding more than a single century,'* Velio initially thought it to be. The latest order proved there was more to it than he first believed. The wall was being abandoned. No doubt there would have been half a dozen names of ambitious officers jockeying for the permanent command if that were not so. However, it was growing clear that ambitious officers were not what Verus needed up here. He imagined Servius would have told the governor two things about him when suggesting his promotion. One; he was a skilled fighter, and two, he was lucky.

Servius believed he was blessed by Fortuna for some reason. Neither of those would seem the key prerequisites for an officer taking temporary command of a fort. The governor's order now explained everything. He was here because things were liable to get a bit lively, one way or the other, and Servius was not going to have his precious legionaries wasted by an idiot. It was a back handed sort of compliment. He was not going to let Servius down. Governor Verus must have been harbouring concerns about the logistical costs of the northern line for a while. Perhaps his predecessor had planted that thought in his head as a parting gift on the quayside to Gaul when he left?

Velio did something he had not done before, he let his officers read Gnaeus Julius Verus' order; the whole thing, personal comments and all, enjoying the surprise and pleasure in their faces.

'Something to break the monotony eh, lads?'

Listening as they passed it around, he pretended to look out through the principia columns towards the barracks blocks. He heard them reading it in twos and threes, craning over each-other's shoulders to see. Outside the snow was easing but it had not given up and drifts in the compound were proving troublesome. In an hour or two the light would be going once again, and he reckoned more was coming. His order came back to him and he put it on the table, debating for a second how best to begin. Impart the facts, or take the opportunity to rejuvenate hearts and minds? Snow in winter did little to fuel the martial spirit. As for the task, in essence this should be a straightforward reshuffling of the Antonine cohorts down the east and west roads. All they need concern themselves with here was the eastern road. Except Trimontium was the northernmost bastion on the road up to the wall. They were all exposed, in varying degrees; in no-mans-land. But his men were Twentieth legion, not the Germanic conscripts holding Habitanum and Bremenium below him. Those sites would be hoping for his assistance if things got tough rather than entertaining ideas of providing it to him.

"A cup of wine gentlemen."

The words were out of his mouth before he realised.

'Dis-Pater be damned, he'll have us all soon enough anyway.'

"As you can all see, the gods have decided we are going nowhere until this passes. The men will worry. Oh, I know it is not the fighting that will bother them. It will be, which direction do they march? Well, you may tell them I share the same feelings. I like to know if I'm heading into trouble or marching away from it."

His servant poured and distributed the wine.

"Gaius, take a cup for yourself," he said.

Gaius smacked out a salute with proud eyes and retreated to leave them to speak. Velio knew he would not eavesdrop.

"There are several fingers to this puzzle. The first is, how will Habitanum and Bremenium cover their sections of the road? The next is, which road will the forts choose to retire south. I, and you, must only worry about the east road. But, if Blatobulgium retires before we do, or is attacked and overcome, I expect the west road becomes our responsibility too. And you may rest assured all my plans so far go up in smoke."

He waited for their dutiful laughter to pass, before raising a finger.

"And, as you know there is no overall commander up on the wall, every fort's praefectus is responsible to the governor himself. So, there is no one up there to give co-ordinated movement orders. Personally, I would shuffle the cohorts east and west towards the nearest road and move one down each day until the wall was empty. That way the whole wall could be evacuated in a week, in a trail of broken-down waggons and tearful sweethearts I expect."

They smiled again.

"Remind me, how many forts are there on the wall?"

A subtle cavalry question from Fufius.

"I think it's fifteen," one of them answered him.

"Then that plan only works if the roads stay open. Any blockage and the cohorts will back up and could end up having to fight their way through," Tacto, his second in command replied.

He gave Tacto a *'so be it,'* tilt of his head.

"When will it begin?" asked the junior cavalry decurion.

Fufius gave him a pleased look. Velio thought it was a good question too. It was just a pity he could not give him the answer.

"Gentlemen I expect this to go badly. I expect weather and heathen savages to combine to frustrate us," he said, "and there are civilians we are obliged to think about. Some of our retired comrades over there in the village, busy selling us wine. They must be escorted with their wives and children safely down the road too, or at the very least offered the chance to leave under our protection. As for the rest, any broken hearted Votadini and suchlike, can tag along. We will not prevent them travelling under our protection, but we won't aid them. The governor is clear, you read it for yourself. I am to save all that I can. That does not mean I am required to aid everyone. The third question is whether we need to guard the road north to the wall. We might expect the cohorts on the wall to do that bit for us but it's not clear to me that they will. Our men will not want to march towards the insurgency, but we may need to assist the cohorts getting back. The road, gentlemen, is everything. As soon as the weather clears, I want an update on the condition of the bridges and working parties out on any repairs. Fufius, your men are going to be busy. I want patrols out every day and intelligence reports on the Brigantes, Votadini and the nearest Selgovae villages."

He raised his wine cup. If they thought he was worried they would only worry more.

"Success flies on the wings of surprise; so, we drink to success and surprise," he said.

He drank and dismissed them.

Tacto nodded a sympathetic smile as he left. The governor really had laid a snapping eel in Velio's lap this time. He nodded back. They both knew what had to be done. He looked out at the principia's empty forecourt. For a moment he wondered whether he had erred in giving them sight of the governor's personal message.

There was a second order, delivered a day later by separate courier direct from Servius. It put the governor's one in context and required the telling of a few lies. That bit he had just done. Tacto and the others did not need to know the complications for the moment. He sighed at the Gordian knot.

"My name's Velio Pinneius and I've got to try and save all your miserable lives," he admonished the fort outside.

Chapter 3.

Twentieth legion barracks; Deva Victrix, several years earlier.

"My name is Marcus Hirtius and I'm going to teach you all how save your miserable lives. You, what's your name?"

"Pinneius sir."

"Pinneius what?"

"Velio Pinneius, sir."

"Pick up that sword Velio Pinneius and kill me."

He took a hard nudge from the legionary standing behind him.

"Go on mate, show 'im."

Marcus Hirtius went on all-out offense and in the blur he created with the wooden gladius felt both a nick of pain on his forearm and the surrounding soldiers' sudden silence. He risked a glance. A red crease, four inches above the wrist marked a clear stroke to Pinneius. The young soldier's face was a hard mask, and he was coming forward. They stood toe to toe exchanging volleys of blows and parries. The optio took a nod from the centurion and took a solitary step forward.

"That will do tesserarius, I think."

Afterwards as Velio was walking into his barrack block thinking about it, a voice yelled at him. Velio almost ran the entire length of it to the lion's den. In the private room at the end, the centurion and the senior weapons instructor for the cohort, Gallus Tiomarus, were waiting.

Tiomaris was a scary man, chewing bread, letting crumbs stray down onto his lorica, sitting there indifferent to them. More powerful than the centurion himself. Not tall, but with chest and forearms like a bull. Marcus Hirtius was standing by the window with his arms crossed, both leaner and taller than Tiomaris. There was a kind of easy going, unspoken sunniness to Marcus Hirtius' disposition that almost settled his sudden nerves.

"Salve, Velio Pinneius. How long have you been in the Twentieth legion Pinneius?"

The bearded centurion asked. He smiled his usual, affable smile.

"Ever since I joined sir," he replied, "three months."

"You're a *one legion* man then?"

"I like the Twentieth sir," he replied again.

"So, you have not served in another legion? In Gaul or on the Germania frontier perhaps, before you came to us?"

He shook his head knowing the centurion had the answer to his question already. The centurion pointed his index finger at him and waved it backwards and forwards a couple of times before carrying on.

"Well, these good gentlemen are wondering exactly where you learned to use the gladius. It was not from them. And you haven't learned it in the three months I've had you. None of my other recruits can use a training sword like you can. Some still act like they're working out which is the dangerous end."

Gallus Tiomaris' eyebrows rose a fraction. He wondered if the centurion had managed an accidental insult. Marcus was examining the fascinations of the floor.

The forefinger stopped waggling and pointed at him.

"So we want to know who taught you Pinneius? Was your father in the legions? An uncle, older brothers?"

"None of that sir. It just comes easy."

Gallus Tiomarus rubbed his fingers over his chin a couple of times before flicking his crumbs onto the centurion's floor.

"Marcus here, tells me you landed a blow on him that could have been a kill in a battle situation," he said.

Marcus turned his forearm to let Velio see the red welt. Away from the training field he looked only four or five years older than him. He did not appear to be bearing a grudge.

"I trained Marcus and I know exactly how good he is. And now you come along and because it *just comes easy* manage to land a disarming strike on him," Gallus Tiomaris growled.

Velio decided there was no safe way to answer that point. He looked at his centurion. The forefinger returned to its scabbard. There was a short silence. The centurion waited, letting the pressure mount, curious to see how this young recruit was going to dig himself out.

"Sorry," he said at last.

The centurion burst out laughing. Marcus raised his eyebrows, amused. There was a short silence.

Gallus turned to the centurion and said, "I'll take him," as if he was buying a chicken for a family sacrifice. Velio half expected a couple of coins to hit the table.

"Gather up your kit Pinneius, we're going to make a disciplined killing machine out of you, not just the gifted amateur you are now," Gallus said, "if not, you can have him back," he grinned to the centurion.

And without further explanation he moved into the block of the First century, Fourth cohort. All new faces. They regarded him with interest and tested his youthful inexperience with a degree of foolery Gallus allowed, curious to see if he could deal with it. Velio knew it was a false peace; eventually he would have to show them all. So, with Marcus' tutoring, he set about improving his shield work, spending extra hours in the evenings working at the wooden training posts, *'the dead gauls,'* building and improving his stamina. And every time, when he felt he had done all he could and the lead-weighted training sword was sending burning pain through the muscles, he put in another one hundred strokes. He could feel a boiling point coming.

*

It was late one afternoon and the last group of eight were coming in from the training hall, putting the world to rights as they threw their water bottles on their beds, slumping down, complaining and bitching. Marcus had worked them hard. Velio was lying on his bunk, eyes closed, feeling bored after the drudgery of six hours on routine watch. A slap on his stomach told him the water had come to the boil. He looked up. The block's unofficial leader was standing over him with two training swords that should have been left in the exercitatoria.

"Let's see how you're getting along?" the soldier sneered.

He bouted the swords against each other with a noisy crack. Velio looked up at the legionary, knowing the time had arrived.

"Drilling is over for today," he stalled, "get some food. Your 'eight' are on the walls tonight, aren't you?"

"Never mind about that, you cheeky little bugger, get off that bed and fight me."

"Here, in the barrack room? The hastiliarius won't like that," he worked the hook in deeper.

The man's face flushed. Velio was much too young to talk back like that

"I don't care what Tiomaris thinks, you get up and fight me or we'll all know who not to ask for help when things get tough out there," he waved the sword as if there were barbarians pressing the gates as he was speaking, "and I'll break this over your skull to teach you manners."

"Fine," Velio snapped.

He got up on the opposite side of the bed. The legionary flung a sword at him and stepped back into the centre isle between the bunks on either side. The man was older and taller.

'Ten years of experience. Enough to have seen some real fighting, will not fight clean. It'll be forehead, boots and fists,' Velio guessed.

The legionary waited, smirking and grinning, not deigning to take the guard stance at all.

"Come on then. You're the one who wants to fight," he said, egging his persecutor on so he would make mistakes.

The bets were getting laid as the others crowded in to watch him get a pasting, sealing off the top end of the block. They did not see who entered at their backs.

Rugio did not require a second invitation. He stepped back into the contact zone and tried to pummel Velio into the ground with a swinging, lunging frenzy of real hatred. Any single blow landed would be sufficient to split skin, break a bone, wooden weapons or not. There was a brief 'crack, crick, cruck, crack' of swords and a sharp slap and a hiss of pain.

Velio admired the slap mark his blade had made on Rugio's cheek, just missing the eye itself. Rugio had rediscovered Velio's left handedness, though it was not a secret. The side of the body usually open to attack was closed off, because Velio's sword arm was there. His 'open-side' was on the wrong side. Left handedness earned men permanent postings to the far right-hand end of the infantry line where their shield arms could defend the weakness. Not today.

"Patience and speed Rugio. You need to learn both," he chided.

The legionary barged in once more and he rattled the flat side of his blade off Rugio's other cheekbone. This strike even closer to the eye and Rugio knew it.

"You fight like a girl Rugio," he taunted.

Rugio looked like he was ready to fling the sword aside and lunge into a fist fight. Velio whipped his sword past Rugio's slapdash guard, to touch the skin at the centre point of his throat, stopping him in his tracks. The room went quiet. No one had seen that amount of ease and flickering speed before. The unseen man at the back of the block waited, intrigued.

"Dead. Rugio, you are now dead," he said.

He held the sword in place and refused to let the older man to step back. Rugio dared not slap the sword aside. Rugio glared at him. Velio could almost hear coins beginning to drop in some of the thicker skulls. Someone snickered a mocking taunt. Rugio flushed, angry and impotent. The mockery was worse than the heat burning his cheeks.

"Most definitely dead. Who will write to tell the emperor he has lost you I wonder? The centurion perhaps? Anyone else fancy their chances? No? I didn't think so. Want to make it real swords next time, Rugio?"

"Dead, Rugio, quite dead," echoed Marcus Hirtius.

Velio thought for a second someone else was taking the piss. The barrack block went silent. Marcus walked up the centre aisle taking his time, letting the sound of his hobnails on the wooden floor send a warning. The century peeled away on either side letting him pass. Rugio snapped to attention. Hirtius did not mess about.

"You are a lucky man. Had that been a real gladius, your head would be down there on the floor looking up at you, saying *'we didn't see that move Rugio,'* not that there's much in that head of yours."

Another wider snicker of mockery rubbed salt into Rugio's red face. Velio wondered if any of Hirtius' ire was for him.

"I have news for all you girls. Tomorrow we are on route march. The centurion is taking us on a little expedition. A maniple is going out to arrest that Brigantes hothead Orgidor. And you, Rugio, you will have the honour of marching alongside me, so I can watch how you perform when it matters. Got that?" Marcus said.

Rugio gave an almost imperceptible nod of compliance.

"How far are we going?" asked a voice from the safety of the crowd.

"Two days march, there and back, with full kit and spades," Marcus said.

"Might be longer if he sees us coming and disappears into the hills. Make sure your weapons are clean and sharp, I have a feeling you will need them," he opined a little more.

He turned to Velio.

"You will not offer to fight a fellow legionary with a real gladius again. Understand?"

"Sir," he said.

"That goes for all of you," he barked.

The next morning the centurion marched them out of Deva Victrix' east gate. It was Velio's first active patrol. The nerves in his stomach kept him sleepless through the night with imaginings, fed by suggestions in the block of what was to come. He woke early and lay waiting for the trumpet call to rise. It was raining and the river by the fortress walls was rising and turning brown. He felt his nerves vanish as the gate fell behind. Two centuries, one hundred and sixty-three men. Two centurions, two optios, a signifier with the 'Running Boar' emblem, two trumpeters, two drummers, Marcus and another tesserarius from the other century. Four mule-drawn short carts, each laden with five goatskin tents, plus one extra for the officers, two spare horses for the centurions. The legionaries of *The Boar* were out to police the distant hills so '*beware all*.'

He pulled the brim of his helmet down, like the rest of them, to keep the worst of the rain out of his eyes and concentrated on striking a steady pace behind the soldier trudging in front of him. The long road led all the way across country to Eburacum itself, fortress of the Sixth legion. They marched across a flat featureless plain and up through high ground overlooking that plain. An obvious stronghold for insurgents.

The centurions wanted silence. The trumpeters marched along with the rest of the column. The rain came down in continual thin mists, in grey curtains, drifting ahead of them, in sudden ominous black bursts that made the road a torrent of ankle-deep waters and every dip a shallow pool to wade. It was mid-summer and every step of the way felt like autumn. The first encampment was dug in soft yielding earth and the rain rattled on the goatskins without letting up. Just like a training exercise. There was no trumpet call on the second day, only the head of the tesserarius poking through the tent flaps with his pleasant invitation and cheery version of '*good morning.'*

At least the rain had passed.

Towards late afternoon hills straddled the whole of the eastern horizon. The centurion stayed on the road that was now rising toward a low pass splitting the southern hills from the northern. Over to the left, in plain sight of the road, wooden stockade walls of a village rose from the dull landscape. The leading centurion veered off the road and led them up the incline. Velio waited for the call for a flanking movement. It did not come. As they drew closer, he saw the gates were wide open and the centurion was riding past. Inside, the burned out remains hosted weeds and debris. Crows and birds. Flowers made incongruous patches of colour along the base of the blackened, ruined stockade.

An optio and six men broke off to check it. They caught back up with the column within a few minutes. Nothing was said but the hitching of sword belts and adjustments of shields were too widespread among the older men to be mere coincidence. Velio searched the landscape for the danger signs they seemed to be picking up, but it all looked the same to him as it did an hour ago; grey, wet, and miserable, empty hills and the backs of the heads of the four legionaries in front.

They kept marching for what felt like another hour. The coldness of the morning left him as he got into a steady stride. He could keep this pace up all day, but it did not seem fast enough to catch anybody let alone a Brigantes mischief maker. And then, overlooking a shallow valley and a decent sized stream of water, they found small, irregular patches of ripening wheat and numerous cattle and livestock pens; geese in small platoons, barking dogs and noisy children going white faced at the sight of legionaries appearing on the slopes above them. It was a pretty spot for a village and no mistake. The fire-smoke from the houses was hanging low and fetid in the valley like an unfriendly welcome. Their centurion took the lead, marching them down into it. Velio reckoned it was not good ground. A mounted attack right now could put them in difficulty. The second century remained behind on the high slope with the tent carts. The trumpeters burst into action making the air shiver. He gripped his shield and pilum tight and waited for orders. For forty minutes he stood whilst the centurion parlayed with the locals.

Their bird had flown north to deeper heartlands, leaving others to make excuses and wring their hands. Later, when he thought back on it, he could not remember the precise moment when swords got drawn, nor the orders preceding it. One minute the village was calm, the Brigantes busy negotiating and explaining to the centurion, the next, it erupted. Armed warriors seemed to rise out of the grass, out of the small round houses, from everywhere. It went downhill fast. The century broke into an encircling position. It became man on man combat; awkward and messy. He stood his ground waiting for any of the Brigantes to rush him, wondering if this was going to be it, his last day. Marcus was bellowing to draw a nucleus around him. There were not enough Brigantes warriors to go around and it turned into a slaughter. He had no inkling what set it off.

When it was over, they looked at each other. The centurion remounted sheathing his gladius.

"Burn it all, leave no one alive, secure the food stores. A lesson must be taught. We only needed the surrender of one man. They chose to fight instead. So be it."

Velio looked at Marcus.

"I'm not for killing women and children," he said.

"Leave an enemy to grow at your back Velio? Is that what you want? So you have to come back another day and go through it all over again. Best do it now and have an end to it," Marcus snapped.

"No brother, but these people are beaten," he dared.

Marcus' normal cheerful face darkened.

"It's not my order," he shrugged, "and I won't lose skin or pay for not following it."

The trumpeter began blowing the 'Alert,' the pre-alarm call.

"Hostiles approaching in numbers," a voice called out from the second century.

"See, it's not over Velio," Marcus warned.

The trumpet changed to '*Stand to the Eagle.*'

"Fuck, we've stumbled into a right rats' nest here," Marcus said.

Velio nodded, watching the second century trumpeter on the slope. The centurion up there was shouting and pointing to a hill crest further away. His men began descending to the village in support. The native women and children started fleeing as a wave of mounted Brigantes flooded down to attack.

"Form circle on the signifer," their optio shouted.

The signifer moved a few yards to a flat spot and dug the pointed butt of the standard into the earth as the centurion got back off his horse. There was not the slightest sense of rush about that dismount. He led the horse into the circle and handed the reins to the signifier to hold. Velio checked about for casualties from his century. There were none. A couple of lightly wounded but nothing more. The supporting century was not going to get down in time before the Brigantes hit them. He hefted his pilum knowing what the next order was going to be.

Marcus stepped in at his shoulder.

"Gently does it soldier. They're coming on fast. Put the horse that comes at you down with the pilum, then you kill the man with the gladius. Do not waste the pilum on a horse that is not coming at you. Do not let the horse get too close or it will break our lines up. Imagine it's Rugio," he murmured.

He moved on to the next man.

"Rugio," Velio replied and relished the prospect.

They did not know it then, but that skirmish was the start of an uprising that crackled through the northern lands for the rest of the summer and on into the autumn.

*

Years passed and the faces changed. There was time spent up on the emperor's wall, enduring strange, magical mornings of piercing, encrusting frost; waiting and pacing, cold and expectant for sunlight to come out from the dark. Rugio faded from his life at some point; victim of a winter fever.

He became a watch commander, cum junior instructor. Part of Gallus Tiomaris' informal sword school for officers willing to pay extra for a personal lesson or two. Velio 'Swords' Pinneius, the young soldier with the fast left arm, taught tribunes and optios. He made allowances for neither category.

Then the rise to optio. Then promotion to centurion followed. All achieved by the age of thirty-seven. Nineteen years of soldiering had drifted past, not in a flash, but time had not dawdled either. Not bad for a boy from Misenum who walked away from father's profitable garum business because the legions passing on the Via Appia one day caught his teenage eye. Marcus Hirtius became his closest friend and now, when procrastination contrived to make it almost too late, there was something he needed to put right for Marcus.

Velunia fort, the present day.
On the turf and timber wall of Antoninus Pius.

The commander read his casualty lists for yesterday, couriered in from every fort and surviving watchtower on the line. None of them were getting fresh reserves to make up for the diminishing complement of men. A few more 'eight-hundred garrison' forts would be useful right at this moment. It was beginning to feel like the forgotten place of the empire. The wall of Hadrian, *'the Stones of Hadrian,'* once despised as the last outpost was becoming more and more desirable.

'Stand to the Eagle' began its familiar, hateful tormenting.

The notes rasped their way into his head, demanding obedience, warning of danger. Inside the principia he heard the duty centurion shouting men to the ramparts; two centuries of them. The rest in reserve. It just happened that the junior of his centurions had the watch.

"Hades' Arse," he complained, "there is no rest for honest men."

The snow muffled the sound of boots running. A scorpion catapult began firing, its distinctive *"whunk"* vibrating through the air like a flat harp-string. The other five machines joined in to make their odd song of different timbres. Another attack. He swore again just for good measure before grabbing his helmet and cloak.

Outside the centurion was sending a third century to the ramparts leaving the other three formed up in the open compound ready to support any part of the wall under pressure. The military horns ceased. Arrows began flighting down out of the sky into the fort

"Testudo," the watch centurion ordered.

His centurion colleagues followed his general order and the shields went up. The commander nodded at the salute as he passed to the rampart.

"Can you see them?"

"Archers from below the escarpment sir. I expect they have sent men over the lip, and we will get an attack on the gates very soon."

"Very well carry on."

"As you command sir."

The centurion kept rapping his vine stick on the palisade posts, scanning the open ground outside the walls.

"I will put the reserve centuries under barrack-cover if this is just archers. No point in leaving them exposed, sir" he added.

"Good. But don't be hasty. I'd rather they were immediately available if something develops," the commander replied.

"Understood sir."

He descended back down into the compound and checked on the north gate. The lip of the escarpment was bare rock and grass, every tree and bush having long since been cleared away to remove as much cover as possible. The fort lay on the forward slope of the low escarpment dominating this section of the defence lines, rising out of the ground as if it had always been there. The rampart, ditch and outer rampart did provide a small degree of temporary protection for warriors getting that close, but once they rose to mount the outer rampart, they were exposed to all the defences. From the high gantry-walk of the north gate, the outer rampart could be monitored. The unseen archers ceased firing. There was a surge thereafter: Damnonii.

"Pila at the ready," called the tesserarius in charge of the north wall defence.

Thirty legionaries stood waiting for him. The Damnonii were now in the ditch area struggling through the wet trap at the bottom. The commander thought the tesserarius was holding back the order for the first spear volley a little too much, but he trusted his men.

"Pila now," the soldier shouted.

"Porta Sinistra defence at the ready. Pila."

Warning of a second attack. He left the tesserarius to his duty and turned his attention to the western gate now under assault.

"Pila now."

The command from that side came quicker than he expected.

The Damnonii kept at it for around two hours, swirling around all sides of the fort before they started pulling back across the open marshlands into the winter's gloom. He sighed; they had this wearing down process perfected. Attack as the light began to fade, push hard for an hour or more, get as many of the fort's buildings alight even with just a few arrows; retreat into the gloom, wait a few days then do it again. He left his centurions to deal with the stand-down drills and went back to the principia, sitting back down in his office while his servant and secretary hovered trying not to get in the way of each-other, one with food and another with a pale expression. He regarded yesterday's casualty reports once more with a feeling of impotency and frustration rising in his chest.

"Mars and Jupiter, why doesn't the governor just give us more men? Is that too much to ask?"

In a sudden rage he picked them all up and dumped them on his fire. They were already out of date now. His secretary stood looking on appalled. His servant poured some wine and offered a clean towel to dry himself.

"Get the standard back inside, cleaned and dried. I want it back in the aedes straight away," he barked, "and I want reports from the medicus and a recount of men able to stand at the ramparts. Within the hour."

The numbers must be getting to the low point, he surmised.

Three hundred including all walking wounded if I'm lucky? Forty of them with arrow wounds. When does it reach the point where the garrison is ineffective as a deterrent?

The fort was still defendable, courtesy of its scorpion bolt throwing machines and ramparts but out in the open the diminished cohort would not be so intimidating. He could field one decent maniple of a hundred and twenty plus another strong century to support it, perhaps a little more.

Of all the wounds a man could suffer, he hated arrow wounds the most. You could lose a man to a simple piercing in the body even when that wound was tended by a medicus without delay. An arrow falling from out of an empty sky from bowmen hiding below the fort. How do you defend something you do not know or see is coming? Take an inspection on the other side of the fort and risk an arrow as you strode over there. Answer a call to attend the headquarters and risk an arrow. Then for days it would be as normal. Forty arrow wounds: they could only do that mischief because they knew the cavalry screen was stretched too much to chase them off.

'Sons of Dis Pater,' if the barbarians would only stand and

fight, he would fancy his chances toe to toe, shield to shield, with the men at his command. Good, decent, reliable men. All the cowards were long gone. It was getting relentless and without better cavalry support along the communication lines his cohort was under the cosh. The tribes had worked out the weakness. The wall only worked when it was manned. Undefended, it could be crossed with relative ease. The southern side had few defences but many small civilian villages. The impregnability of the line was now compromised by several burned out watchtowers and unmanned signal stations, sitting there like rotten teeth. It would be better for his men's morale and worse for the enemy's to have them pulled down. The support road had not been ceded, but the fight to maintain control of it was proving too much of a challenge for the four cavalry forts on the line. Like the infantry, they were understrength in horses and men too. The local horse traders were no longer willing to sell them new animals or proclaiming they had none to sell, hiding them.

The local spies would be sending reports out, feeding the unrest, encouraging more attacks, stoking up the priests. At least the collateral destruction of the workshops and taverns in the civilian compound had given the men less reason to fraternise. He had never liked its closeness, its distractions, not liked it being there at all, if he was honest. It gave the natives far too much insight into the calibre of his command, a hotspot with too many ears listening to off duty soldiers, drinking, gambling, and attempting to wench the local girls. It was now a charred remnant of what it had been.

He watched the recent reports turning to curling black ash on his fire and regretted his rashness.

"Just as well I know yesterday's numbers were the same as the day before," he smiled at them.

All in all, it had not been a good demonstration of calm authority. Both were Twentieth legion men. The cohort might be decent Gallic auxiliary, but the officers and staff he relied on were from the legion.

"Thank Mithras, Mars, Jupiter thou Best and Greatest, and all the Holy Mothers of the Parade Ground for good men," he prayed aloud in exasperation.

"Perhaps a bath sir? Before you eat? To ease the back," Lucius said.

"Is it still safe for me to go to the bathhouse?" he said.

He raised his eyebrows, grateful to Lucius for his intervention.

Atius looked up, "I'll get you an escort sir."

He shook his head, "get up on that rampart with your shield and pilum and don't come back until the calends pass," he growled.

"Shall I note that, sir?" Lucius chimed

"Enough," he replied, "but if they come back, you will let

me know in time, won't you?"

He picked up his helmet and gladius again to reinforce the point.

"I'll bring a fresh tunic over directly sir," Lucius replied.

Chapter 5.
Trimontium fort.

The snow thawed and vanished, but Velio had the feeling the northern winds would come again. Saturnalia passed and the real weeks and months of winter were on them. He saddled his horse and went for a ride towards the three hills that gave their name to the fort. Atop the nearest one was the fort's new signalling tower and the ditches and ramparts of an old tribal hill fort, long abandoned, overlooking the garrison and the civilian sprawl that had grown in its shadow. Quite ironic in the circumstances that the legions were now readying themselves to do the same. He enjoyed the thought. Identifying which tribe had ruled these lands from up there was a little difficult. The locals he had asked on that point were reluctant to say either way. Perhaps abandoning such a strategic point was an old disgrace no one wanted on their doorstep?

These people had been powerful long before the Twentieth legion marched along and set stone on stone. It was an uncomfortable reminder that all things passed. All rulers were transient.

Scattered around the base of the hills numerous round-halls and livestock pens of the local Votadini made for a peaceful, harmonious scene. Time had resolved whatever conflicts Agricola may have encountered during his time. Trade with the Votadini was brisk. Everything from wine to jewellery, to girls and sweethearts. A few miles further on to the west were the beginnings of the Selgovae territory and they were a different type of animal. They pretended to ignore the invaders as much as possible. But he knew it was a sham. There were more forts in the western territories than in the east. When retreat happened what would they make of the passive Votadini? Would a bit of spite be in order?

The orders did not require their king to be alerted. What the commander at Blatobulgium chose to tell the Selgovae king in the southwest was, *'not my problem,'* he told himself.

Perhaps it was better not to tell them anything lest they all unite and turn on the retreating army in a desperate attempt to prove to each other they were not lapdogs. It could be a bloodbath.

He rode out past the civilian huts and workshops, the wine taverns, and brothels, smithying sheds and horse yards, away from the noise and the smells of woodsmoke and cooking; the shouts and laughter of local children, the polite waves from people who knew his name and position in the hierarchy. His horse knew the way. She had been along this path many times. As he walked on, he wondered about Voccia and what he was going to tell her that was different to what he had decided to tell her father.

*

Eidumnos was Votadini, Segontio was a Selgovae. They were not natural allies. Abutting tribal lands made for some unpalatable necessities. The stars were turning and news from the north was growing for resumption of all-out war on the legions. They were both in a tricky situation. Segontio's people were policed into submission by Blatobulgium and its string of forts. Eidumnos' people were free to trade and gain wealth. And now they required each other. If all-out war were coming, the tribes to the north would be the ones driving the invaders south through Votadini and Selgovae lands. Best then they agreed to be seen participating.

Eidumnos stared at the Roman wending his horse to his hall, wondering how he was going to explain this to Segontio. It was the worst timing possible. Of all days why did the stupid Roman want to come today? In his heart he already knew why.

"Why's he coming? Does he know I am here?" Segontio hissed.

Eidumnos folded his arms and sniffed, the Selgovae was younger than him and fractious, reminding him of an unbroken horse, all whinny and rearing.

"From time to time he comes and takes porridge with us. His way of being friendly I suppose. And Voccia seems to have caught his eyes."

"He comes and eats porridge with you, Eidumnos? And looks at your daughter? And you let him? What are you thinking Eidumnos?"

"Occasionally he comes here, I do not encourage him of course, but what can I do? They are here and I have responsibilities. My people elected me to speak on their behalf whenever we have a problem. The king is too far away for most things. So, I must keep my people safe. Besides, they are good to trade with. Anything I cannot get or make for myself, I can get there," he pointed at the fort, "you understand what it is like."

Segontio frowned.

"Yes, but I don't let them come to my hall uninvited and take breakfast whenever it pleases them, and I wouldn't let them eye my daughters."

"As if you and me have a choice about when they choose to visit? Come Segontio, we know how it is," he said.

"Tell me you don't go to the fort and eat porridge with them in there? By our gods of the waters, do not let those be words you say to me. When the next war comes, we must make sure the Veniconi and the Dumnoni have no cause to point their spears at our people as if we were the Romani," Segontio said.

"Never," Eidumnos replied, "still, we shouldn't let him

know you are here. He will get nosey, and it will only lead to questions. I will come and get you when he leaves. My people know you are my guest. Go and take a walk among them until this one is gone. If anyone asks, tell them I have business with the Roman commander."

"I'd cut him to pieces if he looked at my daughter," Segontio snarled with rising anger.

He made himself turn away. It would be quite a coup if he could get an alliance to work and take that news back to his king. There was no reason the two tribes could not unite; it was only the fear of failure that was staying their hands. A weakness that was unbecoming to warriors.

Eidumnos raised his hand in greeting, watching the soldier picking his way along the snow-covered path. Just the head and fancy bright helmet showing atop the big red swathe of woollen cloak, with his pale booted feet sticking out below, chivvying the glossy flanked horse on, white breath fuming around its nostrils.

'That is a nice animal,' he admitted.

A single well aimed spear would take the rider from its back. All that was required to unleash death and destruction on his family. His spear throwing alter ego, fretting in his head, surrendered to diplomacy and common sense and vanished back into its cave.

"I am sure you will get your chance to throw the spear, Segontio my friend," he muttered.

"Greetings centurion. Salve," he forced himself to smile.

"Salve, indeed, Eidumnos. How are you and your people this fine winter's morning?" Velio replied.

"We are snug in our halls, we have wood for our fires, our pots are full, and our women are content. You will have hot porridge with me centurion. I insist, I won't hear a refusal. No one makes porridge like my Bractia. It would be a pleasure for me to hear your news and have you share my fireside. Please come with me. I'll have your horse taken care of. Some good grain for her too I think?"

He held the bridle and stroked the mare's muzzle with genuine affection. Velio was not surprised to see the Votadini kiss the horse's nose. He dismounted and let Eidumnos lead him through the gate. He knew he did not need to be so polite; his officers might snigger he was showing so much deference to a minor local leader, but little gestures counted in these lands and Eidumnos had played things straight with him ever since they had first met.

*

"Where's our esteemed commander?" Fufius asked.

He rested the side of his head against the warm shining coat of his favourite mount.

Tacto kept his eyes peeled, concentrating on avoiding two

of his recurring hates; putting a boot in all the horseshit lying about, and getting kicked. Horses were not beasts he really liked. He had to ride them when leading his century, but he did not enjoy it much. The stable block was full of horses and troopers, and they appeared to be getting along very well with each other. It was not the ideal place for discussing the commander's personal life. Fufius liked to get to the point, and he had a way of hauling you into awkward conversations at the most inappropriate times and places. He was like a whirlpool you had to sail past at a safe distance, or he would suck you in and drown you in gossip or intrigue.

"He's gone off to visit his girl's father. Courtesy call, that kind of thing. Check the lay of the land," he replied.

Fufius grinned and waved the currying comb.

"Gone off to visit his girl's father indeed Tacto. He's not got a girl, has he?"

He rolled over the comment.

"Well, he seems quite keen on the chief's daughter. Wonder how he will break the news when we march south?" Tacto replied, conscious of all the ears listening.

Velio was camp commander, and when all was said and done, he was Velio's second. It did not hurt to let them know Velio was human, but indiscretion at the wrong time could cause trouble. Centurion in command Velio Pinneius was not to be mocked. Certainly not by the young cavalryman who owed his first chance to command a few turmae to the same soldier. Fufius now seemed intent on being less than wholly respectful. That sort of attitude could spread through the stables like the vapours. He was going to have to pay attention to the ala. Some of them were too naïve, too stupid to realise the snake they were taunting. Velio was too dangerous a man to fall out with, for one thing. He was not nick-named Swords for nothing and he had at least two missions north of the wall to his credit. Not every soldier sent north in a small patrol survived to recount his story. Personally, he never wanted to see that particular gladius pointing at his ribs; and then there was Velio's famous, Medusa-like, death-stare.

"Voccia?" Fufius teased in mock surprise.

He ceased his horse-combing for a moment and regarded his comrade's solemn face

"The one with the nice hips, eh Tacto? Velio and Voccia, how sweet sounding. I'm sure they will be happy in Rome, one day," he jibbed.

"That's the one," Tacto said.

He kept his arms folded inside his cloak. The stables were warmer than this most days but with the doors open for 'mucking out' there was a fearsome draught whistling through.

"He'll have to watch himself there. Votadini and all that. You never know when they might decide to wake up and cause a bit of mischief. I would like to cause a bit of mischief with a little wildcat like Voccia if I could get her alone," Fufius smiled.

"Unwise to mess around with a commander's girl I would say Fufius. Don't you think?" he replied.

"Well, if he wants her, he should just get on with it," Fufius answered.

"You'll never make a politician Fufius." he vouched.

"Well at least I'll never be lonely," Fufius said.

He looked at Fufius and knew this conversation had reached the line he feared. He waved goodbye and left the cavalry to talk to their horses.

"Centurion," Fufius called after him.

He turned to hear the last words Fufius appeared intent on having today. Fufius put down the comb and came out of the stable, wiping his hands on a rag.

"Well," he said.

"I mean no disrespect, but do you think it is wise to let the commander go over there on his own each time? I know he is Swords Pinneius and all that, but they could lay a trap for him, and he would ride straight into it. We could never get over there in time if he needed help."

Fufius kept his voice down low.

"Fufius," Tacto said, "you never fail to surprise me. One moment you mock him and now you have concerns for his safety."

Fufius smirked a little.

"Oh, it's not that. But one of these days, you know? They might just decide to have a go. Just when he's full of romantic thoughts and poetry, not paying attention, they'll have him."

He clicked his fingers.

"I will bring it to his attention Fufius, although I'm not sure what good it will do," he replied.

Fufius nodded and grinned.

"Well, none of us like an audience when we're busy with a lady, do we? Most of us don't anyway. I'm probably worrying too much," he winked.

"Get back to your bloody horse, Fufius Pulcher, or I'll have you on a charge," Tacto growled.

He turned and marched back to the principia.

'It will be a brave Votadini that tries it on with Velio,' he fumed, but the thought of the damage a successful ambush would do chewed away at his concentration all day. He could suggest to Velio that he take an escort in future, half a dozen, a turma perhaps. They would sit around, while their camp commander made sweet talk with a young lady.

'Who am I kidding?'

Velio would have a fit. He made the stiff finger sign against the scene Fufius had made possible just by speaking of it and hoped that was enough.

Chapter 6.
Deva Victrix barracks.

Servius Albinius felt Gallus Tiomarus was too long in the tooth to still be the legion's principal weapons and tactics instructor.

'He must be sixty if not older,' he mused.

Another of those soldiers who had done their 'twenty-five,' and more, and find they have nowhere else to go? The post demanded stamina and patience, relentless supplies of them.

'Gallus always had the patience, but does he still have the stamina? Perhaps I need to replace him?'

He lost interest in the reports on his desk. They were both close in ages. Grey bearded Gallus maybe had the edge on him by a few years. He had more scars to show for his time. Servius put his clenched fist to his mouth and coughed. Time for a chat. Procrastination never built a marching camp. He rose from his chair, waving aside the questioning looks from the coterie of clerks and tribunes. A full morning's-worth of paperwork lying untouched on his desk and now where was he off to?

"I'm going for a chat with my lead-hastiliarius," he boomed, "all this paperwork you're feeding me is making me fat."

He left before the sycophants had time to fashion replies and clerks protest their invented deadlines.

He found the hastiliarius in his room in the First cohort block. They jumped off their bunks when they saw him marching down the centre aisle and saluted him the whole way to Gallus' den. They were his favourite men in the legion. They knew it. He could have asked for a detachment to go and retrieve the armour of Achilles and they would have queued for the honour; he knew that too.

"Gallus, bring some swords I want to feel like a soldier again. Bring a couple of the heavier ones you use yourself." he told him.

Outside they went looking for a quiet spot but could not find one.

"The drill hall sir? I think you will have an audience unless you order it emptied," Gallus said, "there should be a century rostered to be in there now."

"Let them watch Gallus. We'll show them how old soldiers fight," he decided.

They cleared a space in the drill hall as soon as he put his face around the doors. The junior soldiers at work all told to sit down and watch.

"Shields? Helmets?" Gallus asked.

The men formed an impromptu ring on the floor.

Servius glanced at their eager faces. How many optios and

centurions of the future were sitting down to watch two old men sparring?

"For real," he replied.

They picked shields and loosened off for a few moments and when he turned back, Gallus was already in the guard position. His grey wolf's beard and his thinning hair had changed colour over the years but the astute expression and calculating eyes were the same old, formidable Gallus. They set to, swinging, and blocking, pushing, and heaving, feinting, using the hammer blow attack to weaken the opponent down, though with wooden blades it did not have the same arm numbing impact.

The hall echoed to the slap and set of lead-weighted wooden blades on wooden shields. To and fro, like it was no drill, but without communicating, taking turns to practise their defence. When they broke Servius accepted water from the watching century's centurion. His face was hot with running sweat. He swiped his brow with his forearm. The centurion waited for the water bottle. Gallus was sweating too but looking like he was just getting warmed up. Servius nodded and stepped back in to face him again.

Ten minutes later Servius put his head back a fraction, Gallus read the message, knowing full well the legate would never want to make an overt sign of surrender in front of these young pups. How Gallus could keep coming at him was a mystery, but he had answered his question. There was a short silence before they began chanting.

"Boar, Boar, Boar."

Their centurion was senior enough to risk a joke with his commander but decided a sharp salute was better. The century leapt up and crashed out a salute. He felt pleased. He was in better form than he had expected and so was Gallus.

"Come Gallus, there is something I want to speak with you about," he said.

He put the shield down and gave the sword back to a soldier he selected at random. The mule's eyes shone. It was the stuff of keepsakes and tales. It was not impossible that piece of wood and lead would live on long after they had all gone to their ancestors. They left the drill hall and the outburst of youthful voices behind and found a vacant spot away from prying ears.

"I'm sending you up to Blatobulgium. We are about to have a general withdrawal to Hadrian's line and order and discipline is going to be crucial. I do not want to send any more men north and the governor has said as much to me as well. But I can send you. You know Velio Pinneius is now centurion commanding Trimontium so I will have two of my old and best instructors in the places where I need them most. I will write an order to the praefectus of Blatobulgium to include you in all his planning. This withdrawal has the potential to become a messy retreat. Auxiliary troops are better going forwards not backwards in my experience. Legionaries do it far better. You know how Trimontium is garrisoned with our lads but Blatobulgium is the 1st Nervana. Better than average for auxiliaries. Cocky enemy tribes and auxiliaries keen to retire south. It's not a good mix Gallus. And they will get cocky once they realise what we are doing. Only the emperor himself knows whether we will ever march north again once this is done. He might even pull us out of the province entirely. Who can say?

But for the moment this is the position. We cannot have a debacle on our hands here and I cannot send more troops to cover the withdrawal. The legate for the Sixth agrees with that assessment. We will reset the frontier at Hadrian's line and just doing that requires work there too. Then there is the small matter of the Brigantes to deal with."

He stopped to check the hastiliarius was following him. Gallus had never had the compliment of such a long explanation from a commanding officer in all his service.

Two days later he was through the gateways on the wall of Hadrian, on the bleak snowy, west road towards Blatobulgium. Servius gave him a squad of cavalry, just to make sure the old lad got there in one piece.

Chapter 7.
Eidumnos' hall, in the valley below Trimontium fort.

Eidumnos waved to his Roman guest as Velio looked back. He waved once to return the gesture. Eidumnos breathed out. Voccia was gossiping with the servants. He sat back down in his chair at the fire. Segontio came in.

"Has he gone?" he asked.

It struck Eidumnos as a stupid question in the circumstances. But this was not the time to lose patience. The stakes were making him edgy too.

"He has gone," he replied.

"Segontio, there is someone else sharing my hospitality that I want you to meet. Forgive me for not introducing him before but I wanted to be certain you and I can be brothers. There was no offence intended I assure you. You may have heard of him."

Segontio waved the apology away as if the thought of offence would not have occurred to him in any circumstances; it was another polite necessity.

"Oh, and who is that?"

"His name is Asuvad, one of the war chiefs of the Dumnoni," he said and waited for a reaction.

Segontio handled it better than he expected. No histrionics, no petulance, a nod that said he accepted his was not the only tribe with an interest in what the garrison here was doing. Asuvad came in at the sound of his name.

"Greetings to you, Dumnoni, I know your name," Segontio said.

He got to his feet and offered his arm in friendship. They sized each other up for a second before Asuvad clutched the Selgovae's arm and shook it.

"And I have heard yours too, my friend," he replied, "the Selgovae are spoken of with respect in our halls."

"You have a reputation of a man who never tires of bringing war to the *sons of the wolf*," Segontio said.

Asuvad smiled at the compliment. Eidumnos indicated a vacant chair.

"We and the Veniconi under young Aulercas have long believed the wolf-skin soldiers can be beaten," he said.

"Aulercas has become chieftain?" Segontio queried.

"He is now one of their principal war chiefs. His father, my old friend, Heruscomani no longer speaks. He wanders in the twilight world and talks to things you and I cannot see. Things that even our priests cannot fathom. Age has taken him. It is a tragedy for everyone who know him; all of us," Asuvad said.

Eidumnos thought before he spoke.

"He is possessed?"

"I think he is an old man, and his body still yearns to live but his head and his heart perhaps do not," Asuvad answered.

There was no need to be cruel. Heruscomani had attacked the wall with him many times. The two tribes raised the spear together before the barrier was even finished. Now, talk to him of the wall and the Romans, and not a ripple of concern or interest would cross the blankness of his once implacable face.

"So, it falls to Aulercas to lead his people in war?" Segontio pursued.

"He has been fighting them since the first days and moons of the wall. He has proud blood. His father taught him well. And cause enough to hate them. They killed his brother-in-law Pasnactus, his sister's husband. The boys were close," Asuvad answered.

Later, once they had eaten, Segontio stared at the fire while Asuvad and Eidumnos exchanged glances. Dumnoni and Veniconi, north of the wall, had been resisting for years. Votadini and Selgovae, south of it had not; until now. He felt hot and embarrassed for himself and his people. This Dumnoni must think him a coward and the way he spoke of Aulercas was putting him at a disadvantage.

"What did the Roman really want? He has plenty of

porridge up there," he said, still gazing into the fire.

"I'm not really sure what he wants when he comes here, apart from the obvious,"

Eidumnos sent a glance towards Voccia still chattering at the back of the hall. His other children had absented themselves without needing telling. She was much more interested in listening in what her father's visitors had to say.

"Did he tell you anything interesting?" Asuvad said.

Eidumnos sat back and shouted over to the women.

"Leave us for a few minutes, go and talk outside, I am in counsel and all I can hear is your nonsense, can't you see?"

Segontio and Asuvad smiled. Eidumnos kept looking at the women until he cleared the hall. She made a playful little bow to her father. His moustaches twitched as he tried not to smile. Segontio caught her eye, and a flicker of a smile touched her lips. She led them out. Eidumnos rolled his eyes when they were gone.

"A fine one, Eidumnos," Asuvad remarked.

"She is so like her mother I have to look twice sometimes," he answered.

Segontio pushed the distracting thoughts of her out of his head, still waiting for Eidumnos to answer. Eidumnos leaned forwards.

"They are preparing for something. I can feel it. He did not say exactly what that might be in so many words, but he said he had always liked these hills. Perhaps he has been recalled. It would make sense."

They digested that for a moment. He began again.

"He keeps his men in line. He flogged the men who raped one of our girls last year, even invited me to watch. I did not go. I do not think he is a bad Roman. We could have worse."

"A bad Roman," Asuvad spat, "you jest with us Eidumnos, forgive me. He is not a bad Roman. Really? And what does a good Roman look like? Does he look like the centurion with his pretty feathered helmet and his red cloak? Does he say 'please' before he takes whatever he wants, your cattle, your women, your daughter?"

"Asuvad, you go too far," Segontio butted in.

"Asuvad, you are my guest," Eidumnos chided, "your mistrust of them, I understand. But my friend, you have never had to live alongside them."

"No, we have not," he replied.

He found his hand had strayed unbidden to his hip-knife

"Please Asuvad, we must not argue. That is how we fail. Eidumnos only meant that the Romans in the fort have not robbed or raided these lands. Is that not it, Eidumnos?" said Segontio.

Eidumnos put his hands on the arms of his chair and patted the carved pommels of wood. He began nodding.

Asuvad raised a hand in a semi apology

"It is the same for us," Segontio continued, "our yoke is different from yours Asuvad. Your yoke I believe, is the loss of brave young warriors. Ours is perhaps worse because it leaves no glory or songs to sing and remember. We lose no warriors. Instead, we grow old and wither. There is no honour in that. We pass to the afterlife having lived our years with the sons of the wolf always around us. We are prisoners who must make the best of the little mercies our guards permit us. It is not a thing I like to admit. I feel ashamed. You will think we are cowards. But do not be mistaken. We will fight as hard as you when we get the chance to beat them. But our young women mix with them. It shames me that we have children among the Selgovae with Roman blood in their bodies. Why do not they bring their own women with them or some of the Brigantes whores? Why do they need to take ours? I will tell you. It's because they have been here so long our women are their women too. That is our yoke Asuvad. It is not so easy as you think to live side by side with them," Segontio sat back.

Asuvad looked at him, impressed by his passion and vehemence.

"What did the good Roman want Asuvad? I think he wanted to tell me something, but he did not know how to," Eidumnos said.

He paused, thinking whether to say more, then decided he

had nothing to lose by telling a truth his guest might find uncomfortable.

"They train out there on the low ground below the fort, Asuvad. I can look over and see them in the distance. Their horsemen are always training, and they play some kind of game in the summer evenings to keep their horses fit. Their foot soldiers train most days. I can see them too. They are strong and they are ready. Sometimes they run in their armour and with their shields to where they train, and they run back when they are finished. These soldiers are not to be taken lightly. I have seen the formations they practise, and they can make them quickly. What do my people practise? They practise with their swords and shields, with the bow and the spear.

We can give good account of ourselves against any tribe. But the Romani are different. War is their craft. And they are exceptionally good at it. Their commander, the one who has just gone, calls himself Centurion Pinneius and he has them like a dog on a leash. I am glad that so far, he has been a decent man because if he were not, I fear I would not be here to warn you, and my people would be slaves. I am Votadini, but I am neither a high chief nor the king. My power is limited but I know the mettle of this Roman. And I am wary of raising a spear until I know we can beat him because I have nowhere to run to if I fail. I have no wall."

Chapter 8.
Blatobulgium fort; the western road, north from Hadrian's wall.

Gallus knew why it was quiet when he arrived at the south gateway. It was bread and porridge time; jentaculum. His stomach told him so. He dismounted at the principia entrance, dismissed his escort, and went in to report to the fort commander. It was a cursory perusal of his order cum introduction that summed up how things were going to be for him.

"I'm grateful to the legate for sending you to me Tiomarus, but I don't really need you. There is no pressing need for extra training. The locals are passive. The withdrawal will not happen for some time until the weather clears, or the roads for that matter and we can begin to co-ordinate movements with the wall. But I suppose it would be pointless to send you back. Why don't you keep yourself occupied for a while? I'll send for you if I need you."

Dometius Barrus put the order down.

And that was pretty much it. It fell just short of an order to 'get lost.' Gallus saluted and stood his ground.

"Well, hastiliarius, something to say?"

"With permission sir, I have a friend over in Trimontium.

Permission to visit him while we wait for further orders?"

"A friend in Trimontium. Is it anyone in particular, hastiliarius?"

"Centurion Pinneius sir."

"Ah of course. Silly of me to miss that. You and the centurion go back aways, don't you? Wall builders both, eh? Very well carry on. But Trimontium is not the easiest place to reach from here. You will have to cut through the hills between us. There are a couple of valleys that run in the right direction, that will help. I suggest you continue up to at least the next fort, perhaps even the one after and cross east from there. I cannot send another escort with you, but you should be safe enough, reputation and all. The Selgovae are quiet for now. Most of them are to the west of the road. Hardly good weather to head up into the hills Tiomarus, even these little ones. Boreas alone knows what it's like up there right now."

Dometius Barrus almost sneered.

'And if you don't come back, you will be a grievous loss, I'm sure.'

Gallus saluted again before he said something he regretted.

"Oh, one more thing Tiomarus."

"Sir?"

"If Centurion Pinneius can find a use for you, you need not rush back. I will sign things off if required. Otherwise, be back in three weeks. We may have a better picture of movement orders."

"Thank you, sir."

"Dismiss, hastiliarius."

He did not wait for a change of heart and went on the scrounge for an extra cloak and some rations before setting off. There was enough of the day left to make a dent in the journey. He gambled he could do the high section of the crossing with a single night halt, provided he nursed the horse a bit and the mare did nothing stupid like breaking a leg and letting him down.

*

He reached and passed the first small fort on the road north. At the second, an even smaller outpost, the light was beginning to fade on him, so he decided to seek a billet for the night. He was gratified to get a different tenor of reception. A quick explanation at the gate was all that was necessary. The tesserarius in charge shook his arm and said he could eat with him when he finished the watch.

The next morning, well rested, he set off towards a deep, whitened valley where the tree lines halted halfway up the slopes. For a while, the valley was arrow-straight, heading northeast. Save for animal trails, he appeared to be the sole fool up here and he pressed on along the valley floor, staying cautious of drifts covering streams he could hear but not see. He climbed higher through the pass with a razoring wind kicking up dry powder. The trail began to bend. On the trail's summit he rested his horse and took a drink from his icy water flask. The sharpness of the air made him cough but it was a sharp pleasure to be above the world, unconcerned by men or warfare. Only the urgency of getting down to a safer, less exposed level spoiled the moment of solitude. He took the horse by its reins and began a slow steady descent, favoured by the shoulder of the pass cutting off the worst of the wind. By the time he reached a loch, he and his mount were done in. He had pushed her too much. The snow was not as deep but common sense told him to stop and make a billet.

There was a good piece of shelter near the southern end and he led her into the relative warmth of a stand of trees, out of both snow and wind, giving thanks the ground underfoot was dry. One cold night and they would be on their way at first light.

The next morning, he kept both cloaks on and got moving as soon as he could get his circulation going and see the path. Passing around the loch's edge he found the ground beginning to descend. It got easier and then, he was through it. The distant triple peaks of Trimontium told him his course.

*

"How long have you been out there, Gallus?" Velio said.

He pumped his shivering old friend's arm, and almost

dragged him indoors to the fire in his house before the older man could reply.

"The fire in the principia is never as hot as this one," he confided, "you can have a soak in the bathhouse when you're ready."

Gallus laughed and surrendered to his former protégé's admonishment. Food arrived and dry caligae for his feet, dry socks too. The ice laden cloaks were whisked way to be thawed and dried and one of Velio's own provided. His house servant stood poised like a hound.

"Stay here, eat and rest, we'll talk later. I have a few things to attend to today," Velio said, "it is good to see you Gallus. I've been thinking a lot about the old days recently. Ask Lentulus for anything you need."

"A dry bed for a couple hours Velio," he murmured.

"Lentulus, see to it please."

And Velio was gone.

Afterwards they took a stroll around the fort. Gallus was well known within the legion and this welcome was more to his liking. After all, a senior hastiliarius deserved a little respect. He sniffed the horse odoured air.

"You could have frozen to death out there, my friend," Velio chided.

"Freezing up in the hills or freezing under the Blatobulgium welcome was some choice, Velio," he said.

"And I preferred to take my chances and come and visit an old comrade," he added.

"I admit I am surprised Gallus. I would have thought they would have been delighted to have you in their walls," Velio replied.

He was puzzled but tried to be diplomatic. Gallus smiled.

"You've done well Velio, a first command of a fort. And not just any fort. One of the most important forts north of Hadrian's Stones."

"Hush Gallus, you will embarrass me."

"No more than you deserve, it's no more than you deserve."

They paused at Velio's thinking spot, on the rampart overlooking the river before it ran under the bridge.

"What's bothering you Velio? There is something going on in that head, I can tell. If you cannot tell Gallus Tiomaris, I don't know what has become of us. Unless it's top-secret orders?"

He gave Velio a fond look. A soldier called Brutus Carruso had been ordered to murder Velio once and he had to sort Carruso out in the style he deserved when Velio found himself caught disarmed at the wrong end of the soldier's gladius. A gifted soldier might have been murdered by a poor one. No thug was going to get away with that; Velio was one of his boys. He did it the 'old legion' way. Sort it out and never speak of it again. Velio saw that look and knew the game was up.

'How do I explain this to him?' he wondered.

He leaned his back on the stone parapet and took in his domain. A fort full of busy legionaries. The noise level alone vouching for their industry. Somebody was whistling. He scratched the side of his mouth and turned around to face the countryside around them.

"It's like this Gallus. We have orders to evacuate the wall."

"That's common knowledge now Velio."

"There's another order that I must keep to myself for the moment that won't be popular," he went on.

"You have to stay until everyone else has evacuated? Some unlucky cohort is always last off the field. Best it is the lads of The Boar that do it. Make sure it's done right," Gallus brogued.

"It's something like that Gallus."

"Well, if it's not that, what is it?" Gallus enquired, his curiosity piquing.

Velio looked at Gallus.

"Remember the day I came back from that northern patrol and told you Marcus was dead?"

Gallus' face changed. Velio watched Gallus' eyes go a

neutral, baleful grey, yielding no insight to what he might be thinking.

"I remember it quite well Velio. You were very distressed about it as I recall. He was a good soldier. And he was a friend to both of us."

Velio dug his fingers into his arms as the memories flooded back.

"He was both those things and more. And I am not leaving the wall we fought to build until I've put a marker down where he fell. If he had died in the garrison, we would have buried him in the cemetery, and he would have had a stone with his name carved on it. Well, he died up there in the wilds of nowhere and I can't leave until I have marked where he fell."

He started shaking as all the pent-up words came out of hiding as a real promise. Gallus pursed his mouth and turned his eyes to the rolling land beneath the fort.

"You told me he fell into a river Velio, so his bones aren't where he was killed anymore," he felt duty bound to point out.

Velio clenched his jaw and raised his fist.

"Well, I'm going to put a marker down on the spot where he took the arrow. May Mars and Jupiter, thou Best and Greatest, curse me if do not carry this out. I vow I will do it Gallus, *Willingly, Gladly, Unreservedly,*' you know the words, I vow, do you hear me? I'm not going to let this go."

"For the glory of the Emperor Antoninus Pius, Father to his country, Centurion Velio Pinneius of the Twentieth Legion did this. Willingly, Gladly, Unreservedly, he fulfilled his vow," Gallus expounded.

"Don't mock me Gallus."

"I don't mock you Velio, is that what Marcus' gravestone will say? Look, Velio, you are not going off to do this on your own. You've got a fort to command for one thing. We can't just head off for the north."

"We, Gallus?"

"We, Centurion Pinneius, sir," he assented.

"I see. It so happens I have another order to deliver to an old friend of ours who is up on the wall."

Velio tugged his nose for a moment.

"Fancy a last look at the barbarian north, Gallus?"

"Have you even got a marker for Marcus, Velio? Sorry, what a stupid question, of course you have," Gallus sighed before he continued, "could you even find the place again? Were you planning on riding up there alone? What if you, what if we I mean, get caught by one of the tribes?"

"I can find it again," Velio replied.

Once the thaw set in, the snow vanished from the road in

the space of a day or so. Velio ordered Fufius and his premier turma to accompany them. They travelled at a decent clip and got first sight of the northern defence zone on the second day. It gave him a strange jolt to think that a few steps over those lines, Rome declared no further interest in what lay beyond. There was nothing worth having: no mines, no bloomeries, no timber stocks or fields of grain and cattle, no recruits for the legions. The tribes were welcome to the marshes and moors and all the cruel gods of the dark places that went with them. It was the end of the world.

They paused on a low rise. Over on their right-hand side beyond the Hill of the Resting Lion and that odd, barren stump of rock with its tapering tail, the waters of the Bodotria lay placid and blue. He let the horses drink and took in the sight, recalling the fight that had occurred on the lion hill and how close Brutus Carruso had pushed him towards death, until Gallus stepped in. Now, fifteen years on, they were venturing back into that past.

They made camp and set off early the next day. He led them past the turn off to Carumabo harbour and kept on, over the wide, well-trodden plain. It was all old familiar ground. Further on they reached the summit of the final low ridge and saw the wall and its network of signalling stations. Despite the constant pressures it had been subjected to, the attempts to burn and harry, he still found it an impressive sight. From this distance the continual repairs could not be seen. Clusters of native round houses coalesced at the forts. But there was something else, smoke palls that were more than just domestic cooking fires. Palls from destruction and looting. The wall was a false oasis of order and calm. The guerrilla war that had been foaming for years against the turfed ramparts had managed to lick out the willpower to resist. Like the sections where the sods were crumbling, the cohorts were beginning to lose the contest.

He let them gather their breath and rest the horses, though he did not want the gravity of the situation to take hold. Fufius and his men were going to talk about what they were seeing and while the duty to honour Marcus was everything to him, he knew their opinions could spread like rust on an old lorica when they got back to Trimontium. Everyone wanted to know how things were up here without wanting to come and find out for themselves first-hand. He glanced at Gallus and Fufius. They nodded back; no words needed.

The guard on the Decumana gate at Velunia picked them up in the distance. The camp praefectus came to have a look. He began to smile.

"As I live and breathe, it's Velio Pinneius and Gallus Tiomaris," he said.

Minutes later Velio pulled his men up to a halt and dismounted.

"Salve, Hanno Glaccus. How goes the war?"

"Salve Centurion Pinneius, getting better on a horse I see," he grinned.

"It's the practise, do you know Fufius my cavalry lead? It amuses him to make me ride horses."

"Welcome Fufius, and you too Gallus. Quite the gathering, is it not? You've come to rescue me?"

Hanno Glaccus grinned wide enough to make his face split. His guards found it hard not to join in.

"Rescue you? I can't think of a soldier who needs less rescuing than Hanno Glaccus," Velio replied.

"Come, let's get you some food. Welcome to the splendour that is Velunia. I hope you brought warm cloaks," Hanno teased.

Velio left Fufius and Gallus to the hospitality of Hanno's staff and sat in Hanno's office.

For a second Hanno looked at him. Velio was leaner if anything than when he was younger, a bit greyer at the temples too, but no disgrace to bow to age's touch. But the same resilient eyes looked back at him. He had matured. Hanno surmised it was the final promotion that must have driven that home. The responsibility for other men's lives and all that. Their leader in battle. Their source of courage and their judge. Here was an example of what a good soldier could do with his life, becoming the emperor's man. He believed it was the power of the vine-stick. The wooden symbol of centurion power. Once you had held one, it imbued a tangible and unshakeable confidence. He had witnessed it many times. Hand an experienced optio, ready to make the jump, a vine stick and you could tell by the wheels and cogs turning behind his eyes that nothing was ever going to remove that rough piece of wood from his grip, except death.

He offered some wine and Velio took it before clearing his throat.

'Now it comes,' he thought.

Velio dug into his military document case and pulled out a scroll, passing it across the table.

"I have brought you an order," Velio said.

"Do you know what it says?" he asked.

"I don't. I have just received two orders myself." Velio replied.

"Why did you bring it in person at a time like this? A courier was all that was necessary Velio. You did not need to take the time or the trouble."

"I have something to discuss with you Hanno, and truth be told, bringing your order gives me the chance to do exactly that," Velio replied.

"Ah, I see. Well first, let us see what the governor wants me to do shall we?"

He slit open the waxed seal with his pugio-dagger, and unrolled the message. For several moments Velio sat and waited, examining Hanno's expression for a clue. The older man put it down, gazing at the far wall of the office in deep thought and then he shrugged.

"He orders me to organise the retreat from here and to liaise with you and our friend Dometius Barrus in Blatobulgium. He says I can commence issuing the forts' decommissioning orders to the commanders as soon as practicable. I think by that he means immediately, and," he paused to secure Velio's attention, "explicitly in the order I am to protect both those who are leaving and those garrisons awaiting movement orders. Mars give me a soldier's death, that is quite an order, don't you think? Does he know how few men I have? Here read it for yourself."

Velio knew Hanno and Dometius Barrus hated each other with a vengeance. It was one of those unreasoned instant dislikes. No amount of flim-flam was ever going to disguise or cure it. They just did not like each other, plain and simple.

'You must liaise and co-operate with a man who dislikes you as much as you do him. Excellent prospects for success there,' he reckoned.

He scanned Hanno's order. This one had no personal messages of support nor explanations other than a hope Fortuna would walk at Hanno's side.

'Perhaps Hanno's too experienced to need all those encouraging words I got?'

He tried not to feel slighted.

"I don't think anyone has ever attempted this before Hanno, not even in Germania," he said.

"Retiring a single legion or an army from a fixed position would be easier than out of this long line. There must be nearly two legions worth of auxiliaries up here if you counted up all the garrisons," Hanno said shaking his head.

"I mean, is it wings first and centre last, or shuffle the centre out to the wings? No suggestions about how to do it, just *'get on with it Hanno Glaccus.'* Mithras, that's some order."

Hanno snarled into his wine cup.

Velio had not expected Hanno to be quite so agitated by the orders: he waited.

"So, what's your news Velio?"

Hanno took a longer pull at his wine and indicated the jug.

Velio shook his head and patted the arms of his chair to gee himself up. He could not imagine what the older man was going to make of this. Hanno was still shaking his head at his order. He handed the scroll back to him.

"It's like this, Hanno. First order, in accordance with yours, I am to support the withdrawal and maintain the road. Liaise appropriately, so on and so forth. The second order, and not yet released to my officers, so strictly between us, is this; Trimontium is not to be abandoned. All forts to the north of it will evacuate, including Carumabo; but Trimontium will assume a new role. We will be the northernmost outpost of the empire. We'll be famous."

Hanno sipped some more wine.

"Save that guff for your boys, Velio. That is going to be challenging given the state of tribal relations right now and given the fact Trimontium is currently understrength. Though perhaps not for much longer, I would hazard, young Pinneius. When will you tell your men?"

"I haven't decided," he replied.

"Best done soon if you want my opinion," Hanno said.

Velio spread his hands out and clenched his fingers a couple of times as he weighed it up, nodding as he reckoned the odds. It made a lot of sense. The longer he kept it from them the more disgruntled they were liable to be when they found out the truth. It was not going to be pleasant dreams when you knew you were beyond rescue if things went tits up.

"Good of you to tell me Velio, but why are you here?" Hanno pushed, "and why is that old wolf-wrestler Gallus here? I thought the emperor might have retired him by now?"

"You know Gallus. A Boar man. He will not leave. They'll find him cold in his bunk one morning and throw him on a fire, then use his bones to build a stockade."

"I expect so," Hanno mused.

"Hanno, I need you to buy me some time," he said.

"How so?"

"Do you remember a tesserarius called Marcus Hirtius?" he said.

"Not really, why?" Hanno replied.

He flooded more wine into Velio's cup.

"Marcus and I were instructors under Gallus when that little prick of a tribune Paterculus Vatinius was up here," he spat.

A light went on in Hanno's face.

"Cornelius Paterculus Vatinius, now there is a name from the past I have tried hard to forget. Insufferable little rat of a man. He was the one that came looking to you for a sword lesson with real weapons, wasn't he? Did not want to use the wooden swords if I remember correctly. Yes, and you gave him a cut on the wrist to remember the lesson by. I had to do a bit of fast talking on your behalf about that. Wanted you flogged for it. You had Servius Albinius on your side. He was not going to allow that to happen, flog a man he had just promoted, most unlikely. An insult to his judgement in fact. I don't think Paterculus ever really grasped what it was all about. A real charmer and of course he was the one that got himself and a whole turma of cavalry annihilated up on that hill to south of here. We never found his body. Did you no harm in the long run though, Velio. Servius promoted you eventually. Right, so; Marcus Hirtius is dead I presume? Cornelius Paterculus Vatinius I know is dead. Enlighten me Velio, I'm getting old and stupid, though I can just about recognise a bad order when I see one," he said.

He poked his finger at the scroll with an ironic, lopsided grin. Velio opened his mouth to speak but Hanno had the bit between his teeth.

"And he led the first patrol to find the officers of the old Ninth legion didn't he? You were on that one too. Except, it was you that found the first piece of evidence," he concluded.

"It was both of us, Marcus and me, who found the first helmet. He took an arrow in the throat and died up there. That is what I'm trying to tell you Hanno. I'm not leaving the wall to the barbarians without going back to where Marcus fell and putting down a marker. Gallus agrees and is coming with me. I'm asking you to do nothing until we get back. Hold back any evacuation orders until then. I want to be back in Trimontium before you set waggons on the road. Would you do that? At least consider that for me. As a favour, Hanno?"

Hanno sat back, changed his mind, leaned forwards, and topped up both their cups.

"I can't order you not to do it Velio, but it's a rash idea all the same. You must know that? For a commander to go off on a personal tribute, no matter how justifiable you feel it is, at the present time and with orders such as these on the table is highly irregular," he paused.

He could not prevent a fellow centurion and he was going to need to rely on Velio once all the movement started.

'Asinine, hare-brained nonsense. What are you thinking of? What possible difference will it make now? The man's been dead for fifteen years.'

But he could perhaps do something to make sure it did not turn into a fiasco of pointless bloodshed.

"These orders are damned betrayal of every soldier who served and fought for this ground. Fifteen years of sweat thrown away because the governor will not send enough men up here to stamp down on the tribes. So, what was the point of us ever being here? I ask you Velio, what was the bloody point?"

Hanno knew he was going red in the face. Velio watched and kept quiet. What Hanno Glaccus had not seen and done in his career was not worth knowing. A veteran in the days when he himself was only a twenty-four-year-old instructor. He had never seen him so angry. He sipped his wine and waited.

Hanno threw his cupful back and served them again, laying the silver wine tankard down without any trace of the angry squall unleashed seconds before. There was a curtain somehow descending between them. Hanno had moved a piece on some internal gaming board, and he had no idea which game was playing or even if he was included in it. Hanno managed a crooked grin.

"If my memory serves, Velio, Paterculus' patrol was a ten-day mission. I will give you that much time. That's fair, isn't it? It will take me that long to copy out my authority-order to the forts and plan the evacuation movements. I'll have to decide how I'm going to do it first. I will need returns of transport and draft animals: you know the drill. And like Servius told our late unlamented tribune, I cannot send troops to rescue you."

'I don't want rescuing, I just want the time to do this,' Velio breathed.

He made himself smile. Hanno really was playing with him.

"Thank you, Hanno, that is all I need. Here's to Marcus Hirtius, and every brave soldier who died up here. May they never have cause to rebuke us."

"To Marcus Hirtius," Hanno replied.

Velio had just decided an issue for him without even knowing what his problem had been.

Fufius joined them later, then Gallus. The hastiliarius started feeling a little uncomfortable sitting with the senior ranks. They were younger men and higher ranking. Educated and better with soft words, though how Velio had acquired that skill eluded him. Somewhere over the last few years he must have found it. He could feel there were things they wanted to discuss and excused himself at a suitable moment. The final thing he heard as he left was from Velio.

"You will take the patrol back to Trimontium tomorrow Fufius, Gallus and I have a little errand that will delay us. We'll be back in Trimontium as soon as it's done."

"As you command, centurion," Fufius replied.

It sounded like an answer of food and wine.

Chapter 9.
The Veniconi heartlands, north of the turf wall.

Aulercas saw his arrow hit the deer a few inches behind the left shoulder. Straight to the heart and lungs. It staggered and turned, seeing them for the first time. They had played the wind direction and the folds in the ground so well she had not seen or smelled a thing. She moved a foreleg and grunted, blood coughing from her mouth as she sank down to the earth.

"Good shot father," young Aulercas burst out.

The elder of the name, smiled and gave him a pat on the shoulder.

"Well, we did not want to chase her all day over the hill and through the woods, did we, Little Owl?"

"No father but she didn't even know we were watching her."

"It was quick and clean, the way it should always be," he preached.

Together they tied her to the pack pony, little Aulercas stroking the fur that was still warm, and began heading home. The whole day beckoned much brighter with fresh deer hanging from the rafters. They crossed the three streams between the high ground and the village, happy and laughing, little Aulercas leading the pony on the flat. They were spotted from a distance and waved back to tell everyone their hunt was successful.

"Live where you can see your enemies coming," Grandpa Heruscomani used to joke with him: before the sickness stole his kind smile and his silly jokes.

To the north a wide moorland of ponds and mosses lay apron-like below the high mountains. And up in those fastnesses was the *'valley of many bones.'*

Aulercas untied the deer and laid her down on the outside table. He went inside for his favourite skinning knife and Little Owl heard his mother's happy greeting. When he returned there was a huge happy smile on his father's face. The servants had already tied the animal up ready to be cleaned. He offered the knife to Little Owl.

"Time you did one," he smiled, "you stalked her, you saw her killed, you helped carry her. Clean her, say a thanks for her, and when you eat her, you will know how she found her way into your belly and made you happy and warm."

"Can I have the hide as well, father?"

"Oh, so do you think you can take it off without any mistakes? No damage? Well, let's see. If you do it well and make a good job of it, I might let you keep it. First you must clean her insides out. Take the heart to your mother."

Young Aulercas set to with sudden concentration. Aulercas patted his shoulder and left him and the servants to it.

*

Ucsella stared at the man in the long grass at the foot of the fence and he stared back at her. She reached out and touched the metal around the forehead and flaps protecting his eyes and the sides of his face, tapping it with her nails. It made the familiar, thin musical note. Her fingers wandered from the metal to the high points of the cheek bone. He did not flinch. Then the nose, brushing the bone with the fleshy parts of her fingers. He did nothing. She sighed; he never wanted to play with her. She withdrew her hand and sat back on her haunches. There was no amusement to be found here. The head and its metal covering were incapable of interaction. She could talk to it and tell all her problems to it, but there was never an answer forthcoming. She wondered where father had found it and why it was lying here. It had been here for as long as she could remember. She could hear her brother trying to claim the new deer hide for his own. She would have to find a way of getting it away from him.

Chapter 10.
Velunia fort.

Velio and Gallus slipped out of Velunia in the early hours before the dawn bugle. Hanno sent them on their way with good packhorses to carry their kit and plenty of rations, waving a solitary farewell from the Praetoria gate as they headed towards the first river crossing lying a scant few thousand paces away. It was just one of the several they were going to have to cross before they passed out of passive Votadini lands into the disputed territory. Velio decided they would take their full armour, helmets, shields, a spare gladius for each of them, some pila-spears, all packed on the spare animals. They would travel in warm tunics and cloaks better suited to camouflage. It was a strategy that would do them little good if they were caught by surprise. Gallus got it though, better to die fighting as a Boar legionary if they had the few minutes needed to kit-up in the loricas. The shields were worth ten extra men to them. Food, some wine, water bottles, a couple of clean bandages from the medicus, and the precious bundle containing the small dedication with Marcus' name on it. They did not need more.

Gallus' question at Trimontium, *'can you find it again?'* had been dogging Velio as he tried to recall the steps they had taken getting there and back the first time. They rode in silence for a while, making their way up to the Bodotria crossing. Finally, they were over it and Gallus felt a real flutter of anticipation in his guts. They took the road north for a few miles before bearing off and settling in a defensible spot for the night, making a low fire and taking hot food while they could.

"We could do a bit of scouting while we're up here," he suggested to Velio, "on the way back I mean."

"That's an idea Gallus. It could be useful, but for now I think we should concentrate on getting up there and getting back out."

"It's not too late to change your mind about doing this Velio. Marcus would not hold it against you. He's probably sitting somewhere thinking the whole idea is bloody daft," he teased.

"In soldier's Elysium?" Velio winced.

"He'll be in a wine shop, if they have such things in the afterlife," he averred.

"Well, if they have, Marcus will find it and if they haven't, he'll be moaning their ears raw. Do you think we'll meet him again Gallus?"

"I don't know Velio, but hopefully not in the next ten days," he said.

They pressed on, heading to the old legionary fortress on

the Tavae because that was the route he remembered. It was a bit of a dog leg but from there it would be a swing to the west towards the big moor. Beyond that were the mountains and the glen where it all happened. He intended to find the spot, put down the stone marker, say some words, whatever they might be, and then they would get out, sharpish.

It started getting difficult about the time they reached the vicinity of the fortress. The price of staying off General Agricola's old road, away from prying eyes, forsaking the speed of its still pristine stone surface for ground that was either wet or still under patchy snow, became clear. There were more native halls, protected by wooden stockades, than Velio remembered; more eyes waiting to track their movement. Travelling off the road under cover of night was going to be far too risky. The ground was unknown and treacherous. And that was not the least of it. Who knew what was out there in the dark? With snow still on the hills it was easy to see Trimontium's thaw had not reached this far north.

Several hours passed of dodging around what appeared to be an endless sea of native dwellings that popped up blocking their path with annoying regularity. Any one of which could raise the alarm.

"I don't think we can make it, Gallus. Not without being seen," he said.

He was no longer certain they were still heading in the right direction after one laborious diversion brought back them too close to the road again.

"And if they see us, we're as dead as Marcus," Gallus replied.

He bit his tongue and let it go. Gallus was entitled to his opinion. They pushed on and on, mile after mile, wrestling with their misgivings. If Gallus began losing his enthusiasm for this it was going to get difficult. Perhaps he had been too quick to drag him into this? Perhaps this was why Hanno had agreed to delay the evacuation orders; Hanno had worked out the lunacy of what he was attempting to do and kept a diplomatic silence?

Evening came as sort of blessing, pressing the need to halt. They were losing direction again in the oncoming darkness, hunting for another safe hideaway. Traversing around a low hump of ground, without warning they struck what could only be the lesser road that had once serviced the supply of Pinnata Castra. There was no other reason for a manufactured road to be in this area and it was clearly of legionary construction. The packed gravel surface was all that had been laid before the fort was abandoned. Weeds and vegetation had made some inroads. Stunted tree saplings and bushes had taken hold, but it was without doubt an army road.

The tale of the whole construction effort at Pinnata Castra was Twentieth legion folklore. Massive efforts for a fortress big enough to house the whole five- thousand strong manpower of The Boar in one location. Sweat and blood and toil for three solid years and then, *'pack up lads, the general has changed his mind. He doesn't need this fort any longer. Oh, and pull it all down again.'*

Who would want to be a stone mason in this army?

The sound of the nearby Tavae water guided them. Velio dismounted and walked on. It was time to get that safe billet. Within minutes they found the outer ditch of the fort. The ditch was no good. Too easy to get trapped and cornered down in that place. Good for hiding the horses and making a small fire but too big an area for a man to mount a safe night guard while the other slept. They hid the horses in a stand of alders and willow right down by the icy river's edge and hunkered down within touching distance of the water among some large awkward sized rocks. With the swift running water at their backs, they had a beach of heavy stones in front that would be noisy and awkward to cross. It was not the worst position to defend or spend the night.

"So, do we go on Velio? Or find the best place we can, lay the marker, and call it quits?"

Gallus huddled down to rest his bones. Velio looked at his old mentor. There was not a trace of fear in his eyes but there was concern in spadefuls. It had been a gruelling day and

Gallus was not getting any younger.

"You and Marcus came this way with the tribune, didn't you?" Gallus continued.

"We did," he answered.

Gallus looked around in the gloom where the fort had once stood; a low plateau cradled and protected by the sweeping arm of the river. A magnificent site: was it fanciful to imagine Mars had selected the place himself to bring Rome's message to the north? If it had been completed in stone, he suspected its mere presence could have quelled tribal resistance for generations. Perhaps the emperor's turf wall would have been unnecessary. And that brought him back to the very reason for huddling here in the cold and gloom: Marcus.

"Then Marcus is here as much as he is in the glen you're trying to get us to," he said.

"You mean put his marker right here?" Velio queried.

He settled against a convenient stone to protect his back and shield some of the cold air coming off the water.

"Well, this was our great fortress of the Twentieth legion at one time, wasn't it?"

"It was," Velio replied.

"Marcus would not want us to get killed for the sake of a few more miles. He'd appreciate a marker wherever it is. But here makes sense. This might even be the same river he died in," Gallus opined.

Velio shook his head, it was probably not the same water.

"Just think on it Velio, before we go beyond the point. Sleep on it, centurion. That is all an old hastiliarius can ask," Gallus pleaded.

The first attack came that night.

Chapter 11.
Trimontium fort.

Fufius brought his men over the bridge and up the hill into Trimontium. Tacto observed the furore of the arriving, muddy, horsemen. The commander and the hastiliarius were absent from the front of the squadron. Perplexed, he returned to the commander's office to resume the tasks Velio had left in his care. He did not have to wait for long before Fufius came bustling into the principia looking for him, spurting out incredible news that the two men had gone over the lines into enemy territory. It got a bit garbled after that and he let Fufius splutter on to an eventual halt.

"He's not going to come back Tacto. It's a suicide mission. I think he's chosen to die up there for some reason," Fufius said.

"You had better read that," Tacto replied.

He pushed an order-scroll bearing the governor's seal across the table.

"Are you supposed to read this?" Fufius worried.

"Just read it and keep the message to yourself," he warned.

Fufius laid down his helmet on the floor by his feet and took the scroll. Tacto sat back and waited for another outburst.

"Fuck," Fufius murmured, "Sons of Dis," he added for good measure, "well, what do you make of it?"

"We're to stay. Last outpost in the north, while everyone else locates back to the 'stones?'"

Fufius shook his head and clenched his fist in a handful of his hair, letting out a howling moan of despair.

"Fuck."

"Precisely. We are being hung out to dry; I think it would be fair to say. A target for every war band. If they lay siege to us, things will surely get interesting," Tacto said.

"Why didn't he tell us?" Fufius' asked.

"I'm sure he intends to, and he must never find out that we found the order and have read it Fufius. Never," he raised his finger.

"Perhaps, he doesn't intend to tell us. May be that why he's gone over the wall?" Fufius replied.

"I'm sure there's more to it than that," Tacto demurred.

"He even left his girl behind," Fufius went on.

"Fufius, I don't like whatever it is that's going on in your head. You have no reason to think Velio has chosen to desert us because of this order. There must be another explanation."

"Well, if there is, he didn't bother to tell me, and I was up there with him the night before he left with that hastiliarius. I sat and dined with him and Hanno Glaccus, sat right beside him and he said not one word," Fufius jibbed.

"Careful Fufius, he doesn't tell me much and I'm his second and for what it's worth that hastiliarius is one of the most senior soldiers in the legion below optio," he hissed back.

"Well, that may be but I'm thinking if we are to be the last link in the chain and our commander has abandoned us, leaving you and me to command, then I'm going over to that Votadini pigsty and having his woman," Fufius fumed.

"I hope that's a joke. Not wise Fufius, not wise. For a start there are more things you should be thinking about, like doing what you have been ordered to do for a start. Frankly, I do not care if you and all your troopers tie her to a waggon first but let's just wait a while before you start another war down here. Velio will have his reasons. A bit of loyalty would not go amiss don't you think Fufius? Go and get yourself some dry clothes and some food inside you and then get rid of these thoughts. That's an order."

Fufius stormed out.

'Mutinous little bastard,' Tacto thought, *'arrogant, mutinous, little bastard. Twenty-seven years old and he thinks he knows it all, thinks he knows better than Velio Pinneius. Who knows what Velio sees in him? If he touches Velio's girl, I will cut his balls off. Bloody cavalry, the whole lot of them are a pain in the arse. His horse has got more between its ears than he has; what are you up to Velio?'*

*

Marcus was there in the moonlight. The arrow that killed him still jutting out of his neck. He was soaking wet, water dripping from his armour onto the rocks. Velio blinked at the outline on the other side of the fire. Behind him the river was busy and yet quiet also, lullaby-ing past. Marcus must have come from out of there. His eyes were open and despite the appalling arrow, he was smiling. Velio sensed he could not speak. The arrow saw to that.

It was impossible. He had seen Marcus fall in the forbidding, gloomy glen, he had been powerless to prevent the light in his eyes going out. Then, there was the split-second choice to let the river have him or leave him to be mutilated by the heathens who launched an attack from out of nowhere. Running to save his own life hurt as much as seeing Marcus die. And his punishment for making that decision was having to endure remembrance of those moments down through all the years since. Marcus had died because of the actions of a cocky young tribune out to prove a point of principle about a legion that was already dead for thirty years. The unlucky Ninth.

'We should find them and recover what we can as a sign to the tribes that even in death we rule this land,' or some such claptrap.

And against all odds and logic that patrol had stumbled upon a valley where some of the Ninth's higher ranking officers had been murdered. He and Marcus had found the bones and helmets.

'Bloody impossible unless the gods wanted it to happen. If that was so, what was Marcus? Some kind of blood-payment for showing them the place? It feels more like a barbarian god's condition than a Roman god's. Nothing makes sense.'

Even now he could not believe what they had done. But what a useless waste of Marcus' life. Paterculus' bombast had killed him just as much as the barbarian arrow in his throat.

He sat up, "Marcus? Brother? Is it you?"

His friend had not aged. He was still young.

"Is it really you Marcus?" he repeated.

Marcus was silent.

"Sons of Dis, is that you Marcus?" Gallus croaked beside him.

He turned, glad that his old mentor was witnessing this vision too. Gallus' face was pale even under the moon light.

"It can't be. Velio? Marcus?" Gallus repeated.

Marcus saluted them both with full legionary decorum and then banged his fist on his chest making his phalerae discs rattle. He had always been proud of them. Velio threw off the cloak and started getting to his feet.

"Wait, Velio," Gallus said, "get your lorica on. It's a warning."

Marcus turned his gaze on Gallus and smiled. And then he vanished leaving the stones where he had been standing, wet.

"He is trying to warn us Velio, get the armour off the horses I'll get the shields and helmets, be quick. There may not be much time."

They scrambled to the horses, keeping low down, conscious of the time it would take to strap each other into their armour. Gallus pulled the shields and pila-spears from the horse. Velio adjusted his helmet.

"Fuck them, let them come" he said, "this Boar won't go down easily."

"What about the fire, centurion?" Gallus asked.

"Leave it. They know we are here, and we may need it," Velio ordered.

They had two spears each, both with narrow shafted metal heads designed to bend on impact so they could not be used by an enemy and thrown back. Gallus put one butt first between some rocks, leaving it sticking up like a nasty welcome and held the other ready, with his shield held close. Velio did the same.

"The rocks will slow them down. And the river is too difficult," Gallus said, assessing the ground.

"Hold the pila and we can pick them off," Velio said.

"Agreed," Gallus answered, "and pray to Mars they have no

archers."

"It would be impossible," he replied, "they would hit their own as well as us.

"Prayers to Mars anyway," Gallus retorted.

Seconds passed. The sound of breaking sticks. A low curse of unknown words. Something skittered off a rock and flighted away into the darkness. Velio checked the moon. It sailed above them clear and bright providing the only source of light apart from the fire. From out of the shadows on the high ground they spotted movement coming down to the river.

"How many?" he hissed.

"Enough to go around centurion," Gallus said.

"Time to kill the fire. Let's not make it any easier if they have a bowman."

"Agreed," Gallus said.

He kicked the low burning pieces of branch apart, letting them carry on burning. An arrow thudded into his shield. He switched the pilum to his shield side, picked up a burning branch and hefted it at the line of men. It did enough to make them move.

"I count seven or eight, Gallus."

"Good odds Centurion Pinneius," Gallus chuckled, "come on you dirty arsed heathen scum, come and taste some good Roman steel."

He launched the most comprehensive insult in Brigantes that he knew hoping it would spur them into rashness. Then he flung the pilum to provoke them on further. The longer they stood, the longer they had to organise an outflanking attack.

'Don't give your enemy time to think' was always a good maxim when the odds were against you.

Velio flung his first pilum. A definite grunt of pain made him smile.

"Hold fast Gallus, let's not lose the advantage of these rocks," he said.

Then the tribesmen were on them, bounding over the rough ground, one slipped with a yell and was left behind and the others came on. Three of them homing in on Gallus, five aiming for Velio's helmet. Nine of them, counting the one on the ground, where was the bowman?

Gallus let them come and then fired the second pilum into the guts of the leading warrior, it pierced his long leather jerkin and he pitched forward, bending the spear shaft, and rolling sideways as it went right though him. The other two dodged around him. Gallus drew his gladius, swishing it once to loosen his wrist and blocked, parried and jabbed them both down, plunging the gladius into them until they ceased moving. He looked up. Velio's more decorated helmet crest was visible over the heads of the warriors encircling him.

Gallus heard a flurry of clashing steel. The first one went down. Like flashes of lightning, sparks blossomed as Velio first parried and then killed another with a pull back of the blade past the head to open the side of the neck. His favourite strike. He stepped in to help and killed a third in the back. Two left now plus the one who had fallen, now back up on his feet and an unseen bowman. He grabbed Velio's remaining pilum and nailed the one who had fallen. It hit him in the thigh. A mortal wound in the circumstances because he was running nowhere now. Gallus left him for later. Two on two. He began rotating his gladius in a circular action as he closed in to Velio's side.

"I like these odds better, centurion," he smirked.

The warrriors faced up to them for a second longer and turned to run. As they passed their fallen comrade, he said something and with the briefest of hesitations, one of them killed him with a thrust into the chest. They were off the rocky beach and up into the darkness of the grassy embankment before either he or Velio could stop them.

"Think they've gone?" he said.

"They've not gone. They've just stepped back for now," Velio replied.

"If they get the horses Velio we're walking out of here."

"Then they'd better not get them, Gallus."

"We can build a barricade with the bodies," he replied.

"Let's do that. They can take an arrow for us just as well as we can," said Velio.

They held their shields up and dragged the bodies into a low pile. It was not much of a defence, but it was something to wait behind, another obstacle for their assailants to master.

"Find the pila, there might be one of them we can use again," said Velio.

He pulled the one from the thigh of the unlucky warrior. It was undamaged. Where was the first one Gallus had thrown? The one that missed its target. He hunted up on the grass until he found it. It too was still serviceable.

"I'll set them at an angle. They might hook a fish if they come in a rush," he said.

"Well, it settles one thing Gallus," remarked Velio.

"What's that?"

"Marcus is going to have his marker here. If we get out of this alive," he retorted.

"I wish he was here, as Mars and Jupiter allow, that extra sword, I wish he was here too," Gallus muttered.

"He was here, that is why we are still alive, remember? Look out, they're coming again," Velio grunted.

More arrows this time but the sky was darkening with cloud, lessening the moonlight. They glanced at each other at the clear omen and took some heart from it. They locked their shields in a mini testudo and let the arrows thud into the wood. Others hit the rocks around them. Velio risked a look in case they were being stalked as the arrows rained down. Nothing. Then the aerial assault ceased.

"We could try and ride out now while they reorganise," Gallus suggested. He shook his head.

"I reckon they've got one more attack left in them and if we get through that, we'll put the marker up there at the fortress at first light and get out of here. Agreed?"

"Agreed."

Twenty minutes drifted past. They looked at each other. A yell in the night then a full war cry and they stood up to meet whatever was heading their way. A group of warriors surged towards them. They stepped back letting the rocks and the impromptu barricade of dead warriors impede the attack and then set about it. Gallus knew Velio had always had a fast hand with a gladius but something godlike took his form tonight. While he could still chop them down, he was getting more and more tired. Velio was getting stronger and somehow more intimidating as each warrior fell under his blade.

He stepped back, just out of reach of his last duellist to grab an extra breath. His adversary fell from an unexpected lateral rib jab from Velio as he managed to take his own man as well. Velio had become invincible: an Achilles. The darkness left no chance for them to read his blows and with his shield covering his own body, he could take chances. The tribesmen fell back, shouting insults and pulling their wounded away. Gallus had no idea how many had made this assault, but Velio had killed and incapacitated more than his share. Within a few moments the riverside beach was empty once more.

"The horses Gallus, have we still got our horses?"

"I think so Velio."

"We'll move over there. We mustn't lose them now. Stoke the fire back up. Let's see if we can fox them a bit more," he said.

*

Aulercas saw the returning warriors and knew something was wrong. There were bodies strapped to some of the horses and the riders looked despondent. He kneed his horse and trotted down to the king's village, forgetting all about the trades he had come to make. A crowd was gathering outside the palisade walls as he rode in from the hill behind them unnoticed. The warriors reached the crowd and began untying the bundles of men. He could hear the first cries of anguish breaking out. A leaden fear started working knots in his stomach. There was no reason for so many men to be dead. The closer he got the clearer the numbers became. There were fewer men bringing the bodies back than actual bodies themselves: there were too many empty seats. He swore and tethered his horse.

'Has Asuvad got a rogue Dumnoni sept in his midst? He has never suggested his people harboured evil towards us?' he wondered.

'Taexalii warriors on the maraud?'

He did not believe either possibility.

'So that leaves only one thing it can be. A Romani patrol has come north of the river.'

It must be a strong patrol judging by the number of dead men. They made way for him to inspect the bodies.

"Romani?" he grunted his suspicion.

"Yes, Roman pigs."

"How many? Is it a big patrol? Do they have an emblem pole?"

It would be a sure sign they meant business. The men shuffled before his questioning.

"Where did you meet them exactly?" he went on, unable to take his eyes from the sight of so many dead men. They deferred to him, edging back before his questions.

"At the old fort on the river," one answered.

"So how many were there in the patrol?" he probed.

"There is no patrol. There were only two of them," the warrior admitted putting his hand on his sword as he waited for a chorus of jeering.

"Two?" Aulercas said, "and they did all this?"

"We caught them at night. They were camped down by the river among the rocks. It should have been easy, but they fought like twenty men. They fought as though they were attacking us."

"And where are their heads?"

The king's voice reached them, he had sword buckled and his face was face red.

"Why did you not bring me back their heads for their punishment? I want their heads on poles outside my hall for this," he demanded.

"Their heads are still on their shoulders my lord. Forgive us. They fought like nothing I have ever faced before. They were possessed. Their gods were at their backs, my lord."

"They did this, and they still live?" he snapped.

He glared into their faces.

"There may have been a third one. It was hard to tell in the dark. Two of them, but perhaps there were three of them, I could see two of their faces but not the third one, I think he must have been hiding in the river. He must have come out of the water. At first there were two and then three. My lord it was dark. I am certain there were three. I do not know my lord. I don't understand how they beat us," the same warrior replied.

"Three is no less disgrace than two, you fool," he snapped, "they cannot be allowed to return to the wall, nor can they be allowed to come any closer or go further to the north. Aulercas, I want you to go and kill them. Our enemies must never hear of this defeat. Two of them, three, twenty, what does it matter? Let me see who is down. The bear's breath, they have killed Rucleotius, Eriscus, Locasses, Redorix, Diatuanis, even Gobbanitio? They were good men, experienced men, so were the others. These Romans will dishonour all of us as long as they have their heads."

Aulercas nodded.

"How many men do you need?" said the king.

"I need to find them and track them," he paused.

He thought fast in the face of the king's fury and the evidence. These men would not have died without fighting. They were not cowards, nor youthful, thoughtless gallants letting exuberance get the better of judgement.

"To bring back just two or three as prisoners, or dead? What do you prefer my lord?" he boasted.

"I want heads Aulercas. Bring them to me."

Chapter 12.
Eidumnos' hall, Trimontium.

Segontio left early the next day, bearing scratches on his face. It was best to get up into the high pass before Eidumnos or anyone else found Voccia. His face stung from the raking of her claws. What a raking before he got her arms pinned.

She was the one shining personality in Eidumnos' household. The moment he set eyes on her; he knew what he wanted. When she grinned and bobbed in response to Eidumnos' chastising the women out of the hall he was, he admitted to himself, smitten. That little, daughterly bob, so full of mischief, and the grin, such a delicious flash of white teeth.

Once they finished the discussions, Eidumnos insisted on taking them to see his cattle. So, they praised the beasts, admiring the rich glossy flanks of well-kept cattle and he was content. Then it was on the horses to go further afield. She simmered away in his head all through that ride. The thought of her under him kept him tense. Keeping clear of the soldiers' bridge they crossed the river upstream and cantered, seeing the rich fertile ground of the valley.

As the evening wore on, they shared wine gifted by the

centurion. He managed to stay out of an argument with Eidumnos about the good Roman. Asuvad refused to drink it and left first for Eidumnos brother's hall a short distance away. Eidumnos smiled at the Dumnoni's refusal to take anything from the invaders.

"He can afford his principles," he said, "good wine is good wine. I see no harm in accepting it. I was not trying to poison him. The gods won't turn in the sky or the woods tonight because he took a cup of Roman wine."

Segontio kept his thoughts on that to himself. Asuvad's denial of wine summed up the difference between those on the north side of the wall.

You might take more notice, old man. That man will bring his warriors through this pretty valley one day.

Eidumnos seemed to let it go and turned to questioning him about his father and his capital town. Voccia sat with them awhile, listening to him speaking with her father. He tried his best not to keep looking at her, but it was hard. She left early when her mother Bractia left. The door closed behind her as she went visiting.

"Does she have someone?" he felt compelled to ask.

Eidumnos regarded him over the rim of his ale cup. The wine was finished.

"You like my Voccia?"

He smiled back, "she is lovely Eidumnos," he admitted.

Eidumnos nodded, pleased.

"She has a young man, but it is just a friendship, nothing serious, if my wife's spies are to be believed," he joked.

'Well, that is good to know.'

They joined in the simple pleasure of the hot fire. He stretched his arms, a gentle sign to Eidumnos that he was ready to sleep.

"If you were to marry my Voccia, we would have a pact that is deeper than promises," Eidumnos murmured, almost into his own beard.

He started in surprise.

"You mean it? She is not betrothed to the young man or one of your warriors?" he said.

It seemed too good to be true that she might be free. Eidumnos nodded.

"I think she likes you and you obviously like her. I am not blind Segontio. It would make a good match."

"I say yes Eidumnos, I say yes indeed."

Eidumnos leaned over and patted his shoulder.

"Then I will tell her in the morning. And now my bones are telling me to lie down. There is much to do and discuss with Asuvad too. This problem of ours is not like morning mist. No, it will not simply fade away when the sun comes out."

Eidumnos got to his feet leaving him to the thoughts

burgeoning in his head as he enjoyed the fire for a bit longer. Then he realised he was intruding on Eidumnos and his wife's privacy. He emptied the cup and headed next door to where that relative of Eidumnos' lived. He struggled to remember if it was a cousin or was it a brother?

'Think, you fool.'

It was dark outside. Dark enough for the souls in the heavens to shine. He stopped to admire them. Voccia appeared, walking in the opposite direction. He grabbed her arm, not meaning to be so sudden, it was clumsy.

'I have good news for you,' he wanted to say.

She whirled around and retaliated with a slap. The warm happiness in his head vanished. It got worse, out of control, she started pulling away. He tried to make amends; the drink fuddled his words. Whatever looks passed between them in the hall were ghosts of what was happening now. She made a quick grab for the small knife in her belt, astonishing him. He pulled her behind a goat pen, down onto the straw, one hand on her mouth as he tried again to explain, but it was all going wrong. A whiplash stung his face, and the knife was out of its fine, decorated leather sheath. Dangerous as a viper fang. The hot fury flooding through him turned to lust.

He hauled away her clothing, ripping down his breeches and forcing himself into her, pounding her as she wriggled and fought. His left hand pinned the wrist and the viper-fang to the ground. Still, she was defying him, with her furious, outraged eyes. He intended a slap, but it became a fist to her temple to make her behave.

Voccia lying so quiet, so still; letting him do it to her as though she was absent from it. That was better. So pretty. Not saying anything. He grunted it out, in pleasure. She said nothing at all.

'Voccia, say something. Call me a pig. Tell me I must marry you or your father will go to war on me, because Voccia, we have already agreed this will happen. I did not want our love to begin this way. I promise you; I swear to you I will be kinder next time.'

Voccia still lying silent.

'Spirits of the river, is she dead? Have I killed her?'

Shaking her made no difference. He pulled her dress back down and sat back feeling a hot surge of panic in his chest. He had killed her and all the possibilities he had only just finished exploring with Eidumnos were dead inside her.

'But it was only a tap, just to make her obey.'

The world was spinning in front of him. He felt sick. He had to get out of here before anyone found her. It was not possible she could have died from that little tap.

'It was an accident.'

But they would never believe that. They would string his body up from an oak in revenge and never believe this was not a calculated and ruthless act of war.

*

He urged the horse on and on higher into the pass, past the loch where an aging Roman soldier had spent a cold and sleepless night among the trees, higher still towards the summit. Past the ancient marker that said to all who knew how to read it,

'These are the lands of the Selgovae.'

He decided it was not safe to halt so he kept walking, leading his mount, afraid that any stop longer than a few minutes to rest would be fatal. He watched the north-south Roman road for signs of cavalry patrols. It was deserted. He chose a place well out of sight of the forts before he risked crossing and pushed on for the citadel, feeling a lot safer now that the road was behind him. He had no doubts he was being pursued. Nor that he had enough of a gap to reach sanctuary with his exhausted mount. He changed horses at a farmer's hall, swapping over his tack, promising to return the animal in a few days. The man knew him and waved him on his way.

Chapter 13.
Trimontium fort.

"I've been thinking," Tacto said in the middle of the compound.

The legionaries were changing the guard on all sides, chased by a little optio intent on demonstrating his authority because the deputy commander was watching. He raised one Umbrian eyebrow, but otherwise kept his peace, returning the salute and waving the officer away so he could talk in private. Fufius was holding his mare by her reins with his hand on her muzzle. She batted her deep, liquid brown eyes at Fufius, and his arm went under her jaw to pat her cheek. He smiled. Fufius had left it late in the day to decide on exercising the horse. The sky was darkening. Two hours of decent light left. Perhaps he was just exercising Fufius?

"I think you should take a turma back up to Velunia and make sure our praefectus gets back. And Gallus too. Losing the old boy would not be good for the lads' morale. He is a bit of a talisman around here," he said.

"Always assuming he gets back to Velunia, Tacto. From wherever he went," Fufius pointed out.

"Well, that is just it Fufius. You may have to go and find him. He is perfectly capable of getting himself into trouble up there. You know the stories as well as I do. All that old heroic Ninth legion stuff. Miraculous discoveries of lost helmets in hidden valleys. Escaping from war bands, pah."

Fufius wagged his head. Velio Pinneius was an easy man to follow, charismatic in his own way. Perhaps because of that, he was just as easy to dislike, if the magic was not to your taste.

"I'd be reluctant to go north of the wall with less than the full complement, all four of my turmae, Tacto," he said, still patting the muzzle of his mare.

"Too many Fufius, I can't spare the whole detachment. I am not leaving myself without some cavalry cover. Remember the road north and south is now our priority. I cannot do it effectively without your boys. Look, take a troop and go up there and have a look. Talk to Hanno Glaccus. If the two of them are there, bring them back. And if you do have to go over the lines for a look, just be careful. Something is brewing. I can feel it. I want you to set off tomorrow. Find out what in the name of Hades is going on. Hanno Glaccus might be able to lend you some men," Tacto went on.

"I doubt that Tacto. I have seen what he's got and frankly he is not flush with troops. Far from it," Fufius said.

Tacto did not take the plea.

"One turma, as you command centurion. I'll brief my decurions before I go," Fufius acquiesced.

He paused to mount up and looked down. Rain was beginning to drift in the wind..

"I'd best push on Tacto, lots to do before I leave, and I've been neglecting this fine one," he said, patting the mare's neck.

"I will see you in the morning if I don't see you later. Enjoy the ride," Tacto replied.

He went to watch the guard change. The optio had raised his head above the parapet rather on purpose: so be it.

'You wanted to be noticed sonny, well I've noticed. So, beware.'

The next day *'Farewell Brother,'* was blowing its wake up for the neighbourhood and surrounding area. Fufius saluted Tacto at the gate before leading his troopers down towards the bridge over the river. It was not a tune Fufius much liked. Nor the connotations that, whomsoever the 'brother' was, if he ever actually existed at all, he might not return. Either it was a poor omen or a miserable bloody tune. He could never quite decide which category fitted best. His *Augusta Vocontiorum* boys were indifferent. It was not their superstition being pricked by the trumpets.

Tall and blond-haired, sculpted cheekbones, they rode out, silent and smart in the saddle, spears upright, horse decorations bright, chain mail polished. Moustaches of men and manes and tails of animals brushed to equal perfection.

He would have preferred to use the most experienced of his men and the best riders, his First turma. Fairness dictated they could not always be the favourites in the fort. Legionaries could accept the pecking order of their cohort within the legion as a fact of military life. Certain cohorts ranked higher and got privileges. It was just the way the legions were structured.

'You don't like it brother? Go and ask the centurion for a transfer.'

Auxiliaries from the conquered tribes always performed better, in his opinion, under a freer touch. Their discipline centred on their perceived personal honour. It was pure and it was simple. He liked it. No flogging was ever required with his men. Dare to prick their courage with a measured slight and they would deliver bloody war for you just as well any regular legion cavalryman. If only they got the chance, once in a while, instead of their routine diet of scouting and patrolling and more scouting and patrolling. He could read their frustration when they got held back from joining in the fun.

The Fourth turma were delighted to get out of barracks. Who knew, they might pick up a few trophies for a change? Tacto stood at the gate until they disappeared below the lip of the plateau down towards the river. They were a magnificent sight and the full ala when on parade was a thing of joy to see. He sniffed. They were not a bad lot for a Germanic auxiliary one generation removed from their oak trees and mud-hut, barbarian ancestry.

Chapter 14.
The riverbank below the razed fortress of Pinnatra Castra.

Velio had the second watch. Sunrise crept over the sky, bringing the trees and hills back to life. He was grateful the night had ended. If there was to be more fighting, it was much better to do it in daylight. He looked around; this camp had served them well in the circumstances. If they had camped by the fortress last night, they would be dead. Enemy warriors were lying on the stones, abandoned in the last attack. He observed for signs they were faking death. They had not moved or made a sound. He considered going over and checking but as the light got better it was clear they were dead. Instead, he watched the remains of the fire burn itself out and decided not to save it. The blackened stones around the ashes were still warm. He poured some wine from the wineskin into a cup and put it by the stones to warm. Gallus stirred himself awake and warmed his hands. He offered him the cup and a lump of bread. In the old days, when he and Marcus served under the hastiliarius together, Gallus could be relied upon to utter his two favourite reminders.

One; *'don't forget the fee for the lesson.'*

Two; *'go past the ovens on the way back and bring me back some bread.'*

"He thinks I'm a bloody baker, Swords," Marcus complained more than once.

'I wonder what you would have made of this lemon?' he grinned at the memory.

They were far north of the wall and well short of the valley where he wanted to lay the marker. Three enemy attacks during the night and they were probably surrounded, with scouts observing and counting them.

'Let's get our arses out of here Velio and back to the lines,' he reckoned would have been Marcus' perceptive suggestion.

Gallus held his cup out for more wine.

"Can't do any harm now can it?" he said with a lopsided grin.

"It surely can't Gallus," he replied, "the question is what is the best step to take now."

Gallus turned the backs of his hands onto the stones to warm that side through, placing the wine cup down in a convenient ledge. There was little chance Velio did not have a plan, but a bit of advice would not go amiss. He coughed and spat wine coloured phlegm out of his throat.

"It seems to me we have four horses and the element of surprise if we act now. We ride the first two horses into the ground so we can get out of here. Leave them behind when they are finished and use the second pair to get us a bit further down to the Bodotria crossing. No stops. Ride all day and night if we must. If both sets of horses die to get us there, then so be it. We strike out from here for the old marching road of Agricola and hope Glaccus might have a patrol out somewhere on this side of the water. Who knows, he might be missing us? No point in hiding now, it's all about speed. If we fight on the road at least we'll have firm ground under our feet. Let's get off these old tracks and get onto a proper road. That's what I think."

Gallus thought for a few seconds.

"And if you agree, let's give Marcus his marker. Put it up there on the grass. We both saw him last night. It is a good place. It will make him happy. It'll set him at rest," he finished up.

"You think he really came to warn us last night?" Velio asked.

"We both saw him Velio," Gallus answered, "we both saw him."

Velio read the agitation on Gallus' face. A dead man had come out of the night to warn them. Such things were not possible and yet they had both seen him. He shivered a little.

"Well, we could use him now, by the Holy Mothers of the Parade Ground, we could," he said trying to put the best shine on it for Gallus' sake.

Gallus looked sideways at him.

'What are you thinking Velio?' he wondered.

He finished off the cup of wine and leaning back put his hand over his head to wash the clay vessel in the river. Velio looked up towards the wiped-out smudges of Pinnata Castra, the stone-faced ramparts had been thrown down by the Twentieth before they left; no stronghold was going to be gifted to the northern tribes. Marcus could have his memorial smack in the middle of the fortress where the principia had stood for all he cared. He reached up to rub the stubble on his chin and realised he still had his helmet on. No, that would not do. Not at all. It was the coward's way out. Marcus had not served here. And no soldier was ever buried inside the walls.

He sniffed and untied his helmet, laying it down on the stones. There was dry blood-spray across the dome and down one cheek-plate. He felt Gallus watching him, waiting for a reply to his suggestion. His plan was sensible. Ride the horses as hard as possible to get to the Bodotria. Get away from the savages who had launched last night's attacks. Very sensible: he picked up a stone and lobbed it into the river. It plopped and sent out a ripple that vanished, overwhelmed by the current.

"Mount up, Gallus. We'll put the helmets and shields back in the sacks, cover our lorica with the cloaks, try and sneak out of here."

"Back to the road Velio?"

"Gallus," he shrugged.

Gallus nodded a slow understanding.

"So, we're pushing on?"

Velio took the wine cup back and tucked it into his saddle bag.

"They will never expect us to go deeper. It would be madness after all," he said.

They stood and looked at each other, acknowledging the reversal of authority from old master and pupil to pupil-now-commander of the self-same old master.

"Aye, centurion. That would indeed be an act of madness," Gallus answered.

He clambering to his feet, tugging at his own helmet straps.

"Check if there is a bow. Could be handy. It may buy us time," Velio said.

Chapter 15.
Deva Victrix barracks.

Servius Albinus read the note from Blatobulgium about Gallus' safe arrival with equanimity. He had an escort after all, so it should not be surprising that he got there intact. He was less sure Dometius Barrus should have sanctioned Gallus' onward journey to Trimontium even allowing that it would do those two some good to spend time together. On his own, travelling over the top of the lowland passes in winter? However, it was a die that had already been cast so there was little to do except send a silent prayer for his hastiliarius' safe arrival. It was not very subtle of Dometius to spurn his secondment. Perhaps Dometius needed a few days in Deva Victrix to relax with other officers of his own grade? A chance to relax in a proper bathhouse, decent food and wine. Or perhaps he needed his legate's caliga up his backside to make the point his gifts were not to be dismissed?

The legate of the Sixth legion, Eburacum, had also written to him. His counterpart sending even less cheering tidings he could summarise as *'Brigantes, Brigantes, bloody Brigantes.'*

Casualties incurred on a cavalry exercise; bodies had to be carried back to Eburacum for burial. Frustration and anger among his men. Disruption on the roads. Then two supply trains ambushed. The attacks were assumed to be evidence of attempts to stir wider revolt. Murmurings of an old unwelcome name; Orgidor.

He snorted at the idea. Orgidor must be ancient by now. The Sixth's legate needed to get a grip of himself if he thought Orgidor was behind the current spate of unrest. It sounded much more like a petty revolt. Or a breakaway of hotheads perhaps? The principal seat of the tamed section of the tribe was right next to the Eburacum legionary base. It was not where the trouble was coming from; of course it wouldn't be, would it? No one would be so stupid as to start a resistance right under the noses of the primary fortress in that part of the province. It was coming from the hills, where all bad things in the province birthed.

The hereditary lands of the Brigantes straddled the country from shoreline to shoreline, rising in the middle with enough hills and valleys to make a safe nursery for new leaders. The more roads the legions built to join up the province, the more opportunities for brigandage they provided. Only seven years had passed since the last major insurrection. A similar pattern. No massing for a head-to-head with the legions like the old post-invasion days; that was far too risky and costly in men lost. The days of set piece battles had long passed. Now it was passive resistance, withholding taxes and sporadic raiding, random mischief, and looting, factions and splinter groups. Young-buck war chiefs in the making all on the lookout for an opportunity to carve up a few careless Romans. Two or three were enough to make it worthwhile entertainment. Like street thugs on the Aventine.

Sometimes they were brave enough to take on a full century or even have a go at a maniple moving on the roads. Small scale stuff but not good for legion morale. No chance to stand shoulder to shoulder and fight till the grass was painted red. And they were a big tribe. There were thousands of them out there over hundreds of square miles. It was a minor blessing they were not a seafaring nation or the coastal supply routes would be threatened too.

'Mars, forbid they could be contemplating a real war,' he prayed.

The last event had ended in boring, standard fashion. Execution of ringleaders and heavy fines on their families, others taken as slaves, livestock taken in lieu of silver. Parades of the standards in front of every village of note. Judging from his letter, the Sixth' legate was of the opinion enough time had slipped by for them to recover their courage and have another go. All in all, it was quite an incredible situation. Quite a stubborn intransigence against taking the hint. They would have taken the hint if it had been *The Boar* whispering in their collective ears and not the Sixth. Executing civic leaders would have no purpose except firing up the bad ones up even more. Well, it would be fire and sword to every village this time around if they carried on with their little insurrection.

'It's the wrong damn side at the wrong damn time,' he growled to himself. The 'stones,' as the legionaries had nick-named Emperor Hadrian's edifice, ran across the northern limits of the Britannia- Secunda sector which also happened to match, more or less, the northern territory line of the Brigantes. So, they were causing trouble in the most awkward place; south of the wall, not north, where all the heathen savages were supposed to be pinned back. Gnaeus Julius Verus was going to have a senior fit. Hadrian's line had not been in use since Antoninus Pius built the new frontier. There had been no purpose. At the most basic level the manpower to do it was unavailable, let alone the lack of need. Verus' order to re-align the defences now put a lamp on the current unpreparedness of the Stones to resume its frontier role.

"It would need some tidying up," as the legate phrased it to him.

A sweet euphemism, he reckoned, for at least ten years of benign neglect. Putting it back on a first-line footing would take weeks even with both their legions working on it. The Brigantes getting cocky was not helpful. He put the letter down and frowned.

'We should burn a few villages to the ground.'

He clicked his fingers and his senior clerk sat down on the opposite side of the desk.

"General order, today's date. Effective immediately.

'To all officers commanding routine patrols and troops escorting supply trains, etcetera.

Manpower to be doubled in numbers. No legionary troops under single century strength to proceed without twenty five percent cavalry support. Expect hostile activity from all Brigantes encountered. No overnight halts at native villages permitted until further notice. No trading for wheat or livestock to be done except at legion headquarters. Bring prisoners in alive for questioning at every opportunity to the headquarters duty tribune.'

Get that written up and I will sign it. I want copies in the hands of the tribunes and every centurion in the legion by the end of today. Send a copy to the governor. And I want to see the commanders of the scouting alae. They have work to do."

"Are we at war with them again sir?" the clerk asked.

"I will know more once we have interrogated a few prisoners but for the moment we are back on alert. The Sixth have lost some men apparently. Tell the tribunes I want to speak to them all in an hour's time. Carry on," he said.

He clicked his fingers as another thought occurred to him.

"Send copies to the praefectii of all forts north of Emperor Hadrian's lines. It's best they are aware of the situation down here."

Chapter 16.
The hill pass, west of Trimontium fort and Eidumnos' hall.

Asuvad knelt over the trail. There was no doubt the tracks were very fresh. The animal was being pushed on. It would not go for much longer in this uphill landscape if Segontio kept thrashing it to its limits. At least Eidumnos had the consolation the culprit's tracks were as readable as a storm riven sky.

"You won't catch him before he is over the high point. And after that he'll be down and out of the passes before we can get close to him," he said.

Eidumnos nodded back. He knew where Segontio was fleeing to. What had happened was shocking, but it was even more than that, it was insane. It would have been one thing to make an inappropriate move on the girl and get slapped aside by her. Embarrassing if she had told him about it later. Voccia, apple of his eye.

'My Voccia, how could he have done that to you?'

He knew she wanted to be betrothed to a local boy, and live in the home valley all her life, beside the people she had grown up with, but Segontio was just a better suitor. The Selgovae were important people. She would get over her disappointment in time. She would have to; she was not getting a say in the matter. He could have put up with her anger at being forced to obey his word. She would have been haughty and cold with him. She would have used the only weapon she possessed to make him suffer and withdrawn her affection. But he could have won that affection back: in time.

'My Voccia.'

But all that was gone because a guest he had encouraged overstepped the mark.

'Had it been that way? Did I give him permission to take what was not yet his? Did I say as much? Surely not?'

Segontio was a noble guest. He could not have believed the suggestion of their marriage to be anything other than a political match. Well, he might have to feign respect to the Romans, but he would lie dead in a bog before he knelt to a Selgovae. First, they would castrate Segontio and then they would skin him and cut him into pieces and put his head on a pole.

Asuvad kept his counsel to himself. A step too far, a refusing woman; a nightmare had unfolded last night. He felt guilty for sleeping through a crime committed outside the very hall where he had bedded down.

The high pass led to the west. He eased his horse forward and looked at the ground for himself. The Votadini beside him was seething in pent-up fury, too angry even to dismount for a cursory inspection of the prints.

*

The farmer knew trouble from the moment he picked out the Votadini faces. Eidumnos brought his mount to halt at the farm gate.

"I seek Segontio of your tribe. He passed this way?"

"He did."

The farmer wrapped his spear in his arm, like a staff against his beefy shoulder. He stood his ground with a calm confidence. They looked at him and understood the message.

"Where is he going?" Eidumnos asked.

"He did not say but Carubantum would be my guess, my lord."

"You are an honest man my friend," said Eidumnos, "I shall have no fight with you."

"Nor I with you my lord," the farmer replied, "cattle do not like the smell of blood. It would be a pity to spoil the day so early,"

'And you would die first my lord.'

Asuvad thanked him before words undid a courteous encounter.

*

The stronghold of Carubantum was well placed with robust defences, a stout palisade, and alert watchmen. Beyond its earthen ditches the sea estuary cut in from the west. Other towns lay beyond it, even further over to the west. The Selgovae had a lot of fertile land to protect and a lot of warriors to do it. Eidumnos reined in half a mile from the gates and walked the horses towards it. Let there be no mistake over his identity; he was the Votadini farmer from over the passes, from the vale of the eastern legion. Asuvad rode along-side still debating whether to say anything or let things unfold. He decided to hold back. There were more than enough Votadini to do what was necessary.

Eidumnos dismounted and stood at the gates. His neighbours and friends drew closer at his back, stony faced, resting spears over their horses' necks; shields hanging from saddles. A hunting party in any man's tongue. If this was southern diplomacy, Asuvad mused, it looked very familiar.

Segontio appeared at a raised platform overlooking the gateway in the palisade, hot faced and angry. He was joined by several men whom Asuvad supposed were friends and elders. The scratches stood out on his face, plain for all to see. Voccia had inflicted some damage before he took her honour. His admiration for her rose. Some of those scratches could leave scars, which was a pity because the Selgovae would claim them as proof of his warrior prowess to those who did not know better, or when the tale of the Votadini girl faded from peoples' memories.

The gates stayed closed. Eidumnos stared up at his former guest, calm and cold, icy revenge pumping in his chest. He waved a 'come down' gesture. Segontio shook his head. Asuvad sucked his teeth. There was not going to be any admission. And without that there was not going to be the single combat that could end all of this in a few minutes. A wounding might be sufficient: a death was not inevitable. Segontio was not going to explain his unannounced departure and the scratches on his face. Asuvad almost laughed. What price Eidumnos' hopes for an alliance now? It would be the sons of the wolf who would laugh when word got out. A three-tribe alliance thrown into the dirt because one man could not keep his hands off a woman and lacked the courage to face up to it. Only the claw marks on his face proved he was the assailant.

Eidumnos walked his horse to within a few feet of the men up on the palisade platform.

"Has he told you what he has done? To me and my family? Are you not wondering why I come here with warriors at my back? I think you know. Your gates are closed to me. How is this? A visitor denied entry? If you do not know what has happened, why are your gates closed to me? I thought Segontio wanted to make alliance with us to fight the Romani. Be warned Selgovae. Turn Segontio over to me or prepare to bleed. This Dumnoni warrior is my witness. The Votadini will fight the Selgovae before we fight the Romani."

He pointed his finger at Asuvad. Asuvad felt duty bound to tip his spear in acknowledgment.

'It's just a shame a girl had to be dishonoured for the Votadini to find some anger,' he thought.

"You understand my daughter has been dishonoured and she lies unconscious, drifting in dreams. We cannot waken her. He did not just rape my daughter; he has sent her where we cannot reach. If she dies, it is murder. I will have a life in payment."

They stuck their chins out, staring back, like treed cats flicking their tails at a fox. There were more than enough warriors in Carubantum to slaughter them. Segontio shook his head in defiance, but Asuvad could feel they were discomforted. Perhaps they did not know the whole story? Well, they had the facts that mattered now, and it did not look as though they were willing to hand Segontio over. He wanted to say something to help, something that would make them reconsider.

"Let them think about it Eidumnos," he whispered, "they may still honour your grievance. I'm sure you are putting questions in their heads that only he can answer."

Eidumnos inclined his head.

"My Dumnoni friend tells me I should give you time to consider my words. He is wise. Very well, I will wait for an hour. Ask Segontio yourselves if he ravished my daughter? Ask him to swear on your river god. But if you do not give him to me for justice, I swear on our gods you will live to regret this."

He gave Asuvad a chilling look that made him wonder for a moment if he was still welcome among them.

"I still know what a good Roman looks like and now I know what a bad Selgovae looks like. I can tell them apart perfectly easily. Can you say the same?" he hissed and turned his horse.

Asuvad parted company with Eidumnos and his men before they took the track back up to the hill pass. The hour had passed and Segontio had not surrendered. Turning the horses around had been an indignity but the message had been delivered. They shook arms.

"If it comes to war, I will plead your case in our council hall," he said.

"Where are you going now?" Eidumnos asked.

"To scout the fort to the south of here," he said, "it is best to keep the wolf-skins, under our eye. I am so close it seems foolish not to go and have a look."

"We keep an eye on them too," Eidumnos grumbled.

"Yes, but if you go to war with the Selgovae you will need

to be looking in two directions, won't you?" he chided.

"Perhaps I should ask them to help me get justice?" Eidumnos mused, "the good Roman might help? A few of his men and a couple of their war machines outside the gates would have the Selgovae shitting their breeches. If the centurion's men take Selgovae heads, particularly that bastard Segontio's, my Voccia is avenged."

"That's true Eidumnos, but don't side with them. Eidumnos, the Votadini will not be forgiven if they use the Romani against another tribe," he pleaded.

"It's not the Votadini, it's me that wants their help," said Eidumnos.

Asuvad sat and waited as the men departed, growing smaller in the distance. He pulled his cloak around him. It was getting colder again. The sky was full of rain clouds and when it fell, it was going to be in torrents.

Chapter 17.
Velunia fort.

Fufius reported back to Hanno Glaccus, much to his amusement and delight at seeing him again so soon. Seeing them leave before had been disappointing. Now, the arrival of another full turma of the *Augusta Vocontiorum*, with a good commander, was just what the situation on the wall needed.

'Except Fufius Pulcher wants to go over the lines and find his lost leader and the hastiliarius. Damn him, we're not having that nonsense.'

"I need you here Fufius. Your men are crucial to the exit plans for the wall. Every cavalry turma is precious don't you see? Eyes and ears, scouting, I cannot permit you to take a turma of the best auxiliary in the area out there."

He waved his hand in the general direction of the *'out-there.'*

"The centurion will just have to take his chances. It is a damn fool idea even if it is well intentioned," he said.

Fufius remained at attention, the principia was agog with the news of his troop's arrival. He could feel curious eyes inspecting him and the faint whispers even as Glaccus started berating Velio. A pang of resentment welled in his chest, he itched to say something loyal about centurion Pinneius. Tacto would have gone in headfirst.

"The acting commander at Trimontium, Centurion Tacto Oscius has ordered me to find him sir. With the greatest respect sir, you cannot overrule that order from my direct superior. I have it here," he said.

He knew he was pushing his luck. Up here on the frontier the word of any officer more senior to him was law, except he had an order, in writing. He produced the small scroll in Tacto's careful hand.

'Blessings on you and all your forefathers for once, you ugly, short-arsed Umbrian footslogger,' he thought.

Hanno took it from his outstretched hand and broke the seal. It was direct and explicit. From a comrade who would soon be aiding every step of his own mens' withdrawal. The cavalryman was right. He could not over-rule it.

'Damn him for a second time. Perhaps there is something to be diced for, though?'

"You don't require thirty men to find two. Take ten men and go and find Centurion Pinneius and the hastiliarius. You will leave twenty troopers here with me. I have despatches for every commander on the wall and your troop is all I have immediately to hand to expedite the governor's orders. I have no cavalry based here."

Fufius gulped, he had no answer to that inexorable logic. The fourth turma could do courier duty along the line. However, leading ten men into hostile ground was like unsalted bread. Not a very palatable thought if there was another alternative available. Glaccus looked down at the scroll pretended to peruse the order for any hidden truths he could have missed.

"As you command me sir," Fufius conceded.

Hanno Glaccus beamed up from his chair, his face transformed.

"Good man Pulcher, I knew you would see sense. Now here are the facts as I know them."

Hanno proceeded to fill in the enormous gap in his knowledge of the situation.

"Centurion Pinneius and the hastiliarius have gone over the wall to lay a memorial at the place where one of our old comrades died. They intended to use Pinnata Castra as a stepping off point. I have an understanding with him that I will not order any movements from the wall until he returns. He has ten days to do all that he needs to and there are now seven days remaining. Good luck finding him."

Hanno sat back happy and contented. Whatever way Fufius chose to toss the coin, he was going to win.

'Good luck in finding him. Well, gratitude is my gift to you, centurion, may your backside never feel a nettle's kiss when you squat,' Fufius fumed.

He saluted before he said something he would regret and left. Outside the building he nodded to the guards and inhaled a long suck of air.

They tried not to look interested but the best part of being on headquarters guard duty was the entertainment provided by the departing players. The forum in every major town struggled to find new material. After the local criminals have been slaughtered in a variety of complicated ways, the hunt is on for invention. They should try coming to a frontline fort and standing at the headquarters door for six hours. They would have entertainment by the cartload.

They noted his rank and buttoned their lips up tight. He put his hands on his hips and surveyed the innards of the fort like they were entrails from an unfortunate goat. He spat a glob of perfect fury onto the grass and headed for the stables. Later he decided Hanno Glaccus was a malicious old bastard who needed watching, or a barbarian spear up him. That mutinous idea warmed his heart as he and the decurion decided how best to split the troop.

*

Aulercas knew the river was a couple of hours ride from his hall, through the gap in the hills, towards the fortress, flattened long before he was born. He had suspicions it was drawing them back; there would be a kind of attachment to it in their stories. Once spades were put in the earth men staked something of themselves with each shovelful lifted. The Romani were not so different from anyone else. The men had come back like moths, perhaps they believed its spirits would shield them. And they had been right. The place had power. The river god had power. How else could they have withstood three attacks by his neighbours? They would have moved on by now of course. There was no point expecting them to sit around waiting to die at his pleasure. Behind him five of his most reliable trackers and fighters trotted along. Enough to deal with two Romani with four horses, or was it three Romani? The report had been garbled. Well, whether it was three or two, the Romani were in a bad place.

Over the years the sons of the wolf had left indelible marks on the ground. A network of trackways, leading over ridges and valleys until they joined a hard stone road that served a series of outposts and signal towers covering the exits from the Grey Mountains; set like a net, for catching his people and others. The towers were empty now, cast aside like so many things the invaders had laboured over. It was imperative he caught them before they got to the hard stone road. Six against two or three; the enemy would be tired, worried, hungry. They would panic and run, and he would sweep them up in his cloak.

He stood on the stony beach by blood washed rocks. There were piles of horse dung by the grassy slope, under a stand of alder. His birds had left the roost. He sat on a rock to enjoy the waters.

"Find their tracks. They'll run south," he said.

"They're walking west, my lord Aulercas."

"Walking? West?"

"These wolf-soldiers know what they are doing Aulercas. The tracks are several hours old. They are nursing the animals in case they have to dig the heels in later."

He pulled the end of his moustache and smiled.

"Good. There is no honour in killing fools. We follow west, silent as owls. Once we have them in sight, I will decide how we will do it. They have no roads leading west from here. They ride on our hills, over our streams, and they can only go as fast as we can."

"Slower than us my lord. This will be strange to them," his chief tracker replied.

They mounted up and cantered over the levelled Roman fort for spite. He decided to split his men. Three to check the old road south and two with him in pursuit of the westing horse tracks. He tried to guess which pass they would pick. There were two obvious choices. He was chewing it over when he had a spark of inspiration.

"Get the others back here, I know where they are going."

There was a story that had been allowed to fade but it made perfect sense now. He reined his horse in.

"We will wait until our brothers rejoin us," he ordered.

"You are certain my lord?"

"No," he replied, "I am not certain. But I cannot see another reason for them to head west from here. There is no reason for so small a group to ride into our lands."

"Perhaps they are a sacrifice to their gods, my lord, allowed to die in battle rather than by a cord around their necks. A decent death lying on the grass, better to be food for the hawks, not feeding creatures in the bog."

Aulercas looked at his man.

"A sacrifice here? Or riding towards a place of sacrifice."

The tracker shook his head at Aulercas and avoided making an answer.

"I don't know either. I do not understand what they are doing. The king wants their heads. That is all we need to think about," Aulercas said.

Adjusting his helmet, he bit his lip and permitted himself a shrug.

Chapter 18.
Pinnata Castra.

Velio and Gallus mounted up once they were clear of the old fortress.

"I think we should push on Gallus," Velio said, "it's not too far from here. Once we're over the moor it's only a few hours away."

Gallus looked at the snowy remnants of winter on the hilltops. The passes beneath them should be clear. If Velio did not get them lost they might be back here in a couple of days. The sooner they were riding the road south the better.

By the time they got to the far edge of the moor the light was fading.

"How long from here?" Gallus asked.

"We'll be there tomorrow with enough time to lay the marker, but it'll be a push to get back here tomorrow. If we make camp there, we can ride due south at first light. Let's find ourselves a decent dry spot for tonight."

"Sounds good to me Velio."

"Only one problem?" he replied.

"What's that?" Gallus asked.

"If we get spotted, we might have a serious number of those

dogs at our throats," he said.

"Could we make it by night, could you find the way there tonight?" Gallus said.

They had done well so far but it would be silly to antagonise the gods' sense of mercy.

"There are a lot of pools and bogs on these moors. I don't think we should risk it," he replied, "one bad step and you or I could be horse deep in the afterlife."

"It's just one more risk, Velio, added to a pile of other risks. But it might give us the edge," Gallus said.

He unhitched the bow and the two solitary arrows he had salvaged from the fight.

"I say we rest, eat, sleep a couple of hours then get back in the saddle."

Velio nodded. If Gallus was willing, it might be safer to travel on after resting the animals here for a few hours.

"I'm going for a rabbit or anything else that only needs two arrows to kill it," Gallus said.

"Don't get into any trouble and don't lose the arrows."

"I'll try not to, centurion."

*

Fufius began his day with a silent prayer to Epona, kissing the horse amulet around his neck before sending two scouts ahead to push up the military road. There were a few parcels of Votadini held ground on the northern side of the river, but they lay further to the east, opposite the river fort of Carumabo. It was all considered hostile ground now, but he felt hopeful his tiny patrol would not arouse any responses. The trick would be to keep moving and not become a target. As well as relying on local apathy towards a handful of horsemen.

Two days later at Pinnata Castra his premier trooper picked up a fresh trail of six horses. Too many to be the centurion and the hastiliarius. He ordered the dismount and a fire. Time to take in some food while he pondered his next moves. If the centurion and the hastiliarius had been here, they could have gone anywhere.

If they are still alive, that is,' he fretted.

He waited for his men to make a porridge while his tracker continued pursuing the horse trail.

*

Aulercas was surprised by the sight of the still warm, stamped out fire and the animal bones around it. The dung told him whoever this was had four horses. It had to be his quarry. But the empty camp in the early dawn said only one thing. The Romans had already moved. Did they realise they were being hunted? No, he did not really believe that was possible. Crossing the moor and riding deeper into Veniconi lands was either a very brave or very foolhardy thing for so few of them to do. He watched his men checking for further signs, was it three men or was it two?

'Which is it?'

Six against two felt better than the alternative. If he was correct and had outguessed them, there was only one place they could be heading. Though why they would want to revisit it now, perplexed him. Old griefs, the ones he thought he had gotten over, began to stir inside him; things he thought had healed. The loss of his brother-in- law, Pasnactus, and the sorrow it brought to his sister. The sorrow he brought because he was the one who broke the news to her. After all these years it still hurt to remember.

"They ate a young deer or part of it, so we know they have fresh meat with them," a warrior said, "there is blood smear around the fire, so they must have made a kill yesterday or the day before. They burned the guts as an offering."

He nodded.

"We know they can kill. And they are not afraid. They have spare horses and fresh meat. I believe they are making for the Valley of the Many Bones. For what reason, only they know. We can either follow them or wait for them to return this way and take them when they least expect it. I favour waiting for them," he said.

"But what if you are wrong, or they choose a different path back? We will lose them."

"Yes, we will," he admitted.

"Why the Valley of the Bones, Aulercas?"

"Perhaps some ancestor lies there. Perhaps they go to honour them?" he replied, "you know the story. Our forefathers killed many of their leaders up in that place. These men's gods may demand some gesture, who knows? It does not really matter as long as we catch them and take them back to the king," he said.

"I say we should follow them Aulercas. If we stop them doing what they are trying to do, it will make their gods angry," the warrior growled.

He sat back. He liked that idea very much. He was not convinced waiting here for their return would work, but the possibility of thwarting whatever they were trying to do and angering their gods into the bargain was too inviting to ignore.

*

Gallus stood at the exact spot Velio and Marcus had been at fifteen or more years before, gazing over the lip of the valley, towards the screens of trees and the high hanging valleys up on the left-hand side. He blew out his cheeks and took a long look. Velio pointed up to the furthest of the high corries.

"It was up there," he said, "that was where we found the very first helmet. And over there," he pointed to the river rushing down the left-hand side of the glen, "over there was where he died. They caught us as we were bringing the helmet back to the tribune. He wanted evidence."

"So, this is where the Ninth met their end? I never thought I'd ever live to see it," Gallus said.

He could not help the sense of futility clutching him as he stared at the utter bleakness of the place, the dark trees and the enclosing, claustrophobic mountains, the sighing erratic breeze in their faces, bending and straightening the tough grasses. A tribal, disordered, unyielding wilderness, a feral place. Not a place for honest soldiers. How in the name of Jupiter Optimus could an emperor think this was worth the honour of being part of the greatest empire in the world? The glen's bend in direction broke his line of view.

'So this is how they were able to sneak up on you and Marcus. You were lucky to escape Velio, alone down there.'

He grunted. Mars Ultra had made the place difficult to charge through. That was how Velio escaped. A man or a patrol could be stalked, but on this terrain, they could not be charged at speed. In some ways it gave a defender every advantage. He imagined what it might be like trying to dig an overnight camp and shivered, pitying the men, who fearing and respecting the gods to the end, died here.

"It's where some of the officers met their end. But as to the whole legion, no one knows Gallus. We just don't know, but it was not here," he corrected.

Gallus looked at the short, sheer waterfall in front of them that tumbled down a natural step into the glen.

"The horses will have to be haltered here. They won't get down there Velio."

"Agreed," he replied.

"Well let's get on with it Velio. This place is giving me the creeps. Put Marcus' stone down where he fell, and let's get out," Gallus grunted.

"You think this is bad, you should go up there where we found them. That gave Marcus the creeps too," he replied.

Gallus declined with a stiff finger sign.

Velio tied the four horses together and staked them with the two remaining pila making the knots as tight as he could. If the horses got away, they would be in serious trouble. He surveyed the glen once more, reliving the memories of the attack; the three young warriors he had chopped to get back here to the waiting patrol. The hairs rose on his forearms. Gallus was getting to him. This was a stupid idea. What had he been thinking? He reached into his saddle bag and took out the small stone plinth the Trimontium stonemason had carved for him. It was not much bigger than a loaf of bread, but it was enough.

"Shields Velio?" Gallus asked.

He shook his head. They were both in their loricas. Besides, the shields would be hard to manage up and down the waterfall.

"Just helmets and swords, I think Gallus."

Gallus snorted back, regarding the wet black rocks and the two tumbling streams uniting into one vicious torrent. The grip of the iron studs in their caligae would be worse than useless.

'You're getting too old for this nonsense, Gallus,' he told himself.

He was tempted to say, "go on Velio, I'll cover your back," but that would never do.

Velio had the dedication stone in the crook of his arm. Gallus waited until the centurion helmet was fastened on his young protégé's head and began clambering down the rock face. At the bottom he turned and watched amazed as Velio managed the descent single handed. Cradling the stone block all the while.

Velio gave him a glimmer of encouragement, "right, follow me, it's not too far and it's on this side of the river."

Gallus gave Velio a half salute, bumping his right fist on his left breast, making the metal strips of his armour rattle. Velio returned the salute though it felt odd in the middle of what they were doing. He did not wait to see if Gallus was coming, stepping in awkward fashion across the tough heathery ground towards the river. He reached the waterside after a few minutes, but it did not look like the fateful place he and Marcus had rested to drink.

"Must be further down," he said.

Gallus drew his sword and followed, covering their backs for signs of danger. The bottom land of the glen had more hollows and dips than it appeared. The minutes passed. He concentrated on scanning the ground, determined to get the precise place. Putting it close would not do. It had to be the actual point. He sensed Gallus getting more and more tense at his side. The horses were now several hundred yards away and if Gallus had to run for his life, he would not make it back.

'Gallus won't even try; he'll stand and fight and the shields we left on the horses might as well be in the weapons store in Deva Victrix for all the use they'll be.'

He stopped. This seemed to be the right place.

"I think it was here Gallus," he said.

The hastiliarius turned to face him, sheathing his sword.

"He fell here?"

"We were kneeling in the water to drink when he was hit. I dragged him over here, but he was gone before I could do anything. I had to let him go and the current took him Gallus. So, the bank here is where we'll put his stone."

Gallus watched the water gushing past trying to imagine what it must have been like.

'Swords Pinneius and Marcus Hirtius, up here on your tod. It must have been frightening, only the gods and your fast sword work got you out of the hole. And poor Marcus didn't make it.'

He pulled his thoughts together.

"Right, so Centurion Pinneius, give me the marker. Have you decided what you're going to say?".

The past was a dangerous distraction. Whatever, whoever, killed Marcus felt very close at hand. Velio bit his lip as he handed over his burden.

Gallus kicked a few flood scattered stones from the river aside and cleared a square space on the grass, laying the inscribed funerary stone down before settling it with a circle of smaller stones. When he had it as best as he could make it, he got up and stood at Velio's side. They looked down not speaking for a moment. He began wondering if Velio was going to speak at all. Velio put his hand down and grasped the pommel of his gladius pulling it free and raising it up, out in front of him. He followed suit.

"Farewell Marcus Hirtius. Tesserarius of the Fourth cohort, Twentieth legion. Goodbye my friend. Forgive me if I let you down that day," Velio said.

He wanted to say more but what was the point? They were only words and Marcus too long dead for him to hear now.

Gallus sheathed his sword and saluted.

"Farewell Marcus," he murmured.

Velio scanned the glen. Dull grey clouds were seeping across the tops. Staying any longer was serving no purpose, quite the opposite in fact. Gallus decided the Trimontium vow had been fulfilled.

"Horses, centurion?" he said.

Velio seemed calmer now. It was not just the stone he had been carrying.

"Horses," he agreed.

*

Fufius decided that following the six horsemen was as good a course to take as any other. Better than pounding up and down the road hoping for sight of them or knocking on the nearest village gateway. Their exposure to ambush was acute. The German auxiliary said the trail was aiming towards a distinct notch through the mountains, easy to follow. He ordered the remount. This extra stride into the unknown could be a dreadful mistake but thinking too much about it only magnified the fears. They would push on and close the gap. Once he had them in sight it would become obvious. He had no doubt of that simple fact. Meanwhile his men must carry on believing and trusting in his judgement. He pulled the rim of his helmet down and waved them on.

*

Aulercas took his men onto the moor pathway. The one leading to the Valley of the Many Bones. The pools and bogs were full of snowmelt, rippling in the chilling breeze. Halfway over, in the lee of the looming mountains, he halted. In the distance he could thought he could see them, his quarry.

"Two men," a warrior murmured, "with pack-horses."

He looked harder, straining his eyes at the indistinct distant shapes. His eyes were not as strong as they used to be.

"Coming this way?" he said.

"Yes, my lord Aulercas, coming this way. Two men. The men we hunt."

"Then we will let them get close, then mount and take them prisoner. There is nowhere for them to go except into the bogs."

"And if they turn and retreat?"

"Then we will follow them. They have nowhere to run, and they cannot get past six of us, alive," he added.

They let the enemy horses draw on towards them, then he urged them from a walk to a trot, then slowed again and then halted. They had now spotted his men.

"The foxes have seen us," he said, "it is time to avenge our brothers."

*

Velio pulled his horse to a halt.

"We've got company," he said.

Gallus squinted down the track and gave his horse a pat on its neck to comfort it.

"Now's the time for swords and shields," Velio ordered, "ever hear of a place called Thermopylae, Gallus?"

"I have not," Gallus replied.

He pulled his helmet back on and slid off his horse to get the shields from the packhorses.

"Well, it was a lot like this," Velio joked.

He waved his hand around at the bleak wet moor.

"We can take them here. Where the numbers won't help them."

"How many of them are there?" Gallus asked, peering over the back of the packhorse.

"No more than a handful," he answered.

"Wasn't much of a battle then was it, this Thermopylae of yours; two against a handful?"

"Oh, it was, Gallus, but we've got a bow and two arrows as well," he grinned.

"We should use the pila; the horses don't need tethering here. Where are they going to go? Back to that glen we left?" Gallus opined.

Velio took a look at the path gauging the width. It was about wide enough for four men to march side by side, or two legionaries to swing swords together.

"Agreed," he answered, "I'll take two with the pila, you use the bow and if they still fancy it, we'll have the heads of the other two hanging off our saddles before the bastards know they're dead."

He pulled the two pila from the horse and pushed its rump away to make space. It took a couple of hesitant steps back, tossing its head. Gallus' mount was a few paces beyond watching them as if interested in what they were up to. He dug the javelins butt-end into the soft ground. They rested their shields against their legs and waited.

*

Aulercas saw the two Romans ready themselves in an ideal position to neutralise his strength in numbers. The older one with the bow was chanting something. The leader with the fancy helmet was covering him with his shield. They had, by luck, found a stance at one of the narrowest sections of the moor-path. Their horses were behind them. They intended to make a stand. He made a quick decision. Fighting on foot against their armour would be foolish. It would be easier to ride them down on horseback. Get either of them off the path into the marsh and it would be all over. He flicked a glance at two of his men.

"Take them," he said.

With a whoop they kicked their horses into a canter side by side. As they closed in, they blocked out his view of the two Romans. Foot-soldiers would not withstand the impact of mounted men. The animals would brush them aside. The path they had chosen to defend gave them no space at all to step aside and avoid the collision that would kill them. It would be over in a moment; his best men would taste an easy victory.

He heard the horses screaming as they both plunged, one to its right and, almost straight after, the other one down onto its knees, spilling the warriors onto the ground. The leading Roman ran forward and killed both men before either could defend himself. His men cried in outrage and the three of them surged forwards without waiting for him. The Romans advanced to the dead horses using them as barricades. The three warriors hurtled down the path, raw with fury. He had a twinge of unease; they were rushing at the two Romans too fast. One mistake and they were as likely to career off the pathway into the bog as the men they hunted.

One warrior jumped his horse clear of the fallen mounts, taking an arrow at close range and falling. The soldier with the bow discarded it and drew his sword. He saw his men swinging their swords. The two Romans were hiding behind their shields. He saw the glint of a stab into another of the horses. Its horrible agonising scream reached his ears, its legs flailing as it toppled. A warrior's blade cut down on a helmet and the man staggered but did not fall. The warrior had another swipe, but the man blocked it on the shield and thrust up through the warrior's midriff. He tumbled off the other side of the horse. The one with the big-feathered crest stood over the last of his men and plunged down twice.

"It is not possible," he heard himself shriek and before he

could control himself, charged at the scene of carnage lying all over the path.

He saw the Romans stepping back as he hurtled towards them. His horse tripped over the leg of the first horse that had fallen and sent him flying. He saw the ground rushing towards him before he smacked into the earth. It drove the air out of his chest, but instinct forced him to roll clear until he felt the wetness of the bog on his neck. He forced himself up. Somehow his sword was still in his hand, but the shield had gone. His horse got up, blocking him from the two Romans. He sucked in air.

"Gallus, I want this one alive," one of them shouted.

A hand hauled his horse's reins and pulled it aside. One of his men's shields was right by his feet and he grabbed it.

The Romans took positions on either side of him. One made a speculative jab at his shield. It was an easy fend. The other laughed at him. He was too angry to care and flung himself at them, butting his shield at the older man and swinging at the other. They gave a step back and let their shields take the impact. Their swords were down and in the small space their changed tactics were obvious. They were going to wear him down and let him exhaust himself. The moment he understood, he surged at the younger man trying to force him from the path into the bog. He was too nimble to be tricked and Aulercas found himself with the morass at his heels and the two Romans reunited on the opposite side of the path; shields up, swords now poised. He rushed at them once more, desperate to get one of them at a disadvantage. If he could wound one, then he could concentrate on killing the other. They danced away out of reach keeping the two shields in his face giving him nothing to strike at. He paused to gather his breath and they reunited before he could prevent it. There was no way past the two huge shields in such a confined space.

'So, I am to die, taunted and begging? Never,'

He flung himself at the younger of the two, hacking the rim of the shield. The Roman swung his sword and he caught it low down on his blade, inches above his hand. It was harder than any other sword strike he had ever received. It was like the blow from a bear. He recoiled trying to keep a hold of his sword, but the impact had gutted the power from his arm, his fingers trembled. In a sudden wash of anger, he saw he could not win this fight. They had him exactly where they wanted him. Another blow like that on his sword arm and he would be beaten. They would take his head. He feinted to attack the older one, but his arm would not respond. The soldier stared into his eyes with an implacable disdain. A shard of fear started rising in his head. He was not getting out of here alive. They were going to kill him just like the others. All the proud boasting had come to this; defeat at the hands of the enemy he most hated. He took a last look at the five warriors on the ground, his promises to the king of retribution, nothing more than a vacant taunt that scared no one. It was unfathomable how these two soldiers had managed to kill them all. Worse than that, he had failed the king.

Little Owl would never know his end and Ucsella must never know. In a sudden squall of outrage, he flung his arms out wide inviting the thrust that would end it. They stood and looked at him. Neither of them moved in for the kill.

"I am Aulercas of the Veniconi, and this is my land," he screamed and stepped backwards into the green, wet, mosses and rushes.

He could feel himself sinking and took more steps back.

"Get him, Gallus, or we'll lose him," Velio shouted.

The water was already up to Aulercas' waist, and he struggled to get himself deeper into it. To cheat them of his death by dying this way.

"You will never take me, Roman," he shouted defiance.

The icy water was halfway up his chest, stealing his breath. He sensed the bog licking its cold chops, wanting its meal.

"Get one of the javelins for me to hold onto, and I'll go in," Gallus said.

Aulercas kept his head above the water. He let go of his sword and it sank out of sight. The shield lay floating alongside him. Velio hauled one of the two pilums free of the horse it had killed, and Gallus unclipped his cloak. He stepped into the bog clutching one end of the javelin in his fist and his shield in the other.

"For the love of the Mothers, don't let go of your end, Velio," he said.

Velio stood at the edge of the path clutching the other end of Gallus' lifeline. Gallus waded out and smacked the boss of the shield into Aulercas' defenceless head. Then he flung the shield back towards the solid ground of the path, grabbed Aulercas by the shoulder and shouted, "get me out of here, Velio."

"Don't lose him, Gallus."

"Just pull, Velio."

*

Fufius' scout picked up the men approaching from a couple of miles out.

"Sir," he called, "horsemen are coming this way."

"Hostile?" he asked.

"They are riding slowly, I see helmets," the scout answered.

'Could be a trick,' Fufius thought, *'perhaps I am too late, and it is all over?'*

He signalled the halt and fanned his men out in an arc with two watching the rear. Were they being scouted themselves? The horsemen in the distance drew closer.

"Fortuna be praised," he breathed "it's the centurion and

Gallus. We've found them."

He raised his fist in salute. A fist lifted in reply. He resisted the urge to go and meet them. The sooner he could retreat from the edges of this place the better.

"Salve centurion," he said, relieved.

"Salve, Fufius, we are glad to see you. We have half a deer to eat, and I don't think we can manage it all," Velio said.

The men laughed.

Fufius nodded to Gallus, "hastiliarius, salve."

"Thank you, sir," Gallus replied, "we have a prisoner."

He cocked his thumb at a bundle tied across a horse.

"And they may already be looking for him Fufius, so explanations should wait for now. We'd best ride, I think," Velio suggested.

Chapter 19.
The Dumnoni territories, the western end of the turf wall.

Asuvad suppressed his surprise at the sight of Eidumnos at his gate. He surmised the Votadini edginess arose from the fact they were surrounded by more Dumnonii than most of them had ever seen. He was surprised to learn they had ridden cross country from Dunpeledur. That was just the beginning of it

"The king offered me my head in a basket for attempting to make alliances behind his back," Eidumnos explained.

"He will not lend men to my cause. So, we are only a few to threaten the Selgovae for Voccia."

'And you come to me to lend you men,' Asuvad waited.

But Eidumnos let his statement rest.

'Hmmmnn,' he wondered, waiting, and waiting.

'Ask me Eidumnos.'

The silence grew until it was disconcerting.

"The Dumnoni cannot be pulled into your quarrel with Segontio no matter how much you have been wronged. That is not to say we have no future alliance, but it must be to fight the soldiers who follow the wolf-capes and their spirit poles, not the Selgovae," he said.

"So, you will not help?" Eidumnos said.

"Eidumnos, please understand. I do not have absolute power in my nation. I can help, but I cannot stand up in our council and tell my king how his warriors will fight. He must release them to me to lead before I can help you. I told him of your proposal and what happened afterwards to your daughter. He was grieved for the girl, and he is not opposed in principle to an alliance. But you must understand the Veniconi are closer to us than you are, and he favours them more. We have shed blood with them. He reminded me and our high counsel that we have never shed blood with you. The Votadini have never brought sacrifices to our pools or offered hospitality to him. Perhaps you should consider that. For the moment my king has already decided, and I will not try to persuade him otherwise. What good will it do if we are both made unwelcome by our kings?" he explained.

"Asuvad, I have few men I can order to ride at my command. I am not a war leader like you. I am a farmer. Yes, I am a local chieftain but as to matters of fighting and war, we are chasers of brigands and stealers of our cattle. That is what we do. No one takes our cattle lightly, though many try. We will give a bed in the grass and bloody faces to those who steal from us. We are a generous people; we only ask to be left alone. This boy here has wetted his spear defending our property. But ask my men to gird themselves for war and you would see how few we are. Did I not explain all this in my hall? That is why alliances are needed, despite what my king says."

The young man at his side fidgeted as he spoke.

"Speak," Eidumnos said, "what have you to say to Asuvad, war chief of the Dumnoni, that will interest him?"

Asuvad smiled; the lad was a decent, fine-looking son. He had not noticed him in Eidumnos' hall until they went riding over the river on the tour of Eidumnos' land. He was a natural horseman, there was no doubt of that, but was he any use with sword in his hand? Was there any gravel in his heart?

"I cannot bring you a sacrifice, but I will fight for you if you help us get the man who raped my sister and sent her into the dreaming," he said.

He looked to Asuvad like a determined weasel watching a nest. Eidumnos turned, startled. This was obviously unplanned. He saw Eidumnos wanted to quash the notion, but his son was quicker.

"I offer my blood promise to you for as long as you wish, in return for the blood of the Selgovae bastard who raped my sister."

Asuvad nodded, impressed by the lad's sincerity. The lad put his hand out and nicked it with his hip-knife. Red blobs of blood welled up and he tilted his palm to let them drip into the flames of the fire.

"I am Tianos, third son of Eidumnos of the Three Hills and I offer my blood to defend the Dumnoni in return for the justice I seek for my sister Voccia."

Asuvad did not let his eyes move from the lad's own.

"Eidumnos, I cannot, with any honour, refuse what your son has done of his own will, in your presence and the memories of the forefathers here in my hall. You know this. So, I accept. Here is my blood."

He pulled his own knife and slit the heel of his hand letting his blood follow into the fire. They gazed at the fire and then each other. He regarded Eidumnos' face, twitching with things he wanted to say to Tianos, his jaw working as if he was chewing. He decided to help the old man recover his composure.

"You can choose to stay here with us Tianos or return home for now. Do not forget your vow. I will send messengers when I am ready to use you," he said.

Eidumnos sat forward.

"I have to go back Tianos," he said, "stay if you wish."

"And our king, father?" Tianos frowned.

"The king had a chance to help us. Now we help ourselves. There is just one thing more I want to try. I am going back to speak to the commander of the fort."

"The one you told me is a good-Roman?'" Asuvad queried.

"Yes him. I will ask him if he gives me justice," Eidumnos growled.

"We should not involve them, father," Tianos said.

"The commander is going to find out about Voccia. I'm going to make sure he finds out," he replied.

"If he acts, the Selgovae will know it was you who told them. They will see it as an act of war, father."

"Good. I want war. I will give the king a war he does not want and then let him hide in Dunpeledur behind his walls of silver and gold."

Asuvad smiled.

"My king may not let me bring his men to help you, but I can bring my own. Send me word what your good Roman decides to do. Segontio's life is worth less now than it was this morning. You have my word on that too.

Chapter 20.

Velunia fort.

Velio opened his eyes and blinked. Hanno had no centurion rooms to spare in the fort, but he had not wanted or needed privacy, only a dry place to sleep. Hanno listened to their story, shaking his head at how the two of them managed to traverse through enemy lands and return unscathed.

"But you've got a bit of a reputation for that sort of thing, haven't you Velio?" he teased.

He fed them and took them to the First century block. There had been no need to move any of the legionaries because the gaps in the rows of bunks were plain to see.

Gallus was somewhere nearer the door in the same room. He would be snoring and farting like an old man. Young, brash, Fufius too was somewhere, full of well-earned wine; his men in another block, tellers of a tale that defied invention, of the moors and bloodshed and long dead comrades.

For a moment, the dark room was blurry and then he saw a shape at the foot of his bunk. It was the outline of a man. The silhouette of a bareheaded soldier in armour; there was no definition, colour or texture to him, simply the outline of a man standing at the foot of his bunk. For an instant it crossed his mind that it was an assassin from within the ranks of the First century. Some centurion-hater, with a vendetta to settle, taking an opportunity with an unguarded, slumbering officer at his mercy. He blinked again. This was no assassin. It did not move

'You came back Swords. You brought Gallus too. We are square now. It is so cold. Don't ever die in a river my friend.'

He blinked harder and the shape at the foot of his bunk was there one moment and gone the next. He checked on each side of him. All the legionaries were sleeping. The room was cool but not uncomfortable. Under the blankets every soldier was dreaming of warm days, pretty girls, food, and wine. He sat up looking for Marcus.

The centre passage between the rows of bunks was empty. He lay back onto the shallow pallet of blanket sewn straw. An immense sorrow swelled up and swallowed him, black and dark and despairing. Tears trickled down his cheeks. He let them run. If the men around had seen them, they would have turned aside, disturbed and embarrassed.

'The centurion is weeping; our omens are bad if Centurion Pinneius weeps in the night.'

Except they slumbered and he had tight fingers of grief throttling him. Marcus Hirtius was dead; he had come back to say farewell. The marker stone had roused him from the depths of wherever he had gone; Elysium, Hades, who could know? He knew it would be the last time. He felt a key turning in the dungeon of his soul and he locked down the pain so nothing would ever dare tap on the door of that cell for fear of what lay inside.

Chapter 21.

"Where is he," Velio asked.

Hanno pointed to a small storage building built as an addition to the long horreum - the grain store, dominating the fort's lower left-hand quadrant.

"I put him next to the grain store with two of my men. They will extract all the information he has before we chop him," he remarked.

"Good," Velio replied without thinking, "he was their leader so he must know something useful. And one less tribal leader up here can only help spread confusion. What with all that's coming."

"He will be a dead leader before the buccinas blow 'lamps out,' tonight," Hanno grunted, "I'm going over later to see how they're getting on with him. Want to come?"

"Another day to rest here would be good if we're not imposing on you, Hanno. I will head back to Trimontium tomorrow and find out what Tacto has for me" Velio replied.

"I will send an orderly to fetch you when I'm going," he promised, "now I must make sure I give your man Fufius all his troopers back. Though if you are intending to go back with him you may need to wait a day or two longer. I am afraid I made good use of them to courier my orders along the line. They have been in the saddle more or less since you left. Well, perhaps not quite, but their animals might need a day or two."

Velio waved away the half apology.

"If it weren't for Fufius I would not be here talking to you now. His lads did well for us. I know he'll want them all back under his wing before we head off."

Hanno waved and went about his tasks leaving him in the middle of the compound. Except for the lack of stone buildings, it was built to the generic army model used across the empire. He had time to kill. Gallus, he suspected, needed another day to regather his strength. Horse riding was tiring. Gallus would be soaking his bones in the bathhouse until he turned into a prune. Fufius was away along the support road searching out some of his twenty men. He went to the north facing gate and climbed up to the gantry walk and stared out over the landscape, conscious he would never come here again.

Later that day, when he arrived with Hanno at the annex to the grain store, two tesserarii had the Veniconi prisoner on his knees. His face was a contused mess of blood and lacerations. The front teeth had succumbed to the attention. Red froth bubbled out between bleeding lips and nostrils each time he tried to breathe. What was left of his nose had drifted to the left. The eyes almost hidden by the rising, swelling cheekbones. The soldiers saluted them as they entered the shed. He stepped to the side and let the locals get on with it. He was not squeamish, but seeing men tortured was not an appetite he enjoyed. The tesserarii on the other hand gave the impression they held no qualms. Quite right: it was one of their functions to inflict punishment dictated by superiors. He doubted doing it to a native counted as work in their eyes at all.

'A bit of light relief. Take all your frustrations out on a tied and bound prisoner.'

Hanno went to the prisoner and pulled his face up, inspecting their efforts. The usual blue markings were indistinguishable from all others he had seen. Forearms, shoulders, back and chest all a mass of swirls and suchlike, blood adding its contribution. The torc at his throat was interesting. Twisted silver and heavy. Same as the arm rings. This was an important man. For all they knew he might be a great warrior or a rich farmer. He could be both; it was an interesting thought. Somewhere out there in the bog lands was his absence already causing agitation? Whether the fates of the other barbarians he had led were already known or suspected was also not worth worrying over.

Velio and Gallus said they had heaved the men they slaughtered into the bog, the horses had been less easy to move. From Velio's description the simple ride back had been like many things in these lands, a contradiction. He reckoned Velio was as shaken in his beliefs by that easy exit as anything he set store by.

"Is he talking?" he asked.

The brawnier of the tesserarii shook his head.

"This is a stubborn one sir. I think we will need to do more than give him a beating. Needs a bit of iron I think, this one."

"What tribe," Hanno asked the pulped bloody cushion of his face in fractured Veniconi. It seemed the likeliest bet.

"Veniconi," Aulercas lisped through the wreckage of his shattered mouth.

Bubbles filling on his lips as he answered. Hanno blinked, surprised to get an answer. If the tesserarii broke the jaw he would get nothing further out of him.

"What name are you, Veniconi?"

"My name is Aulercas."

Hanno glanced at his two tesserarii and frowned in doubt.

"We've gotten that far sir, but not anymore," the other one answered this time.

There was a patience in the soldier's tone. Hanno nodded and accepted they were telling the truth.

"I want to know why you keep attacking the forts, "he said.

'Bloody silly question Hanno,' Velio reckoned.

"Aulercas, Veniconi, water, Roman."

Aulercas replied in single bites of Latin.

"When are you going to attack next?" Hanno persisted.

Velio shook his head and scratched his forehead, looking down at the shed floor. It was a complete mystery what Hanno expected to get out of this man. It was not as though there was an army out there poised to strike that could be outmanoeuvred if this man could be made to talk.

Kill him and forget him. You cannot let him go now that he has seen the strength of the garrison, so better to chop him and have done with it. Hide his body and the Veniconii will be none the wiser we ever had him,' he judged.

"Centurion, may I have a word," he murmured.

Hanno turned around and assented with a nod.

"Carry on," he told his men.

They stepped out of the shed for some privacy.

"Are you intending to make an assault on his village?" he asked.

Hanno did not need to answer that.

"Pinneius," he said, "you've done what you came up here to do. You have put a marker down for your friend. Tomorrow you will mount up and head back to Trimontium. You will keep the roads clear, and I will send the cohorts back in due order and together we will comply with the governor's command, the emperor's command."

He nodded. Hanno was senior to him. A coldness in the pit of his stomach began creeping fog-like up into his chest. It was becoming clear Hanno had decided to start laying down the law to him. The wafer of friendship only lasted so long before it was eaten.

"I am too old to retreat from the Veniconii or any other tribe up here. I am going to send my lads down the road when it is our turn, but I am staying. I refuse to retreat from these filthy savages and if the emperor does not want to have our men defend his line, then I will do it myself," Hanno said.

"Hanno you are mad. It will be suicide to stay here once the cohort leaves," he blurted.

"I'm sure there will be others willing to stay. The forts must look occupied until everyone else is either at Trimontium or past it," Hanno vowed.

"One attack and it will all be over Hanno," he said.

"Then this old boar will go down fighting. And that Veniconi might help me kill a few more before I go down. Don't you see, timing the evacuation will be the key? If they are planning to keep attacking, perhaps I can deceive them."

Hanno looked pugnacious. Velio put his hand on the pommel of his gladius and scratched his chin. A rear guard was one thing but a man pretending he could hold back the Veniconii or the Dumnonii was parting companionship with his wits.

"It's better to die this way Velio. I do not think I am fated to die drinking wine in the sun. What was your friend's name again?"

Velio saw Hanno was trying his best to soften after his out of character demonstration of authority.

"Marcus Hirtius," he said with a prescient conviction of what was about to be argued back at him.

"Well Marcus Hirtius did not give his life to Rome for nothing. I will not abandon all the Marcus Hirtiuses that lie in the ground up here."

"I don't understand Hanno," he said.

Hanno shrugged as though indifferent to his confusion. He half turned to go then decided on a final question.

"Then why bother with the Veniconi in there? Why not just kill him, Hanno?".

Hanno gave him a weary smile.

"My lads deserve a little fun and he deserves no mercy. You and Gallus would have been trophies on his gateway had things panned out the other way. You would give him a merciful end?"

"Not necessarily, but if he has nothing to tell us that is useful?"

Velio gestured and conceded the point.

Chapter 22.

Hanno was ready to have 'Farewell Brother' sounded for the Trimontium men's' early departure when someone else ordered 'Stand to the Eagles' instead. He cocked his head at the opening notes. The dawn centurion pounded up the rampart steps to a sentry pointing in the direction of the fort two miles westwards.

"Signal fire from Volitanio, it's the general alarm," the centurion bawled across the compound.

The barrack doors opened, and the six depleted centuries of the garrison surged out as if they had been expecting the call to form up. Hanno turned back to Velio and Fufius and the reunited turma of cavalry filling the yardage by the Decumana gateway.

"Might be wisest to remain inside the walls until we get this sorted out. I could use the extra men," he said.

"Dismount the troop, Fufius and get the horses under cover," Velio replied.

Fufius nodded to his decurion. The men, having just got mounted and settled began muttering amongst themselves at the contrary order.

"Silence," the decurion barked, "or I'll have you out there on foot. I want those horses secured on this side of the barrack blocks, immediately. Every other man, get your shields up for enemy arrows."

Velio kept a straight face. He could not have put it better himself.

"Where do you want me?" he said.

Hanno made his 'let's-get-to-it' fist.

"If they come on at us here, then you can join me on the walls, Gallus too. The men will take heart from seeing you up there with them. You know what auxiliaries are like. Regular legion at their side makes them twice as brave. We have some spare bows. Some of the troopers could help with that. Fufius, what are they like with a bow?"

Fufius handed the headstall of his horse to a trooper.

"I'll get my decurion to pick out the better shots. No point in wasting your arrow stock."

"Thank you, Fufius," said Hanno.

Fufius saluted him in reply. Velio smiled at Fufius' response. The signal fire in the west flared smoky, black clouds, reiterating the general alarm. The duty optio brought Hanno word the scorpion bolt firers were primed and in place.

"And now my dear Velio, we have to wait to see what transpires. It might just be a minor delay for you. Damned annoying all the same," he frowned.

His second centurion, Tacto's equivalent, joined them. He

was another officer from the Boar but from the Seventh cohort. Not one Velio knew too well. He shook his arm, but he could not remember meeting him before.

"What do you think," Hanno asked him.

"Bad feeling about this sir. I'm thinking they perhaps know about our prisoner."

Velio pricked up his ears.

"Oh, how so?" he said.

"Last few attacks have all been harassments, nothing serious. Plenty of disturbances on the military road. Your couriers did well to avoid them."

Fufius listened hard for criticism, but it was not there.

"But we've not had a real push at the gates for several months. They are getting bolder; it is just a matter of when it is our turn. And I hope I am wrong sir, but it feels to me like it could be us today," he said, "it's the sort of time they like to have a go."

Hanno gave him a comforting pat on the shoulder plates of his decorated lorica

"Come now, the more we kill today, Pomponius, the less are left to annoy us tomorrow," he said.

They went to the Praetoria gate gantry and looked out over the low ground that ended in a distant haze in the dawn light. Groups of armed men were moving in from the north, converging towards the wall. Some mounted, others on foot. There was an absence of the uncoordinated rushing that often marked their attacks. Today it appeared they were moving at leisure to assault their favourite foe. Their stolid calmness was somehow more unnerving than the usual frenzied battle cries and demented horn-blowing. The light began to brighten and from the immediate frontage of Velunia, to the west, where the men of Volitanio and beyond were looking out on the same plain, hundreds of what Velio presumed were Veniconii were moving in for a major assault on the two forts. It could be even bigger. It could be a whole scale assault on the line. Each fort would have its own battle.

"What price would you ask for Servius Albinius and the First cohort of The Boar to be standing here with us right now?" Hanno murmured.

"The First cohort would be a happy sight; indeed, our eagle, the emperor's standard, the cohort standard, the best men of the best legion of Rome," Velio replied.

Hanno kept his gaze fixed on the tribesmen.

"Maybe this was a mistake," he said.

Velio flicked a glance at his older comrade, waiting for him to elaborate. Hanno tutted and began pacing off to the corner of the gantry deep in thought, Pomponius three steps behind him, his own optio at his side, hound-like, poised to act. Velio turned away. Fufius had a dozen of his men on the western wall of the fort spread out, bows and full quivers, another dozen were there with their cavalry spears and shields. Down in the compound the thirty horses were reined together and tied off on a row of large nails in the walls of the barrack buildings. Archers were bearing small copper pans of fire up to the parapet, ready to for the order to fire. The thought of being hit by a burning arrow made him shiver. The garrison numbers, all told, looked reasonable but only because of Fufius' extra thirty troopers. Without them Hanno would be pushed to the utmost to hold off a sustained attack. Perhaps Pomponius' had good reason to be nervous? Perhaps Aulercas was someone of note?

The attack came about two hours later. The wall in the intermediate ground between the two forts was scaled and the warriors began sweeping along the road to encircle them. Fufius hissed in frustration at the ease with which the boundary breach was made but even with the rest of his detachment from Trimontium he would have struggled to hold them back. Only the north gate, an integral part of the wall rampart itself, was for the moment not under direct threat. Velio knew it was an illusion. There would be barbarians lying out there in the grass ready to join in once the other gates came under pressure. Horns blew and the Veniconii surged forwards to the closed sections of the ditch in front of the entrances: like fish in a barrel. Flights of incoming burning arrows began thudding all around, supporting the weight of numbers heaving their way towards the gates. He could hear cries of anguish as at least one arrow struck home.

'Where is Gallus?' he wondered.

Leaving Hanno and Pomponius to their command he hurried down the steps into the compound. The scorpions began firing and he stepped inside their firing lines. There was hammering at the Porta Sinistra and Dextra gates. Up on the ramparts the German auxiliary were hurling pila down into unseen warriors. The buccinas and cornus were blowing a staunch rebuttal. Fresh pila were being manhandled up the steps to the rampart. Fufius' archers were now engaged on the west side: things were holding. Bit by bit the noise increased at the gates. Spears started fusillading over the rampart into the compound. More cries of agony. The Praetoria gate was calling for support. He could see Pomponius descending to the compound as the gates began to creak. Hanno too was striding along the rampart despatching enemy warriors with his men.

'Get out of there, Hanno,' he fumed, *'leave it to your men.'*

The first solitary heads of Veniconii warriors appeared at the north-western corner. A knot of them succeeded in fighting off the nearest auxiliaries. They took aim at the men inside the gate and sent a shower of spears down. He drew his gladius and hastened towards the danger, forgetting Gallus.

He was almost at the rampart steps with reinforcements to sweep the danger off the walls when a spear hit Pomponius in the back just above his waist. Pomponius pitched forwards onto his knees. A scream of rage behind him sent a torrent of auxiliaries piling up the steps, snuffing out the Veniconii in a few clinical seconds of hand-to-hand fighting. The bodies were thrown back over the palisade.

"Centurion, we need you," someone shouted.

Hanno was barking out orders in his stentorian, chaos defying, roar. Auxiliaries were sprinting across the compound. Velio turned searching for the voice and saw more Veniconii on the Dextra rampart. He prayed the medicus was on hand for Pomponius.

Chapter 23.
Carubantum, citadel of the Selgovae king.

Segontio knew he had a problem. The effects of Eidumnos' dignified appeal at the gates rippled through the halls and alleyways, influencing his friends as well as his foes. He tried laughing off the nail gouges on his face but could tell by the way the womenfolk were looking they were siding against him. Apart from his close friends, the older men who could and would fight when the wolf skins gave an opportunity, were tight lipped: smirking at his discomfort. A leader depended on their loyalty and the story of the Votadini girl had shaken them. It was not simply a bit of amorous horseplay gone wrong. They believed what her father had said at the gates, and he could feel a latent simmering of disapproval.

There was also the reaction of the Dumnoni, Asuvad, to think about. Though Asuvad must still have been sleeping when Voccia got hurt, he had tipped his spear when Eidumnos cited him as witness to his revenge. That would bother the king. If he jeopardised the king's position, he would be in real trouble.

'Stupid girl, why didn't she just listen to what I was trying to tell her. Why all the fuss? You would think it was her first tumble. If I kill

Eidumnos, that's the end of it.'

It was a convenient idea. But the elders might decide to throw him to the Votadini as the price of peace, even though they stood with him at the gate. The Votadini would strangle him as a criminal and throw him in the nearest bog. It was not the sort of end he fancied.

'What to do? What to do? Stick it out and let it blow over? Deny it all? Admit I took her, but I did not kill her? Deny that bit. That must have been somebody else. They will not believe me. Offer compensation to Eidumnos, give him all my horses? Yes, he might nod to that, after all I didn't kill one of his sons.'

He decided to keep out of sight until he could find a plan. Let them talk about him if they wished. Gossip was harmless but his next move needed to be surefooted.

Chapter 24.
Trimontium fort.

Tacto had always felt the principia should have a mosaic on the floor. Without it, headquarters felt a bit shabby. It lacked the stateliness of legion headquarters at Deva Victrix. Trimontium was big enough to have some decent decoration and thus a little bit naked without it. After all this was not the real frontier. Up there, an extravagance like that would be out of place. It might even be misconstrued as presumptuous. Pinneius' personal quarters in the praetorium boasted the solitary heated floor inside the fort as well as his private bath. The rest of them had to make do with the bathhouse outside the walls. They were the only two places in Trimontium that could be relied upon to be warm, with men tasked to keep it so, day and night and he had sole rights of access to neither of them.

He glared at the floor. There were sufficient stone-smiths in the garrison to make it possible. But Velio would not entertain the extravagance. What extravagance: the stone chips could be waggoned up from either Deva Victrix or Eburacum? The work would keep the men interested, distract them from the tedium. Instead, plain flagstone was the order of the day. Plain and simple, with nary a chisel groove of decoration. A bit of painted plaster on the walls was a concession, but only geometric lines and shapes permitted. No sweet green gardens of home, no painted birds, fountains, volcanoes, and abundant fruit, garlanding in streams beneath the ceiling lines.

The commander's chair was a nice piece of carved oak. His desk was nice piece of furniture too. And as for the rest, it could have been rescued from the campaigns on the Germania frontier with Varus, a hundred and fifty years prior.

Velio's clerk Marcellus hovered close by, waiting for the right time to burden him with an extra appointment not on the list. He sat back, stretching his back and looked at Marcellus.

"I'm not a trout and I'm not going to bite Marcellus unless you tell me what is bothering you."

"Ah, thank you centurion. I have an embassy from one of the local Votadini headmen, Eidumnos. I've questioned him closely and I believe he merits a few minutes if you can spare sir."

"Obsequiousness, Marcellus, do you know what obsequious means?"

"Ah, I do not know sir, I have to admit, that I do not," he said, shuffling his feet.

Tacto toyed with the thought of tormenting Marcellus a little bit more, extracting a couple of tail feathers just to watch him squirm, then let it go.

"Very well I'll see him today."

He let the Votadini stand awhile. He knew the name, Velio might be soft on his daughter, but the old man could stand for taking time out of his day. He completed the letter he was working on and gave Marcellus a peremptory nod. The Votadini entered past the guarded room of the cohort standard. He had never come this far inside before. The front gateway was his previous horizon, standing outside and looking in at the world of soldiers within. Now he was in the commander's own room. It was all alien. Almost hidden away like a prisoner from his men. There was no lofted high timber in this hall and the lord's chair was small, no great fire was burning. There was a hole in the wall that he could see through to the outside, but no draught coming from it. This room was smaller than the space outside between the columns. All of it made in stone. There was not a single wall of wood. What kind of a people would set their soldiers to carving stone into blocks when timber was freely available? Squared off blocks of stone set layer upon level upon layer.

'A people who mean to stay,' he tutored himself.

It was not the monumental amount of work required to raise such a building, but the mindset behind the order he found frightening. Had the commander clicked his fingers and set his men to make him a hall out of stone blocks? Was it just another order? No more special or difficult than building one of their marching camps? The difference being a matter of degree and time? He could understand ordering a bridge to be built over the river. It was not an unwelcome addition to the landscape for everyone's carts and waggons, though he abhorred it all the same. It smacked of Votadini weakness and somehow, their consummate Roman strength in equal, contradictory measure.

They have us beaten in everything,' he mourned.

It was not the good Roman centurion Pinneius looking at him. It was another man. Where was the centurion? This one was mean faced and gravel chinned, sitting in his armour as if waiting for the next trumpet call to march or fight. He recognised him but could not recall his name. No doubt he had campaigned and murdered tribespeople in their hundreds. Or ordered their murder. He stood in front of him feeling like a child seeking permission to speak. He half snorted in his nose to make him pay attention.

The soldier looked up and he told him his story. Tacto listened with growing horror.

Eidumnos leaned back a little on his hip, waiting and wondering whether to cut his losses and throw this visit down the well. There was Asuvad and Tianos' oath to rely on. The soldier gestured to a solitary vacant chair in the room and asked him to sit. When he spoke, he rumbled in the throat, like the slow onset of a chesty cough.

"Centurion Pinneius is not here. As you can see. When he returns, I will tell him about what has happened to your daughter. I know he will want to bring his sword down on the heads of those who did this. Centurion Pinneius has often spoken to me of his warmth and regard for the friendship of the Votadini people. And for your family. He knows the wise counsel you give. Let me assure you we look after our friends."

Eidumnos waited.

'He says nothing. It's all just words.'

"He came to visit you, did he not?" Tacto asked.

"Yes, he did," he answered.

"What did he say to you," Tacto enquired.

Eidumnos recognised there was a trap in the question.

"Nothing that helps me now."

He stared at Tacto, frustrated and confused.

"That is interesting. He said nothing of his plans?" Tacto said.

"Centurion, I do not understand what you want me to say. Your commander came, as he sometimes does, and ate my porridge, complimented my horses, and smiled at my daughter. He is always welcome but, his plans? I do not know anything of plans."

Tacto breathed a long slow breath.

'So Velio, you've kept the order secret from everybody. Blessings on your sword and the soldiers who fight for you.'

"My commander is a skilled warrior, but he understands the value of peace. I believe he would want me to intercede on your behalf, but the Selgovae nation falls into the jurisdiction of Blatobulgium. It is to their commander, Dometrius Barrus, you must make your appeal. I will write a letter on your behalf and ask him to arrest the Selgovae, Segontio and escort him here for questioning. Odd though, Selgovae and Segontio. The names are so similar."

"He is a prince of their royal family," he replied.

'Oh, he just has to be, doesn't he? I should have seen that bolt coming,' Tacto mused, *'where is outright war and bloodshed when you need a bit of harmless, safe diversion from politics?'*

Chapter 25.
Velunia fort.

When Velio arrived, Pomponius was lying face down on the infirmary bed and Hanno Glaccus was kneeling at his side. The medicus had untied the armour and cut away the leather shoulder padding and his tunic. There was a thick, red stained pad just above Pomponius' hips. The infirmary at Velunia was a barracks block configured in a square around a small, open courtyard. A low, veranda covered walkway overlooked the courtyard on all sides. Pomponius was lying in the third of twelve beds in the north wing. The rest of the room was empty, the centurion privilege even in times of pain. He had no exemption from the sounds from the other wings as the medicus' assistants dealt with slash wounds and punctures and smashed bones. It was otherwise quiet outside now that the attack was over. Along the ramparts and in the compound, men were taking stock and counting their friends, but in here the sounds had just begun. Velio dreaded the prognosis. His men had picked him up and carried him face down from the gate to the infirmary like a damaged starfish, the spear rising from his back like a foul fin.

He unbuckled his gladius, untied his helmet, and sat down on the bed opposite, Hanno's head blocking his sight of

Pomponius' face. The spear that caused the damage was propped up against a wall. The leaf shaped blade was long and narrow; a throwing spear for hunting rather than a heavy, close-in-fighting, weapon. It had hunted out a centurion. He did not really know Pomponius, but his face was a tight, pale parody of the earlier professional, amicable expression. He lay still, drawing deep and slow draughts of air, as if trying to breathe the pain away. His eyelids fluttering each time he inhaled. He had not shaved this morning. Most likely he would have turned to that little task once Velio, Gallus and Fufius had set off for Trimontium. A little personal act Velio feared Pomponius was never going to complete. Hanno laid his hand on the large taut muscles of Pomponius' shoulder. He opened his eyes like some deep-sea creature peering up from the ocean at a worried fisherman staring down at what he might have caught.

"Are we secure, sir?"

"The fort is secure my friend, have no fear. Your boys saw them off," Hanno smiled.

He put all the personal warmth he could find into his smile. Pomponius breathed and his eyes fluttered again. Velio dared not look away. The sand was running near to the bottom of the jar.

"Can't feel my legs, sir. I cannot feel my toes. Have I still got my boots on?"

"No, the medicus had taken them off for you," Hanno replied, "your legs will return once the pain wears off. I am sure of it. Just rest easy for now."

"If you need me to stay and help there is no problem. Fufius can go back. I and Gallus can stay on until Pomponius is back on his feet," Velio said, and hoped the outright lie would settle the centurion's mind.

"My gratitude, Velio. Pomponius will appreciate your advice," Hanno colluded, "I'm going to let you rest now Pomponius. Take all the medicines the medicus orders and don't argue with him, do you hear me?"

"Aye, sir," Pomponius managed.

Hanno gave his shoulder a squeeze and stepped back. The medicus looked him straight in his eye and did not blink. He did not have to; they all understood the centurion's wound was not survivable.

Velio made a minute, almost subconscious appeal with his hand, afraid to trust his tongue in the sickroom, wanting the medicus to give his approval that Pomponius' chances were good. The doctor edged outside drawing Velio and Hanno after him. Gallus loitered with intent on the opposite veranda, his face still streaked with gore, his armour wiped and smeared and unrepentant.

"The centurion will not survive this wound. It is too deep. A barbarian spear has given him the numbness of Socrates. I think Socrates' poison would have been kinder. That spear has severed his backbone. He has no feeling. I will give him everything he asks. Every poultice known in the civilised world. But the pain will overwhelm the parts of him that still feel, and as much as I know him, he will ask for his pugio to end it when he can take no more," the medicus whispered.

He ducked his head as if to screen his real opinion from all of them.

"It would be less painful for him to end it now."

Velio crossed his arms, scabbarded sword in one fist, helmet in the other.

"Let us give him time," Hanno murmured, "he may rally and prove you wrong."

"Praefectus, there will be no trained medicus in the army of Rome less embarrassed at his poor diagnosis if that comes true. Until then, make a sacrifice to Aesculapius and hope the god hears you."

"Where will we find a cockerel here?" Velio fretted, thinking of the Greek tradition.

The medicus smiled a fraction.

"In my experience, Pomponius is no philosopher, so whatever you can get hold of will do. The gesture of sacrifice from a soldier is more important than which actual beast he uses. This is not Rome; we do not need a white bull or such nonsense. Only Aesculapius can heal that wound, believe me.

It is beyond my care. I can help with the pain, but I can't heal him."

Gallus sidled close enough to catch the last words.

"There were some wounded Veniconii in the ditch, I'll try and get one before the lads slit every throat out there."

Hanno nodded.

"Thank you, Gallus," he sighed, "Aesculapius might enjoy the joke."

The medicus scowled, "a man's life for another's life, that might work, though it's an odd thing to give the god of healing if you think about it. Be quick, the centurion's life depends on it."

Gallus sped as fast as his sixty years let him, shouting his way out past the sentries at the gate for a prisoner to be held back.

"Hanno Glaccus needs a sacrifice, get me a Veniconi."

He leapt down into the ditch stumbling over dead warriors, avoiding the sharpened stakes, shouting at the pitch of his voice for a live warrior. Heads jerked around as the auxiliaries carried on despatching the enemy, filching souvenirs and rifling trinkets from arms and necks with the edgy, cruel laughter of men released from their fear.

Two Veniconii died in front of his eyes before he could get to them. He smacked the guilty auxiliaries' chests as he passed.

"Are you deaf, I need a man alive. I will flog the next man who disobeys me. Kill another Veniconi and I'll have the flesh off your backs, the whole lot of you, as Mars is my judge."

An optio on the ramparts, shouted over his head.

"All men inside. Stop what you are doing. Carry on, hastiliarius."

That did it. He saluted without looking, still searching for the first live barbarian he could find.

"You, come with me, on my order," he yelled at a young soldier.

The lad looked confused and unhappy with two different orders, but Gallus' expression was more intimidating than the optio's. Together they searched their way along the ditch. The clearing squad had been busy, it was looking like he had witnessed the ends of the last two living warriors.

"Sons of Dis Pater," he swore, frustrated.

He glared at the legionary.

"Well he's your sodding centurion, you find me a barbarian we can offer up."

A light came on behind the auxiliary's eyes.

"I will find you one," he promised.

Gallus sat down on the edge of the berm with his calves and feet resting on the downward slope of the ditch. The auxiliary disappeared around the corner as the ditch tracked along the eastern rampart.

'*Just give me one lousy barbarian, for the love of the Holy Mothers*', he prayed.

His throat was parched. He looked up at the rampart and called out to one of the sentries staring off into the distance, leaning on his pilum for support. He knew that feeling, the post battle fatigue, the sudden draining of the last scraps of energy, the raging thirst, the slow welling up of pain in places he did not realise had borne contact; the stunned surprise that he was still alive. The awkward sense of not knowing what to do or say. Coarse and crude unfunny jokes at the expense of enemy dead.

"Throw me some water, will you?"

A lead bottle landed on the turf beside him. He unstopped it and drank the cold fresh water until it was gone. He put the stopper back in place and got up on his feet. The young auxiliary was coming back. He read his face: there were no prisoners to be had. He took the salute and returned it.

"It's alright lad, not your fault. It cannot be helped. We'll just have to use someone in the cavalry."

Not a flicker touched the lad's face.

Velio and Hanno were unfazed by his failure. Gallus scratched his chin perplexed.

'What is going on?' he wondered.

Velio was grinning like a boy with an entire plate of honey cakes to himself.

"I was forgetting our friend from the moor," he said, "come Gallus I have something to show you."

He nodded and followed at Velio's heels. Outside the grain store Velio turned around and faced him.

"Tell me what you see in the little shed," he said.

Gallus was too tired to argue. He drew the locking bar sideways in its track, pulled the door and peered inside. Velio heard a chuckle.

"Is he still alive?" he said.

Gallus gave the prostrated, blood spattered body a kick in the ribs. There was an immediate answering groan.

"Oh yes, but only just. He's been well worked over, I'd say," Gallus replied.

"Aulercas the Veniconi," Velio announced, "has nothing of interest to tell us, so he will serve Pomponius' needs perfectly. My apologies for the earlier panic."

"The cavalry will be relieved," Gallus said, walking back.

Velio raised his eyebrows as Gallus rejoined him. What on earth was Gallus gibbering about?

He smiled back, "sorry sir, private joke, sir."

Which made Velio even more worried. Too much courtesy

was usually a hair's breadth from an old comrade's piss-take.

Chapter 26.

Carubantum, citadel of the Selgovae king.

Segontio knelt in front of the king with his father's hands on his head. Three days had passed. Three days to invent excuses. Three days skulking, surrounded by his retainers. The king summonsed him and here he was, being tugged like a river current to the inevitable.

"Eidumnos seeks justice for something you have done, my son. I assume it is true. His accusation sounds like your kind of rash stupidity. A prince of the Selgovae will not start war with our neighbours because he has caused a wrong. We admit the wrongs we do. I know who we should be fighting but I think you have forgotten. Your penance will be to attack the fort they call Flour-Sacks as atonement for your foolishness. If you survive and return with Roman heads as proof, I will speak to Eidumnos on your behalf and see if he and I can find an honourable way to appease the gods. I should have you tied up and handed over to the girl's mother and let her slice you up for dog meat. But you are my son, and I will permit you to find a better death fighting the wolf-skins. If you die, I will tell him you took your own life in repentance and that we have both lost children through this unhappy event. Hear me well Segontio, you spat on our good name when you took the girl by force. What made you do it when all I asked was for you to explore terms with the Votadini? You did not even get as far as Dunpeledur. This cannot be repaired."

The king took his hands off his head. He kept still, knowing his father's anger had a habit of rolling out in waves like thunder. You never could be sure when the last of it had passed until the silence came. His father's voice began rising again.

"But you went further because you have a sickness in your head. Now you will lick back up what you spat out and stomach it. You will go alone or with only those fools who choose to follow you. I will not condemn my warriors to help. You have your own gang itching to see you king, itching to see you sitting in this chair. Let them lift the spears and ride with you."

He paused again.

'Now it comes,' Segontio thought, *'the final rumble.'*

"Do not come back to me unless you bring proof you have washed your crime clean in Roman blood. Now get out."

He got up off his knees and bowed.

"As you allow me, father," he said.

His father dismissed him with an angry glare and wave of his hand. When Segontio was gone, his adviser and his chief druid stepped forwards from the side of the hall.

"A wise decision, my king. This will pacify the Votadini. They do not want war. And attacking the fort with so few men will be Segontio's suicide. The Roman soldiers will swat them aside and the insurrection you feared will be over," his adviser said.

"I will send prayers to the gods my lord that if he returns your son is a wiser man," said the priest.

The king looked at him.

"Pray hard my friend. I do not choose to lose him or his loyal men, but there can only be one bear in this forest. This folly over a woman tells me he has no wisdom yet. Of all the tribes, I think the Votadini are the most useless. I wonder what the Dumnoni would think if they heard of this stupidity?"

The priest shook his long shaggy head.

"Asuvad and me have shared the same bowl on occasion," he said.

The king turned to leave. The king's advisor laid his hand on his arm.

"I don't think the Votadini are without courage my lord. They are poorly led and counselled by kings who have forgotten what damage the Romani have brought. It would only take a king's death and a brave leader to change their outlook."

"Huh, well that will never happen," the king growled.

Chapter 27.
Trimontium fort.

After the attack Fufius led his men down the Trimontium road with Velio's order ringing in his head.

'Maintain and patrol the road at all costs. I will follow with the hastiliarius in a couple of days, leave me four troopers.'

Tacto listened to his news. Hanno's second, Pomponius had been wounded and was quite possibly dying. Velio was remaining to assist until that situation resolved itself.

He found that odd. Hanno Glaccus did not need another quasi praefectus sitting in his fort. Velio should be here now with Fufius, fulfilling the governor's order.

'Damn you Velio, what games are you playing now? Fufius ordered to get on with maintaining the roads; not good but not wholly bad either. The cohorts must be readying to move. Time to make sure Habitanum and Bremenium do their parts.'

He rubbed his chin, his initial irritation draining away. At least Velio was in the best position to keep the evacuation in order while he and Fufius could handle this end.

'Typical of him, always wanting the upper hand. He's quick to talk about saving people. Sometimes Velio, you think everyone can march at your speed my friend.'

"Well, it must be happening soon," he said.

Fufius assented, taking the cup of wine Marcellus was offering them both.

"Leave the wine Marcellus, I need a few moments with the commander," Tacto said.

Marcellus put the jug down, saluted and left, closing the door behind him.

"There is other news Fufius," he said.

Fufius sniffed the wine, finding it to his liking and taking a hearty mouthful.

"It's a bit delicate really. Not exactly a military matter and yet I have a bad feeling it could develop into one."

Fufius felt a cold unease in the pit of his stomach.

"Oh?" he said, "cavalry or infantry?"

"Very much a bit of both if it sours," Tacto went on.

Fufius drank a bit more, waiting for the centurion.

"You know that girl Velio is fond of? The one with the nice hips, as you so delicately like to put it?" Tacto purred.

"Indeed, Voccia, our headman's daughter. One of the lads has pushed his luck and I bet the old boy's upset?" Fufius grinned.

"A bit more than that actually. We've had a couple of whispers that she may have been raped and left for dead by a Selgovae prince," Tacto said.

"Why in the name of the gods would a Selgovae prince do that?" Fufius replied.

"Crime of passion, we think Fufius. A cheating lover perhaps, who can tell?"

"Well good luck telling Velio that," he said.

"Exactly my point, that's the delicate bit. What to do Fufius, how do we play this?".

"I suggest we do nothing. If it was not one of our men then we have no duty to make any kind of amends, if you follow me? Anything that keeps the natives distracted is exactly what Velio would want at the present time," he answered.

"And if it blows up into something that we could have prevented?"

"Tacto, his last words to me were to protect the road and keep it open. That is what I intend to do, subject to your orders of course."

"It's alright Fufius I'm not asking you to go behind his back. Merely that if the Votadini and Selgovae set to, then the western road is in the firing line of all cohorts using it," Tacto explained.

"We can send a courier to Dometius Barrus. Tell him to expect trouble. Tell him to get his road secured, though he won't thank you for stating the obvious."

"Would you take it Fufius? If I write a report of this

intelligence?"

"As you command, Tacto I will take it, if you're certain this is going to blow up, but not today my friend. Let me give my turmae some orders for the next week. Day after tomorrow suit you?" he grinned.

"I'm not certain Fufius, but I have a bad feeling about this."

Fufius took it on himself to pour them both more wine, Tacto was too absorbed to realise he was thirsty. He thought about the centurion's unease and despite his light-hearted comments had no intention of dismissing Tacto's experienced opinion.

"We could do without trouble around the roads. I'm happy they might start slaughtered each other, Tacto, just as long as they do it on the other side of the hill, if you know what I mean?" he said.

Tacto sipped his wine. Fufius' willingness to courier a message to Blatobulgium was all he wanted to hear.

"Good Fufius, that puts my mind at rest. Your arrival at Blatobulgium will reinforce the seriousness of the message," he decided, "now what about some food? Let's get Velio's cook working for his pay."

Chapter 28.
Velunia fort.

Aulercas was on his knees in the open centre-space of the infirmary building. His head lowered down in submission, his chin touching his bare chest, hiding some of the damage he had suffered. A bucket of water had been dowsed over him and his head was still wet and matted with gore. Velio examined the wretched man at his feet and felt his own doubts growing. The medicus was not the arbiter of prayers and offerings within the cohort. That was part of Hanno's role as praefectus. It was his too, within the confines of Trimontium. He did not have to do it very often, but he accepted the responsibility of maintaining the garrison's good relations with the gods was part and parcel of a commander's burden. But the probity of using a foreign warrior's life to appease Aesculapius was tricky. What if by doing that they offended the god?

He folded his arms and paced up and down for a few minutes. With Fufius and his turma's departure, Velunia seemed spacious again. The garrison had taken more wounded and killed, whittling Hanno's numbers down further. Yet of all the men who could not be spared, the man lying waiting to die here on the infirmary bunk was second only to

Hanno Glaccus.

"I don't like it," he decided.

"Beggin' your pardon sir," Gallus went all formal, "it was your and the praefectus' idea and now you're changing your mind?"

Velio turned, facing Gallus and the medicus.

"He does not have much time sir," said the medicus, "I think the commander would take the chance of an honest, well-intentioned sacrifice."

Hanno came into the infirmary, nodding to them all, "any change?"

"None, sir," said the medicus.

He nodded again. Gallus thought he was convinced the offering of Aulercas provided the best hope for Pomponius. As ever Velio confounded him.

"A sacrifice must be performed perfectly at all its stages as you well know. There is a piaculum to be said even when we think we have done it perfectly. And if it is not done properly then it must be repeated, step for step. It takes time and I am not sure the god will accept the blood of a man, tempting though we find it, as an acceptable offering to heal the centurion," Velio argued.

Hanno began nodding even as Velio began outlining his concerns. He held up his hand.

"I have decided to make a personal vow instead. I will vow the Veniconi's blood to Aesculapius if he heals Pomponius. If he does not want him to live, then we will not have mistakenly insulted him by slaughtering the Veniconi," Hanno said.

He fixed his gaze on the man lying unconscious on the bed. The medicus cupped his chin in his hand.

"I think that would meet with any god's approval. If he does not choose to act, we have not insulted him with an inappropriate offering."

"Gallus?" Velio asked.

"It makes sense," Gallus said.

Hanno smiled his appreciation. The old wolf-wrestler had seen a lot of things and lived to tell the tales. His agreement helped assuage the doubts.

"Very well, leave me with Pomponius and I will vow on his behalf and then we will wait," he said.

He paused, his instincts jangling in this unforeseen territory.

"Gallus, if the centurion dies, you will execute the Veniconi and put his head on a pole above the north gate."

Velio thought about protesting the duty was more appropriate to one of Hanno's men but let it go. The Boar men were going close rank to save one of their own or execute a prisoner whose life was now meaningless.

*

Hanno sat with Pomponius watching him breathe. Rush lamps burning in place of precious oil that had been long since used up, lent an unpleasant smokiness to the infirmary room. Sitting on the adjacent bunk the medicus was also keeping watch on his patient. Four hours had passed since Hanno made his vow. Outside, the watch that had the stint through midnight was taking up position. Over in the shed by the grain store a barbarian warrior was sleeping for a final time, perhaps, before he journeyed to his ancestors. By dawn tomorrow the god would have spoken and Pomponius would either be improving or worsening. The Veniconi was going on that journey regardless of whether Pomponius survived.

The room was cooling down. Pomponius began sweating and nerves sparking in his arms and shoulders made his muscles dance under the skin. Then he went still. Hanno eased down onto his knees so that he could listen to anything Pomponius tried to say. His face was wet and cold with the sweat. His eyes opened.

"Praefectus Glaccus," he murmured, recognising him, "how is the grape harvest looking?"

"They tell me the harvest will be a good one this year." Hanno paused, '*say something else to him you fool,*" he scolded himself, struggling for words.

"Bacchus smiles and waits with his cup," he managed.

"Good," whispered Pomponius, "I have a feeling the wine

will be extra special this year. We will need more slaves to help with the picking, I think. Yes, I think we will."

The creases around his eyes deepened a fraction and then relaxed as he drifted away, his eyes open to the last. Hanno looked across at the medicus who shook his head.

"It was not the kind of wound a man can survive on his own, sir. It rocked his spirit as well as his flesh. I am sorry Aesculapius has seen fit to let him die. I don't understand why he did not intervene," he said, halting short.

It would be too easy to offend his most personal and sacred of gods. He got up to leave Hanno in privacy to mourn.

"That must have been his plan," Hanno sighed, "once he was out of here, I mean. Retire, buy some land, and make wine: either that or his mind had wandered."

"I prefer to think it was his plan, praefectus."

*

Aulercas turned back in disbelief and looked when he reached the far side of the ditch. His breath rattled under his broken ribs. He coughed blood and struggled to focus his eyes. In place of the weapons, he had been captured with, a soldier had given him a stick-pole to lean on. In the fog of confusion swathing everything, the gesture of the stick was too strange to understand. The dawn, the opening of the shed door, both had heralded his death. No, it seemed they did not; death walked past and sat down to wait for another day.

The Praetoria gate began swinging back into position leaving him outside the walls and alive. The sentries up on the gantry walk were studying him. The smell of rotting warriors' bodies beyond the upcast mound of the outer rampart reminded him his people had tried to get him back. They had known he was here. The bodies were in scattered clumps. He tried not to dwell on the friends and kin who might be lying there. Gripping the stick-pole tight he swore to return, on the lives of his children.

Gallus waited until the Veniconi began limping off towards the north. He doubted the man would made it back across the bogs and mosses. He would most likely stumble at some point and in his weakened state be unable to survive the first night out in the cold. It might have been more merciful to have chopped him there and then for a clean way out. But Velio had ordered his release after a brief discussion with Hanno and, in truth, he would have taken no pleasure in killing a broken man. Hanno Glaccus had not demurred. It was an inexplicable turnaround. One minute the Veniconi was condemned and the next, his execution was no longer necessary. It was as if Hanno Glaccus had lost interest. Perhaps he and Aesculapius were no longer on speaking terms. Pomponius' passing put a shadow in Hanno's eyes.

Up there on the moor, when they had been fighting for their lives the Veniconi had been something quite different. The man Gallus could see now was not the same proud warrior. What message would he take back to his people? It did not matter. If it was Velio and Hanno's half-handed mercy that the Veniconi should live, Gallus Tiomaris would not argue the toss. He sniffed and went looking for the nearest bread oven.

Chapter 29.
Velunia fort.

"Little tender wand'ring soul,
Body's guest and comrade thou,
To what bourne, all bare and pale,
Wilt thou be a faring now,
All the merry jest and play,
Thou so lovest, put away?"

Hanno stepped forwards and lit the first bier in the row of dead soldiers, the one under Pomponius. Velio looked sideways at him wondering where those words had come from, not the usual kind of words from a soldier's mouth: a poet perhaps? When the time was right, he would ask, perhaps write them down himself, for another day. He moved away from the pyre once it began fuming with the stink of Pomponius' singeing hair and incinerating body. The wool cloak, the tunic and the leather would go first. Then the metal armour would blacken and distort. He wanted to vomit at the stink. There was no glory in this. Nothing pleasant or glorious in the smell of a dead man roasting. Nothing to mark this part of Pomponius' courageous act. His assailant had not looked him in the eyes. So busy keeping the north gate secure he fell, unable to defend himself, to a spear from an unseen enemy. It was the only thing worse than a burning arrow.

Afterwards, he sat with Hanno inside the principia, his clerks hovering in attendance. He reached inside, scouring for their names.

'Lucius, his personal batman; Atius is his military clerk.'

"Bring us the wine and the best maps we have of the fortification lines," Hanno said laying down his helmet and gladius.

Lucius poured the wine for him. Atius unrolled a map replete with Hanno's copious scribbles and drawn arrow marks on the table. There was a small note written over the winding river web lying a thousand paces to the north of the fort. The river that fed into the Bodotria itself. His hand had posted his most ultimate, strategic questions.

'All at once, or alternate cohorts east and west?'

The neat, printed words dominated the map.

"This was Pomponius' personal stock," he said, "I think it's only right that we toast him in his own wine."

Velio swallowed Pomponius' good wine and could not help wondering if there was much of it left and who was going to drink it.

"Now, have a look at this and tell me what you think?"

Hanno said.

He stepped back, sipping the wine as though the funeral had been in another time and place. Velio drank some more. The two soldiers looked at the words on the map: the clerks waited. Atius looked like he wanted permission to speak. Velio nudged Hanno.

"Well, Atius, give us your wisdom," Hanno said.

"Begging your pardon sir, if it was me waiting in the last cohort off the wall, I'd be praying those barbarian bastards out there were busy slaughtering virgins or whatever else they do to keep their gods on their side."

Hanno smiled and indicated the wine jug to both. He turned to Velio as they helped themselves.

"Do you ever let your clerks into your thinking on such matters?" he asked.

Lucius choked on his wine. Velio did not buy it.

"Come now. I don't know a centurion that's never tested a plan out first with his staff," Hanno said.

Atius exchanged looks with Lucius. Velio shrugged and wiped an errant wine dribble from his chin. Praefectus Glaccus was playing games.

"Sometimes," he admitted.

"So, how would you do it?" Hanno persisted, looking this time at Atius.

Lucius pulled himself together.

"I'd order a wholesale retreat on whatever day in the month you deem best. The outermost forts to signal departure to the next as they leave. At two to three miles apart, the cohorts should be able to keep an organised gap."

"Do it all in a single day, every fort?" Hanno frowned.

"There are four cavalry forts sir on the line, use those alae to screen and protect each road. By evening the whole wall would be empty. By the end of the second day the last cohorts from the centre ground would be twenty-five miles down the road. The savages wouldn't know we'd gone until the signal fires burned out. Every cohort would be able to support each other if attacked."

Atius began nodding too. Hanno smirked in delight as he weighed it up. He smiled at both.

"Very well gentlemen, that's how we will do it."

They both began to protest but he would have none of it: the twin elements of speed and surprise, perfect.

"Just like that sir?" Atius said.

Hanno poured Velio more wine. Velio admired the ease with which the older man could command an opinion, hear it, and adopt it without giving out the faintest sense of being given a lesson in tactics by a military clerk. Hanno appeared more at ease than at any time since he had delivered the order.

"To success gentlemen. The best plans are the simplest

plans Lucius, but I think we'll keep the trumpets quiet that day."

Velio ran his eyes over the map considering Lucius' idea with growing enthusiasm. Damn him, Lucius had just solved the problem, not by being inventive but by a soldier's infallible belief in the army's ability to just get on with it.

"Everything from Medio will funnel west. Everything east of it will come past us. I fancy the Ides, that is what, three weeks from now? Gives the ground some time to dry out. Tomorrow we will issue the movement orders in detail. The Ides it is. A day earlier for the Carumabo garrison. Give them a chance to get clear. I always thought it a stupid place to put a supply base. You cannot signal a bloody thing to them without three relays. Typical of the navy to want to put it there, I suppose. Drink up Velio," Hanno toasted.

Chapter 30.
Aulercas' hall. Veniconi heartlands.

Aulercas' journey was eased in the latter stages by kindness of Votadini strangers who took him in and provided a horse and a diligent young warrior to escort him as far as the Veniconi border. Frequent stops to drink, dousing his face, head and body in chill running water helped to restore him. At times Heruscomani spoke in his head, urging him to take vengeance, telling him not to falter, to keep going. Cold water brought out a rainbow of colours across his face and body, but the swellings and the pain lessening. Water could not heal broken ribs or grow new teeth. He was still a wreck of the warrior he had been when he set out with his men to track and kill the Romans at the fort.

Ucsella screamed at the sight of him, fleeing as he hobbled towards the gateway, a bloodied scary wreck in place of the smiling papa she knew and loved. He stopped, gutted, realising that he must look bad for her to be so afraid. Revenge and anger flooded back into him. Anger for the fearful little girl they caused to run from her father. Revenge for the brutal beating they had given him.

Eithne wept at his battered face, her hands fluttering as she attempted to touch the wounds without hurting him. As he lay on his bed under a blanket, she sent a servant to the king. She was at his side when that overlord asked permission to enter. He was sleeping face up. He could not mask the pain in both his sides any other way. They had done a good job on him.

*

The king accepted a cup of her brewed ale, sitting thoughtful and calm, yet angry too. He had never seemed so polite, so respectful as he was now, sitting, waiting, for his bondsman to awaken. After all he was just a man in her house, where she ruled. She accused him with her eyes for Aulercas' injuries and let silence punish him. The king finished the ale and went outside to carry on waiting, sitting on a wood stump with his single retainer: an ordinary man she liked better.

It was early evening when Aulercas next stirred. Eithne had a water cup at his lips before he had time to ask. Behind her back Ucsella came venturing closer, clutching her doll with the ferocity of a shield. The king smiled and she wriggled up and took refuge on his lap before Eithne could intervene. She turned her thin-lipped attention back to Aulercas. He had seized up, every muscle tightened into knots by the hours of sleep and the warmth of his bed. He tried to sit up and had to stifle a groan at the pain. Even that sound was harsh and new to all their ears. He looked at Ucsella and Eithne.

"Where is my Little Owl?" he lisped.

"He's with the druid and the smith. He wants a sword to kill the men that did this to you," she said, hot eyed.

"Uhuh," he replied.

He looked past her to Ucsella leaning back against the king's chest, the doll upside down, her eyes still wide. He could see that first fear at the gate had gone. Replaced instead by something almost worse. He could deal with that later.

"How is my little Ucsella?" he lisped, disliking the new sound of his own voice.

"Papa" she said.

He smiled as best he could.

"It's still me. I know I look a fright. Tell your brother I want to see him too. Will you do that for me?"

She nodded, brightening. She slipped down from the king's knee, ran over to him, gave him a hug that made his ribs twinge and raced out of the hall to find Little Owl.

"My king," he said.

The king smiled with his eyes, but it did not touch his mouth

"Aulercas, I am glad to see you back with us. When I saw you earlier, I feared for you? I cannot afford to lose a man like you, my friend."

He paused.

"Only you came back so I know whatever happened was

bad. Was it two Romans or was it a trap?"

Aulercas decided to go back to the beginning. He drank some more water and told him how things had gone from bad to worse, climaxing on the path on the moor. He skipped over the hours in the fort. Her worried frown deserved that much consideration. When he finished Eithne poured him more water and the king more ale. He drained the water and held his cup out for the ale.

"Help me up," he said.

"You should be resting, your ribs are broken," she fretted.

"In front of the king in my own hall? I will not," he said.

The king raised his hand to placate her angry glance. Perhaps he had outstayed the welcome.

"You'll heal quicker if you listen to Eithne," he smiled.

Her eyes softened a fraction, conceding his support. Aulercas lay back as she pushed down on his shoulders.

"I should not be lying down," he complained.

"I can hear you lying down or sitting up, Aulercas. When you are recovered come to my hall and we will talk more. There are things that need to be done."

Eithne had no clue as to what that meant. Aulercas smiled as best he could and then she twigged, sick at the thought.

Chapter 31.
Blatobulgium fort.

Eidumnos thought long and hard about going. The Roman said he would "write a letter," whatever that meant.

What good this thing would do had not been explained to him. But he had the commander's name, so that was something. Was he supposed to sit back and wait for Segontio to be apprehended and brought here for punishment? He wished Tianos had not been so eager to pledge support to Asuvad. Well, it was done now: Bractia gave him enough food for the journey and managed to say 'farewell' to him civilly enough, but he feared he was forever condemned in her eyes for what had happened to her child. He could tie Segontio to a post in the barn, strip off his clothes, hand her a butchering knife and leave her to it, except even that would never be enough. Segontio had dishonoured not just Voccia. He had dishonoured them all. Bractia would burn at the injustice until the day she took the journey to her mothers.

Once he was over the high point, he saw a fog brought by a far off, incoming tide. He rode towards the great estuary, smelling the salt. His horse plodded on and with its quiet resilient pace came the dim outline of a fort.

He swallowed and braced himself for an arrow or a javelin. To a stray warrior coming out of nowhere in these parts, what price an invisible death flying off the ramparts? A Romani guard would plead 'care' and go unpunished for doing his duty. He swallowed again and kicked the stallion forwards, shouting his business as loud as he could to the unseen sentries. They kept him waiting until the gate began creaking like an oak in the forest. The guards covered him on both sides until he dismounted and surrendered his sword and his spear. They considered his hip-knife and let that go. The horse got a pat as it was led away and although altogether strange to him, the guards seemed alert but reasonable. What harm was one ageing tribesman?

*

Now that he had met him face to face for the first time Fufius decided he did not like Dometius Barrus any more than Hanno Glaccus or Velio did, and now he knew why. Barrus was a robust framed Spaniard with jet black hair, a beard that was combed to perfection and clipped to the point of effeminacy with not a hair out of place, and just the suggestion of a personal scent. He wore the full toga of a senior soldier, lounging in his praetorium awaiting his next meal. It was all too unworkmanlike. Whatever Velio Pinneius' faults, and he had a fair few, he always looked like the senior officer in charge of a frontline garrison, and there was none of this perfume or elaborate grooming. He hid his feelings and suffered the praefectus' attempts at pleasantry. Sharp minded though, no fool, he had not forgotten sending Gallus to Trimontium.

'Was he still there?'

'No, he was away, acting as batman to Velio'.

It seemed to satisfy the point. Barrus bitched for a while about Hanno Glaccus' ability to screw up the evacuation procedure for the wall. He smiled, Velio was there right now, so it was not given to be any sort of fiasco. He watched for the reaction as Barrus read Tacto's intelligence report: there was none.

"Well, let's go and get him," Barrus said waving the report in his hand.

"Do you think they will surrender him up to you? Without trouble?" he said.

"I don't much care either way. They can hand him over or face the consequences," Barrus snapped.

"Mmmn. How have they been, co-operation wise, sir? I mean." he asked.

Barrus considered that a sensible question. Plainly not all the cavalry were horse-centred fools. He pointed to a map of the northern province.

"We are here. This is the west road. Straddling it are the Selgovae, but their various strongholds are all sited to the west of the road. Beyond them are the coastal Novantae. So long as the Selgovae carry out no predation east of the road, and confine their cattle stealing to the Novantae, I am perfectly happy with them. When they step over the line, that is when I have a problem. This girl provides the Votadini a pretext to cross that line too, from the other direction. I have never been convinced, unlike some others I could mention, the Votadini are the soft touches we all seem to want to take them for.

'Beware the dog that never bites.'

That my thinking. Do you realize how many warriors the Votadini could raise potentially? They are the largest tribe north of the Brigantes before you strike the lands of the Caledonii. And because they have never fought against us, we have no idea, not even the faintest, as to whether they are dangerous opponents or not. It is only their lack of recent experience that should count. And so, until you brought me this letter all I had to concern myself about was seeing the cohorts safely down the road and falling in behind them at the tail end. Though even that last part might change."

'Careful Fufius,' he told himself, *'he is very shrewd. And he may not have had an order to stay, like Velio has.'*

"That, and the small matter of decommissioning the fort."

Barrus went on, "we can't leave it intact for the barbarians, can we?"

'Question answered.'

He tried not to smile at the little dig about the Votadini.

Just as well the boss was not here.

"So?" he asked, trying to posit it as a reasonable query rather than a challenge.

Barrus put the report down and began rolling it up. Fufius waited until Barrus had tied the closure and laid it aside.

"So, I can either send a messenger and a few men to extract this man Segontio and bring him here, I assume you will want to escort him back to Trimontium for a hearing, or if they refuse that, it's a question of sending a maniple in and threatening to batter down the gate. That usually works with these people. Once they see the cohort standards and the steel outside, they normally come to their senses. The mistake of sitting idle while a new tribal war gets suckled cannot be allowed. Servius Albinius would have me on the first boat to the Germania front," Dometius Barrus replied.

It sounded pretty much like the approach Velio would use if it was his problem. Parade the standards, blow the buccinas, parade a couple of centuries and see how willing they were to fight over a single wrongdoer.

There was a knock at the door. One of his centurions wanted to come in. He gave a polite nod to Fufius.

"Come in," Barrus clicked his fingers.

"Fog's rising sir. Oh, and we have a Votadini asking for you. He's saying centurion Tacto Oscius in Trimontium has referred him to you."

Fufius exchanged looks with Barrus.

"Timely, wouldn't you say?" Fufius observed.

Barrus smiled.

"Useful to take him with us," he said, "might just force their hand for us. Well, I think that settles it. We'll take a maniple and not waste time asking politely."

He stood up.

"Centurion, I want a maniple ready to march on Carubantum immediately with two turmae of cavalry in support. You will be in command. Go and arrest the man called Segontio and bring him back here. This man is a prince of the ruling family so you may need to be firm. The commander here will accompany you and take the Votadini along as well so you can be certain you get the right man. The fog will help disguise the numbers. If you think there is going to be real resistance, retire and report back. Do not engage in a fight."

The centurion saluted and left.

"Half an hour, Fufius, you have time for a bite to eat."

"Thank you praefectus," he paused, "are you going to speak to this Votadini?"

"I don't think so. Let us wait until we have our man."

Chapter 32.
Blatobulgium fort.

Only a full day later Dometius Barrus had the centurion commanding the maniple and Fufius back in his office. They were looking pleased with themselves. Pinneius' man had an insufferable smugness about him he found distasteful. His centurion was wearing his habitual glum reserve. He stifled the temptation to take them down a peg until he heard what they had to say.

"With your permission sir I have him in the courtyard for your inspection," said his centurion.

"Why on earth would I want to inspect some ghastly little Selgovae? Has he said anything useful? I assume you have offered him the chance to save his miserable, nit infested life," he grimaced.

"He has been uncooperative sir, but some of his men were only too quick to save their own throats from the pugio."

"And what have they delivered unto Caesar?" Barrus purred.

That smug look on Pinneius man's face was beginning to fade into uncertainty.

Pinneius does not speak to his minions this way. How very

provincial.'

"We caught them on their way here sir. They were planning to attack us if you can believe it? Ran smack into us in the fog a few miles from Carubantum. No bloodshed was required, their people will not even know we have them," the centurion reported.

"Delightful. Now take him away with you Fufius and do what you must. Commander Pinneius will be pleased with your efficient work I'm sure," he purred again.

Fufius could feel himself colouring up at the jibe. There was no need for that like little snipe.

"There is one piece of intelligence I need to report sir, it can't wait," the centurion went on.

"Well, put it in your report. Have it on my desk by this evening, dismiss," Barrus said.

"As you command sir but with your permission, I should report to you the unconfirmed presence of Dumnonii in the area. One of the prisoners said as much," the centurion said.

Fufius could see colour draining from Barrus' saturnine face as he considered his options, with his gold ringed fingers as counters.

"Do you believe him?" Barrus asked.

Fufius felt himself shiver; this man was as cold as a snake.

"It's plausible sir," replied the centurion.

"Plausible, eh? It could also be a lie to divert our attention, centurion," Barrus said.

"With permission sir, I'm not sure I see the point. Divert us from what?" said the centurion.

Barrus marched over the top of that question.

"Selgovae join with Dumnonii? What if the western Novantae wake up and decide to join in? No evidence of that, have we centurion?"

"Not so far sir," he answered.

"What does our outraged Votadini father have to say on the point? He is," Barrus paused, "I was going to say more reliable, but is he? Could we rely on him? Even if I hold him back to assist us with the interrogations, how could we be sure he was telling us exactly what the Selgovae say?"

The centurion coughed.

"Em, I have not asked him sir."

Barrus sat back and steepled his fingers, turning his hands and admiring his manicure that, like his combed beard and glossy hair was a work of art. He raised his brows in mock surprise and smiled.

"I'm sure it must have skipped your mind. Have a word before Fufius Pulcher takes him and this Segontio back to Trimontium. Interrogate the prisoners on that specific point. Are the Novantae involved, do you understand?"

The infantryman nodded.

"That would be a sour lemon for you, gentlemen. A veritable nightmare. We would have all three tribes within our area joining up and at our throats. Effective strength of enemy hostiles could be up into the thousands. That is a lot of spears. All this for the sake of a Votadini girl? Surely not, no woman since Boudicca has caused a tribal uprising in this country. This girl is no more than some headman's daughter. Unlikely she could be the cause of this, but stranger things have happened," Barrus wondered.

He closed his hands and began rapping his desktop. The solitary gold ring on his right hand had a red intaglio inset with a design Fufius could not quite make out. It was the plain decoration of a working soldier: Barrus was a contradiction.

"Is it possible they have got word of our plans for the wall? Surely not?" he mused.

He chewed it over, ignoring their presence, a gambler's shadow hinting at calculations. Fufius glanced at the centurion. Barrus looked at Fufius.

"You may take your man as soon as you like. As you doubtless know, keeping the road open is all that matters. If by chance the Selgovae come asking for their man, I may need to tell them you have him for questioning. Outright denial is not likely to play well with them. Best you get moving. Give my regards to commander Pinneius," he repeated.

Fufius saluted.

"Torture the one who told you this Dumnonii story, centurion. Torture them all if you must. Find out everything there is about these Dumnonii. Take your man, Pulcher before I change my mind and have him tortured as well. I assume you have sufficient men to get the prisoner over the hills to Trimontium? Good, now, if there really is nothing else?"

Fufius saluted with the centurion, and they about turned and marched out.

*

Fufius separated Eidumnos from Segontio from the beginning when the Votadini eased his mount right up behind the bound Selgovae, tapping him on the shoulder with his spearhead, running the flat of it over the top of the beautifully tooled and decorated leather armour. He suspected that whatever Eidumnos was planning it would happen when he was not looking.

"Eidumnos, why don't you ride with me," he said, "you there, ride alongside the prisoner."

One of his men moved forward to take position.

Later, they escaped the low-lying fog and rode out into fresh clean air. There was a decent spot for a camp in the upper part of the hill pass. He let Segontio piss, then had him propped up, with his back against a boulder. He set two troopers the task of watching him. All he had to do was keep the Votadini and Selgovae apart. In the morning he would hand him over to Tacto.

They settled down for the night around him, leaving him pondering which god decided to send the Selgovae blundering into the arms of the patrol in the fog.

*

A nervous trooper woke Fufius in the first light of dawn. He rolled out of his cloak. The other troopers were rising. Something in the man's demeanour chilled his stomach. Were they surrounded by hostiles, trapped in this less than perfect spot?

"Come, you must see, sir, it's bad," the trooper said.

Fufius stared astonished at the body of a dead trooper no longer guarding a bound prisoner. Segontio was gone, with a horse.

'How in the name of Dis Pater? How could he do this and take a horse from under the noses of the Ala Augusta Vocontiorum without wakening anyone? The best auxiliary troopers in the legion. Tacto will have a fit.'

He tried to clear his mind and think. The Votadini, Eidumnos, was glaring at the vacant spot. His clothes had blood on them. His hands and arms were red.

"He found Lantor's body. A pity he was a good man," the trooper guessed his question.

"He was until he fell asleep on watch. If Lantor had stayed awake as ordered, he would still be alive," Fufius snapped.

He decided there was no purpose in discussing this with Eidumnos. He looked as outraged at they all were.

'Give chase, or go back and alert Dometius Barrus? Not very appealing either. Pour holy bull's blood on the altars of Mithras. What a mess.'

"What now sir?" his senior trooper asked, bringing him back.

"You and one other, get after him and see if you can find out where he has gone. If you can catch him and he resists, kill him. I will wait an hour for you here before going on to Trimontium. Bring him to me alive and you will be well rewarded."

The two men vaulted up into their saddles and after the briefest of checks of the horse-prints, set back off in the direction of the Selgovae lands.

"Put him on his horse," he said, indicating Lantor's body

"Shall I make porridge, sir?" one of them asked.

"Why not? There's nothing else to be done," he sighed.

*

Tacto heard the clamour from his troopers in the compound and got up to investigate. Fufius and his men were still mounted and from the crush of men around them he could not see what problem was causing the furore. The duty centurion spotted his presence and barked them to order. He waited for calm to be restored and then eased his way through the broad shoulders of the Augusta Vocontiorum. Fufius saluted him as he approached, his face grim and troubled. He saw the empty saddle and the dead trooper tied across it.

"Who is this?" he demanded.

"Lantor," Fufius replied.

The gaping wound had finished draining but it had run across the coat of the horse and the smell of blood was making it skittish. A ripple of dismay ran through the troopers crowding around.

"Did he die well?" he asked, for their benefit more than his own.

Fufius straightened himself up and looked around at his men.

"Lantor died because he fell asleep on watch. The prisoner we were escorting here for justice, took Lantor's life and escaped. If Lantor had not died last night, he would be flogged today."

His words carried for a moment.

"See to him," he told one of his decurions.

Tacto stepped back and let a trooper lead Lantor's body and horse to the stable. His friends rested hands on its rump, stroking its neck as if it too was grieving. A low song that was quite unknown to Tacto broke out. He had not the faintest notion what it meant but he understood it. Perhaps trooper Lantor had been more than he realised amongst his own kind?

Fufius dismounted and shook his head. Off duty legionaries were beginning to gather in knots as word spread. A sombre mood enveloped the compound.

"No sign of him then?" he said.

"None once he reached the road," Fufius replied, feeling tired.

It did not take a military master to pass the obvious judgement that he had failed in a simple task.

"Go and sit in the bathhouse, get changed, eat something and come to the office when you have done all that," Tacto said.

"As you command," he replied.

The rape of 'Velio's girl' had ceased being just an unfortunate piece of news for their missing commander. It had grown into a bear of a problem. They had moved not a single step forwards in resolving the matter of a Votadini and Selgovae dispute impacting the security of the western road. In fact, if anything, it might now be worse.

"I should have just let Eidumnos kill him when I had the chance. Left his body up there to rot." Fufius admitted.

"Perhaps," Tacto returned, "you should have, but that was not your order. Segontio either has power over rope or he was helped. Now that he has shed legion blood he is fair game. What our commander will make of all this, you had best turn your mind to, because he will want answers and not excuses."

Chapter 33.
The Ides of Aprilis.

Velio heard them in the distance even before dawn broke. He cocked his ear and leaned out over the Dextra gate rampart. It faded away for a while and then rose in an almost imperceptible degree, second on second, minute on minute, like watching the tide rising a quayside dock-post. The steady distant rumble of their nearest neighbours' waggons. Not a buccina-trumpet blowing, nor a drum beating. The musicians would be heartbroken. His mind had not slept for two nights and now the day was here. Velunia's waggons were packed and ready in the compound. Carts for the marching camp tents, carts with extra spades for digging and every spare pilum from the weapons store. Low fires already burning. Jentaculum bread and cheese, with a mouthful or two of watered wine to fortify the soul, for the soldiers coming off watch. The optios doing the rounds of barrack blocks, where no one alive was slumbering. Not a single voice audible above a low general murmur of preparation. Like a giant beehive with its tangible sense of purpose. It was not so different from the last hours before a battle except from the fact no one was expecting to die today. They had taken Hanno's order at face value, for what it was, from the moment they woke.

"We will depart in silence."

By evening, if the gods favoured them, Velunia would be the last garrison to hit the road. Even now, other cohorts based inland would be moving. He waited until he saw the first standards passing the Decumana gate and took the salutes of their officers. He walked out and saluted the column back. The 'mules' smiled at the unexpected compliment.

"Whatever you do, don't stop today until it's time to dig," he called over to them.

Their praefectus raised his left hand as he passed.

"May Fortuna favour us all commander," he replied.

"No breakdowns," Velio called after him.

"I know commander, I know," the praefectus murmured to his grinning youthful aide riding alongside.

Centurions raised their vine sticks to him as the centuries passed.

He waited to watch the last waggons passing before he decided he should eat too. Where was the hastiliarius hiding? He and Gallus had nothing to contribute to the packing up.

By the time he had finished breakfast and gone back to check on progress the Volitanio cohort was moving off into the distance and the light had grown from the suggestion of dawn into full daylight. It should be Colanica coming next then Subdobiadon. An hour passed before the advance cavalry screen heralded Colanica was on the move. The ramparts were beginning to crowd with men. He knew they were ready for it yesterday. In some ways it was just like a day's training march to build an overnight camp, except this time they would not be coming back. They would take their own memories of serving here with them. Those camps would take them all the way down to the Stones of Hadrian. And after that, would it be a posting on that wall or back to Deva Victrix or Eburacum for these men? That part was in the lap of Verus.

"Doesn't feel right, does it sir, not blowing the trumpets? A bit of 'Farewell Brother,' as they pass, if you know what I mean?"

A tesserarius, of his old rank, dared an opinion.

"Can you keep a secret tesserarius? I have never liked it," he replied, "it's too damn gloomy for my taste. I had a friend when I was a tesserarius. He liked everything the trumpeters play. But then, Marcus was tone deaf," he raised his eyebrows in mock horror.

The tesserarius grinned.

"A question if I may, sir?"

"Go on," he indulged him.

"Are we really opening the gates and marching south? Not burning the fort, or anything?"

"It's the same on every post. If all iron supplies have been secured, every nail and every wheel rim, the barbarians can have the fort. We leave nothing they can make into weapons. But as for the rest, the emperor has ordered us south and that's all you and I need to know. Make sure every man puts every weapon that's broken, bent, or otherwise buggered, down to the last hip-knife, on the transport waggons. And if they've never scratched **'I was here'** on the wall above their bunk, now's the time for them to go and do it."

"And the wall markers sir. The cohort slabs?"

'Now we're getting to it,' he realised.

The distance markers on both sides of the wall told every passer-by that could read, which century of men had sweated and toiled under their centurion to build the wall for the emperor. Stonemasons carved the words and numbers to order, until every slab was as straight and perfect as they could make them. The slabs said,

'We were here. We did this. Look on and wonder at the men of this cohort.'

Hanno's Germanic auxiliary would not give two stuffs for the stones but a legion regular like the tesserarius had invested something more.

"What would we do with them if we took them down? No, they stand for all time or as long as the wall stands, telling their gods who we were and what we achieved. Those barbarian dogs have nothing to match this. They never will be anything more than savages. Let them look at the wall when we are gone and dream they might become like us."

The tesserarius looked like he wanted to continue but Velio turned away, disinclined to give him any more chances to moan, descending down from the ramparts. Hanno's office felt like it might be a refuge from twitchy soldiers. Giving them too much time to think was never a good policy. Hanno would have papers needing burning now that the cohorts were moving. Perhaps he would appreciate a hand?

'Broken, bent or otherwise buggered,' the tesserarius cackled, 'the lads'll get a kick out of that one.'

Atius and Lucius were back in uniform and full armour. The small forecourt of the principia had a stack of wooden chests piled up. The aedes with the cohort standard and the pay-chest would be last to be cleared. The signifer was brushing his already resplendent wolf-skin cape but his eyes never left the entrance to the aedes and its treasure. A waggon was backing up to begin loading. Hanno's stuff was also piled up outside his residence: the lesser impedimenta of a bachelor careerist. He wondered if he piled his own gear alongside which pile would be higher.

'No wife, no family, not even a hound. Not much of a return for fifteen years on the wall is it Hanno? And no one in Rome cares in the slightest that a centurion named Pomponius died here less than a week

ago.'

All day, men and waggons passed by on the road that veered towards the south. In late afternoon Hanno performed the last lustration prayer in the compound in front of all his men. Afterwards the two of them went up to the north gateway for a last look at the barbarian lands.

"You said to me you were going to stay. You said you were going to defy the order, Hanno. What's made you change your mind?" he asked.

Hanno swivelled around, his muscled forearms resting in the wooden beam of the parapet

"It's a damned bad order, Velio, but it is an order. What kind of soldier would I be in the eyes of my men if I disobeyed it? Forgive me, Velio, I was angry that night. I cannot ask any of my men to stand here and commit suicide merely to keep me company. The gods would say I had lost my mind. And me staying would be a useless gesture 'contrary to the purposes of morale,'" Hanno murmured the old dictum.

Velio relaxed, grateful that one of Hanno's gods had whispered some sense into his old head. Only fools sought death.

"So, you're coming with us?" he probed, medicus like.

Hanno nodded.

"There's still plenty of Brigantes needing a good

hammering down south, from what I hear. The truth is I would like to get back to the legion, Velio. We are men of The Boar, you and me. An auxiliary command is all well and good but," he paused to lower his voice, "this is not the legion, is it? And I am getting sick of hearing German auxiliary voices and their language. I've never spoken it. Pomponius had it off well, but I insisted they spoke to me in the mother tongue. Bloody heathen savages. The Britunculi and the Gauls are trustworthy once they get enlisted and get over the shock, but these ones are descended from the ones Arminius led against Varus. We should have no truck with them."

He flexed his fingers and drummed the wooden parapet.

Velio smiled. These auxiliaries were not from the same tribes that took out Varus and his three legions, but that sort of minor detail would cut no ice with Hanno. The old soldier had finally had enough.

'You've just been up here too long Hanno. You are beginning to see enemies where they do not exist. This order has come just in time for you.'

"No, it is not the legion," he said trying to divert him.

"You and I, Velio, I think we deserve a bit more from Servius. Nigh on twenty years up here give or take. We have built forts and defences and manned them. A legion cohort to command, that is what I want. That would be something. Commander of the First cohort Velio; that is what I want for all the miserable wet dark winters I have waited up here for

Mithras knows what to happen. I am nothing more than a bloody tax gatherer and counter of cattle passing through the gates. These last few years have at least brought a bit of soldiering back to me. And now, I want the First cohort of the Twentieth legion. Best legion in the world. That would make all this worthwhile."

Hanno took out his pugio, nicked the tip of his finger and stabbed the blade deep into the timber.

"Here's to the First cohort of the 'Boar.'"

"That would be something, Hanno, I'd serve under you if you got that command," Velio promised.

Hanno brightened up, "then let's you and me agree to make that our aim, Velio. You and me. You will have the First century in the First cohort. You will be my 'First Spear' of the legion. Now that would be something to savour."

"What about our legate Servius Albinius?"

"Pah, leave him to me," Hanno growled, "he's not the first legate I've had to explain the world to."

He offered his bloodied hand. Velio took out his pugio and followed his example. They shook arms, their blood a sign of their pact.

Hanno led his men out with a certain panache, sitting erect in the saddle, helmet set, one fist on his hip, the reins in the other hand as if he was parading through Rome: signifer and silent trumpeters at his back, century after century following him. Out on the road, the last turmae of cavalry were waiting in line for them. Velio waited until the end, casting around the compound for any final last job left undone, knowing full well the optios had ensured there was nothing left for him to do. Hanno's optios and centurions knew their duties. In front of the headquarters building the grain sacrifice from the lustration still smouldered, grey smoke hanging low in the air. Not an unpleasant smell at all, welcoming in fact, almost like bread. The north, west and east gates were bolted shut. It was an eerie feeling. The barrack block doors were closed. The well had been blocked up with broken equipment and smashed amphorae. Every pot not required thrown down there along with odd chunks of stone and discarded ore from the smithying shop. No one would ever be able to drink from it now. The principal streets were empty. The low verandas where the men sat of an evening to talk, and joke were silent. The natives might salvage some timbers out of this but not much more. The ovens around the perimeter line were growing colder as the minutes passed. No soldier would bake bread in them again, or wait, impatient and hungry for the rough dough to cook. Bread, olives and cheap army wine, a bit of local cheese, endless porridge, and an occasional bite of meat: these wooden walls had seen and smelt it all.

He clicked his tongue. There really was not anything more to do. He knew he was stalling. Gallus was waiting with

Fufius' four troopers to escort him. One was holding his horse. The auxiliary saluted as he walked through the Decumana gate. He mounted and drew the horse's head around for one last look. So much had passed. Beyond expressing. Tomorrow or the day after, or next week, it would be burnt to the ground; just as soon as word of their leaving got out. The torches left burning on the ramparts would not fool the locals for long. He nodded to the trooper, and they trotted to join the column, thoughts careering, one after the other through his head.

'Four hours of daylight left. Enough time to get down the road a bit. Enough to sever the cord. How are the waggons holding up? Are they keeping the gaps? The Volitanio cohort should be setting camp by now. Has word leaked out to the tribes?'

He turned to check the mood of his men. Gallus wore a serene expression of perfect contentment.

Chapter 34.
The hill pass from Blatobulgium.

Segontio could feel his hands going numb from the tightness of the ropes

"If the Romans do not kill you, I am going to let my wife cut off your balls before we skin you alive, and know this, I'm prepared to pay them to release you into my custody, Selgovae. So whichever way the knife swings, it is not going to be a clean death for you. I may hang you from a tree once she's finished just so I can watch the birds picking at you every morning."

Eidumnos' promise kept rattling around in his head no matter how hard he tried to push it away. Now it was dark. The soldiers were asleep, and his skin crawled with the thought of that knife.

He wriggled his fingers trying to stem the creeping dullness and rolled onto his side moving his knees a few times to keep the pain in his feet at bay. Much more of this and walking, let alone riding would be impossible. The Roman commander, the one they called Fufius, had set a single guard on him. After a few hours the man changed over with another, who regarded him briefly, tapped his sword in warning and after a brief check to see no one was watching, settled down to sleep. Off to the side, he could feel Eidumnos watching him like a stoat.

'I'm dead as soon as that soldier starts to snore,' he thought.

It was not going to be a warrior's end, more the ignominy of a trussed-up goat. Eidumnos' attention had switched to the single sentry. Little by little his eyelids began drooping. Eidumnos flicked a malevolent glance at Segontio.

'Shit,' he fretted.

The sentry's head nodded, jolted, nodded, and began the slow downward dance to sleep. Eidumnos uncurled himself from his cloak like a glass eyed snake, moving in deft silence behind the sleeping guard.

'Shout and waken them all,' he shouted in his head, but a tiny part of him was already accepting death as his price for hurting Voccia.

Eidumnos paused halfway across the gap to the trooper and looked into his eyes. He looked straight back at him.

'A prince of the Selgovae is not afraid to die. But I did not think it would be to an old Votadini woman like you.'

Eidumnos crept up to the guard, listening to his deepening regular breathing. His head lolled forwards, jerked, and then lolled sideways. With a quickness Segontio could only admire, Eidumnos slid his hunting knife under the man's throat, clamped his free hand over the mouth and slit the soldier's throat from ear to ear. The soldier bucked and twitched like a deer. Blood fountaining over Eidumnos' hands and arms. The

Votadini held him in a vice and in a few shorts moments the soldier went limp. Still holding him, Eidumnos scanned the sleeping soldiers for signs of discovery. The fire crackled as it settled. The nearest horses had pricked up their ears. Fufius was just an outline under his blue cavalry cloak. He laid the dead soldier down on his side facing away from his comrades. When they woke, he would face abuse for falling asleep. It would buy vital seconds of time.

'It's time to make amends before my journey,' Segontio realised.

Eidumnos slipped over to him shielding him from the Romans with his back. His face a strange mix of fury, and sorrow.

'He expects to die here too, I suppose,' he reasoned, *'why should I let him have the silence he needs? One shout and they'll kill him for killing me and the soldier. We all die. The Romans win.'*

"I'm sorry I killed Voccia. I did not mean to do it. I admit I raped her. I am truly sorry Eidumnos. But I did not intend to do it. Take your knife and have your revenge. I will not betray what you do. You can blame that Roman," he said soft and low, nodding toward the corpse on the other side of the fire.

Eidumnos' bloody knife touched his windpipe. He felt blood start to dribble. He refused to take the cowardice of closing his eyes.

'Face it like a prince,' he told himself.

"I can kill you now and her mother will smile. My daughter

Voccia, she is not dead, you failed to steal her light, but I am taking yours now," Eidumnos breathed in his ear.

"What if I marry her and swear a vow to you to put things right between us," he said before he had time to think.

Eidumnos stroked the knife back to the other side of his windpipe, drawing more blood. Nothing resembling mercy touched his eyes. But playing with the coward would sweeten the thrust that finished him. Segontio saw that with the fire at his back, Eidumnos resembled a hunching crow poised to take his eyes out.

"What kind of vow could you make that could possibly end my mistrust of you?"

The older man lifted his eyebrows and mocked him.

"Name your price," Segontio whispered.

Eidumnos' face flickered his surprise. Segontio read the expression and dared to hope, *a chance.*

"There is no price to remedy dishonour except death. Honour is not paid in coin," Eidumnos reminded him.

He took the knife away from Segontio's throat and wiped the blade clean on his shoulder, smearing the rich leather.

"But if I were to let you marry her, if she wishes it, you would pay me every horse you ever own or steal in battle. I will let you keep two for riding. For as long as I live you will send me all of your horses. And men will ask you 'why do you give away your horses Segontio?' and you may choose whether to confess what you did or tell more lies. You will also bring your father's men to our fight with the legions," he murmured.

He pressed his lips against Segontio's ear.

Segontio gulped: it was a virtual death sentence to any man with aspirations of leading men. No self-respecting warrior would promise his every horse to another. He nodded, surprising Eidumnos for a second time.

'You're too quick to agree Segontio.'

He added another condition.

"Voccia's brother, Tianos, is free to kill you if he wishes for the dishonour you caused. He is his own man."

"I will take my chances with your son and if he gives me a chance I will explain. Forgive me, I went too far. I did not think she would not like it. Let me speak to her and if she refuses marriage, I will kneel under your knife. You will not have to look for me. I won't hide."

Eidumnos felt his anger ebbing, despite himself. There was nothing he could think of that brought sufficient dishonour to make this Selgovae gag. He swallowed and acceded.

"I'm only doing this because our peoples must stand as one or the Veniconi and the Dumnoni will roll over us like a tide. No one will survive the reckoning."

"Free me Eidumnos and I will rule instead of my father. I pledge to stand with you Eidumnos," he whispered and glanced at the Romans.

Time was running short. The point of the knife whisked up to his right eye: he blinked.

"Make it right with Voccia. If you have seeded her, her child will be yours: a half prince. If you cannot, you are a dead man. I have had you on the end of this knife once, I can do it twice. Your life is in her hands now. And all the rest will not matter to you if she decides the answer is 'no'."

He nodded back, not daring to break eye contact with the Votadini. The knife flashed and he felt the ropes part. He flexed his hands, arms, and legs, biting his lip, expecting pain. It was not as bad as he feared. Eidumnos pulled him up to his feet. Together they paused waiting for a challenge from the prostrate soldiers. It was only the fire rustling. Eidumnos gave the dead soldier a soft kick. The man's shoulder gave at the impact but there was no feeling in the flesh. He pointed to the horse-lines and together they stole past their sleeping guards. Eidumnos untied a horse and handed the reins to Segontio, keeping a hand on the animal's nostrils to keep it calm in the night.

"You are not coming?" Segontio frowned.

Eidumnos shook his head at the naivety of the question.

"You must escape alone, or I am implicated. Find your way to my hall. Do not bring the horse. They must believe you acted alone. You killed the guard and escaped. Now go before we are both discovered," Eidumnos said.

He turned back to the camp and Segontio realised with a jolt he was on his own.

*

He rode through the gates of Carubantum and gave a jocular grin and wink to the astonished warrior watching from above. The reaction was better than he could have hoped.

'No, I'm not in the land of the ancestors yet my friend.'

Let them gossip about him now. His name would be on everybody's lips before nightfall.

'The prince has returned alive, he outwitted the Roman dogs, they could not hold him,' he could hear them now and his heart swelled with his own prowess.

'Come see what a true warrior prince looks like. Come see your next king.'

He rode through the main street that was busy with trade, dogs and children. The usual women and stalls of every kind of food and items imaginable. Jewellery and knife stalls, side by side with butchered boar and cow. Geese in wooden framed cages. Escaping the Roman patrol had cost him all his weapons, even his helmet, so it was not the spear and shield-bearing entrance he wanted. But it was enough to sit erect in the saddle and let the horse pick its way through the shoals of townsfolk. He dismounted at his father's hall and handed the horse reins to a servant, outstaring the king's champion guarding the door, prudence kept him from starting an argument. He entered the hall feeling the burn of the champion's eyes on the back of his leather jerkin. One day they would have to resolve such discourtesy.

His father was standing with his back turned away from him and his arms folded. His long hair was tied around his head with a favourite decorated leather band inlaid with scrolls and whorls of gold wire. Not quite a crown, it was the mark of a rich man. He waited to be noticed. Father would not deign to be the first to see him even if only the two of them were standing there. An urgent whispering made him feel better. His father whirled around, his face a mix of pleasure and confusion, as startled by his arrival as the common folk out in the street. Had they all thought him dead?

"We thought you were dead Segontio, my boy. We heard the Romani had you?"

"They did and yet here I am," he said, "they could not hold me," he bragged.

His father almost smiled.

'I've finally done something he has never managed,' Segontio warmed at the thought.

"Where are my Roman heads?" his father said.

He put his hands on his hips wondering whether the old man was serious after all that had happened? To turn so fast from flickering concern for his wellbeing to demanding his tribute.

"I dropped them," he lied, "and I have made peace with the girl's father."

His father put his hands on his shoulders, looking at him as if Segontio was a stranger who had on a single stroke become both useful and important.

"Indeed? How did you manage that?" he said.

"Did any of my men return?" Segontio changed the subject.

"No," the king replied, "now answer my question."

He ate with his brothers that evening, chewing over more than the food. As he watched them, he felt sure they would fall in line when the time came for the coup. The question was, would the king's own men do the same? He chaffed them and afterwards went walking alone to ponder the next step. Death would need to be more subtle than a blade in the chest. A hunting accident was too unlikely to arrange. A fall from a horse was one thing, to make it fatal was quite another. That only left poison or strangulation at night. And then it struck him: do it at a meeting with the girl's father. A poisoning at a feast of reconciliation. Wiping them both out at the same meal would remove any stain of treachery by either side; all would be fooled into thinking it was an unfortunate mis pick of a mushroom. Why would anyone wish to poison them both? Why indeed, it would not be explicable. It would make him king, give him Voccia, or not if she chose to be difficult. If she said 'no,' it removed his obligation. There were plenty of willing Selgovae ladies to choose from. And as king, the Novantae to the west would be more inclined to help him fight the Roman forts along the road.

Another piece moved on the board in his head. What if the poisoning of father and Eidumnos happened during a visit to the Votadini's hall instead of Carubantum? That would give him another option of laying the blame of the double poisoning on the Votadini? Use the outrage as an excuse to invade over the hill pass and take their land. The Votadini overlord in Dunpeledur would never fight back if a thousand summers passed. He would huff and send emissaries and protest, but getting off his throne and retaliating, no, that was most unlikely. A swift victory in the three hills valley would feed his claim as nascent king.

Once he had the idea of a double poisoning in Eidumnos' hall in his head, the details started coming. There would be no need to overdramatise it by waiting for a wedding with Voccia because, really, that would be far too obvious. If he could arrange a reason for father to cross the hill pass it should be possible. A meeting with Eidumnos' good Roman perhaps, to express regret at their leaving? Some friendly farewell gifts of compliance? Then afterwards in Eidumnos' hall, perhaps,

perhaps, perhaps. No, father would never countenance giving gifts to the wolf-soldiers. There must be another way of getting him to cross the hill pass.

He bolted his own door tight shut and lay down on the fur-robes to sleep, tired beyond the point of caring what anyone thought anymore. Tomorrow he would speak to his men. Tomorrow their reaction would help decide how much longer he would put up with his father.

Four days later news came that a Roman cohort was marching down the road from the wall. He rode with some of his brothers to observe them from a hill. The rumbling carts made his fingers itch to lift the spear. They were such easy targets when spread out in column. He returned inside the walls. He had scant time to settle his horse before news came of other cohorts moving on the road. Other messengers repeated the incredible news. The Romans were moving south. It was beyond any doubt. A major event was happening just a few miles from Carubantum's walls.

The next step after the poisoning must be to avoid contact with all Romani and keep out of sight of them. He would have power before they had time to react. Not that they would care over much now they were retreating. He sent two of his more trusted men to see for themselves if the wall was being abandoned. It seemed too good to be true. The gods were smiling, the plan was good, but he needed help to make it work.

Part two.
Foxes and wolves.

Chapter 35.
Orgidor's war.

Orgidor had the legate's column in his sights as he tracked them parallel to the road, knowing the contours would keep his men out of sight. He knew the course, dips, and hollows of the stone road so well it was no great challenge to shadow the horsemen. It was disappointing they were too numerous to try a direct attack. He had almost enough men with him and if the ground had been better, he could have sneaked closer before launching them. But on this exposed section the odds were not auspicious. It stayed that way until a small patrol detached and fell right into his pocket. He had a hunch where the column was heading with such confidence.

He split his men, keeping a handful with him to follow the enemy and sent the rest on to the pool to set an ambush. The advance cavalry picked up pace and the gap between them and the main column widened. In his head he saw it develop, the horsemen descending the short slope from the road to the waterfall and its pool. From that moment they would be lost to sight from any following body of men. With the gap increasing every second he watched, there would be time to spring an attack when they rested by the water. The road disappeared into the folds of the undulating ground taking them with it. He had seen enough. With a swift tug of his horse's reins, he led his band in pursuit of his own men.

*

Now the bodies of that rash, advanced, group of cavalry lay arranged around the small pool below the waterfall. He thought about stealing the horses and decided he would. Free horses plus tack including some weapons, it was a good day to be a Brigantes. He waited until the young officer's head was removed and presented to him in homage by the swaggering young bucks. He hefted it by the feathered crest and stared at the white face of the dead young cavalryman. Quite a good-looking young man really. At least he had been, up until he led his men off the road and trotted into the trap and became a dripping trophy.

He rallied them; it was time to move. The main column could only be minutes away. He would have liked to have waited and watched their reaction, but common sense made him take a last glance at what they had done and kick the stallion forward. They yelped and shouted the war cries. He joined in, caught up in their exuberant joy. It had been so simple. The Romans had gifted their lives to his men. Their horses galloped amongst his own with the faithlessness of animals that had once been traded by the Brigantes. He led them up into the rough bounds of the moors and on to the hills and corries of their homes. This was not the way the great leaders of the past waged their wars but the old days of head-to-head butting against squared-up legions was over. His own ancestor Venutius proved courage and swordplay were not enough. The lessons were hard learned. He was not ever going to make that kind of mistake again. The long game was everything. Outfox the legions at every opportunity and find out which side had the stomach to withstand the loss of blood and men in a land where winters were his friends.

His druid surged on ahead to spread the news of their foray. He urged his horse onward and gave the soldier's gory head over to one of his followers to carry. The lad's face lit up in delight. His old bones and thin bony backside were not made for horses anymore. His back was beginning to hurt again.

'Too much riding, you old fool,' he told himself and clenched his jaw as the stallion thundered on.

'The long game Orgidor, pray that you live long enough to see it won.'

The village turned out for their arrival, spoiling them, and fussing over him. He laughed and pretended to struggle to the seat at the fire, mock wrestling with a couple of small boys, catching a little girl and sweeping her up onto his lap until she giggled to burst. They felt his aura and the love of the gods exuding from him bathed them all, filling the hall, overflowing through the village. Night fell over hot fires and plentiful meat. Harps began thrumming as they fell into tune. Songs and praise-poems for long-ago heroes. They sang the praise poem of Orgidor, for him, then cheered long and loud. He breathed deep contented breaths of pleasure. It was just as splendid as the old days when he had been the one kneeling at his father's knees, listening, and soaking it all in.

So many happy faces, trying to visualise the great deeds that caused songs to be sung about Orgidor. Later he felt himself beginning to nod. His eyes felt heavy. It had been a long day; a fine day, no one had been lost in the attack and those keen young warriors had not let him down. The trap had been perfect. The horror on the faces of the Romans had pleasured him as much as their deaths.

'They rode to give themselves to Brigantia at her pool; what fools they are. They learn nothing. They will never succeed in defeating us as long as we respect and honour her.'

He maybe did not feel as young as he used to feel.

'Ah, but in my prime I was a force to reckoned with. And now my back hurts more each day and the horses get bonier.'

Excusing himself from the company, he let his daughter lead him through their warm wishes to his own hall.

"You must go back," he said.

He smiled as his dog beat the rushes on the floor with its

tail.

"Go back and enjoy yourself. I will be sleeping before you are back at that fine young man's side."

She smiled at the reference to her husband. He was always 'that fine young man,' when her father was content and at peace with himself. She waited for the usual follow up comment about the lack of grandchildren, but his head touched his pillow, and he was asleep before he had time to tease her. She closed the door and left *'the old grey man of the hills'* and his favourite deer hound sleeping in their respective places.

Chapter 36.

From Deva Victrix to Eburacum.

Servius stood in front of his maps, tapping away with end of his stylus in a relentless unhappy rhythm, with one hand up on the wall, the other staccato-ing the pen onto the parchment, threatening to puncture it. His shorn head gleamed from his fresh shearing. A nick from the morning razor had sealed yet left a tell-tale red slit under the chin. His political tribunus laticlavius and his chief military tribunus augusticlavius stood poised on either side on the map as he drummed. His astute young laticlavius standing without his armour, arms folded, all attention to detail, focussed, senses running like a stallion. Dressed in his working toga. The augusticlavius ready to pick up his helmet and sword and set the cohorts into action.

This Brigantes nonsense had to end. The exchanges of messages through high command were getting terser and terser as the weeks of spring rolled by. The governor already making his lofty opinions of the unfolding strategy he had instigated, plain. He was now apoplectic that the land they were reverting to might be drifting towards to a similar state as the land he was vacating. Insurrection simmering below

Hadrian's wall as well as beyond. The situation had him worried.

"The walls are in the wrong places," was only one of his frequent complaints.

'Not much we can do about that.'

Servius got so close to reminding him on more than one occasion that it troubled him later. The last interview had not been pleasant. Abundant shouting and spume. It was sheer spite to lay all the blame at his door. There were two legions charged with keeping the peace up here after all. The Twentieth did its share. Let the Sixth do likewise.

'He could start by stopping handing out medals for frightening children and get a grip on the eastern sector,'

The words had been so tempting he had almost said them.

'Start by stopping.'

What a critique of a colleague's entire strategy.

Rattle, tap, tap rattle: he felt a wicked delight that the sound of the pen transmitting his anger was stifling conversation in the principia. He could hear some of the other tribunes busy with the clerks at their desks behind him. No one daring to speak above a whisper this morning until he gave permission. He had, he admitted to himself, made things a little tense in the headquarters. He enjoyed the frisson. That was what he intended it to be, that was how he was feeling, so why not them as well?

'Let them hate me, so long as they fear me.'

Mad old Caligula got that bit right but then he was a soldier's boy. He had seen the black trees of Germania in winter.

But, *'let them understand my anger,'* was more constructive, *'then they understand better what they must do to please me.'*

The map was specked with red crosses where the Brigantes had interfered with troop movements. Scores of them. It was time to clean off the old ones because they were starting to confuse the situation. Last year's blood was dry. What was happening on the ground today mattered. The hills in the middle divided the country into the sectors controlled by, and under the jurisdiction of, the Twentieth and Sixth legions. So why was Gnaeus Julius Verus so keen to bite off only his ear?

'Why am I taking all the spade for this?'

He chewed the thought for a bit. The sphincters of the clerks were twitching so much he could almost hear them.

'Time for a meeting Servius,' he told himself. *'this needs sorting out.'*

One more narky comment from Verus, and he would be forced to explain the obvious to him. He stamped down an impromptu vision of seizing and shaking the governor by his windpipe. The map tore under the pressure of his pen. His hot suppressed rage made a hole through the paper on a little settlement in the mid-ground, almost on the unmarked border between the two legions.

The settlement obliterated by the hole was a short march from the hill pass road. He had burned it before on campaign and now he had torn it from the map. His dry sense of humour began bubbling and he made himself take a long breath. He curled his fingers around the stylus and relaxed. Current reports from tame Carvetii tribesmen suggested it had been, or was being, rebuilt. They could not confirm what state it was in, which was a bit of a concern. A rebuilding had the hallmarks of deliberate provocation.

"Come back and burn us again?" he murmured aloud.

"A trap sir?" the augusticlavius offered.

His laticlavius' jaw clenched and relaxed a few times, but he had nothing to add. Servius stood back regarding them for a moment.

'A trap sir?'

He was not convinced, but it could be seen as a symbol of resistance.

"Take a letter, best paper we have," he called out.

"To the legate of the Sixth.

'My dear friend, Hail and fraternal greetings.'"

The laticlavius rolled his eyes at the military tribune. Servius gave them both a grin. In an instant the hitherto restrained voices rose. He rubbed his almost bald head and laid down the stylus, turning to the young tribune.

"There, I've started it for you. You finish it. Write a letter that invites me to a meeting in Eburacum."

"Immediately sir," the laticlavius replied, surprised.

He turned to his augusticlavius.

"We are going over, you and me, to sit in the latrines for ten minutes and get a feel for what the mules say. Dealing with fractured skirmishing is never popular."

He turned back to the laticlavius.

"It's a lesson my own first commander impressed upon me. Men always tell the truth to each other when they think no one of higher rank is listening. Where better to hear the truth?"

A courier left within the hour for Eburacum with enough of an escort to control the forum in Rome on a festival day. The servant at the latrines, with no escort, took all day to calm down after the legate and tribune's sudden appearance. At first, he feared it was an unannounced inspection. Then it was evident the visit was a great deal more prosaic. It was not fitting. After all the legate had his own private, much superior, facilities in the praetorium, but as Servius reminded him, "my backside is no different from anybody else's."

A bit of warning would have given him time to get fresh sponges for the ablutionary part. This time of the morning was busy. But the legate did not seem to mind. When they left the two officers were wearing contented expressions. Nothing unusual in that, he supposed.

*

The flying silver wine cup bounced off the floor, took a ricochet and glanced off the wall before landing on the chief clerk's desk, shedding a remnant of wine on his pristine, first, and thereby tidiest version, of the daily orders.

"Balls of Dis," he exclaimed before he remembered whose company he was working in.

There was visceral silence that might have graced Pompey's theatre when it became clear Gaius Julius Caesar was in fact dead; no longer breathing, they really had dared to, and had in fact killed him. Caesar was dead at their hands.

The order was despoiled. The legate glared at the exclamation but only to the degree he had not uttered the profanity himself. High command meant decorum must be exhibited but sometimes a vent of honesty was required. A good swear was like a good and noisy fart. It might not appeal much to the audience, but it rendered immense satisfaction to the performer. Why should the clerk be alone in saying what he felt? The clerk took a furtive look in his direction and lowered his head, wishing he had kept silent. The Twentieth legion were coming to patronise the lesser experience of the Sixth.

"Balls of Dis," failed to sum it up. Though it did its best.

"Those bastards invite themselves to my garrison to tell me how to police the Brigantes filth a spear's length from my front wall, can you believe it?" the legate fumed.

The dented drinking cup was retrieved and replaced on his desk. A servant scurried to find a cloth to clean up the wine.

"I want all the headmen brought here. I will have answers from them, or I'll flog the skins off their backs, so help me."

He picked up the cup he had thrown and inspected the damage. The wave passed and he took a deep breath.

"See if this can be fixed, will you? Apologies to you all. Is the order ruined Surus? My apology to you too."

The chief clerk risked a head shake and a faint smile. The damaged cup was whisked out of sight before it engendered another outburst.

"We should be able to master our animal emotions, but we are not all born with the emperor's grace," the legate continued.

A dutiful flutter of laughter, delicate as a butterfly, broke out.

"Get them here tomorrow. Make sure they have answers to why these raids continue despite my patience. Make sure they understand I do not wish to use the whip, but the tribe must not carry on with these, mischiefs. I will not have it. Make it plain to them and I will see them tomorrow. Servius Albinius is not coming here to tell me how to rule the Brigantes. That, he is certainly not."

He strode out leaving the carnage and a room still stunned at his outburst. Surus turned to his junior clerk.

"Another fresh order-scroll if you please young man."

*

The First cohort saw their legate delivered to the gates of Eburacum fortress and retired to make camp outside the town. Servius saluted them as they paraded past in the rain. The standards and the feather crests dripped. The joy of wet armour and wet cloaks. It was going to be chilly and uncomfortable in the eight-man tents tonight. He was glad it was not for him. Fires would be awkward to get going; hot food slow to prepare. The genus spirits of Northern Britannia were cold and unwelcoming at this time of year.

'They call this early summer,' he mused, *'they would call it winter in Gaul.'*

Eburacum watched the cohort counter-march under its walls and retire into the distance while its commanders shook arms with their counterparts in the Sixth and took shelter in a warm headquarters already prepared for their arrival. Adroit as he was, Servius found it heavy going to agree progress on a summer campaign. He ate a frugal mouthful or two, knowing the evening meal would be significant and let his presence and that of his men seep into the consciousness of the Sixth's high command. The noisy sound of rain on the tiles overhead was depressing.

*

Orgidor spied the tent lines being erected beyond the last houses of the sprawling civilian vicus and knew the soldiers were being stationed away from the fortress on purpose. Perhaps the two sets of soldiers were likely to argue and fight: like tribes? He had heard of such things. If they regarded themselves as two tribes, if this was true, there might be opportunities to turn that to his advantage.

'That is wishful thinking, Orgidor,' he chastised himself.

The wolf-soldiers were not like the tribes at all.

'If only they were.'

The spades were soon out, and the customary ditch and low out-fill mound grew before his eyes

'Functional and simple. The same as always. They never deviate.'

In the centre he could see the large tent of their leader and torches getting set. The wet grey afternoon was turning to dank early evening. He watched the defences getting inspected by officers and the camp settling down.

"Which cohort are they?" he asked.

"Twentieth legion, First cohort," his spy said.

"The First cohort? You understand who they are? These are the best of their warriors."

He tried to keep his surprise in check.

"Then their legate must be here," he reasoned.

The young man nodded to the 'old grey man of the hills.'

"Night is coming," he said.

Orgidor smiled back.

"Who knows what gifts the darkness will bring to the First cohort," he whispered.

Chapter 37.
First cohort camp, Boar legion; Eburacum.

The Primus Pilus surveyed the damage and snorted in contempt. It was insignificant, given the fact that overnight camps tended to attract unwelcome attention. Last night's drizzle had helped dampen everything down; so, it could have been worse, much worse. Even so, a bit of provocation of his camp was either a deliberate taunt to come out and fight, except there was no enemy standing outside the rampart, or a gesture of defiance. He put his hands on his hips and sucked through his teeth. A few burned tents, some of the night guard wounded by spear and arrow; a "Stand to the Eagle," blown at some unholy hour just as he was getting off to sleep and then nothing. The legate had taken the cavalry escort and the tribune leaving the camp in his charge until he returned. He was not going to tolerate this mess. There was not much time to tidy things up.

He called the centurions together. Their mood was grim, but he kept things focussed on what was required. No one had slept after the bugle call. No one had had time to get themselves dry again. Breakfast had been a quick and tetchy refuelling.

"Get this tidied up before the boss gets back. I want full

injury reports from the medicus. Are any of the burnt tents salvageable? If so, get the lads working on them. There is no guarantee we will be leaving today, and these clouds aren't moving so there'll need to be some doubling up in your centuries or some fast stitching before tonight."

They grimaced at the thought extra men doubling up in tents made for eight.

He gave a bleak, *'that's the way it is,'* kind of gesture.

They saluted and got on with it. He stalked out of the gateway abutting the road into Eburacum. Doubtless the local Brigantes would be wondering if he was going to make reprisals. A small group of villagers were walking towards him as though to prove that point. Four of them, all mature men, two had swords but otherwise they were only armed with their work-knives. They raised their hands in greeting as soon as they realised he had sighted them. He removed his helmet as a little reciprocal sign of peace. They halted several paces from him. The squad on guard at the gate behind him moved out to support him, their tesserarius leading. He stood to attention at the centurion's left shoulder.

"Problem sir?"

"I don't think so. They look more worried we're about to go in there and chop the lot of them," he replied.

"That'd bloody teach them," said the tesserarius.

He nodded back, agreeing. It was tempting to wave the steel

at them even if they were not responsible.

"Garum bloody sauce if you ask me, sir," the tesserarius went on, "pushin' their bloody luck."

"Let's hear what they have to say," he replied.

Junior officers did not always have the wisdom of patience. Out of the corner of his eye he noticed the Brigantes waiting until they had ceased speaking.

'Definitely worried we'll hold them responsible,' he assessed.

"Salve," the leader raised his hand.

"Salve," he replied.

The tesserarius 'harruphed' under his breath.

"Not us, Orgidor," the leader pointed to the camp.

"Orgidor?" he queried.

He decided to play for information, biting back the thought they seemed well informed for men who had done nothing.

"Bloody would be someone else, wouldn't it, sir," the tesserarius fumed.

"Where is Orgidor?" he frowned.

He raised the hand and vine stick, pretending to wipe his brow. The tesserarius took the hint.

"Gone to the hills. We are amicus - friends to the Eburacum legion. The Sixth are good to us. We trade. They buy our horses, our cattle, our wheat. We do not fight you. Orgidor fights you," the Brigantes spokesman went on.

The centurion chewed his lip.

"I need goat skins to repair the tents Orgidor burned last night. I am not going to pay for them. You can get Orgidor to pay for the skins. I want fifty goat skins this morning."

He tapped the vine against his decorated greaves. He could sense the tesserarius tensing up in anticipation of a refusal.

"Fifty skins, you will have them sir. We have skins for your tents. Centurion, do not punish us for Orgidor's actions. Ask your soldiers in the fort. We are amicus of Rome."

"That'll be bloody likely," said the tesserarius, unmoved.

The centurion let it slide and stepped forwards until he was face to face with the four Brigantes.

"Some of my men were wounded last night. Best pray to your Brigantia goddess they do not die. Otherwise, it might be that I do speak to the soldiers in the fort, your friends in the Sixth legion. Got it?"

The men nodded, too eager to pacify him, and his instinct like his junior colleague's, was they were a bit too quick to accept his demand for free skins to repair the damage.

"Keep them away from the gate, tesserarius. Don't let them see inside, I don't trust them," he ordered.

"My pleasure sir."

"Keep the swords sheathed. No bloodshed. Do not make things worse before the legate and the tribune return. When the skins arrive have them unloaded here and get a couple of the lads to carry them in. Strictly no visitors, and definitely no bartering. No excuses, tesserarius."

He reeled off the order as if ordering food in a tavern. The Brigantes had their ears cocked but he doubted they understood what he said.

*

Servius listened to the report inside the cohort's headquarter's tent. His tribune was busy inspecting the camp damage on his behalf. Caninius, his Primus Pilus, made a good job of masking his annoyance that the events last night had happened at all. He was also succinct and to the point.

"Local sympathisers sir. Night-time probe at our defences. Vanished once the alarm sounded. Nothing to pursue, without cavalry support. By the time Eburacum sent out its cavalry they had gone. It feels like a reminder to the vicus that we are still the enemy."

"That is an interesting proposition, Caninius. A reminder to the vicus? To stir them up under Eburacum's walls? We heard the alarm call. Rather embarrassing for the legate. Makes it look as though he is not in control," Servius shared his thinking.

"How did it go, sir?" Caninius asked.

Servius tugged his chin, "exactly as I expected."

He paused, debating whether to let the primus into his

personal conviction that the Sixth were sitting on the job.

'Possibly best to let that go. Caninius is not here for politicking tribunes and legates.'

"Get the tents repaired, we are not marching back to Deva Victrix. Not anytime soon, I fear. Put the wounded on the carts and take them into the fortress. They will have to wait for our return. In answer to the question that is undoubtedly in your head Caninius, we and the Second cohort of the Sixth are going out to capture this Orgidor fellow and put him to the sword along with as many of his followers as we can. If we cannot find him, or they will not give him up, we are going to herd their women and children together like goats and threaten them with slavery in Gaul and Germania unless they give him up. The governor has made it clear. The lands below the wall must be secure. He will not be made to look a fool by a few Brigantes, and quite frankly nor will I. What the Sixth want is not important."

'There, Caninius, now you know.'

Caninius did not even twitch.

"Cavalry sir?" he said.

"The Sixth are providing four turmae, that will give us six in total. I will be in overall command of all forces. They are sending a tribune of course to command their cohort. The tribes will run at the sight of us, so this is going to be a messy gathering operation. We'll have their cattle too, I think, they can feed us for their impertinence."

"Begging your pardon sir, but what are we going to do with the women and children we gather up?" Caninius asked.

"I'm afraid the women may end up in the tents with the lads. Should be just the thing to provoke a bit of betrayal don't you think? These Brigantes are used to betraying other tribes' chieftains to us in return for securing peace, remember Caracticus and all that, years ago, long before our time. A little bit of the hammer will do them good. Get hold of those goat-skins and get those tents repaired Caninius, I want to march tomorrow."

Chapter 38.
Scouring for Orgidor.

Orgidor's spies had the two cohorts' movements within hours of breaking camp. They took him to high point where he could see the numerous standards and hear the trumpets blaring. There was a small screen of outriding cavalry keeping pace with the foot soldiers on all four sides. He lay down in the grass to watch them pass across his front, heading north. Were they marching to the great wall of stone? He scratched his head.

"You are certain this is the First cohort?" he asked.

The distance made the too details fuzzy for his eyesight. He could see them moving but they were too blurry for him to distinguish.

"They are strengthened by a cohort from Eburacum. It's their Second cohort," his spy replied.

"So, they have sent out two cohorts of their best men with horsemen, and they are heading north," he scowled, "our little wasp sting two nights ago has nipped them. They are hunting for us I think," he said.

"They will never catch us with all those men my lord. They

are too slow."

"Not unless there are other horsemen searching that you have not found for me," he warned, "were there eyes on the fort all night? Could they have sent out an advance patrol ahead of this one? Tell me honestly, I do not want to be caught between two forces. Are you sure they have not sent more horsemen out secretly?"

His spy shook his head.

He gave him a hard look, "if you are lying, you know what I will do to you?"

"Orgidor, I swear no troops left the fort before the men you can see now."

Orgidor leaned over and patted his spy's shoulder.

"Very well, I trust you. There is no trap. One thing is clear, the wall of stones has new troops on it. These men are not needed there. The question is, where are they going and why?"

"Orgidor, the word is they are looking for you. They want to say they captured 'the 'old grey man of the hills' from the Brigantes so they can execute him," his son in law hissed.

He was forced to agree that was the most likely reason. He moved his head from side to side.

"All those men for one old man?" he played to make them laugh.

"Are you going to attack the wall from this side, Orgidor?

Strike at their belly?" his spy said.

His son in law waited. It was not Orgidor's habit to reveal his plans to anyone until he was ready to strike.

"If I could lift all of our people over the wall to safety, we could strike bargains with the Votadini and never have to see another one of these curs again. They offend me. They always have. They should offend you too. They are like a stupid hound that never learns, no matter how hard you punish it when it bites," he scowled.

"But this is our land, as you have always said. Why should we leave and go north of the wall?" the spy said.

"Do not worry, we are not going north of the wall. But if we do not leave and we do not fight, we will eventually become Roman in everything but our names. In the end it will be a sacrifice that you and I pay, but so must our families. I believe if we defeat another legion, it might be enough to make them pull back. Some of the priests agree with me but not all of them. They say the signs are not clear. But that is what priests always say. They will not tell me the signs are in my favour until I have gone out and won the victory. And when I do that, I will be able to judge the signs for myself. But the priests are not wrong. It's just that they are careful: too careful. It can be a bad habit for warriors. If I teach you all one thing it is this; no songs are sung for careful men. I can tell you that much. Careful men achieve only one thing, a long life, long lives of slavery. Imagine what that would be like? I would rather die. I say, if the northern tribes have managed to chase them away, the signs the priests are so desperate to see are there already. Perhaps we need to let the signs grow stronger. I believe it is possible to do what our fathers did it. Aren't we men, the same as them," he reasoned.

"We cannot beat another legion without all of our nation lifting the spear," the spy reposted.

His son in law tried his best to hide his agreement. Orgidor wanted to reach out and hug them all. They cared, that was all that mattered: sometimes it was enough to care. The things that followed for men who cared were gifts from above.

"Then we must do what we can to persuade them," he said.

*

Servius sipped a decent cup of Falernian at his camp desk, settling his stomach from what had been an indifferent evening meal. The scouring had got off to a good start. Two villages mopped up in the first day. Women and children seized; the women hauled off to the tent lines this evening for the men to enjoy. The sounds of that distress already audible. Let them remember what it meant to raise weapons against Rome.

The smell of roasting meat still floated on the evening air. It had been a good day, all things considered. Tomorrow he would send the prisoners back to Eburacum under escort and carry on the search. A bit more provocation, a few more villages pillaged, and it should not be long before the Brigantes came boiling out of the hills to fight. He was counting on causing enough rage to dull their tactics into full-on, bloody, meat grinding: let the gladius chop them limb from limb.

He sipped his wine and almost bit into the lip of the cup. He laid it down. His hand was shaking. A vehemence was in him, he could feel its powerful surge and it surprised him. He should try and make himself step back, staying cold and calm, and assess the men fighting him. This Orgidor had reached deeper under his skin than he had given him credit. The lads would stand in line; swords and shields at the ready, battle chanting the challenge and the Brigantes would make their stupid, arrow headed assault, rushing in to break his lines and after a half hour or so they would be dogs' meat.

He took a long pull on the wine. That was how it would be. The First cohort would be the grinder and the Brigantes, the dog meat. It was merely a question of how soon the brigand could be lured to his fate.

'*Roma Victa.*'

He took a fresh letter from his campaign trunk. It was from Hanno Glaccus.

'*Hanno Glaccus, wants to come back to me, asks to come back,*' he grinned.

Hanno was the best of centurions and the worst. Brilliant as a commander of men. In the cruelty of life's counterbalance, he was equally poor and blind to the nuances of strategic command. For a soldier he was an intelligent blacksmith. He judged the weight of the hammer without fail, like a master, in fact. Could he relinquish the tasks he enjoyed doing, to other men? Could Hanno Glaccus take a map and plan a campaign, and then send men to die while he remained impartial behind the rearmost rank, observing?   He liked Hanno: modest Hanno.

Hanno Drusus Glaccus Ticinus: Servius knew the answer to his own question quite well.

Hanno had tried to reflect all his good deeds on the page and made a decent stab at it. His performance on the northern wall required no repetition to a friend, and he was writing to a friend, even if he did not always know it. Had he not served his time, he asked? It was a dignified query, with no embarrassing or unbecoming imploring. Was his loyalty to Servius and the Twentieth not clear? Was it not valued? Like Hanno's best qualities, the message was simple and direct.

'Hanno you are valued. Rest assured I owe you much for your unstinting service to the legion. You are bored kicking your heels now that you are back with your men on the Stones of Hadrian. It's too safe for you I expect; the turf wall was a lot more fun for a man like you, even if you won't admit it to me: that, I can tell. I did say it was the sort of

command that would serve your career well. You want me to give you a cohort in the legion now instead. Knowing you, you will want the First. Though you are too wise an old owl to come out and say so. That would be a little too pushy and you know me well too. Hmmnn, the evacuation of the wall was well done under you.

You cannot have long to go, Hanno? You must be about ages with Gallus Tiomaris. How about a short-term command then, Hanno? I could do that for you. That phalera on your armour would be a nice touch for you. Something to remember when you retire, and it could open other doors if that is what you want. Politics, is that it, Hanno, you want to run for office when you leave? It will be a pity when you two leave: you'll be missed, both of you. First cohort, though, hmmnn, I am not sure Hanno; I am really not sure. It is a big favour. I'll need to think about it.'

He lifted his stylus to pen a holding note. Hanno deserved that much consideration while he spent time chewing it over. This one would go tomorrow on its surreptitious journey and the clerks would have no record of it. There were some letters they were better not seeing, even the most faithful of them. He topped his cup and told himself it was for the final time tonight. The bunk and the blankets were calling. Hanno and Gallus were not the only ageing soldiers in the army. By the gods, they were not the only ones.

The weeping of Brigantes women seemed to have ceased. The camp was settling for the night. The guard changed outside.

"Everything you require sir?" the duty optio enquired in a low, polite voice at the tent flap.

"My gratitude for your concern," he replied.

A low murmur with the guard sounded very much like "he's in a good mood," but he was not certain.

In an earlier time, he might have got to his feet at the impertinence. Now, it was only a statement of the truth. He drank a little more wine and laid the stylus down. When he reached the trestle bunk, he finished the cup and laid it on the rug at his feet. He looked down. His caligae were dry and clean. His calves had lost their once thick muscularity. When was the last time he had lain down in a tent with muddy, wet feet, glad to be under the goatskin, within camp-lines, with guards patrolling the perimeter keeping him safe? He lay back and listened to the sounds. Somewhere there were voices. A game of dice? Distant sentries exchanging a supportive joke? The earthy smell of a meadow and fresh dug soil. The faintness of latrine ordure. It never took long to announce its presence.

'Very well Hanno, a reward for a good soldier and an old friend. I will give you the First cohort. For a few months, until you go.'

He would have to find a deployment for the current officer commanding. A delicate task for his tribune to sort out. He closed his eyes, inhaling the smell of horses that pervaded the thick army blankets.

'Soldiering: there is nothing better.'

*

Orgidor knew what they were doing and what they had done, and for a few hours sat by the yellows of his campfire telling himself he had misjudged the response of the First cohort of the Twentieth legion. They were after him and they were making his people suffer for the handful of burned tents. He did not need anyone to tell him, because he understood their ways. It was easy to be so certain when others paid the price; and was not that the most bitter of thoughts? He prayed for guidance and inspiration and was answered.

'All this is nothing but a scourging they were already itching to unleash,' the unknown guide said to him, *'harrying the legionary camp played into their hands, you played into their hands and provided them with the perfect excuse to crush your people.'*

He felt sick; it was as if they never tired of murdering the Brigantes. He sat back from the flames. His son in law sat close by, attending him like a personal guard. He nodded to his daughter's husband, 'that fine young man.' Perhaps he was wrong in his conviction? Perhaps he was not bringing them freedom but only tears and a grave in their own soil? For the first time in years, he rocked, with his arms wrapped around himself and wished there was someone else to lead his people.

He let the refugees tell him their grim messages. Two villages had been burned and the bodies left lying on the ground for the crows and the buzzards. They had taken the captured women and children south for the slave boats to Gaul. It would either turn his people against him or bring them to his side. If they turned, he was a dead man. Was it possible he had miscalculated his own people? He viewed the remains and helped bury them.

'What now 'grey man' Orgidor?' he asked himself.

*

Servius took the column and criss crossed the high bounds northwest of Eburacum. When they came in sight of the ocean, he turned south towards Deva Victrix, then turned northeast back across country towards the ports serving the stone wall and south, back towards Eburacum. For four weeks he marched his men hundreds of miles A giant slashing march that caught villages by the dozen and all the time he knew the word was moving ahead of him. He marched, scooping up prisoners, slaughtering a few warriors, caught with no option but to fight, and failed to coax accurate information of Orgidor's whereabouts out of the Brigantes. By the time he had reached the northeast coast below the stone wall he knew it was time to let things settle. On a sunny morning, he marched south.

When Eburacum's walls were visible in the distance, he debated whether to enter the fortress, or simply detach from the Sixth and march for Deva Victrix. He enjoyed the self-delusion that he had any choice in the matter until the civilian vicus to come into view, its smoke haze signalling they were entering peaceful territory.

"Trumpets," he called.

It would not do to march in unannounced. He coughed, cleared his throat, and spat. There was no alternative to entering the fortress. It would be a gross insult to detach the Second cohort and leave. The legate was entitled to know what had been achieved.

'Not that it will take long to explain,' he winced.

The legate's home was warm, well-lit and enhanced by the beauty of his wife and family. His two senior tribunes provided some challenging conversation which Servius was desperate for, except the laticlavius was just like his own. Young and full of conviction, ambitious, eager and altogether dangerous behind his wide-eyed façade of innocence. When that little viper returned to Rome after his secondment it did not take much imagination to see his tongue could spell trouble for honest legates. As a rule, and as a form of human animal, he found them detestable and self-serving.

There were also some locals with harps to entertain them.

They had been scrubbed and combed. All things considered it was a splendid distraction from a wet tent in the field. He reclined on one of the legate's padded couches and allowed himself to be pampered.

Appuleia was such a delightful name. She was from a wealthy Gaulish family of soldiers who had served time in the Germanic forests.

'Lucky them,' he thought.

He could not work out if she was flirting with him under her husband's nose or he was tired and misreading the signs.

'I'm losing my touch,' he decided.

He played along with a careful eye to his host's face, waiting for the merest sign of displeasure.

"So, my friend, we have not succeeded in trapping this cur Orgidor?" the legate began.

The wine servant moved in tune with every flick of the legate's eyes.

"This is true, though we have worn out some boot studs looking for him," Servius agreed.

"And they won't give him up?"

"Not even the loss of their women and children has been enough to turn him over to us," he sighed, "I have found it an efficient way to bring things to a head in the past but this time, alas, o me miserum, it has not worked."

"Then I think we can assume we, rather you Servius, have cowed him into hiding. For now, at least," the legate soothed.

"They tell me he is an old man now. Boreas may take care of him for us," he replied.

"Forgive me Servius, I don't want the governor nor the emperor to hear I'm waiting for one of the weather gods to dispose of an enemy for me," the legate raised his palm in comic supplication.

Appuleia laughed. Servius grinned at them both.

"So long as the attacks on our transport cease and the roads are safe then I think we can leave Orgidor to answer to his people. I have burned more villages in the last month than Julius Caesar in Gaul," he chaffed.

He turned to the listening musicians. They seemed a little too attentive. His host was on to it.

"You speak Latin?" he asked them.

They nodded.

"You have understood what we are saying?"

They nodded again. The legate leaned forwards in their direction, turning his head away. Appuleia smiled an opportunistic and blatant 'come-on' at Servius.

"If you knew where Orgidor was, would you hand him over to me?" the legate said to them.

The room went silent. She withdrew the smile. The

laticlavius on the opposite couch had his wine swirling up to the very rim of his cup. She gave him a warning eye. He let the cup calm itself. Servius wondered if he had celebrated twenty name-days.

The military tribune was in his mid-thirties. He was sure the augusticlavius must have shaved before coming here but his chin wore a defiant black tone all the same.

Servius waited for the Brigantes to speak.

'How close did we really get to Orgidor's lair?" he wondered.

This little harp player might have been a useful guide if he had only known.

The leading Brigantes stopped playing and held the instrument by his side. The room was warm enough to make a man used to bare floored rooms sweat. The hypocaust was below their feet. He smiled his best attempt at innocence. The question was still unanswered, and each passing moment was like waiting for a prosecutor's flourish.

'You're going to have to lie better than that,' Servius mused.

The laticlavius stirred his cup into a final swirl and drained it.

"Perhaps, sir, you will permit me the honour of getting the answer from this man," he offered.

The hand holding the instrument tightened into a whitening clench. The legate beamed at his young officer.

"That is an excellent idea. You can play on for now," he tortured the musicians.

"You can have a little chat with him later," he promised.

His expression was like a stoat eyeing a mouse. The military tribune caught Servius' eye and raised his brows a fraction. The music seemed to go downhill after that until the legate got bored and waved them to leave. Appuleia leaned towards him, her jewellery clinking as she moved serpent-like into his face. He had forgotten the sound of a wealthy woman's advance. Her light-coloured hair wreathed her face; with blue eyes of playful intensity, she smelled wonderful.

'Venus protect me,' he prayed.

"Servius, why has such a handsome prize like you never married? You can't be fighting the natives every day. You must tell. Are there no pretty, sophisticated women in Deva that catch your eye? Not even one? They do say Deva is like that. Is it true?" she teased and smiled.

"All the prettiest ones seem to be here" he fended, amused by her directness.

The military tribune's lips twitched in appreciation for a perfect defence against dangerous odds. He turned his head away as she detected his minute response and turned her lustrous, Medusa, face towards him. Servius had a sudden pang of sympathy for him. It must be tricky navigating these waters every day.

The legate clicked his fingers for wine. Platters of food came with it. It was looking like a long evening's wait for the poor Brigantes. Servius almost pitied him. Appuleia returned her attention back to him, and he felt the first stirrings.

The bedroom door opened in near perfect silence. Servius touched the hilt of his pugio dagger checking it was where he had left it. The strange bed was too comfortable for him to sleep, though the warmth was most enjoyable. He liked the sensuous irony. Light from the atrium told him who it was, unless the legate been kind enough to send him a female slave. The figure slipped through the narrow opening and closed the door without a sound. He let his fingers release the pugio. This was going to require a blunter weapon and much less force. Appuleia shed her night shift to the floor, standing naked before him.

"Why should you soldiers have all the fun," she said, forestalling his question and slipped in beside him.

Afterwards, she lay back smiling up at him, trailing her fingertips across his chest and shoulders.

"You should get back," he suggested.

He did not want her to leave, but time was passing, and every minute was now getting more and more fraught with the likelihood of discovery. She put her fingers to his face.

"Do not worry, Marius knows."

She smiled a perfect smile of perfect white teeth that made him want to dive in, and curled her arms up around his neck, in invitation

"Marius knows?" he retorted.

Images of retribution flooded his head.

She would be caught in his room, in his bed, naked, *'no, no, no. Caught flagrante delicto. The two of them by the irate husband.'*

She smiled again, reading his thoughts.

"He does not mind as long as the children are asleep, and we are discreet. It is the only fun I get in this dreary, dreary place. There is not even a theatre. And the fights they stage show no imagination at all. They hack each other to bits in the shortest possible time and then look up asking for clemency. My father had guard dogs that were more intelligent. Can you believe it?"

She giggled at his expression.

"Are you going to ask me for clemency, Servius? No, I think not. You must die in this bed doing your duty. I command it. You have time to do it again, if the Twentieth legion are up to it? By the signs I believe they are. And then I will have to leave you to get some sleep. Be brave soldier and do tonight what Rome expects or else, I'll have to tell Marius."

*

She adjusted her robe, taking her time to hide all her charms as he watched. She leaned over to kiss him and let him touch, one more time. She slipped out of the room and he watched the door close like fog on a river. He lay back shook his head in disbelief.

'*Marius knows,*' revolved through his head, over and over.

He grinned. Appuleia was his kind of woman.

'*I'd steal you at the first opportunity Marius gives me and you'd never wander again. "Are you going to ask for clemency?" No, Appuleia I'm happy to take more punishment if it's anything like that.*'

The bed was rich with her scent. Before he knew it, he was in his deepest sleep for months, rampaging through dreams. Marius died in a pitched encounter with the Brigantes, screaming for Appuleia to bring reinforcements. Then she was fleeing a besieged Eburacum and pitching up at his gates in a villa in Capua where the harp players were playing upside down on their heads in the gardens. No words needed saying. The two of them free of Marius, happy in a huge villa outside Capua: and a bed.

The next morning Marius was busy devouring his jentaculum when he arrived at the table.

"Greetings Servius, sleep well?"

He started in surprise despite preparing for the awkward moment so early in the day.

'*What should I say? Deny everything? There is not really much point. Marius has me precisely where he wants me. At a complete disadvantage.*'

He sat and addressed the bread and eggs before him.

"Appuleia will not be joining us, she is eating with the children this morning. Doesn't like to get in the way of military things."

Marius said it in a neutral enough tone. He could not detect any disapproval or sense of betrayal. Perhaps she had been telling the truth? Perhaps Marius really did not give a stuff if she was discreet and selective.

'Legates and governors only, my dear. Quite an order.'

He chewed his bread and kept silent, risking an appreciative nod back for the information. There was an age gap between the two of them, but it would not have been thought to be much of a gap in Rome. Daughters went to political allies. Firm flesh shored up and flattered the ambitions of flabby men. And the servants of male dominated households paid the domina's price every time the master left for the Senate or the law courts. Things were not so different out here in the provinces.

"How did your tribune fare with those Brigantes last night?" he said.

Torture was so much safer ground. Marius took a sip of milk, forgoing the well watered-down wine Servius preferred at this hour.

"She is a little weary this morning."

Marius went on as if he had not heard the change of

subject.

'Perhaps this is his intellectual version of torture,' Servius wondered.

Firing barbs to prick the conscience of the cuckold under his roof, enjoying a little sport at his expense. A perverse pleasure of the deftest kind.

"Oh dear," he lied and tried not to be pleased at his animal prowess.

She had urged him to splendid heights: what a fabulous woman.

"The Brigantes failed to deliver any information for us. Despite some inventive persuasion. We now think he was merely interested to hear the news instead of soaking up intelligence for the dissidents."

"Was, Marius?" he probed.

The legate spread his hands, palms open, like a merchant forced to offer vittles at a higher price than normal. Defending his prices for all he was worth.

"Well, I could hardly send him back, could I? The man comes to play at my banquet and ends up getting tortured for information. I do not think he would be happy to play for me again. Not the kind of thing that needs to get out, don't you think?" Marius smiled.

Servius saw it as a wicked, cynical, smirk.

'I wonder which you enjoyed more? The thought of me on Appuleia, or the thought of the Brigantes being tortured to death? Or did you just chop him because he knew nothing?'

He held back his repugnance. It was time to pick up the cohort and head back to Deva. He cleared his throat and finished eating.

"My gratitude for your hospitality Marius. I am sorry Appuleia is not here. Let me know if there are further problems with the roads. I have a promotion to consider when I get back to Deva. Best I see to it soon, our duties for the emperor don't wait to be invited, do they?"

*

Marius waved to Servius from the walls above the gate.

"Farewell brother," never sounding stranger in his ears than it did now. Servius urged the horse into a trot, leading his two turmae of cavalry through the town. Brigantes children stopped to look up and wave to him. Like Caesar before him, he raised up his open palm in greeting, smiling down at the small faces staring wide eyed up at him. He refused to think about the tortured harp player. Grandfather to one of these children perhaps? The Sixth had to rule here. How they chose to go about it was not his concern.

She refused to leave him alone, haunting his head as he returned to the First's encampment. When they crossed the ridge of hills and left through the pass towards Deva Victrix, the idea of stealing Appuleia from Marius helped while away the miles.

Chapter 39.

They brought word to Orgidor word as soon as the First cohort began moving out of camp. Their commander was holding his cavalry close at hand.

'No fool,' he thought, *'these are ones who have stolen our women and children into slavery.'*

He seethed to strike back. His band only numbered a little over one hundred men. Not enough to take the wolf-skins head on. They waited as the cohort drew closer and closer to the waterfall. Would they veer off to drink? Could he repeat the trick? The soldiers approached the point where he had sprung the trap and kept marching. Perhaps it was just as well. He was too angry to set a trap. They were too many and the ground was a little too open to risk an approach to the road.

"Not today," he said.

But the idea itched him.

"We will shadow them," he decided.

"We could attack when they halt to make camp, Orgidor. They are always vulnerable then. Their horsemen are too few to hold us off. Half of them will be digging as the others mount guard."

He turned to his warriors, liking the idea.

"Good," he said.

He led them in a wide arc to the north, all the while heading for the point in the pass where the Roman road passed near to his old village, long burned out. There was ground there by a river descending to the plain that the legions used for their halts. It was a pretty place, heartland of his nation. True to form, when the column reached the spot, it left the road and formed up on the grass. He was close enough to hear shouts of command sending out a screen of scouts. Two came riding as though they knew he was there and wanted to speak to him, just a word in his ear. He wriggled back off the crest of the slope and mounted up.

"They have seen us," he cried, kicking his horse into a gallop.

"If we don't attack now, we will have no chance," a warrior snarled.

He nodded, calm and sure of himself. The numbers were against them.

"We will try and draw them off and kill them. If they see us and report back, we cannot fight today," he ruled.

A horn sounded at their backs. He turned around. The two troopers were sitting on the crest they had just vacated, pointing at his band, refusing to pursue them.

"Orgidor, you are too slow. We should have attacked and killed those two on the way. We have lost our chance."

The truth hurt. The warrior was right. He had chosen the wrong tactic. It was logical enough, but it was wrong. He should have foreseen the two troopers would not be lured. The rough ground was hard riding. He felt it was all slipping away. He pulled his mount to a shuddering halt. The war band surged on without him for a distance before they realised and slewed around in milling confusion.

"I am going back to fight. I do not ask any of you to come with me. I am tired of running from them and hiding. Waiting for them to make a mistake. I am going to fight them now."

"What about the signs Orgidor? What signs are there here?"

He dismissed the cry with a wave of his hand, not wanting to hear what they were saying. He pulled his horse's head around and kicked it back into a charge towards the two Romans still observing from the low crest. Shouts from his men carried in his ears. He pushed them aside. The horse's hoof beat pummelled the grass. The two Romans were staring at him, talking as he came thundering towards them. The voices of his men faded and for a split second he was glad none of them had decided to share his fate.

'Signs? Signs? The only sign you need is dead Romani on the grass bleeding the sacred earth red. And I am going to give it to you.'

The Roman horsemen separated, levelling their spears, and setting their narrow shields. He levelled his own lance and chose the larger of the two men to attack. The gap closed. Were they going to just sit there and wait for him to crash into them? But they responded and kicked their mounts, surging into the attack.

"Brigantes, Brigantia," he screamed.

They met in a crash of horseflesh and spears. In the distance his men watched, solemn faced at his gesture of bravery. His trusted son in law went galloping back after him. The enemy horsemen whirled at Orgidor, and the old man succumbed. They knocked him off his mount and sat above him thrusting down with their spears like malevolent silver chested birds, their feathered helmets covering their faces. His son in law slammed into them catching one in a broadside. The three mounted men whirled in a desperate dance of war-lances, while the war chief lay on the ground ignored. The lad went down too, and this time one trooper slid off his mount to inspect the bodies. The watching warriors moaned at the sight but none of them wanted to go back. A few seconds later the Roman stood upright heaving one body up over the saddle of his horse. The other trooper's horse kept prancing as he kept watch on them. The trooper leapt into his saddle holding the body in front of him. The other raised his lance in challenge. They turned and rode off towards the camp.

"They didn't take their heads," a warrior said, puzzled.

Chapter 40.
North of the abandoned turf wall.

"Are you just going to go and knock on the door?" Eithne asked Aulercas.

He busied himself hugging the children before he set off. He tugged his moustaches and kissed her.

"Something like that," he said.

*

The fighting elite of the two tribes approached each other with mutual respect, edging closer in the neutral space of the river valley, wary as if half expecting the other to be planning a deception. There was no reason to suspect either would do such a thing, but this was no ordinary day. In the distance, over the wide bogland, the invader's wall was shedding none of its customary smoke into the sky. The wind was blowing over the plain from the northwest. The sky was alive with clouds. The noise of birdsong was louder and sweeter than they could remember; something had changed.

Asuvad greeted Aulercas. They shook each other's arms grinning like boys on their first adult hunting expedition. He knew what had happened to Aulercas. The gapped tooth smile had healed. Aulercas' swollen face had calmed; only his nose testified to his treatment. He clapped his shoulder in real friendship.

"I am glad to see you alive, my friend."

"They did their best but one good Veniconi is worth more than a fort full of Romans," Aulercas bragged, "I did not need all those teeth anyway."

"And this?" Asuvad touched his own nose.

Aulercas flinched and shrugged.

"I breathe through my mouth now, but I'm still breathing."

"It's an improvement to your beauty, Aulercas," Asuvad said straight faced.

Aulercas made to tug at it as though he could pull it back in line and let go, laughing in pleasure that he could admit things to his friend.

"So they are telling me. Eithne's not so sure. Neither is my little Ucsella."

They sat on their horses while their priests huddled and conferred, waiting for their approval to go further. Word had been filtering back from nearby farmers that the normal bugles and trumpets had ceased to sound. They had not been heard for several days. No cavalry patrols had been out to do their routine inspections of the bridges. The gates of all the forts were closed: the support road behind the wall had seen heavy traffic but it was empty now. No waggons were moving on it at all. It was time to go and see what was happening over there. Between them they had brought perhaps two thousand men to find out.

At Asuvad's signal they set off, arriving together at the outer limits of the upcast mounds. Another step or two and they were in javelin range, the edge of the killing zone.

He rose in his saddle and signalled, they halted and sat waiting, listening to the birds and insects. It was as peaceful as the pastureland they fattened their cattle on. Aulercas felt his heart pumping. Asuvad seemed as calm as an oak. A low murmuring of voices rippled along the line. If the Romans were there, the iron bolts, the arrows, the javelins must come flying soon. The moments passed. Asuvad kicked his mount forwards. He followed. The Dumnonii would not say the Veniconii hesitated to confront the wolf. Gazing up at the ramparts of a fort Asuvad reined in again.

"There are no guards up there," he said.

"No," Aulercas replied.

They looked at each other and rode closer, each of them holding their shields at the ready for the pila that surely must be coming. They dismounted at the ditch keeping their horses between their bodies and the wall. Nothing was moving. The birds were still calling. Asuvad raised a finger to his lips and led his horse along the edge of the ditch rampart, halting at the causeway that split the ditch. Once they stepped onto that narrow shelf they would be exposed. Asuvad scanned the wall on either side of the gateway. There was not a single shout, nor a challenge. Aulercas felt the first shoots of genuine hope rising inside him. He glanced at Asuvad. The Dumnoni seemed to be thinking the same thing.

"Oh well," Asuvad muttered and strode over the causeway to the relative security below the rampart wall.

A defender would have to lean out to hit him with a spear. He stepped up to the gate and pushed. It did not move. Aulercas joined him. They pushed the solid timber gate together. Asuvad banged several loud knocks with the hilt of his sword, and they ran back over the ditch to wait for the spears that must surely now come. Behind them their men edged closer, clustering together into knots of horses and men. They went back to the gate and hammered harder. Still no reply. Without a word they stood to the side and began climbing the outer turf face of the wall. At the top they paused to gather their courage then sprang up and peered over the wooden stockade-fence into the fort. It was empty. There was not a Roman to be seen, not a horse, nor a stable hand. The south gate was open and beyond those timbers the lowlands stretched uninterrupted to the south horizon. The sons of the wolf had gone.

Asuvad turned around facing the waiting line of warriors, lifting his arms up high. He clenched his fists and smiled the broadest smile and waved for them to come and see for themselves. A huge roar erupted from the ranks. He whirled about to check the compound beneath him. If that noise did not bring them running then it really was true.

He sent men further to the west, expecting those forts to be occupied. Within an hour the first scout came cantering back along the support road. His relaxed riding telling them there was no danger. He pulled to a halt and waved with an enthusiastic smile across his face. Aulercas turned and sent men to the east.

"Two empty forts? A coincidence? I tell you Aulercas, they have left. We have finally beaten them off," Asuvad cried.

"I am going to burn the fort they held me in," Aulercas said, "I'll set the torches with my own hands."

"What about the others?" Asuvad said.

"The others? We will open all the gates so we can cross whenever we wish and after that, they can rot as far as I care. One day soon Asuvad the hawks will be using the gateways for nests and flowers will grow in the courtyards. These walls will crumble, and the ditch will fill. And when you and I are just songs around the fire there will be no sign the Romani were ever here."

"You believe it is really finished after all these years? We really have beaten them?"

"It looks that way. Which makes me wonder why those two soldiers came into our lands to see the Valley of the Bones for a last time? I tell you it's hidden from me by the gods. What was it all for? What did my men die for, Asuvad?"

"Get your torch lit, Aulercas. This one is going to burn today. We will take gifts and throw them in the sacred pools. The priests will thank the gods. Our troubles are over."

"And tonight, the feasting can begin," Aulercas replied, "it is almost worth the teeth and a nose that does not work anymore to be free of them."

"Aulercas and Asuvad; we two, we will be remembered as the warriors who united their clans and chased the sons of the wolf away forever," Asuvad crowed.

"If only Heruscomani could understand what this means," Aulercas said.

Asuvad patted his arm.

"Tell him gently so the surprise does not kill him. Who knows, perhaps this is the medicine he needs? He led the way to this day. All the attacks, the ambushes, the nights of stalking just to pick off a few guards. Take him something back to show him they are beaten at last. This victory belongs to him too."

Asuvad clapped his consoling hand on Aulercas' shoulder again.

"The only thing missing is a barrel of ale."

Outside carynx horns were spreading the news. Villagers from south of the wall were drawing near, pulled in by the sound and the commotion. Warriors were dispersing in all directions. Before nightfall, Asuvad reckoned all the tribes would know the joyous news. The great yoke was lifted. The old ways had been strong enough to resist all the legions could throw at them. Aulercas nodded at his suggestion and went off to root through the buildings for a gift for his father. That night, bonfires started to break out along the hilltops. The yellow news travelled from the Bodotria to the Clota. Those who had not yet heard looked up and wondered what it could mean.

*

The king of the Votadini people rode out to the roadside soon after the first cohort passed his citadel at Dunpeledur on the road south. Back up the road the standards of another column and its mounted officers were coming up over the brow of the rise. The morning air and the glitter of sunlight off armour and spearheads made it quite a spectacle. He had always enjoyed seeing them marching along in their smart organised columns. So different from the relaxed informality of a tribal army moving en-masse but it was still impressive, nevertheless. But two separate columns with their carts was not normal. His curiosity piqued and he rode out to the road with his champion to find out more.

He put his horse in the middle of the road as the cavalry outriders came thundering closer and waited. They would not dare to ride him down. His champion waited at his back with a casual lance at the ready lest the troopers failed to recognise his master was the king. The cavalry decurion in the front took one look at him and ignored him, clattering past with his turma, the troopers splitting like a shoal of fish and sweeping past so close on either side he could have touched the horses with his hand.

"This is a big patrol," his champion muttered, "there must be trouble at the three hills."

"Perhaps. Maybe they are changing over," he said.

The leading officers came on without slowing their mounts. They nodded as he moved his horse aside lest they sweep over the top of him. There was an unstoppable momentum about it. The foot soldiers were not going to move aside for him.

"What has happened?" he shouted, "has war started?"

They did not reply. It was only when he saw a third column in the afternoon that a worm of concern began moving in his belly. Far off in the distance he saw the moving shape of a fourth coming. And then the slow realisation of what it meant struck him. Fifteen years of profitable, protected living was coming to an end. At last he got an officer to talk to him. A centurion on his horse spared him a second look and waved him to ride alongside. He closed in, raising his hand in gratitude.

"Not what you expected to see today?"

The centurion lifted his hand to encompass everything going on.

"What is happening centurion?"

"I can't tell you what is happening, but we are leaving the wall to your people and the others, if that answers your question?" he said.

He had a good-humoured expression. The king looked at his men. They all looked happy. It had to be true; they were abandoning the turf wall. The northern tribes had driven them out.

"You are going down to the stone wall now?" he asked.

The centurion smiled.

"You know my friend, they haven't asked for my advice so I expect to keep marching until they say we can halt."

"You're leaving us behind too," he said.

The centurion leaned over and whispered, "well you're getting your country back, aren't you? Why so glum? I thought you'd be glad to see us leave?"

The king pulled his horse aside and sat watching as the column passed. They were singing a rhythmic song to make the miles pass. He had sufficient Latin to get the gist of it. A young lady of uncertain morals from a town he had never heard of. A beer song. The waggons with their steady oxen came swaying in the rear. The drivers shouting and cracking the whips over the heads of the beasts. And further back, a raggle of women and children; army detritus, bound to the invaders by obvious bonds. He scowled in disapproval and tried not to fall into the trap of caring. They had crossed the invisible stream separating tribe from wolf-skin. Not that it mattered what he thought. They stood on the other side from him. In their eyes he had crossed the same stream years before.

"Are there more to come?" he yelled at the departing centurion's back.

The soldier put up his right hand and let the fingers tell the story. His champion put his mount alongside.

"What happens now my lord?" he asked.

The king chewed his lip for a moment. Inside, he wanted to weep.

"'What happens now?' is a good question. What happens now is we make sure our gates and defences are in good repair. That our food stocks are full, our water supply secure. They did not even tell me what they were planning because I suspect they did not trust us. We look to our men and our spears and wait for our enemies to stand below our gates."

He paused, thinking hard.

"And we carry on selling and trading with the forts as we always have for as long as they are willing to buy. That is what happens now. And to anyone who asks you what you saw here, tell them the soldiers are moving south. There is no point in pretending now."

"Are they going for good my lord?"

"I doubt anyone can answer that," he said, "not even the wisest priest."

Chapter 41.
Eidumnos' hall.

Velio left his horse at the gateway with one of Eidumnos' younger servants, handing the reins to the lad who always took an interest in his armour and his sword. Not the kind of interest that gave him cause for concern. More like the kind of interest a youth on the cusp of manhood takes in the accoutrements of adulthood and an exotic one to boot. It seemed weeks since he had last stood on the spot. Now the cohorts had passed over the bridge and southwards towards Habitanum, he had time for this. Time to pick up from where he had left off before. He smelled a recruit for the legions and spent a few moments talking to him, hoping Voccia would come and interrupt and make ending the conversation easy. Every volunteer was a victory for Rome.

Eidumnos came out with Voccia at his back, paler than the last time and a hunted look in her eyes that spoiled her face. He roiled at the thought some tribal brute had done this to her. She managed a small effort at a smile and retreated into the hall. Eidumnos caught him looking at her. With the slightest of pauses he gestured for them to walk and Velio let himself be diverted. Perhaps the old man had something to say in private. As the father of a pretty girl, he would be used to setting boundaries in his own home.

They headed in the direction of the river. Eidumnos stopped at a convenient cluster of rocks, and they sat in the sunshine with the river flowing behind them. It would have been a pleasant seat if it had not reminded him so much of the other river: Gallus, and Marcus. This old man would never understand in a thousand years. He wondered what was coming but did not much care what Eidumnos wanted to say. There was only one thing of interest

"So, centurion, your people have left the wall and gone back to the south. I saw the army passing by. The Brigantes entertain them now."

Eidumnos made it almost conversational instead of the cataclysmic shock Velio knew must be ringing round the valley. The cohorts had taken a full day to pass. He had said a temporary farewell to Hanno at the bridge. He watched the old man trying to keep things light, pretending an insouciance he knew was false.

"When do you and your men leave?" Eidumnos said, keeping his face solemn.

Segontio had not long left this morning after making his first attempt at peace with Voccia and now the Roman officer was here. His heart raced. Velio adjusted his sword, moving it to the side and unclipping his cloak, laying it unfolded on the nearest rock

"Is this why we are speaking here? So that no one else can overhear?" he said

"Partly," Eidumnos replied, "centurion, I like you. You are a fair man. You keep your men under control. No one is harmed by your presence in this valley. Many of us have cause to be grateful your soldiers are here and not somewhere else."

Velio waited, intrigued by the Votadini's frankness. Where was this leading? Eidumnos cut to it.

"You have heard from your officer what has happened to my family?"

"Centurion Oscius told me," he acknowledged.

Eidumnos stared up at the blue, cloud flecked, sky for a second before he turned his stare at him.

"The Selgovae have dishonoured my daughter and I asked your centurion for help. We went looking for Segontio. We had help from your fort in the west, Flour Sacks, you call it? A clever nick name."

"Blatobulgium," he corrected, "I've heard this news."

"We captured Segontio and somehow he escaped. Your cavalry officer perhaps thinks I helped set him free. I did not do that. But do you believe me? And if you do, will you help me find and punish the man who attacked my daughter?" Eidumnos continued.

Velio sat back. Voccia was a little bit special. She would make a good wife if she could adjust to the strangeness of army life in Deva far from her relations and friends. It would not be plain sailing for her if she agreed. He could be happy with her despite what had happened. It did not change his feelings. He could feel Eidumnos was searching for a promise. This was not how he had planned to break the news. It was not the right time. Neither Tacto nor Fufius knew the cohort was remaining in Trimontium and it was unfair to keep them in the dark while a tribal leader knew more than they did.

'Stall,' he told himself, *'and pray he swallows it.'*

"I will help you for as long as we are here, Eidumnos. Your daughter will have her good name restored."

Eidumnos snorted.

"Too late for that, centurion. He has robbed her of that. So, I want his head. That is my justice."

"Will the Votadini go to war with the Selgovae over this insult?" Velio pushed.

Eidumnos sagged a little. Some of his zeal evaporated.

"Centurion, I am at war with the Selgovae. My king and my people are not. I fight alone. Have you ever had to do that?"

Part of him wanted to laugh. He choked it down.

"Aaahh, I understand. Then it is a matter of honour as you say."

He bit back from saying *'just a matter of honour'* in the nick of time. The Votadini king's reluctance to intervene was important. Something for the intelligence report to Servius.

"You will help though, for as long as you are here?" said Eidumnos.

Velio straightened up and brushed an imaginary fleck of dust from his parade cuirass, polished to a mirror's sheen, all for the benefit of Voccia. The blacksmiths had done a good job on it for him. It fitted like a second skin.

"If we catch him, I will let you have him in chains. If the Selgovae cause us problems and give me reason to march west, then the Selgovae might come under my sword. Your man too, perhaps. That is all I can promise for now, Eidumnos. I and my men are here. The Votadini have no reason to fear."

"And will the men at Flour sacks stay too?" Eidumnos said.

A sudden alarm horn started blowing in Velio's head. That was one question too far, too direct, too much like fishing. He shrugged pretending he had no view on it.

"May I speak with your daughter Voccia? I'd like to pay my respects and perhaps put her fears to rest personally, if I can."

Eidumnos smiled.

"Of course, she speaks of you often. When she speaks of you her eyes smile even although she was betrothed to another. He has rejected her now. All this."

Eidumnos raised his hands and let them fall into his lap.

"She is alone with her grief. You may be able to help her shake this terrible thing off her shoulders. I have tried but she cannot be comforted. Come, you must be hungry. We will eat and leave Segontio to the gods to deliver if they see fit. Do not expect too much from her. She is not herself and Bractia is likewise."

Eidumnos half smiled an apology.

"It is that bad?" Velio asked.

Eidumnos rose to his feet. He faced the river for a moment, listening to it, ignoring Velio, lost in some deep thought. He bit his lip. It was that bad.

Velio decided to take off his gladius and helmet before going into the hall. It crossed his mind for a moment whether to leave them outside but he would have flogged any enlisted 'mule' who did anything so stupid so he tucked his helmet under his arm and held the sword by the scabbard making his intentions as peaceful as he could. Inside, he blinked in the dimmer light. A sweet smell of fresh rushes on the floor made it pleasant and airy. Bractia nodded to him and gestured to the usual chair at the fire. He sat down. She stepped back and whispered something urgent and strained to Eidumnos. He had a sudden sureness he was intruding. Whatever Eidumnos might think about him visiting, Bractia did not seem to share it. It was too soon to be in here.

"I will wait outside," he said and got back to his feet.

Voccia smiled a wan, tired greeting that was mere shadow of its usual brilliance. He followed her out into the daylight leaving Eidumnos in his chair lost in his thoughts. Bractia filled two decorated clay cups with water and brought them out, handing him one before she sat. She smoothed the front of her dress and held Voccia's hand in support, patting it.

He looked at the young woman who occupied his thoughts more than any other woman in recent years. It was inexplicable how she possessed this power over him. It had been different up on the wall and beyond with Gallus. A different world to this warm peaceful valley with its pleasing river and contented cattle. It was a world of single purpose up there, whereas here, there were many purposes to life. She looked at him a little more and waited for him.

"I have told your father that if we apprehend Segontio we will hand him over. I will let your people administer justice," he said, thinking it would be the sort of thing she wanted to hear.

"Will you go looking for him?" her mother said.

Her eyes flashed a mixture of appeal and latent fury. He straightened the loin armour strips below his cuirass, covering his lap and put his forearm down, fist-clenched, atop his knee.

'How do I tell her No?'

In the village, a hammer was beating out its relentless message of metal upon metal, the sound drifting like a bell.

Cattle were grazing and no doubt out in the meadow grass small boys were playing warrior games with sticks like every other small boy in the world, whether he was Roman, Gaul or German. He rubbed his face and gave Voccia the promise he knew he wanted to hear.

"I have a feeling he is going to make a mistake and then," he paused, opened and clasped his fingers, "I will have him."

He wished her mother would go inside so he could talk to Voccia, but it did not look like she was ready to take the hint.

"The gods will have marked his name as surely as I have," he said, "I cannot send men to look for him but that does not mean I am not looking," he finished.

Bractia frowned at the contradiction. He decided not to explain further. Voccia seemed to understand what he was trying to say. Her smile was more certain this time. He got to his feet.

"Next time centurion you must stay for porridge," she said.

Had things been different he would have dared to put a kiss on her cheek.

Another time Velio, he told himself.

Her mother released her frown and smiled a little more. As he mounted his horse, he glanced at the doorway into the hall. Eidumnos watched him leaving. He raised his hand in farewell.

"Well done my love," Bractia said, "I really think he believes we are hunting for Segontio."

"Mother, he hurt me. How can you think I would want to be with him?" she retorted.

"Because he is more like one of us than that Roman will ever be. Because he is a prince. And because we need his protection. You, my love, will need his protection

"Tianos will protect me," she replied.

Bractia held her close and stroked her head.

"Tianos does not yet understand what had happened since he swore to serve Asuvad and hunt Segontio like a wolf. He will always be there for you but only a husband can protect you properly once your father and I are gone."

"I will never marry Segontio," she hissed, "I would rather go with the Roman."

"Shush now Voccia, don't let your father hear you. The Roman is charming I admit. But he would never allow it. Put it out of your mind. Give Segontio time. We must both give him time. And if you cannot thole the thought of it then say now and your father will finish it. Your father showed mercy and wisdom in giving Segontio another chance, but the condition is that he makes things right with you. You can order his death like that my child," she clicked her fingers, "think carefully because his life depends on it."

"Perhaps I will," Voccia said, "and choose the centurion commander instead,"

'Perhaps I will let him be my lover, to spite you.'

*

"How is the mood down there, Tacto? Do they hate me?" he asked.

Tacto stood at the rampart overlooking the river and folded his arms. Where to begin with that question? Velio had been quirky and sparky since returning from his visit to Eidumnos. He called a parade and revealed the 'second order' to the garrison; terse and brooking no comment. The six centuries stood stock still and took it on the chin.

You are going to be recalled at some point, but the cavalry is staying put. Trimontium will become a full strength millaria cohort of eight hundred men under a new commander. That is all for now.

Dismiss.'

If they felt like cheering, Velio's expression kept them quiet.

"Strange this is sir, the Boar lads are not too bothered, though I suspect they would be happier if we were full equitata milliaria. Comfort in having more swords around you in a fight. There is also a bit of pride in having to be replaced by a larger force. You understand the thinking. But it is more Fufius' boys who seem to be windier about it," Tacto reported.

"Servius Albinius told me in the beginning a milliaria command would have go to a more experienced praefectus. Not that I mind. I'm with Hanno Glaccus when he says commanding legionaries is always better than German tribesmen."

"Oh, so you will be leaving? Am I getting the recall too?" Tacto asked.

'Now is the tricky part,' he decided.

"My understanding Tacto, and it is just my understanding for now, is you and Fufius will remain as officers in support of the new praefectus. I will take the Boar centuries back to Deva Victrix. This is going to be the last outpost north of the Stones, though Blatobulgium will perform the same function in the west. At least they have the luxury of sitting a good few miles closer to the nearest support. If Habitanum and Bremenium stay garrisoned below us, it won't be too bad for you."

'And if they don't,' Tacto fretted, *'we could be stuffed.'*

He resumed his watch of the peaceful river valley and the wooded slopes beyond. There were voices drifting up from the river. Locals fishing for salmon.

"Look, Tacto, I'm not gone yet. And there is this Segontio business to consider. Dometius Barrus may have cause for alarm if the Selgovae decide to extend their territories at the expense of the Votadini. I am sure the intention must be that Blato will be our equivalent post in the west. And once the northern tribes find out we have left the wall they will push south to find out where we are. I expect we may get a bit of action, one way or the other, quite soon. Do you want to leave this and go back to boring drill-halls and recruiting parades? These are good stone walls," he said.

"The Votadini. The girl. You intend we sort out her grievance against the Selgovae before you go?" Tacto blurted out.

He saw no alternative to ploughing on.

"That can easily develop into a Votadini-Selgovae feud if we are not careful."

All the things Tacto told Fufius to avoid saying were somehow tumbling out of his mouth and he could not stop himself.

Velio's face went hard.

"Speak plainly, centurion."

"Apologies sir, I mean no disrespect."

"And?"

"If the Votadini get chewed up by the other tribes, what do we care? I know you like her, forgive me sir. If they are fighting themselves, they are weakening their armies and they are not fighting us."

Tacto stuck to his point.

"True," Velio snapped, temper rising.

A single word reply to Tacto was like a lash on his face.

"Forgive me sir. I," Tacto stumbled over the words, "what I

mean to say is."

"Attend your duties centurion," Velio snapped again.

Tacto flushed despite himself. Velio had never cut him off from speaking before. He crashed out a salute and stamped down off the rampart. Where was Fufius? All jokes about the praefectus' girl must cease. The glint in Pinneius' eyes; the infamous death stare of barrack block legend. Well, he had just had it at close range, and he did not fancy being on the receiving end of it again.

'What you meant to say Tacto is, if I want the girl, I should rescue her and take her with me to Deva Victrix while the rest of them hack each other to pieces. Call her 'servant,' call her anything except a wife. And you think that has not crossed my mind, Tacto?' Velio fumed.

He listened to his fort. Someone was whistling. Someone else was seeking bread. Traders from the civilian vicus were waiting by the Dextra gate hoping for a word with the duty optio. Marcellus would have paperwork waiting for his attention. There was precious little sign of mutiny in the ranks. Tacto was edgy and Fufius did not care about the order. Tonight, it would be appropriate to invite them all to drink some wine with him. Lentulus and the cook would excel as usual.

Chapter 42.
Deva Victrix.

Hanno dismounted, intending to report to Servius Albinius. The cart with his simple belongings creaked to a halt.

The driver gasped, "thanks be to all the gods. I'm back safe in barracks of The Boar. Away from all those bloody heathens."

He glanced, checking Hanno's reaction. Hanno toyed with a comment then let it drop. The driver busied himself getting directions to Hanno's new accommodation.

Inside, Servius was all 'hail and welcome Hanno'. It was as if they were younger men again, charged with building a new wall in the wilderness of the north and keen to get at it. Servius was older and still retained his charismatic authority. In Hanno's eyes he might have made a good senator. The question he really wanted to ask was, what the existing commander of the First cohort knew of his arrival. Servius did not let him engineer such a question.

"You will take command as from now until you muster out in six months. Enjoy your time, you have earned it, Hanno for all the good years' service you have rendered to me. Make the cohort better for having your experience. Make the centurions, and the optios, better. First cohorts need to be constantly challenged in my experience or they get casual. You may wish to spend tomorrow with me and then your centurions. But first there is the not inconsiderable matter of a Brigantes we are holding prisoner, who very well may be the legendary Orgidor, though he refuses to admit it. We have him, Hanno. I think we finally have him," he summarised.

"What are you going to do with him, sir."

"Call me Servius please, Hanno. You of all people," he smiled, "what am I going to do with him? That is a good question. He is too old to pass on to the local games. I doubt anyone would pay to see him killed in a combat. Too dangerous to be a house slave, so he ends up in one of the tin mines or digging lead? Not that he would last long there. Orgidor is an old man now. His fighting days are over. Perhaps strangulation would be the kindest answer."

"It's what he represents that is dangerous, Servius."

"I know Hanno, I know, he is another one of these leaders the young bucks dream of impressing."

"I lost a good centurion to a spear in the back at Velunia not long before we retrenched to the Stones."

Servius waited. Hanno furrowed his brow making the scar on his forehead wrinkle.

"Do you remember Tribune Paterculus?" he said.

"Indeed, I do," Servius sighed, "he had the idea that we should insult them at every opportunity."

He rolled his eyes and carried on.

"He pissed in a river in front of one of their priests just to get a response, if what I was told at the time was true, upsetting not only the druid but the troopers escorting, who had apparently adopted the god as one of their own. Our tribune was too sure of himself to consider the matter of belief in other things."

"Well, I don't believe in making pointless insults, Servius. I believe it's better to either show mercy or give an enemy a clean death," he said.

"I agree wholeheartedly, Hanno. But we can't release this one. He is far too dangerous. What about that centurion? The one you lost, tell me more about it."

"He took a spear in the back whilst organising the manning of my Praetoria gate during the last assault before we evacuated. My point is someone stirred the Veniconii into making that attack," he replied.

"An Orgidor, of sorts?" Servius asked.

"Precisely."

"So, we execute him?" Servius said.

"Indeed," he agreed, "for Pomponius as well as us."

"Then, your first act as commander of the First cohort may be to execute a prisoner. Very well, once he has been interrogated you may have him. Now you will eat with me tonight and I will introduce you to the tribunes and the other cohort commanders. Should be a lively evening, there are some amusing chaps amongst them. I should warn you it will start like an audience with the emperor's mother and by the time it finishes feel like we have descended into the Forum. If you don't mind, I think I will let them have an opinion on how we deal with Orgidor. He is not going anywhere."

Hanno nodded.

"Nowhere with a future."

"Very good Hanno, I've missed your wit. It is good to have you back. Think about your demustering. If you enjoy the cohort, things can be stretched out. There is no rush. The Boar needs you," Servius beamed.

*

It was a room that would have done justice to a senator. The mural paintings were exquisite, and the furnishings lavish. The touch of real old family money was everywhere. He looked and tried not to be impressed. A far cry from the praetorium in Velunia and warm to the point of being overheated for his taste.

"Gentlemen of the Twentieth, let me introduce you to Hanno Drusus Glaccus Ticinus, the new commander of our First cohort," Servius smiled.

"So, you the man who's stolen the First right from under Morenus' nose. Your exploits and reputation travel before you on the wings of Mercury," the senior augusticlavius boomed across the room.

Hanno decided that if the man's waist was anything to go by, he had not seen much action in recent years. Every head turned.

"I shall have to watch you Hanno Glaccus or you'll have my tribuneship before I know it."

The room guffawed on cue.

'Always laugh at any officer's joke if he is more senior to you, show your teeth and smile as if your career depends upon it.'

He knew the drill. A warming flush crept onto his face all the same and he did not like it.

'The new boy is always the butt of the jokes. Enjoy it while you can, you pompous fat bastard.'

"Some of my Falernian, Hanno, a fresh shipment, should have had time to settle nicely I think," Servius intervened.

"Ah, Mithras how I remember this stuff," Hanno grinned, "you always had a good supply of decent wine, Servius. You must tell me your vintner's name."

He sniffed the silver engraved goblet Servius handed to him. Happy memories of confiding as centurion to tribune on the travails of building the wall came flooding back: and other more sensitive things

"Servius commands his officer corps by the simple expedient of threatening to withdraw his personal wine stock from these gatherings."

Hoots of hilarity now.

"Perhaps you have not met the Governor of the province. Hanno, let me introduce you to Gnaeus Julius Verus."

Servius shepherded him to the side.

'Odd that so powerful a man is not in the middle of the room,' he thought.

"I am indeed honoured, sir," he said and shook the governor's outstretched arm.

Verus was tall, lean and aesthetic, perhaps forty-five years of age. His black hair cropped in a severe cut. '

'Dyed at the temples perhaps?' Hanno wondered.

He analysed a possible vanity. A soldier's face though; soldier's hands. Verus may well have carried a shield and gladius in his day. Shrewd grey, green, catlike eyes. Or were they fox-like? They had a feral colour.

"I heard you think we should 'chop,' is that the current way the men call it Servius, chop this Brigantes, Orgidor?" he enquired.

It sounded like he was considering a Christian for the Forum.

'Mithras how did he hear that?' Hanno thought.

The room went silent. The legate's servants, attuned to every nuance, poised with their silver trays of goblets, almost in mid step. Almost comical as they eased themselves back to the fringes of the room while this little drama played out. Servius' laticlavius was busy with the lie of the purple hem of his toga, listening with affected disinterest.

'Nearly as welcoming as the north wall in winter, just not as safe,' Hanno judged and, in an instant, worked out the plays of this little induction-game.

"Better this particular Brigantes loses his head than we lose more patrols or waggons. The trick of course is not to advertise the fact and make him special."

'There, suck on that lemon boys.'

"And there speaks a soldier," Verus replied.

The governor opened his arms to the room, taking credit for his question rather than the answer. The laticlavius saluted the governor with his wine cup, his attire no longer troubling him. The room relaxed.

"Olives, Hanno, taste these," Servius coaxed his servants away from the safety of the walls.

"Let me tell you about the day Morenus got caught short crossing the parade ground and left his vine stick in the latrines," boomed the girthy augusticlavius.

"Not again," the optio's risked a raucous, humoured jeer.

"Well Hanno has not heard it, have you, Hanno?"

"Not if it happened during the last thirteen years," he

reposted.

"There you are then, you cheeky pups, he's not heard it."

Later Servius indicated a quiet chat with an inclination of his head.

"Is it really thirteen years since I sent you to Velunia, Hanno?" he asked, awkward and embarrassed.

Hanno felt his sense of retribution vindicated. His spearpoint had struck home. Servius had given him a heavy order once the wall had been completed; stay here and man it. For the last years he had borne it without complaint. Now he had been rescued

"Time passes slowly on the frontier, Servius, but yes summers and winters pass by, and the tribes wash up against the wall like the tide. They never broke us, they tried, by the gods they tried and until the last two years they made no inroads. Our men remained resolute. They knew we were the edge of the empire. The emperor was watching. But if the governors will not permit reinforcements the winters take their toll, with fevers and whatnot. Men die Servius, resolve weakens. The tribes become bolder, more persistent, but you know all this from the reports," he stated, keeping it light.

He had what he needed. There was no need to fall out with Servius now.

"It was getting precarious, I admit," Servius jibbed, "but I always had confidence you could hold the discipline of the line. Be an example to the other garrisons. Now, put all that behind you. Use your new power lightly. These men are the cream of the legion. They know it, every other cohort and century know it and they are proud soldiers. Punishment is almost unheard of in the First. The centurions and optios will not bring a problem to you that individually or collectively they cannot resolve. Do not be surprised or alarmed if it appears quiet on the surface. Back up on the wall with your Germans, no doubt you might well worry if things went unnaturally quiet on the discipline front. You have served in a legionary cohort, so you know it does not work like an auxiliary cohort. Even more so in a First cohort. I do not expect that to change. Ask them to perform a task and it will be done. Even if it costs them comrades to achieve it. Remember that before you throw them into any fighting that may arise. They know who you are Hanno. They have heard your record. You are too wise to make the mistake of trying to impress them. They do not require that."

Hanno had an odd desire to laugh and swallowed more from the silver wine cup to quell it, swallowing more than he intended. He choked and covered his mouth with the back of his hand. Servius pounded him between the shoulders.

"Don't die on me now, Hanno, I have work for you."

He recovered his breath and drank a slower sip.

"I am grateful for the chance to have a cohort," he conceded, "and if I managed to lead or inspire others that was simply my duty to the emperor."

The lie came out and he saw Servius' face ease; mollified from any implied criticism.

"I never intended it would be so long, Hanno," he said, "just as I never expected to command the Twentieth. Always hoped for it of course, the way a man should, but never dreamed it would be given to me. It takes time, you understand. It takes time."

"Servius, promise me one thing," Hanno said, "promise you won't ask me to go back," he hissed.

"Hanno, I don't believe we will ever go back. Governor Verus hints the troops are needed elsewhere abroad. Britannia's garrison is to be reduced. Who knows where that will leave us? I think you can rest easy. You will not see the north again."

'Unless the First cohort is required to march. And only a fool would make a bet before rolling his dice against that.'

"There is another thing I would like to mention," Hanno persisted.

Servius smiled at him.

"Go on, tell me, Hanno."

"I would like to appoint Velio Pinneius as my Primus Pilus," he said.

"No, I'm afraid not. I can divert the current commander so you can have the cohort but understand me clearly. Once you leave, I will bring him back. I will not juggle the most senior centurion in my legion just so Pinneius can have that post under you. I rate Pinneius but I also rate my Primus Pilus, Caninius. He may get his turn, or he may not. Anyway, it's bad for morale to change both the commander and the senior centurion. You can imagine the message that sends. No, I'm afraid what you ask is impossible. Pinneius will return here when Trimontium garrison is increased. You can have him by all means. Find him a century to command. I don't want the details, but you cannot have him as your Primus Pilus," Servius ruled.

Hanno bowed his head in defeat. After all, to be a centurion in the First was no small achievement. Velio would grin like a fool. At least he had tried for him. His conscience was clear.

"Is that where the cohort commander is going to make room for me: Trimontium?"

"As it happens, no, he is not going to lead the Trimontium garrison."

He heard the warning in Servius' tone and changed the subject.

"So, what am I to do with Orgidor?" he asked.

"My dear chap, just be discreet about it and get it done

tonight or tomorrow. Get rid of the body. No displays. Tell me when it is done. The governor will want to know that menace has been removed forever," Servius murmured.

"And now, my old friend, I fear it is time I listened to more of the governor's opinions on the last appointments to the Senate. Have some pity on me, Hanno. I am in control of less than you may imagine. A few soldiers, a stone fortress, centurion Pinneius' career, but otherwise, I am a plaything of the gods. Send me word when it's done. I owe Legate Marius of the Sixth a letter and he will be pleased to know we have dealt with the Brigantes' most famous living warrior."

Chapter 43.

The tranquillity of the commander's house was like balm after the exuberance of the party. The singing was his cue. Servius winked and Verus nodded. Hanno decided Velio deserved to know he was not getting the transfer to become Primus Pilus. He sat and wrote the letter. The more he thought about Servius' reasons the more comfortable he felt about writing it and the easier the words were to find.

Sitting in another officer's home, surrounded by his possessions was comfortable enough but he took a superstitious check over his shoulder a couple of times to make sure he was alone. The bed was not his and neither were the house servants. Lucius and Atius made light of the move. Nothing much in this villa was his except for a pitiable, small set of trunks and boxes holding all his clothing and equipment and a comfortable chair. He signed the ill news for Velio, sealing the scroll for despatch and laying it aside for Lucius to collect in the morning.

'Orgidor. Tonight, or tomorrow morning? How do we do this? Just send in a guard and have him chop you without a word of explanation; like a street killing. More like the murder of a bound man than his execution.'

He wrinkled his nose. His identical intentions towards the

Veniconi, Aulercas, came back to him and he grimaced at the irony, studying his pen and the blank page. The whole idea of killing one man to save another, by invoking the god of healing was risible. What a stupid idea.

His first order was going to be an execution order. It felt a little bit ominous. How best to make sure it did not jinx his fate? If he went over to where Orgidor was being held at least he would look the man in the face before condemning him. Though Servius had rather given the impression he should distance himself from it. Given the nature of who it was, a famous brigand and all that, did he not merit a little bit of ceremony? Servius certainly knew the man's crimes and whatever mischief he had caused across the years better than he did. Orgidor; his name meant nothing and as far as he knew, it did not mean anything special in the native tongue.

He sighed and glanced over at his predecessor's shrine to the house gods. The serving and offerings bowls had been removed. Servius had not said whether Morenus had a family, Deva Victrix made it at least possible that Morenus was married. Whatever the answer, it was clear he was not inclined to share his altar with a stranger. A pointed reminder he had no personal connection to the gods of this house. Next to it, Atius had been quick to set up his own little personal shrine. They knew each other well. Atius had not sought permission to touch the box wherein his shrine had been packed for transportation and yet unpacking it and constructing it here without requiring instruction, was an act of piety and loyalty.

Was it perhaps appropriate to make a prayer right now before he wrote the warrant? He listened to his instincts and knelt at the altar, lighting its three lamps with a wick. At least Deva had no shortage of lamp oil. No smoky make-does for light. Jupiter Optimus Maximus, Vesta, Fortuna, Mars: he prayed to each in turn, asking the house gods be kind to him and his endeavours for as long as he lived in this house. He would make an offering of salt and milk tomorrow to mark the start.

He went back to his table.

"Pomponius, I dedicate Orgidor to your memory," he said aloud before writing **Glaccus** at the foot of the blank page.

He summonsed Atius from his bed and dictated the execution order. Atius seemed attuned to his temper and wrote it without a single question. He handed the order to one of the two guards outside his front door.

"Take this to the duty officer at the prison. Tell him I want it carried out immediately. Wait for him to confirm it has been done and bring me news. Make sure it is you that brings me the news. Tell the officer that you are ordered by me to wait until the order has been carried out. Clear? Right carry on."

He prayed the officer would recognise his name as the new commander of the cohort. Then he went back inside, untied his boots, and lay down to sleep, forgetting the sentry's order to report back to him in person.

He woke to the hand of Atius shaking his shoulder. Atius looked down. The clerk's face was calm enough but something in his eyes troubled Hanno.

"What is it Atius?" he asked, "Orgidor has not escaped has he?"

Atius shook his head.

"Begging you pardon sir I went along to see it was done properly. The Brigantes is dead as you commanded. It's just that he laughed at us when he heard the order. Laughed like he did not care. Gave me the shivers sir. Not quite right in the head. He really laughed like it was funny. There was something about him. Unrepentant bloody heathen he was, if you ask me. These people, sir."

'Only you, Atius, could summon up an expression like "unrepentant bloody heathen" at such an hour of the night.'

"Thank you Atius, Now go and rest. We have much to do tomorrow."

Chapter 44.
The abandoned turf wall.

Segontio's two scouts reached the turf wall after a long surveillance of the normally busy, cart infested roads. The fringe of towers and signal points had suffered from attacks, but the actual forts remained unburned. An air of desolation was already lurking about the place. They looked at each other, hefted their lances and side by side moved into the wolves' den. Wheel marks cut deep ruts in the soft ground, sure signs the rumours were true. They walked the horses along the line looking for more evidence with growing confidence. After a couple of hours, they turned and began retracing their steps. There really was nothing to see. Neither one of them had any interest in venturing inside the empty stockades to search out spoils. They halted to eat from their food pouches, taking their ease on a cluster of rocks that gave a good view of the rising escarpment further to the east. All was quiet. There was not a Roman soldier in sight; anywhere. They finished and struck out for the road south, fearless now that they had satisfied their mission.

On the distant skyline a large group of Dumnoni horsemen sat watching them. After a quick exchange of looks, they nudged their mounts towards the waiting warriors. As they drew closer, they could see cooking fires and more men sitting in the hollows, eating. The invitation to join them was quick and they accepted. What else could they do?

"The warriors of the Dumnoni nation have been called to gather here. We wait for three days for them all to arrive and then we ride south under Asuvad to attack the fort at Flour Sacks. Two more days until we move."

The war band leader advised them. It felt very calm.

"That is in our land," the older Selgovae remarked.

He ensured it sounded like nothing more serious than the state of a river.

"That is known."

The circled, eating, men nodded and passed leather flasks of ale to them.

"Our king has given no command that we attack the fort," the more experienced Selgovae announced after he had tasted the ale and taken a hearty swallow that drew jeers and calls from the Dumnoni.

"Our king, on the other hand, has commanded we sweep the foul stench of the invaders from our lands. Will you join with us or just drink all of our ale?" the Dumnoni leader chaffed.

The younger scout began to relax. Tales were often told of their northern neighbours' ferocity, but they were quick to smile and open handed with their hospitality. He let his older friend handle the discussion, lying back on the grass on his elbow and pulling a grass stem to chew. He was a dead man if his friend could not parley his way out of this. Much better to show no fear. The ale skin came his way, and he had a good feeling this was going to turn out well.

"It is not our decision. As you can see, we are only messengers sent to see the truth on the wall," his comrade reported.

"The truth of the wall is they have gone. It is our pushing that made them go. Now we will finish it. The Selgovae are welcome to join our men," the Dumnoni said with pride.

"The Dumnoni are known as great warriors," his friend acknowledged, "and after Flour Sacks? What will the Dumnoni do then? Will you ride back north and leave us to our lands? What of the other fort at the three hills?" he probed.

His younger friend felt a sudden jolt of anxiety.

That was a little too pointed,' he thought, but none of them appeared to take offence.

"The Dumnoni do not care about the fort at the three hills. That is for you or the Votadini to deal with. We hear the Veniconi lord, Aulercas, has no interest in helping the Votadini with their problem. They tell us they have no need to venture to the three hills. We think the Veniconi will stay in the north now that the battle is won."

"We will tell our king you wish to pass through our lands

on the way to Flour Sacks," his comrade went on.

The Dumnoni leading the talking paused, waving the offer of the ale-skin away with his hand.

"I cannot speak for my lord, Asuvad, it is not my place, but I do not think he will want to cross your land without your king's permission. We could use the Roman road if he is unhappy, tell your king that the Dumnoni have no desire for disagreement with our neighbouring friends now that the wolf-soldiers have finally gone. Your warriors would be welcome to our ride by our sides and sit at our fires."

'There it is. The open hand. There is only one enemy.'

The young Selgovae grinned.

They set off back to Carubantum once they finished eating, bearing the message and good impressions, for all their opinion was worth in the eyes of their prince Segontio.

*

Segontio listening with growing delight at the news. It just got better and better. His father, sitting on the other side of the great fire pit was keeping a straight face, hiding his feelings about the Dumnoni intention to cross his land. Their invitation to join forces and sack the fort was not something he could ignore.

'But if you sack Flour Sacks you must do the same at the three hills fort or else what is the point? Leaving three hills untouched will only suggest weakness and spark a reprisal.'

He laughed, delighted at the torment most likely raging in his father's mind.

"Very well we will send a rider back. We will join the Dumnoni, let them cross our land and attack Flour Sacks, but thereafter we will not seek to impose ourselves on other tribes. Let every tribe mourn its time of oppression and then light fires for new beginnings. Segontio, you will lead my warriors. We will tell the Dumnoni they may cross our land and we will join them at the river crossing north of Flour Sacks. Set scouts in all directions so that we are not mistaken the Dumnoni are riding in peace to our boundaries," his father said, "it would be a terrible mistake to see the Romani leave without further blood, only to shed it because we underestimated our neighbours."

*

Asuvad pulled up, reining in his mount as the cloaked figure of Segontio came galloping towards him.

'Raper of girls, fugitive from honour. And now you want to ride with me?' he thought, *'Tianos, you will have your chance to avenge your sister. I will make sure it is your hand that returns her good name.'*

"Greetings, my lord Asuvad," Segontio beamed, "I bring my father's warriors you join with you. He grants your request to cross our lands with open hands. Together we will destroy Flour Sacks and send her men to their gods. Our holy pools will have gifts. The priests are eager. I have three of them riding with my men at my back."

Asuvad sat patient and calm in the saddle, absorbing Segontio's bluster and spume, with Eidumnos son's face sharp in his mind. Tianos had honour and courage, unlike Segontio.

"I have twelve hundred men Segontio," he said, "the flower of the Dumnoni."

"I bring seven hundred, Asuvad," Segontio said, "and more have given their oath to follow on tomorrow."

"Then all is well. We are enough to destroy them. But do you lead them or your father?" he said.

"It's my father's wish to see them gone. We will shed our blood as required and they fight under me. But I am happy that we fight alongside each other. There will be glory for all of us," Segontio affirmed.

"Only if we succeed and only for those who live to return to their halls," Asuvad snapped, whirling his horse around, already disliking the casual arrogance.

Somehow the shock he had felt at Eidumnos' sorry tale of Voccia now felt misplaced. He could well believe this young man could overstep the mark. There he sat on his horse boasting of Selgovae courage in battle but had nothing to say about honour to their women. His bit his tongue.

This is not for glory, he wanted to say, *'it's for our land and our people.'*

But this cock-bantam was not worth the explanation. He

was surprised at the anger he felt. It would be nothing to turn back and knock the fool from his horse.

'Seven hundred additional fighters, think of that, forget this strutting little hawk,' he chided himself, *'eagles do not bow to hawks.'*

*

Dometius Barrus coughed into the cloth. There it was again. Spittle-spottles of blood, like a little bird's footprints in snow. He waited until the spasm behind his left nipple passed, tucking the hateful evidence on the cloth under the edge of his breastplate. He was ill and the blood stains were getting more frequent, but the medicus was not getting his hands on him, anything but that. It was a chill of some kind, some flux of the chest. The warmer weather was coming; a few days rest and it would pass. He was Dometius Barrus and the Barrus lineage did not fall prone to springtime coughs.

His cohors 1 Nervana Germanorum was waiting out on the parade ground for him, beyond the fort's walls. They would be drawn up and polished within a finger-span of their lives, the way he wanted them. Men of the best auxiliary in the north. His pride and dedication and their willingness to work had made them the best; Dometius Barrus' German cohort were every bit as good as regular legion troops.

The ache in his chest was receding. Now it was duller and energy sapping. He took a pull on the cup of wine mixed with rosemary and sage and pushed the gnawing fear of a pain he could not see scuttering into the shadows like a rat in the horreum.

Outside the gates the men were drawn up, polished and splendid. The standards gleaming and bright in the sunlight. It was good to command such men. The senior centurion saluted him and ordered them to attention. The buccinas blew the sharp noted 'Commander's Salute.' Then silence.

"Men, you have seen the cohorts marching past these last days. The army has withdrawn from the wall of Emperor Antoninus Pius. I cannot tell you whether it is for all time. We too will soon be marching south to take position on Emperor Hadrian's wall. That is the empire's new line. It will be defended at all costs. We will help defend it. Before we leave, this fort must be rendered unfit for use by the enemy. Not an easy task. We are not."

He stopped.

The mens' faces changed from attention to puzzlement. He raised his hand to hold them silent. Then pointed for the benefit of the officer at his side.

Beyond the hindmost ranks of Nervana, a mass of warriors was emerging out from the distant tree line. His senior centurion had also spotted them.

"Take the men back inside and blow 'Stand to the Eagle' as soon as the last century is in. I will take the ala and scout what is happening over there. Get the scorpions ready to fire on my return. Get every pilum, every arrow, out of the weapons store, every man to the walls. Every man in the infirmary capable of holding a gladius to be armed and formed as a reserve in the compound," he said.

"As you command," the centurion replied.

He signalled the cavalry decurions to bring on their troops and spurred out to the gathering tribes. He picked a stream that was no barrier at all to pull up and assess what he had in front of him. The warriors had formed a front two or three men deep, fronted by mounted warriors and some chariots. It was, he realised, good ground for chariots. His officers joined him to confer. Cool heads and cool blood would help make wise decisions. A little lecture was in order.

"Chariots, gentlemen, not something we are used to seeing too much of up here in these lands. I wonder if they are Selgovae? Used to be a regular thing further south, I recall. And back in the days of the invasions of course the coastal tribes encountered by Caesar and suchlike were formidable charioteers; all flash and pomp, swagger and piss. But I rather like them, all the same. There is something splendid about men who want to rush to their deaths on such machines, don't you think?"

They laughed.

"And their chariot horses are magnificent. Make sure you try and bag them when the fighting starts. We will divide them up in a lottery if you get enough. You will be delighted by them, I am sure. Strong and fast. Good endurance. Almost a waste to have them pull chariots. Now, if we had kept the men out in the open, the chariots could be a real danger. It just takes a few hotheads to drive headfirst into the lines to unsettle everything. Break up the lines, get the junior soldiers jumping, that sort of thing. From what I have read about them in the histories, they will charge in and then dismount to fight and keep the chariot as a means of escape. I estimate a couple of thousands of foot soldiers and fifty or so chariots. Any disagreements? Give or take?" he averred.

He kept his true concerns about the speed of the chariots to himself.

Together his officers sat with him scanning the armed men three or four hundred paces away. The enemy did not shout or demonstrate. Their quietness was more worrying than had the thoughts of chariots crashing into auxiliary lines. 'Stand to the Eagle,' came drifting out from the fort.

"What are they waiting for, sir?"

He swivelled in his saddle. His six decurions were veterans of the peace, less so of the fighting.

'Perfectly obvious question, I just wish you had not asked,' he chided.

"Well, whatever it is, I don't think they are selling us fresh horses today."

More laughter.

"We will not provoke them further. They seem," he paused for a moment to choose the right words and the denarius dropped on the table, "I think they might be waiting to test our reaction and perhaps also they wait for reinforcements. They will attack us at some point, you can save the dice game on that fact. I have seen enough."

He pointed to one of his officers.

"Get your men back inside."

He indicated another.

"You, take ten men and ride down to Castra Exploratum. Tell them they must get word down to the Stones. Tell them we have an attack pending. Tell them to prepare. This may be the start of a reaction to our evacuation of the northern wall."

Waiting until they had begun riding off, he pulled the cloth from under neath his armour plate and coughed into it. He checked the results. More blood, bigger globules. The left-hand side of his chest was aching again. This all-pervading dampness was doing him in, it would be the end of him, he no longer doubted it.

The signal beacon was ready and waiting outside the fort. Resin-soaked timbers atop a stone plinth. The torch bearer was up there on a ladder.

"Carry on decanus," he ordered, "get the word moving

down the road."

The flame licked the timbers like a faithful hound and the flower blossomed.

*

The day dragged on, and he decided it was safe to stand half of the cohort down. It was clear the tribes were sitting, waiting. Whatever was coming it would be ugly, but he was beginning to think it would not happen today.

"Let them eat centurion," he said to his second.

The warriors had moved from the merest suggestion of a low ridge into a thin encircling line surrounding the fort. It exposed their lack of numbers but demonstrated their ambition to cut off the fort. Best to get the men off the walls and concentrating on filling their bellies. No good would come of staring out there and letting imaginations take hold. Once night came, darkness would only feed anxieties. He wanted them rested and eager. The cavalrymen had taken word of this south to the wall. That was all they needed to concern themselves with for the moment.

Campfires started burning in the darkness. Shapes and shadows to feed the rat called fear. He decided to change the wall guards every two hours. Better they did not have too long to dwell on what was out there. Sending cavalry out to harry them on all sides was appealing but scarce worth the risk. If nothing changed, he would have to do something tomorrow to alter the balance. He inspected the ramparts, spoke to the duty officers, and looked at the fires.

'Really rather impressive. There is something about these people, when all is said and done.'

He paused outside the valetudinarium where the medicus would still be up, preparing bandages with his four assistants for the battle that was coming.

"It doesn't work," he said aloud, "your red wine, rosemary and sage does not work."

'Perhaps a hot knife can cut it out.'

The bleakness that picture brought chilled him to the bone.

Daylight brought the Novantae into the picture and others too. He sucked his teeth and checked the position on all four sides. There were perhaps five thousand warriors in the encircling ring now and three or even four different tribes represented. They were not taking long to renew alliances against the common foe. A cavalry foray was out of the question until he had them running in defeat; then he could unleash the horsemen.

*

Asuvad watched the waggons laden with barrels of pitch labouring up the slope. Burning the wooden gates down would be the only way to storm the stone-built fort. It would be a new challenge to take defences made in stone. He grinned at the praise and glory such a victory would bring. It had to be done by storming the gates, otherwise, men would be wasted. Starvation was an option too, but would this alliance stay committed to the weeks and perhaps months it would take? Segontio would not wait that long. Tianos might not let him wait that long.

The men of the Novantae were unknown to him though not to Segontio, which was unhelpful. He sensed discord simmering between them. Their common hatred of the sons of the wolf was all they had binding them together. Once the fort was taken, he imagined they could easily be at each other's throats, fighting over the spoils.

Tianos came to his fireside and sat for a while not speaking.

"He may die in the fighting," Asuvad said to prompt things along.

"His dying is not important, it is how Segontio dies that matters to me," Tianos replied, "if he dies fighting, he will be remembered as a brave man by his people. I want him to be forgotten because he is a coward."

"Do not try and kill him tonight my young friend. That would be most unwise. We need the Selgovae to help destroy the fort. Once we have done that, I will help you if you want," he replied.

"I could find my way to his campfire and do it tonight," Tianos said.

He looked hot faced and he was trembling.

'You're not listening, my young friend,' Asuvad sympathised.

"Listen to me, Tianos. You swore a blood oath to serve me. You will not touch Segontio until we have achieved everything we set out to. Then, then you can have him," he waved his finger at Tianos.

Tianos sat back on his haunches.

"I am going to take my mother back his head as a gift."

"You can cut off his parts as well, for all I care Tianos, but you must wait," he ruled, "taking this fort comes first. Promise me Tianos."

*

The waggon axles were caked with cattle and boar fat. Everything else, the open topped barrels, the waggon sides, was smeared with pitch. Asuvad listened for any tell-tale squeaks as the wheels turned and hoped the darkness would hide the sound. He waved the men at the ropes forward. The laden waggons took a moment to move. Pointing to the gateway of the fort that was a dark silhouette in the night, he sent them to put the waggon where it would do the most good.

"Get it burning as soon as it is in place," he said.

The waggon started moving and bowmen followed. The gates would be defended as soon as the waggons were detected. The fire would make it easy to pick off the soldiers trying to extinguish the flames. He knew of nothing as good as fire to instil fear into an encampment a night. A low throb of confidence rose in his chest. He went around the circle to the part of the line opposite the next gate and send that waggon on its way. The other two waggons were already moving by the time he got to those positions. Gazing up at the clouds he prayed the moon would not shed her light tonight. Every sound now was crucial to success. Fire at all four gates would have the Romani in a panic. The minutes passed. He started walking towards the fort to see for himself and men followed him. There was no use in trying to prevent them. Voices drifted in the night air. And then it began. A battle trumpet began blasting from inside the fort. The noise was matched by simultaneous roars from the men dragging the pitch waggons.

"Forwards," he shouted, "we must get the gates burning tonight."

The Novantae section of the lines yelled agreement and as he ran with them, Tianos was nowhere to be seen. Segontio's men were on the other side of the fort. As were the Dumnoni. He should have been there to lead them. This was not what he had planned but the fire waggons must succeed. Up ahead a waggon burst into flames and a cacophony of shouting broke out. Surging forwards, he saw it had crossed the slender entranceway over the outer ditches to reach the gates. The leaping yellow light painted men and shadows. Soldiers leaned out over the protective walls. Water was already being poured from buckets to quench the flames. Spears and arrows were visible only when they found a target. Warriors were falling under sheathing volleys of spears. He had no bow to help but strode through his men pointing to soldiers needing their attention. The heavy wooden gates were not yet alight. A warrior dashed up onto the back of the waggon and toppled a pitch barrel over, sending its sticky liquid flowing. Others joined him, before arrows took each of them, but more men leapt up to take their places. Unless the pitch touched the base of the gates this was going to fail. But they could all see that once the gates were alight it would be nigh impossible for the defenders to douse the flames because of the way the gateway recessed under the raised walkway. It was an effective dead spot where the defenders would struggle to fight the fire.

He whirled around checking numbers. This had exploded into a night time assault. He had only wanted to get the gates burning but the warriors had decided otherwise.

He pulled back and ran around the corner of the walls. The next waggon was not yet touching the gates. The warriors were struggling to heave the waggon the last vital gasp. He ran on, the third wall had defended the waggon. It was not yet alight and a group of dead and wounded lay around it. The Dumnoni saw him coming and surged again, heaving and pushing the waggon to the gap between the ditches.

"Pride of the Dumnoni," he screamed at them, "you are the pride of the Dumnoni."

The waggon crashed into the gates with a satisfying thud. A torch followed and it erupted into flames.

*

Dometius watched his men hauling water from the well and knew something as stupid as a shortage of buckets was going to make saving the gates nigh impossible.

"Get every amphora," he ordered.

The gates of the horreum and the other storerooms were already open. The horses were scenting the smoke as the watering buckets from the stables were used.

"Get the fires out, men," he called, "we must get them out. Centurion, I want a report. How many of them are out there? Decurion, make sure all the horses are secured. I do not want horses loose in here. Archers, I want you on the walls now. Centurion, keep two centuries in the compound, the rest to the walls. Get that water moving, men."

'Stand to the Eagle,' was deafening on all sides. He could not hear himself think.

"Enough" he yelled.

The nearest buccina saw him and heard. Others carried on. The trumpeter ran to spread the order. He sprang up steps to the ramparts and peered out. An arrow hit him. It jolted him backwards and sent spinning him off the rampart to a shuddering collision with the ground below. Somehow his finest military armour had failed to stop the point.

'How can this be?' he wondered.

He coughed blood and tried to pull his handkerchief out. The pain in the left-hand side of his chest was gone. Perhaps he had shaken it off. He covered his mouth from the stink of smoke and pitch with his forearm. Someone had seen he was injured. He could hear their voices shouting his name. He heard their alarm. The pain that had tormented him for so long really was gone. His chest no longer throbbed and plagued him. He needed to get up and take command. The cohors I Nervana Germanorum, his cohort, his boys, needed him.

'Get up Dometius, you fool,' he told himself.

He tried to lift his head. The smoke was awful. The stink of pitch, suffocating.

'The arrow's a scratch, the medicus will sort this in a moment.'

He laid his head back on the ground and realised he was passing through the gates to Elysium.

*

Daylight came early with its smoke and pitch scents filling Asuvad's nostrils. He got up from the fireside and drank water from his leather flask. Warriors lay around, still sleeping, or sitting conversing in low voices. He raised his hand in greeting and went to find Segontio and the Novantae leader whose name he had heard once last night and forgotten. As he went, he kept his eyes on the fort. The two entrances he could see had lost their gates. The attack was going to have to begin before the Romans had time to rebuild. Food would have to wait. Every minute now counted. There was a roar ahead. The Novantae were charging already. The men on the ground at his feet rose, shields, swords, helmets, axes ready. His own shield was back at his fire. He donned his helmet and drew his blade.

"It begins," he said to no one in particular.

*

The senior centurion tried to conceal Dometius Barrus' death, but the word was out. The commander had been killed. The mood in the fort was low.

"Get out there with spades and extend the ditch through the entranceways. Quickly before they attack. There is no time to repair the gates. Get waggons to bar the gateways. I want a full century at every gate and the rest on the walls. And get those scorpions firing. Blow 'Stand to the Eagle.'"

It felt a redundant order because every man in the fort could see for himself. The digging squads raced out and threw themselves into it. Years of practice marches and overnight camps had drilled the need for speed into them. The ground at the gateways had to be cleared of the timber remnants and the pitch waggons. The entrance ways had been gravelled when the old wooden fort of Agricola had been upgraded to stone. It made for hard digging. Only the Decumana gate had been spared from the pitch. The waggon had been halted by concentrated archery and though it still burned it was too far outside to be a concern. The centurion on that side took a brief look and sent men to put the fire out. There was no need to leave a gift to the enemy. The gate opened and ten men and an optio raced out with buckets. The centurion watched the smoke rising as it was extinguished and decided to save his men's' strength for what was coming.

The attempt to rebuild the defences on the dextra, sinistra and praetoria sides had just got going when the roar from the distant circle of warriors told him there was no more time.

"Get those waggons in place," he shouted, "get archers on top of them. Why are the bloody scorpions not firing?"

"Range sir, too far, soon sir," a cool voice replied.

The Latin was a little fractured. He whirled ready to put the man on a punishment for his cheek. It was a tesserarius, with a face that had seen the untamed barbarian world beyond Rome's frontiers because he was born from it. The Germanic auxiliary looked at him.

"Caledonii coming," he said, "we send them to their gods today."

The centurion debated whether he had time to correct the misidentification of the tribes. It really did not much matter now.

He nodded, "fire on the first signal."

"Sir," the tesserarius said.

The men were still climbing to the walls as the Novantae wave swept up to the outer ditch, rolled over and up again like a dam bursting.

"Pila," a commanding voice bawled out.

"Now."

More warriors fought their way over the impeding ditches, reaching the flat berm between the base of the stone walls and the ditch, leaving bodies strewn and bleeding. The javelin fusillade only seemed to enrage them, and they funnelled towards the burned-out gateway.

"Here they come, archers ready, fire."

Spears started raining back in reply to the auxiliary volley. The senior centurion judged the situation at that gate under control and rushed to the Sinistra that was now receiving its share of warriors.

Asuvad threw his men at the Sinistra and the waggon blocking it. Roman archers loosed a frenzy of arrows, taking men in the face and the chest around him. He leapt forwards, enraged, taking the cream of the Dumnoni with him. A furious struggle enveloped the waggon. Swords thrusting down at them and spears jutting up in reply. Roman archers were firing down from the gantry walk overhead and he shouted for men to scale the stone walls. They got a grip of the waggons wheels and began heaving at it trying to move it aside. It had not been in place long enough for blocks to have been set to lock the wheels. They got the massive wooden wheels to turn. His men got up on the bed of the waggon, but they only seemed to live for seconds before getting cut down. Others followed, the shields of the leading men taking a terrific pounding.

The senior centurion saw the increasing flood of enemy rushing the walls. Scanning the distant area where they had been encamped there did not appear to be any more of them waiting in reserve. He had the full attack. If they could hold this, they would win the fight. But from the shouts he could hear even the unburned Decumana gate was under pressure. The Sinstra was where the most danger was, but the situation at the Praetoria was getting down to hand to hand too. If the gates fell the fort would become a slaughter yard with nowhere to run.

This'll decide it,' he intuited.

If they were beaten off from the main gate the men would take heart.

Segontio pulled his men back to rest. He would have given

his torc and arm rings for a drink of water. An enormous roar broke out on the far side of the fort.

"Forwards," he shouted, "our brothers need us."

They looked at him disbelieving this was all the rest they were permitted and charged the gate with him. Right away he sensed something had changed. He jumped up onto the waggon and killed a blond-haired auxiliary trying to block him. This time the next Roman was slower to come to attack.

'They're tiring too,' he exulted.

On the far side of the fort's compound the Dumnoni were forcing their way through a slender gap in the gateway they had made by moving the waggon. The burned and wrecked timbers did their best to impede the warriors, but he saw them jumping through and in an instant, they had carried the fight into the fort itself. A trumpet call broke out. One he had never heard. The soldiers on the rampart were turning away from the warriors beneath the walls to fight his men and the Dumnoni on the inside. The military standard suddenly appeared and he pointed at it.

"There is their god," he screamed.

The bolt firing engines were facing right at them. One fired and two men were flung back, impaled. Then it ceased. He saw it would kill the Romans as easily as his men and he cheered. The standard bearer was surrounded by horsemen. The third gate yielded to the Novantae and with a snarl of delight he knew they had the wolf-skin soldiers at their mercy. The fort would fall if the attack could only keep going for a little longer.

The senior centurion saw his two gates breached.

"Get your troopers mounted and throw these dogs out of here," he ordered the cavalry commander.

"Get the standard out so the men can see it."

He realised the mistake when the first barbarian spears hit the horses in the confined space. The panic was immediate, and they began a havoc, spelling disaster. He rushed toward the horsemen engaging the enemy warriors. The compound was filling with men coming down from the ramparts.

"Testudo," an authoritative voice shouted.

But it was too late. The fort was breached, the horses were knocking over friend as well as foe. There was too little room for them to manoeuvre. He drew his gladius and prayed Mars Ultor was with them today.

*

Asuvad knelt on his knees and put his sword on the earth. Exhaustion filled him but it could not prevent the elation in his veins. The shouting from within the fort was lessening. He regarded the regimental standard Segontio had presented to him in rightful homage as senior war-leader. Segontio, to his marginal credit, had not tried to usurp the honour. There was blood on the pole, but the decorated metal upper was undamaged. Next to one of their totem birds he could not think of a better gift to take back to his king. His thirst was a torture. He sat back on his heels allowing himself a smile of unadulterated pleasure. There was nothing like this. No song, nor woman could match this joy. It was what Heruscomani and he had always spoken of, driving them out by the sword, adorning the sacred groves with heads. Aulercas and the Veniconi should have been here to share in the spoils. The fort was full of things worth having. He got up and went to find water. The river running past the fort had warriors lying along its banks drinking like thirsty hounds, drinking their fill. It was a good day to be a warrior.

Chapter 45.

"Join me and we will do the same to the fort at the three hills," Segontio crowed.

Asuvad felt the cold resumption of his dislike and decided not to get drawn into another fight. Flour Sacks, was ruined and its wooden parts, burned or burning, but he had lost men doing it. And he had wounded men to consider. The Novantae leader dismissed the suggestion.

"The soldiers at the three hills are cut off now. There is no need to waste men. When they hear about what we did here they may leave. They will be completely alone if they stay," he said

Asuvad reckoned it was sage advice. Segontio scowled, his face red with aggression from his fill of Roman wine. The inevitable argument with the big shouldered Novantae was about to begin.

The Novantae had a good humour in his eyes, and he was brave, perhaps in his middle twenties, but big shouldered and strong. A man who could wrestle a bull. Asuvad was warming to him. The Novantae had done well for themselves. He saw no reason to pick a quarrel. He listened while they sparred. The Novantae declined to join in another attack.

Segontio turned back trying to persuade him next. He shook his head and accepted Segontio's wine. He leaned down and patted the Roman standard lying beside him.

"Segontio, I'm taking this back, plus a few heads and weapons as gifts to offer the gods and I'm going to ask the druids whether we are really free now. And if they say it is true, I will offer a prayer that I never see another one of them ever again," he said.

"So, you will not come over the hill pass with me to the three hills and finish this?" Segontio barracked.

"Segontio, I think we finished it today. They left and we killed those who lingered. The fort in the east will start running as soon as word of this spreads," he replied.

"We have not finished until they are all dead," Segontio argued.

It's a fair point,' he thought, *'but the men are weary and Aulercas might yet be persuaded to take some of the burden.'*

"I would prefer the Veniconi gave help," he said.

"No, I say we go now while the men are ready to fight," Segontio shouted.

"Then I shall ask the gods to smile on you Segontio. But I am taking my men north. If Aulercas is willing to join us, we will return. You won't wait that long?" he asked.

"No Asuvad, I want to kill them tomorrow or the day after

tomorrow. It can't come soon enough," Segontio ranted.

"You should calm down Segontio, the men at the three hills will be fresh. Your men will need to rest. So, will the horses. I have heard they wait in a stone fort like this one," he said.

"I do not fear stone forts."

"No, but they are not so easy to burn, Segontio," he replied.

It was getting pointless. The Selgovae was too stubborn and too intoxicated to listen. He exchanged a glance with the Novantae. His bright eyes were laughing but he could tell he was unimpressed with Segontio's plan.

"More wine Segontio," Asuvad suggested.

'If Tianos finds you now, you won't live until morning.'

He threw a soldier's wine flask at him. Segontio dropped it and scrabbled between his knees to gather it. Asuvad turned away.

All along the ring of campfires the Selgovae, Dumnoni and Novantae were resting, jumbled together in groups of friends and new found allies. Their early strict segregation into their own kind had melted as forgotten pride. Many tended the wounds of others. He walked through them, showing off the standard of the Cohors 1 Nervana Germanorum. Some got to their feet to touch it. Others struck it with their swords. Before he had gone a hundred paces the long wood pole had notches from dozens of blades. Some men stood and offered him their homage.

"Asuvad," they said, shaking his arm.

He smiled and nodded, letting every man who wanted to, have his moment with the Roman standard. Some looked at it and spat. There was no sign of Tianos. He turned and looked at the fort. Carrion crows were strutting around amid the corpses, first to the scene as ever. The bigger hawks would follow soon, the foxes and suchlike, to the feast of men. He could hear the bartering of loot for the best Roman horses. Inside the walls there were more casual pickings over the spoils. There was sufficient grain in the store to feed many families if anyone bothered to fetch carts to haul it away. Some of the chariots raced around outside the walls cheered on by happy, intoxicated young bloods. Once the men had rested, they would begin collecting the fallen warriors, but for now the living celebrated.

He found Tianos sleeping under a tree. There was enough blood on his clothing to vouch for his part in taking the fort. He knelt down at, worried the lad was injured but Tianos was sleeping with his arms wrapped around a beautiful, decorated, cavalry sword; a fine exuberant weapon that would suit his youthful vigour and vitality. A sword that would serve him well for years. It seemed a long time since Tianos had come and sat by his fireside talking over Segontio's death. Should he wake him and tell him Segontio was drunk beyond any ability to defend himself and let Tianos have his revenge?

He took another long look at the standard. The Romans had fought hard to protect it. Up close it did not seem so valuable, but not one soldier survived to see it in his hands. He looked again at Tianos. If Segontio did not succeed in getting himself killed by his own stupidity, he would stand with Tianos and help him put that right. This boy had courage. Asuvad felt a welling of affection for him. Tianos was going to get his chance to put a sword cut into the Roman standard and a bigger one into Segontio too.

Chapter 46.
Trimontium.

Velio looked at the communication scroll Marcellus had left on his desk.

'At least this one's not from the governor,' he thought with some relief, *'can't be as bad as the last order I opened.'*

"Hail and my greetings to you Commander Pinneius," it began in a hand he recognised.

'Fuck,' he thought, *'wrong again.'*

Servius' letter was short, he could tell from the thin feel of the scroll in his fingers.

'Likely to be bad, Velio,' he schooled himself for the worst.

'Velio,

I am informed auxiliary cavalry from Blatobulgium reported to the praefectus at Castra Exploratum the onset of an attack by the tribes in that region. Since then, no further communication has been received from Dometius Barrus. You are hereby advised to assume Blatobulgium may have fallen. I regret the situation regarding supporting troops has not changed. You will bring the existing centuries back to Deva Victrix when your successor and his command relieves you. But until then you must hold out, regardless of the odds.'

The usual closures followed. Then an afterthought so

typical of Servius.

'Velio,

Take no chances. I regret I did not give you a milliaria at the outset. Mea culpa, forgiveness please. I imagine you could use those extra men at this moment. I ask Fortuna to ride at your side. We will take wine when you return. Bring Gallus back in one piece, as a favour both to me and to the legion. You will be interested to hear Hanno Glaccus now commands the First Cohort.'

He put it down. No mention of when the relief column would come. How could Servius have omitted the single most useful piece of information?

'Bloody legates, too far removed from the shitty end of the sword to remember what's important. Tell me the worst and forget the single bit I need to know. The old man's losing his grip.'

He picked the letter up and flung it across the room. He sighed, got up and retrieved it, scratching his initials on it so Marcellus could file it as 'read'.

So, the natives had not interfered with the evacuation of the wall but had chased up with a suspected assault on Blatobulgium. They were neither stupid nor ill informed. He put his head around the door of his office.

"Officers in one hour," he ordered, "and tell Lentulus I want to eat before then."

He could hear the men singing as they scraped out the ditches of weeds and brambles. At the very worst the thought of a bit of action was a tonic to bored legionaries. It could be worse. The signal station atop the highest of the three hills was now redundant. There was no one in line of sight who could possibly see any fire that was set. And even if the garrisons at Habitanum and Bremenium had their eyes peeled, it must be assumed they were under the same order that no local reinforcements were to support Trimontium until the milliaria came.

"Send a message to the decanus up at the signal tower. Tell him to bring his squad back immediately," he added.

Trimontium's position on the steep hill above the river was well chosen. With the immediate ground falling away on all sides he would have all the notice he could wish for if a tribal force came to visit. The men at the signal station would have to cross the valley and up the hill to get back to the fort. Not easy if the expected attack came in from the west. He was not going to lose a single man if he could avoid it. Turning his attention to Fufius' command, he dictated another order.

'No legionaries are to leave the immediate precinct of the fort.
The duty centurion will advise the local village that we expect an attack.
There will be a reward for any correct information supplied to me.
Otherwise, all troops should take appropriate precautions.
Cavalry patrols only until further notice and only under my express orders.'

"Have that issued Marcellus."

Lentulus brought in a tray of food and he ate by himself, alone in his office, ruminating on Servius' order. The information from Barrus' men to Castra Exploratum must now be two days old, older even, because of the legate's knowledge and the subsequent relaying of it to him.

'Four or five days old? More? Unless Servius was up on The Stones inspecting troops when the message arrived.'

Either way the attack, if it was coming, was likely to be soon. He put down his napkin. Outside the sounds of the ditch cleansing had ceased. He picked up his helmet and went to see the results. An optio was peering along one side with a critical eye. Tacto was out there too. The ditch was being inspected to death. He gazed across the valley to Eidumnos' hall, wondering whether the old man and his family would be safe.

'Will you be safe, Voccia?' he corrected himself.

The thought plagued him. There were some obvious options open to him. It was more a matter of whether he should.

He found Gallus at his favourite occupation, drilling a half century of men. Further out on the flat ground beyond the vicus Fufius' cavalry men were performing charges and retirals to a series of trumpet calls. Back and forth they went. The men seemed to be enjoying the work. The vicus blacksmith was hammering. It all spoke of normality. He scowled and returned to his paperwork and chased up the issuance of the order.

An hour later he briefed the officers. Tacto was his usual phlegmatic, stoic calm self. Fufius made a few facial twitches as he digested the news. The rest kept silent, nodding, and listening. It would be the first attack the fort had been subjected to since any of them had arrived. He suspected the legion's records clerk could be consulted to find out whether Trimontium had ever been attacked and the answer would most likely be 'No.'

He waited for someone to ask a pointless question, showing him a little bit of their nerves but none of them did. It would be satisfying to know that some of them were uneasy too, but they were saying nothing. He nodded and dismissed them, then called for his favourite horse.

Chapter 47.
The hill pass, west of Trimontium.

Segontio kicked his horse forwards leaving the bulk of his Selgovae resting in the pass. He made his way along the base of the northern most of the hills to Eidumnos' hall. Over on the ridge he could see Trimontium fort. He was forced to concede it had been well placed to command the valley and river crossings as well as the stone road. The curling river protected one side. He would have to think how to do this. It was not going to be a repeat of Flour Sacks. But first he had to deal with Eidumnos and Voccia. He had thrown away the plans for a double poisoning: it had been a pleasant dream to include his father in with Eidumnos, but the coming battle would take care of the Votadini one way or the other. Today or tomorrow that family would cease to trouble him. Eidumnos was going to die. That was all there was to it. Meanwhile he would pretend to woo the girl.

He slid down off his mount and handed the reins to the same lad Velio had in mind as a future legionary. They did not speak. The boy was beneath a prince of the Selgovae to merit words of parley. He was beneath more than a cursory glance. The homestead was busy. The year was moving towards summer.

"Mistress," the stable lad called out, "the centurion is coming."

Segontio felt his blood freeze. He turned and followed the lad's outstretched finger. In the distance, a feathered helmet on the head of a Roman soldier was coming this way.

"Give me back my horse," he hissed, snatching the reins out of the lad's grip.

Confusion flooded the groom's face. He kicked his horse and took off for the path to the hills. He galloped his mount, knowing full well it would send a signal to the Roman. He heard a shout, looked over his shoulder and saw the Roman pursuing.

'I'll lead him up into the pass and we'll kill him there. The attack will happen today.'

He had a good lead on the Roman and he lashed the horse to its limits. He checked over his shoulder again. The Roman was pulling up. He had misjudged it. It was too late now, far better to get clear and confer with his men.

Velio watched the rider vanish into the rougher round at the entrance to the hills. His instincts told him he had missed something important. Wheeling around, he carried on to Eidumnos' hall keeping one hand on the pommel of his gladius. He reached the homestead but did not dismount.

"Eidumnos?" he asked.

Bractia came out to greet him.

"You are too late for food centurion, but I can make fresh porridge if you are hungry and can wait," she said, smiling.

There was a warmth in her eyes that almost tempted him into accepting.

"Is Eidumnos here?" he asked again.

"He is out with the cattle. We lost some. Thieves have taken four," she replied.

"Who was that man on the horse?" he said.

"What man centurion? I have been inside all morning. Did we have a visitor?" she asked the stable boy.

He looked at Velio.

"There was a man, but he rode off when he saw you," he replied.

'Honest lad,' Velio smiled.

"Oh, that must have been Segontio," she said, "you have frightened him away centurion," she tried to chastise him.

"He's courting our Voccia. Properly now. The way he should have from the start. Still, there is a nice lad in there somewhere hiding under all his bragging. Perhaps if he shows he is sorry we can make amends."

The lie rolled off her tongue.

Velio kept his attention on the stable boy.

"What's Segontio like," he said.

The lad blushed in confusion.

"I don't know sir. It's not my place."

"No, it's not my lad, just you get along with your chores and don't pretend you know things you don't," she scolded.

"Come sir, let me get you some hot food, He won't be long with the cows, bloody thieves."

She waved him to dismount.

"And Voccia?" he asked.

For a moment, her face froze. Her lie came too fast. He saw it in her eyes.

"She is visiting a friend over in the village. You probably passed her on the way here I expect," Bractia said.

"Ah well, another time perhaps. I hope Eidumnos gets his cows back," he solicited.

"You can't un-eat a cow," the stable boy muttered under his breath.

Velio looked at him and he looked away. Bractia wiped her hands on her apron. He pulled his horse's head and waved. Four cows would feed a lot of men. He held the mare back to a casual walk for as long as he could before letting her switch to a canter.

*

Gallus finished up and the half century were marching back to the fort behind their optio. He swung in at the rear seeing Velio riding in from the west. He halted. His old protégé reined in and got down.

"We got your order, just bringing them back inside now. Good ride?" he asked.

They walked in behind the infantry, Velio leading his horse.

"Something is not quite right, Gallus. I went to visit the local headman over there below the signal hill. He lost four cows last night and I scared away a horseman. The man's wife is lying about something," he confided.

Gallus smiled.

"There's a girl, Gallus," he said, not knowing why this was the moment to say.

Gallus sniffed and wiped his hand against his nose.

"So I gather. You and she are the talk of the latrines in case you are interested. And you are keen on her I suppose? Which is why you were over there this morning."

Velio gave Gallus a hopeless, lopsided, and foolish grin.

'Not the response of an officer commanding troops in the field. Not at all,' Gallus adjudged, *'thirty plus years old and I am still watching out for him.'*

"First things should come first, sir. Sort out whatever needs sorting out and once that's done, you can," he waved his hand in a diplomatic waggle and stopped, "after all these years Velio this is a bloody fine time to start a romance," he snorted.

"We're going back tonight, Gallus, you and me. We are

going over there to find out what is going on. That horseman was a spy, I am certain of it and Eidumnos and his wife are in on it. It was one of their servants who tried to warn me. There's something going on and if we don't try and find out we will have them at our gates."

*

Tacto was horrified by the plan.

"You are going to get yourself killed sir. The hastiliarius too," he growled.

"Tacto, we do not know if Blatobulgium has been taken by the enemy. And if it has been it will be the first stone fort ever to fall to the tribes. I do not intend we fall too. Gallus and me, we'll be careful, and you will take over command if we do not return. If we get captured, you will not entertain any kind of swap for us. We'll take soldier's deaths. I will not have you compromise the safety of the garrison. If we are not back by first light, send some of Fufius' men down the track to Habitanum, tell them the tribes are looking to fight," Velio sat back.

Tacto shook his head.

"Nothing I say is going to make you change your mind is it sir?"

"Tacto, I'm not going to sit here and wait," Velio responded.

"Why not? It seems a very sensible plan to me?" Tacto

argued for once, "that's why the walls are made of stone."

Velio sighed, casting around the room for suitable words to use.

"The Votadini have been peaceful for decades Tacto. If they have discovered their courage and want to fight, we will have a hard time of it. We are completely surrounded by them on all sides. But if it is one of the northern tribes flexing its muscles we need to know. There's a battle coming Tacto, and I want to know where the Votadini stand. There will be casualties. Remember the first order to save those I could? I am going to have to make choices Tacto. I cannot even save the people out there in the village. The half dozen old soldiers out there who sell us wine? Yes, them and their families, but the rest? It's not going to be possible. And if the Votadini rise, I'm not even going to try to. They will have to take their chances. Dis Pater, we might have them throwing spears at us too."

*

Segontio returned with the twilight with three of his Carubantum band. A soft rain was falling, low cloud louring down from the heights of the hills and hastening the end of the day. Eidumnos came out to greet them with his cloak wrapped against the wet. The stable lad took the horses and retreated to the barn with his head down. Eidumnos wondered whether to set his marker out so there would be no mistake. He watched the horses being led away to the stables and took his time turning back to the Selgovae. A couple of spare horses tonight would have been a courteous gesture. There was the small matter of the equine promise Segontio had made.

'*No matter,*' he thought but it niggled him all the same.

Inside the hall Bractia had carved up a deer haunch and the scent of roasting meat made Segontio's men smile. They seemed decent enough men.

Chapter 48.

Gallus was ready at the appointed hour late in the night watch. He had two ordinary plain helmets and two slim cavalry shields borrowed from one of the decurions.

"I thought we should not advertise our presence," he said, clapping one of the helmets on his head.

Bereft of insignia feathers they were the headwear of the common 'mules.' Somehow it felt very appropriate.

"Shields like last time Velio. I'm not running anywhere if I have to stand and fight."

"Agreed Gallus," Velio replied.

He turned to the officer in charge of the gate detail.

"Open the gate and don't reopen it until we give the password, and you know it's us."

Tacto pulled back the draw-bolts on the gate himself.

"Mars and Fortuna be with you both," he breathed, "no one will sleep until we know you are back."

Velio shook his arm. Gallus nodded. They slipped outside and the gate eased shut at their backs.

The night was wet and cool. Velio hitched his cloak up and over his shoulder. They crouched low and ran over the ditches away from the night torches. The duty optio had reduced them down to the minimum number. He had not thought of that detail and wondered if it was that officer's brains or Tacto's foresight. The fort wall was not far from the drop off to the plain below. The wild grasses were taller and wetter. They made their way down the slippery hillside keeping clear of the regular paths. The stars overhead were out in their great myriads and the moon was bright. Not ideal: they paused at the base of the slope for a moment. A yellow eyed dog fox was looking at them. He stared at them as if nonplussed by their nocturnal wandering. He sniffed and vanished back into the grass. An owl hooted far away, and Gallus grinned a flash of teeth.

"That's more like it. We don't want to offend the local gods tonight."

Velio waved his hand and beckoned Gallus to follow. The dark massive outline of the three hills dominated the horizon. Eidumnos' hall was to the left of straight ahead. They crouched and moved in short steady stages, lying low to listen for counts of five hundred before taking the next foray. They were soaking and cold. The counting halts were taking the warmth out of their bones. Velio turned to check on Gallus. The hastiliarius' eyes shone bright and clear. He nodded before Velio had time to ask and they pushed on.

The outline of Eidumnos hall was so dim they nearly missed it. Closer, a faint yellow light was visible through one of the walls. They crept to the barn first. It was dark and silent. The doors were barred. Beyond, was the main hall. To the side were Eidumnos' little foundry for working iron and two other sheds. The geese pen lay like a lilia trap of sharpened stakes before them. If they woke them things would get difficult. Much further to the left were the halls of Eidumnos' neighbours. He gestured so Gallus knew what was in front of them. Gallus shook his head in mock disbelief. By an unspoken wisdom they had both chosen to use leather cuirass armour tonight in place of the regular strip iron lorica. The dark coloured leather made no noise as they moved. If there was to be any possibility of success tonight complete silence was going to be vital. The geese slumbered as they eased past.

They caught their breath, hiding by the wall along from the hall door. The door opened and Velio felt Gallus stiffen like a hunting dog.

'Discovered already. Sons of Dis Pater.'

*

Segontio lay quiet as a dead man as Voccia came down from the family sleeping platform, crossed past the fire and unlocked the hall to door to go outside. He guessed where she was going. He nudged the warrior pretending to sleep next to him.

"Do it now," he breathed, "I'll deal with the girl. Do it

quietly, don't make a sound."

The warrior smirked like a bear and padded from his place at the back of the hall to the wooden stairway up to Eidumnos and Bractia's bed. The other two rose on cue and wraithed towards the servants in their corner.

She was holding a rush lamp. She scragged her tousled hair back from her face with the fingers of one hand as she tottered around the back of the hall. She looked like she had been sleeping. Velio followed and peered. Beyond a small wicker gate, she was peeing. He retreated to Gallus and grinned. After a few moments she returned yawning, her hand up to her mouth. Velio shifted away from the wall, and she froze as though he was a ghost.

"Voccia, it's me, Velio," he whispered.

Gallus tore his eyes away and searched the darkness for danger. If she made a noise now, the geese would rise, and he was never going to see Deva Victrix again. He made himself ignore the couple behind him. A hand tapped his shoulder and pulled. He followed the hand and the three of them hunched by the stables. The slumbering geese were shredding his nerves.

"Segontio is in the hall with some of his men. He is telling Father the fort you call Blatobulgium has been destroyed by his men. It was a great victory for the Selgovae, and he will be made king once he returns. Velio, they are coming to attack you tomorrow. At dawn. The priests are saying all the omens are on our side and that your men will be destroyed too."

"Where are his men Voccia?" Velio whispered.

"They are waiting up in the hill passes, waiting for the dawn. They have been there for two days. Father has been feeding them."

"So, he did not lose four cows?" Velio smiled.

"No," she said.

He glanced at Gallus.

"Time to go Velio, you have what we need," Gallus said.

"Velio, they are forcing me to marry Segontio. I will not do it. He hurt me. He does not like me. I am afraid of him Velio. Please take me with you."

Her frightened face was only inches from his.

"Are you sure Voccia?" he whispered.

She leaned over and kissed him.

"Velio please," Gallus hissed.

Velio unclipped his sodden cloak and draped it over her shoulders. Gallus nodded and tiptoed past the geese, daring to think they might get away without detection.

They were more than halfway back to the fort when the sound of geese came floating across the night air. Gallus flicked a look towards Velio. Velio grunted and stood upright.

There was little point in hiding now. Speed was what mattered.

"Run Voccia, take Gallus' hand and run," he said.

She shook her head.

"Perhaps it's nothing, a fox has got in."

He stared back towards the hall. A light had appeared, bright yellow in the darkness of the night.

"I don't think it's a fox," he said.

Gallus took her hand, "best do as he says. There's still the hill to climb before we're safe," he whispered.

"Take the path Gallus," Velio ordered.

Without waiting Gallus pulled her arm and she followed leaving Velio statue-like. The havoc of the geese might be a fox, but something told him it was something worse. If Segontio was in the hall, he was awake now and Voccia was missing. It would not take a philosopher to work out something was up. He saw more lights, heard the distant neighing of horses. He held his breath hoping if men were riding in this darkness, they would have no reason to venture in this direction. The lights grew brighter by shades. They were coming this way.

"Run Gallus, Voccia, they know we have been visiting," he called out.

It sounded ridiculous but it did not matter now. He stormed after the older man and the Votadini woman.

"How far?" she gasped.

"Just run," he replied, "up that hill."

"No!" she said, horrified.

The hill was getting no closer. Gallus began heaving loud gasps and then halted and put his hands on his knees.

"A moment Velio, I need a moment. You two carry on, I'll catch up."

"Never," he replied.

Voccia let go of Gallus' hand and clung to him.

"Do you want to make a stand here Gallus?" he asked.

Gallus lifted his head, "let's keep going. Get closer to the fort. They might be able to cover us."

He knew Gallus was lying for Voccia's sake. No guard could see far enough in this light to send a pilum or an arrow with any accuracy.

Gallus started running once more with Voccia helping him as much as he was helping her. The ground began rising. Velio saw Gallus weakening again but the older man was ploughing on as best he could.

"Just a bit further old friend. We get under the wall and make a fight of it," he urged.

Gallus was too exhausted to speak but he clung onto the shield and Voccia's hand like it was his mother's skirt. The beat of hooves was sudden and close. The path was helping their pursuers, but they were gaining the slope now. They pushed on, Gallus pumping his legs as Velio covered their retreat, staring into the inky night for the first sign of the horsemen. In a few moments they were perhaps a third of the way up the hill, just where it steepened, when Gallus slumped.

"Here, Velio. I will do what I can to hold them. You two go on," he grunted.

"No Gallus. Voccia, stand behind us. Gallus, get up and show them your shield the way you taught me and Marcus to fight for the Running Boar, the Twentieth," Velio commanded.

Something clicked in the hastiliarius' eyes. The battle grey cloak of experience and aged-oak muscles. He straightened up. There were four horsemen. Fewer than it had sounded when they were running. Voccia pulled her knife out.

"Just give me a chance," she spat, "and I'll cut the balls off the one who raped me."

The horsemen reared out of the gloom. Velio struck the first animal in the belly before its rider knew he was there. The warrior tumbled off the dying animal and Voccia stabbed him before even Velio could step around the flailing animal's hooves. The second and third came side by side, the fourth a little behind them. Gallus smacked the second horse's face with his shield, it reared, throwing the rider. Velio cut him down. The third passed beyond them slowing on the hillside higher up before turning. He left Gallus to deal with him and faced the last horseman.

"That's him, that's Segontio," Voccia shouted.

"The Good Roman," Segontio jeered, "is dead Roman."

He slid off his horse like an eel and came at Velio, his sword almost invisible in the darkness. Velio ignored the dog Latin; the insult meant nothing to him and concentrated on the arm wielding the weapon. The warrior facing Gallus was now off his horse and the two warriors were positioning themselves together, one higher on the slope than the other. Velio and Gallus had the disadvantage of the lower incline. Voccia retreated obeying Velio's backwards gesture.

"This is Segontio?" he said, jabbing his sword towards the man in front of him.

"Yes" she shouted again, frantic.

Segontio lunged over across toward Gallus, surprising them. His warrior accomplice stepped around to confront Velio. Gallus sized Segontio up for a second. Velio stepped in with the hammer blow attack. Butting the shield to the head he sent the fourth warrior off balance and then falling backwards. He stood over him and struck down once. The warrior grunted and slid down onto the black wet grass until his head was askew.

Segontio saw what happened and kept his stance on the higher ground. Velio moved in to support Gallus but the hastiliarius had somehow recovered his breath and with it all his normal poise.

"You had me runnin' all over that fuckin' valley. I hate runnin'. At my age, I walk, and I shout. Other fuckers run. And I do not like being chased on horses," he explained.

It sounded quite conversational.

"Stand back Velio, I have this," he murmured, "now that I've got my breath back."

Segontio whirled his blade and laid into him. The shield angled and deflected everything Segontio had to offer. He threw himself down the slope in rage trying to bodycheck the old soldier off balance. Gallus buffered the charge, fending and parrying, easing just out of range of the longer Selgovae blade. Velio could see Gallus was going to take his opponent. Segontio gathered himself and launched another swirling sweep of his sword. Gallus checked the blade, Velio could almost hear the forearm muscles popping, raising bright white sparks, letting the impact push his gladius close into his armour then, with a flick of his wrist put the point into Segontio's exposed midriff. As Segontio fell, Gallus buried the blade deep into his belly for good measure. Segontio's jaw flexed like a dying salmon. Blood fumed up from his throat. Voccia stepped towards him in a flash, kneeling at his head. She took it in her hands. Water dripped from her sodden hair onto his face. He recognised her and tried to speak. She touched his lips with her fingers.

"Justice, Segontio. I am going to have the good Roman hang you up in a tree for the crows to pick at. But first your body will lie here to tell all your warriors that your power is over. And I am going to take your horse and ride him as my own so that he does not follow you to the ancestors. I am going to take your sword and have the blacksmith melt it down for cooking spoons. You pass at my hand, with no horse and no sword to go with you. I will take your torc and I might wear it myself. Who knows? Or I may throw it into the grass. So much for a warrior's death. Justice Segontio. This is my justice," she crooned before she pushed.

His face went blank. She pulled her small knife from out of his ear and stood up.

Lights from the fort came bobbing down the path. Tacto hove into sight with a twenty-man detail. He had his sword already drawn. He pulled a torch from one of the men, inspecting their handiwork.

"Secure those horses," he ordered.

"Commander Pinneius sir," he said.

"Centurion Oscius," Velio replied.

He took a final look at Segontio's corpse.

"Find a suitable tree. Strip this naked, remove the torc, the arm rings, all of it and hang this up. Take the heads off the others and mount them over the gate. The Selgovae may think twice once they see this."

"As you command sir," Tacto saluted.

"And get this young woman to my quarters. Waken Lentulus and tell him to get her something warm and dry to wear."

Chapter 49.
Eidumnos' hall.

Orann woke up at the sounds. He stood up and left his bed in the empty pen and peered out of the gaps in the stable doors. It looked like the entire Selgovae nation was walking beyond the homestead, through the open fields of drenched and weary flowers, heading towards the patient fort on the hill. Lines and lines of men on foot, leather clad and obedient, following the elite class warriors and their leaders on horses. Mail chain shirts and iron helmets for the wealthy, leather for the poor. Shields of copper laced decoration: bucklers of oak, lances upright. They passed silent and composed as though this time of day was for contemplation and not shouting or boasting. He had never seen an army on the march before.

The farmyard was silent too. He hurried to the hall door. It was open. The aroma of a feast gone cold was everywhere. Meat and ale, sweet rushes on the floor and a butcher's pen of death. He baulked at the sights and clung to the door frame.

Eidumnos must have died before Bractia. His body was lying in a dishevelled heap at the foot of the stair to the upper sleeping platform. Eidumnos had not been allowed to take his dignity with him. The sword he had used to defend himself and his family was on the floor beside him. It had a coating of dried blood. Orann hoped it was Selgovae blood.

Bractia had been trapped up there. His mistress had been abused; that much was clear. He was glad her eyes were shut. The servants had been murdered too. His friends who ragged him and called him 'smelly horse-fool.' Everyone except Voccia. She was nowhere to be seen. He shook his head in disbelief. The Selgovae were further away now. Their backs to him, growing smaller as they advanced. A trumpet in the fort began calling.

'What is happening to the world? Is everyone going to die today? Am I?'

Chapter 50.

Velio rose from the chair where he had been sleeping, his back feeling stiff and sore. Lentulus stepped back pretending not to see the Votadini woman sleeping face down in his bed. The commander removed the army blanket revealing his toga underneath.

"It's time sir. The sentries report the enemy under the walls. Selgovae by the look of them. Just them sir. Interesting."

'Safer to stick to military matters,' he decided.

The young woman had wept herself asleep through what had been left of last night. He heard her through the wall while the commander, by all appearances had sat in his favourite chair and drunk a healthy amount of Falernian.

"Thank you Lentulus. Ask centurion Oscius to come."

Velio adjusted the blanket over her, motioning Lentulus outside his bedroom.

"He's waiting outside sir. Let me help you with your armour," Lentulus whispered.

He stepped up the stairway to the rampart. The Selgovae had taken the flat summit unopposed as well as the opportunity to have the rising sun at their backs. He squinted.

A thin mist off the river had replaced the night's torrid weather but up here the sun was burning it off. Beyond the gate, the naked, headless bodies of the naked Selgovae were hanging from temporary jibbets. Three heads were on spikes as he had ordered. The single corpse still with its head was Segontio. Tacto joined him, bringing Velio's helmet.

"No convenient trees sir. Had the lads knock these up, pro tem, just for now, as it were, sorry if the noise disturbed the young lady."

"Splendid Tacto. That is exactly what is required," he said.

The Selgovae were examining the four corpses.

"They don't look too interested now do they?" Tacto ventured.

Velio nodded.

"How many would you think, Tacto?" he asked.

"Five, six hundred perhaps, maybe a few more."

"Pity we let them get up here onto the plateau though," he said.

"Shall I send Fufius out to drive them off sir?" Tacto asked.

"I want to see if they have the stomach for it this morning Tacto. A dead leader hanging up for all to see is never good for morale. Does not inspire the men," he said, glad to see their dismay.

"They are in range of the scorpions," Tacto offered.

"You are only to fire if they attempt to remove Segontio. I do not care about the others. I am going down to eat. Bring me word when they leave."

"As you command," Tacto answered.

*

Orann dragged the last of the master's servants from the hall and laid him down by the rest in the dust. He sat back against the geese pen, and they pecked him, seeking food. He banged his fist at the wattle, and they clucked and squawked back at him in annoyance. The Selgovae were returning. Their earlier proud bearing had evaporated. Their heads were down. But there had been no signs or sounds of fighting and they had not passed by the hall on their way to the fort much less than three hours ago. He stood and saw them pass; moving back to the hill passes. None of them looked in his direction and he fell flat on the ground, hoping they would stay away. They had murdered the family and he survived because he was not allowed to sleep in the hall. Not that he had ever cared about that. The horses were kinder to him than most people around here. 'Daft Orann' had outwitted them all.

When he was sure it was safe, he fetched a spade from the barn and wondered whether he should begin preparing graves for Eidumnos and Bractia. Without Voccia or Tianos to instruct him he dallied at the family plot where the forebears lay. None of this was his job. He cut away enough turf for them and did not dig any deeper. The day was young. Perhaps Voccia would return and tell him what she wanted him to do. He carried their bodies to the plot and sat down to wait. Perhaps the neighbours would come by soon?

*

Velio let her sleep on undisturbed in his room knowing the normal noises in the fort would waken her without him needing to interfere. Lentulus had her clothes dried, courtesy of the hypercaust and returned to the bottom of Velio's bed ready for when she awoke. Mid-morning Lentulus brought her to the principia. Marcellus made himself scarce.

"Thank you for saving me last night. I must go back. My parents and those men," she tried to explain.

"Segontio is dead Voccia. You have nothing to be afraid of now," he smiled.

"I want to be with you Velio, but my home is here. I must find my parents and my brother."

"Voccia, I am leaving here soon. Taking my men to our fortress called Deva Victrix. It's many days marching. I am going back to my legion. Another commander will come here with more men. Rome is not abandoning you or your people. The Votadini are our friends. I saw that this morning outside my gates. Only the Selgovae want to fight us. Or they did. I think they may have already changed their minds."

"Will you be coming back?" she said.

"I do not know," he broke off.

She did not deserve the easy lie resting on the tip of his tongue.

"I cannot leave," she said, "my family belongs here. My grandparents and their grandparents are buried here. It is our land centurion. Can't you stay?"

He shook his head, "Velio, my name is Velio."

"I know centurion. If I came with you, you would be Velio. But you must always be 'centurion.' My father always calls you the good Roman. He likes you."

He sat back.

"I will send an escort to take you back to your father's hall. I have a report to write so I will see you later."

She looked at him.

"I thought I could make you stay," she said, "but I was wrong. Your legion means more to you."

She got up and hurried out of the room. A few minutes later Marcellus put his head around the doorway.

"Scouts have already been out to that young woman's home. Commander Fufius' orders. Looks bad, sir. The Selgovae left no one alive. He's shadowing their retreat through the passes."

'Thank you Tacto and Fufius.'

He could only imagine what carnage had been wrought in Eidumnos' hall at the hands of Segontio and his men. Poor Voccia. What a mess. They had been decent people. Pulling out soldiers was always going to result in casualties.

"Tell Fufius I want her escorted home. And tell Fufius to post a guard at the hall if she wants one. Eight men and a decanus. Just till things calm down. Tell the decanus his men must behave with respect, or I'll have the skin off their backs."

Marcellus assented with a nod.

"So, what was all that about last night and this morning sir?"

He grimaced, "that Marcellus, was the Selgovae rolling the dice. They lost. Unfortunately, I think I did too."

Marcellus gave him a consoling smile, "affairs of the heart sir?"

Velio rolled his eyes and shrugged.

"I'm issuing fresh orders Marcellus and I need to do a report for legate Albinius. I hope to have good news very soon for the men about our return to Deva Victrix. But keep that to yourself for now."

"Absolutely sir."

"Let's hope the gods of this country will be content with last night's blood for a while."

Marcellus saluted with a wry grin and left the office.

'You must always be 'centurion,' those were her words. How had she learned so much about him in such a short time?

Chapter 51.
Deva Victrix - five months later.

Velio waited for the woman to bring the wine. Gallus then decided he wanted to order bread and olives. She smiled and he expected her to say something like, "why didn't you tell me that before?"

But the tavern was busy, and she did not seem to mind the extra legwork back to the kitchen. Velio poured out the third cup as Hanno arrived in his full resplendent uniform. A polite avenue opened for him to pass. Eyes followed his progress, assessing Velio and Gallus. It was a very high-powered table. They earned a space apart. Gallus lifted his cup.

"The Boar, the best. Long may the soldiers of The Boar conquer all her enemies and those of our beloved emperor."

"The Boar, the Twentieth, the best," they repeated.

"Fill them up Gallus, I've got a thirst on me tonight," Hanno said.

When the cups were full Velio managed to secure some of the remaining olives and bread from under Gallus' watchful eyes.

"So, what is this plan of yours Gallus? Velio mentioned something," Hanno said.

Gallus drank and smiled, "what do you think of this stuff?" he asked.

Hanno snorted and waggled his hand from side to side, "it's drink, army style posca, Gallus, it does the job," he replied.

"And you, centurion Pinneius what do you think?" Gallus said, good humoured and not put out in the slightest by Hanno.

Velio sniffed the cup and drank. Did Gallus really want his opinion about tavern wine?

"It's the way Hanno has it. It's legionary swill but unless you're paying for the better stuff it's fine with me."

Gallus smiled back and drank, refilling them without asking.

"I got a letter today," he teased.

Velio exchanged a look with Hanno.

Hanno groaned, "Gallus, we'd love to know what was in your letter."

Gallus leaned forwards to conspire.

"Well, since you've persuaded me to talk, it's this. An old comrade of mine retired to a place in Gaul a few years back. Argentomagus, land of the Bituriges, it's been tame since the time of Caesar. I was not always in the Twentieth you know. Anyway, he secured a piece of land with good vines. Set himself up and went into the wine business. And the town is growing. Plenty of opportunity."

"Well, none of it ever reached me," Velio chipped in.

"No, it didn't," Gallus said, his happy grin broke out.

"You're going into the wine trade?" Hanno asked.

"My pal Priscus has apparently gone to join the immortal legions in Elysium and his widow has invited me to go down and look with a view to buying her out. She says the wines are getting better every year as the vines age. So, as a business opportunity she says there is little risk. She wants Priscus' business to go to a friend. She counts on me to be fair, price wise. As if I would try to stiff the widow of an old comrade. Well, not for business if you get my drift. So, that is what I'm going to do. I'm going down to have a look with a view to sealing the deal," he explained.

"And?" Velio probed.

"And I could use a partner, or even better two partners. A little extra capital would not hurt. I would like to give her a decent price just for thinking of me in the first place. There might be a bit of layout required to get it going more efficiently."

"And what will you do all day while you wait for the grapes to grow?" said Hanno.

'I was hoping to sit in the shade and take all your money at dice. Velio is the worst dice player I ever met Hanno, apart from poor old Marcus."

"That's true, Marcus could play dice with a child and lose

money."

"And when I'm not taking his money, Swords here can make little legionaries for the emperor if he can find a willing Bituriges lass. That will pass the time, Velio," he sat back delighted with his strategy.

He could tell they were interested. Velio tipped his cup in salute and drank.

"Fortuna and Bacchus be with you Gallus, you deserve success," he said.

"Listen you two, this stuff is mediocre at best. What I am suggesting is, why don't we wave 'Vale,' to the army? We have all put in the years. 'cept you Velio, you might have to sweet-talk a discharge. Hanno will put in a good word to Servius for you. Better be quick, cos' Servius can't have long to go before he heads back to wherever he comes from," Gallus said.

"Have you thought about asking him to join you too Gallus?" Hanno wondered.

"Ask Servius? No, I don't think so. I say, let's make wine and sell it to the army. We can do better than this swill. And make a fortune along the way. Drinkable, plain, stuff for the taverns and the mules. Better stuff for the officers. Top notch drink for the generals."

Hanno nodded.

"You want me to head south to where it's warmer. Help make and drink wine and make money as well. It's a tricky proposition Gallus. I'm just not certain," he replied.

Gallus went pale, swallowing it, hook line and sinker. Velio slapped his arm.

"He's taking the piss, Gallus."

"I discharge next month. I am in Gallus. How much is a share?" Hanno grinned.

"Good sir."

Hanno waved the rank aside.

"In thirty-six days I am ex First cohort commander Hanno Glaccus. Morenus returns to take his cohort back. Servius always said it was a short-term appointment. So, it won't be 'sir' anymore, it'll be all the other foul labels you have for me. And my only achievement was on the first day I ordered the execution of Orgidor, chief of the Brigantes. I did not even bother to go and watch it happen. Just sent an order."

He clicked his fingers.

"We've finally pacified this country, or at least the bits worth keeping. There's no fun left in it for us," he mourned.

"How did you know it was Orgidor?" Velio asked.

Hanno snorted into his wine.

"Bloody fool told us who he was."

"Hanno, none of us ever saw him up close in all the time before we went to build the north wall. Did you get someone to identify him?"

Gallus started fidgeting, but Hanno held his hand up.

"Well, Velio, since you ask, I didn't," he said, "Servius told me he had been captured and I had him executed. I rather assumed the legion knew who it had sitting in chains before I got there."

"So, it might not have been Orgidor, is all I'm saying," Velio persisted.

"Never," Gallus blurted.

They laughed. Hanno began heaving in hysterics as the idea grabbed him.

"I didn't even get that right," he cackled, "what a joke."

Gallus waited until Hanno subsided.

"What about you Swords? Are you in? Three of us can put some cash to this and make a go of it. Somewhere warm for Glaccus' old bones and mine for that matter," he moved it on.

Velio sipped the wine.

"It's really not that good is it. Time for a flagon of the good stuff. My treat." he waved to the barman.

"More?" the tavern keeper called back.

"The good stuff," Velio replied.

It arrived quicker than the first round.

"Some more bread and olives gents. On the house."

"See?" Gallus crowed.

Velio poured and they savoured the improved smell and the

taste. Gallus rubbed his thumb along the rim of his cup.

"We can make better than this," he plotted.

Velio sat back, "to Marcus Hirtius," he said, out of the blue.

They toasted and drank.

'It is time to let Marcus rest, Velio my friend, you must let him go. You must forgive yourself,' Gallus thought.

"I know what Marcus would have said to my offer," he persisted, pushing his plan.

A little shiver danced down his spine as if a draught had found its way in.

"If you stay in the legion any longer Velio they'll have you marching back up north to reclaim the turf wall," Hanno murmured, "I'd roll dice on it. Some politician will whisper the poison in the emperor's ear that all this is a mistake and before you know it it'll be 'hello Bodotria and the Hill of the Resting Lion.'"

Velio smiled. Without these two he would be without the two men he counted as closest friends; Tacto and Fufius were decent blokes but, it was not the same.

"Making wine in Gaul with you two? Old Pomponius had the same idea. Retire and make wine. Let me think about it," he said.

He thrust his wine cup towards Gallus.

"Come on, you old wolf, I paid for this."

"It will be quiet and profitable I promise you, the Gauls were tamed long ago," Gallus smiled the smile of a benevolent emperor who despatches his army whilst making the stiff finger sign against evil behind his back.

"You can hang up the sword Velio, the empire is changing, and we have to change too. The only blood red thing I want to see now is our wine filling the cups of thirsty men," Hanno was getting more enthusiastic.

Velio sat back, the tavern was growing rowdier, the drink was flowing. The noise levels were rising as it filled with off duty 'mules.' The early gap around their table had disappeared and soldiers were laughing and eating within touching distance, all rank forgotten. There were boar emblems scratched into the plaster of the tavern walls. Some of them old, others clearly recent, some well executed, others more graphitto than emblem. Gallus leaned forwards divining Velio's mood.

"If Marcus was here, do you think the two of you would have to think twice?" he said.

He tapped Velio on the chest with his forefinger. Velio forced a grin.

"Marcus would have said, 'what are you waiting for Swords? When's the first boat to Gaul?" he admitted.

"Right then, so what do you say, Velio?"

He took a long look around and returned his gaze to both of them, shaking off the sudden, sad thoughts of Marcus. The ghost of a smile was threatening to break out on Hanno's lips. Gallus was still trying to persuade him with everything he had. His eyes focussed as if the universe depended on the answer; the very gods themselves listening.

Gallus Tiomaris, Hanno Glaccus and Velio Pinneius. There would be no trouble with the workforce with these two at his back. Velio put out his cup for more wine, making them both wait until Gallus filled it.

"What do I say? I say, let me think about it for a while," he paused.

Gallus eyeballed Hanno in disbelief. Hanno's face defied description

"He's not coming, Gallus," Hanno cried.

'How can you still have unfinished business with Britannia Velio after everything that's happened?' he paused, astonished.

Gallus was about to wish Velio good fortune but could not quite bring himself to say the words after all the years. In the blink of an eye, the click of a vine stick on the tabletop tonight, it would all be over, all of it. Hanno saw the hastiliarius was bereft. He felt lousy for him.

'I should say something,' he thought.

"But just out of interest, when is the next boat to Gaul?" Velio asked.

Gallus sat back, "Swords Pinneius, you really are a sod. I always preferred Marcus to you, you know. I really did."

The End.

Author's note

It is not completely certain that the Antonine wall was abandoned around the year 155/156. There are views that it was temporarily abandoned but swiftly reoccupied, around AD158. If this was what happened, then it may indicate times of turmoil and perhaps uncertainty in the garrisoning policy of the province, or a shortage of men. Perhaps a confusion of strategy or some sub optimal decision making. It would be a mistake to assume the Roman army and Imperial policy always 'got it right.'

No surprise then that Velio Pinneius could still be there and abouts in that timescale.

Several forts on the western road south through Dumfries and Galloway to Carlisle, including Blatobulgium (Flour Sacks) are believed to have been destroyed around this time. It is not clear whether Blatobulgium was destroyed by tribal attack or simply rendered unusable by the departing garrison. There is some archaeological debate as to whether Trimontium was attacked and destroyed. The modern theory seems to be it was not destroyed and may have remained garrisoned throughout the two phases of consolidation under the emperor Antonine, so for two to three years or so, it may well have been the northernmost fort of the entire Roman empire.

The poetry quoted in Chapter 29 is just one of many attempts to translate the emperor Hadrian's dying composition, "Animula vagula blandula."

Unfortunately, I cannot give credit to the translator as this rendering came from an old brochure from the Yorkshire Museum, though it is my personal favourite.

Velio, Gallus and Hanno's story continues in the third part of the series, Centurion of The Boat.

You can contact the author by email through the website.
www.lochardfiction.co.uk

Printed in Great Britain
by Amazon